My
Guardian
Angel

My Guardian Angel

Kay Hooper
Sandra Chastain
Susan Krinard
Karyn Monk
and
Elizabeth Thornton

Bantam Books
New York Toronto London
Sydney Auckland

MY GUARDIAN ANGEL

A Bantam Book/March 1995

ISBN 0-553-56916-3

Published simultaneously in the United States and Canada

*Bantam Books are published by Bantam Books, a division of Bantam Doubleday
Dell Publishing Group, Inc. Its trademark, consisting of the words "Bantam
Books" and the portrayal of a rooster, is Registered in U.S. Patent and Trademark
Office and in other countries. Marca Registrada. Bantam Books, 1540 Broadway,
New York, New York 10036.*

PRINTED IN THE UNITED STATES OF AMERICA

RAD   0 9 8 7 6 5 4 3 2 1

CONTENTS

Almost an Angel

Kay Hooper

ONE

"Where did he go?"

"I didn't see—"

"You let him past you? You bloody fool!"

"Maybe he didn't come this way. And Charlie shot him, didn't he? Knocked him right off his fine prancer. He won't be troublin' us, you can bet on that, Jack."

"He's already troubled us, Tom! Dammit, I want him found, and I mean quick. You head up toward the boats, and I'll tell Charlie. . . ."

The voices faded away until he could hear nothing except the low roar of the sea. Alexander Drake remained where he was for a moment, but only long enough to make a flimsy pad of his handkerchief and press it inside his shirt to stanch the blood flowing from the wound in his shoulder.

At least, he thought it was his shoulder. That arm—his right—was dead well enough. But it was so damned dark, and his entire body hurt, and for all he knew he'd a dozen bullets in him. . . .

He pushed himself to his feet and eased away from the scant shelter of a thicket of bushes, grimly intent on not making his presence known to the men searching for him. They would not hesitate to kill him, he knew all too well. He used his left hand to fumble inside his greatcoat, until the reassuring thickness of the packet took shape under his gloved fingers. So, at least he hadn't lost the papers. He had not been at all sure of that, not after being shot off his horse and forced to slither along the cold, wet ground for what felt like an eternity.

It had begun to rain. No—sleet. Winter was making its presence felt with a vengeance. He wanted to curse. He wanted to curse out loud, good and loud.

It seemed like hours that he picked his way through the underbrush, but he knew his sense of passing time was as confused as everything else; it might have been only a few minutes. The darkness and cold left him disoriented, as did his steadily worsening physical condition, and there was little he could do about either.

He paused for a moment, leaning back against a tree for both support and balance. He was becoming dizzy and appallingly weak, and for the first time since leaving London days ago, he acknowledged to himself that he was in trouble. Even if those pursuing him had abandoned the search, he was alone, without a horse or other means of transport, wounded—and he had no idea where he was.

Oh, the coast of Kent, certainly. South of Folkestone somewhere. But that "somewhere" was far too vague. He needed help, and if he didn't get it soon, the War Office would lose one of its most effective agents, to say nothing of vital information about the doings in France.

Alex began to push himself away from the tree, but had to remain there when his legs refused to obey him. Dammit, he was weak as a cat! The throbbing in his shoulder had become a red agony, and he had the notion at least two of his ribs had been cracked because it hurt to breathe.

Cold. When had it gotten so cold?

He opened his eyes with a start and looked around in confusion. Had he been asleep? He listened, straining, but heard nothing except the muted sounds of the sea. And though he peered hard in every direction, he saw nothing, not a single sign of life.

With utter concentration, he pushed himself away from the tree and staggered on, hoping to hell he was at least moving in a straight line away from the coast. He thought he was, thought he was making some kind of progress, but then he stumbled and fell to his knees, the fall jarring his entire body, so that he nearly blacked out, and when the agony finally lessened, he heard the sea again. Louder.

Then, abruptly, he saw a light bobbing distantly, and heard a shout, and he realized he had stumbled back to where he had started. The smugglers were still hunting him.

He struggled to his feet and turned carefully, trying to orient himself in the cold, icy darkness, then staggered on once again. He kept his left hand pressed to his right shoulder, trying to stop the bleeding he could feel draining the strength and life from him.

This time he was certain he made it no more than twelve or fifteen feet before an uneven patch of ground caused him to stumble and fall yet again. And this time he remained where he fell.

He was tired. So tired. He needed to sleep before going on, just close his eyes for a few moments and rest. . . .

"You must get up."

He felt himself drifting and wanted to ignore the soft voice, but it was insistent and tugged at him oddly. There was something almost familiar about it, like the memory of a voice or words he had heard long, long ago in another place ... or in a dream.

"Please, you must get up."

Alex forced his eyes open. Darkness. But was that ... the dim flash of white petticoat as a woman's skirt was raised? Surely not. Still, even the possibility of such an absurdity made him raise his head and then shift the lead weight of his body until he could look up.

By God, it *was* a woman.

"What the hell ... ?" His voice was thickened and seemed to him to originate from someone else.

"Please." She bent nearer, and even in the intense darkness, her face and, especially, her eyes, seemed radiant. "Please, they will find you soon. You must get up."

To please her, he would have done anything, no matter how painful. He somehow managed to get his legs under him and then lever himself upright. He swayed unsteadily, but his gaze was fixed on her shadowy form and curiously luminous face, and when she backed away, he found himself following her.

"Who—"

"Shhh," she urged. "They could hear you."

Alex accepted the warning, but after they had gone some distance, he had to ask again. "Who are you?"

She paused as she had several times before to allow him a moment to rest, somehow knowing or sensing when he had reached his limits. Her glowing face was turned toward him again, but she was several feet away and he couldn't make out her features clearly.

"I am a friend," she replied softly.

He heard a rough laugh escape him. "For all I know, you could be leading me into the hands of the smugglers—or worse."

She shook her head. "You need a doctor. You need to be ... safe. I need you to be safe."

"I don't—"

"Please. There isn't much time. You—you're losing blood. Come with me. Let me help you."

Again, her voice tugged at him, and again he found himself following her as if nothing else mattered to him. It was the most peculiar sensation. More than once he glanced down at himself, vaguely surprised to find no line attached to his body and stretched out to her; the feeling of being pulled along by her was that strong.

He had no way of knowing how long or how far he followed her; he knew only that the sounds of the ocean faded away, and that all he heard was the rattle of sleet and the bellows of his own breathing. It remained dark, incredibly dark, and cold. And, gradually, he was moving forward only because she softly urged and pleaded with him to keep going; it simply was not in him to refuse her.

He followed her from the interminable forest into a field, startled from his apathetic daze by the realization that they had at last arrived somewhere. Across the field could be seen the lights of an inn or some other such establishment.

"You will be safe now."

"Wait. Don't go."

But she was already gone, fading back into the blackness of the forest without another word or sound. Alex stood there swaying for a moment, then made his unsteady legs carry him across the field and toward the lights.

•   •   •

"I had the devil's own time of it getting you back here," Lord Sherringham told his friend rather severely. "There you were, out cold and barely patched up by that sawbones the landlord found—would you believe he wanted to bleed you? When you must have lost pints already!"

Accustomed to his friend's habit of wandering from the subject, Alex merely said, "There I was, out cold and barely patched up ... and then?"

"Well, after I paid your shot at the inn—with a little something extra to keep the landlord's curiosity in bounds—we got you loaded into my coach and brought you here. Luckily I was at the country house when the inn's groom arrived with your message instead of in London, where I rightfully belong this time of year—and where *you* were supposed to be, I might remind you."

"And the dispatches?"

Sherringham's voice was patient. "Taken to London, as I told you. Bennet knows to give them only into the right hands."

Alex shifted restlessly. "Are you sure you can trust this man, Sherry?"

The young viscount's amiable face took on an expression of profound surprise. "Not trust Bennet? Alex, if a man can't trust his own valet ... !"

"Very well, I suppose you had little choice."

After a moment Sherringham said gently, "You're quite welcome."

Alex frowned at him, but then the grim expression melted into amusement. "Did I neglect to thank you? How boorish of me."

Sherringham lounged back in the chair beside his guest's bed and grinned. "There's scarcely been time since you came back to your senses. Actually, for most of the past two days the only subject on your feverish brain seemed to be a lady. And since I know you've expended all your energies these last months doing what you can to foil Boney's plans rather than waltzing at Almack's, I assume this lady is someone you've met only recently. Whoever she is, she does seem to have taken possession of your thoughts, if not your heart. Or was she merely a sweet dream brought on by your feverish state?"

Alex didn't answer immediately. Had she been a dream? "Sherry . . . you said there was no one else at the inn?"

"Just that rascally landlord. I had a word with the doctor, of course, before I dared move you. Seemed skilled enough, barring his fondness for leeches." Sherringham's brows lifted curiously. "Was there a lady involved? I admit, given your usual resistance to the petticoats, I assumed you were merely dreaming."

"What did I say?"

"Oh . . . something about luminous eyes and the sweetest voice this side of heaven. It was rather out of character for you to wax poetic, now that I think about it."

Alex felt heat rise in his face. He cleared his throat and shifted once more against the pillows propping him up. "I see."

"I'd like to see, if she *was* more than a dream," Sherringham told him. "From your raptures, she sounds like an angel. Of course, you *were* delirious, I realize that."

After a slight hesitation, Alex said, "I suppose I can't be sure since I'd lost so much blood, but . . . I think there was a lady, Sherry. She guided me inland, through a forest and away from the smugglers I had the misfortune to stumble upon just after I came ashore."

Sherringham frowned. "Who was she?"

"I have no idea. I asked her—I believe I asked

her—but her only reply was that she was a friend.
She said . . ."

I need you to be safe.

An odd way of putting it, Alex realized as he remembered her words. She *needed* him to be safe?

"She said . . . ?"

Alex shook his head. "She kept urging me to follow her, to allow her to help me. I was in no shape
to question her, and I'd no choice but to follow her.
She led me to the inn and then . . . she vanished."

"What, into thin air?"

"No, no—she moved back into the forest. She
said I would be safe now, and she went back into the
forest."

The viscount crossed one elegant leg over the
other and frowned at his friend. "The landlord said
you fell into his establishment sometime after midnight. Where did the lady go, Alex? For that matter,
where did she come from, so late at night and so far
from anything?"

"I don't know."

"You were almost at death's door, in case I neglected to mention it," Sherringham said conversationally. "God knows how much blood you'd lost,
and you had three cracked ribs as well. Exhaustion,
exposure, fever. In such a situation, I imagine most
any man would see what he wanted—what he
needed—to see."

"You think I dreamed her."

"I think it likely."

Alex didn't say anything to that, and after a moment Lord Sherringham got to his feet.

"*My* sawbones says you need rest," he said lightly.
"I've tired you enough for today. Why don't you try
to sleep now? And don't worry—as soon as Bennet
returns from London, I'll have him report to you

the safe delivery of the dispatches you risked your neck for."

Alex nodded, but before his friend could leave the room, he said, "Sherry . . . thank you."

Lord Sherringham smiled. "Think nothing of it, Alex. You would do the same for me—*if* I were mad enough to go careening about the countryside on dark nights. Get some rest."

When he was alone, Alex leaned his head back against the pillows and brooded. His memories of that near-fatal night were certainly hazy. He could, vaguely, remember thrusting a handful of coins at the landlord and asking that Viscount Sherringham be sent for. He could remember fighting to keep his wits about him long enough to be certain the packet of dispatches was shoved under his pillow in relative safety. But he didn't remember the doctor, or having the bullet extracted from his shoulder, and he had absolutely no memory of the journey from that remote inn to Sherringham's country estate some thirty miles from the coast.

But—he remembered her. Very clearly, he remembered her.

He simply couldn't explain her. The smugglers certainly had not included a lady in their activities, and she had undoubtedly been a lady. Sherry had told him that the inn lay some two miles from the shore, with the nearest cottage miles away up the coast; so where had she come from? Why had she been so intent on helping him? She hadn't approached within arm's reach of him, and in the stygian blackness of the night, how had she known he needed a doctor? He might well have been drunk, for all she could tell.

I need you to be safe.

She needed him to be safe. She *needed* him to be safe?

A lady appeared in the dead of night out of nowhere, miles from anything, her face and eyes curiously luminous. She did not shrink away from the
dirty and ragged clothing he wore, nor did she ask
him a single question about his identity or reasons
for being there himself. No, without explaining anything or asking him a single reasonable question, she
simply saved his life.

And he was trying to convince himself she had
been real?

Of all the absurdities! A figment of his feverish
imagination, as Sherry had supposed? That sounded
far more likely. Simply the result of wandering for
too long, dazed and bleeding, on a cold, dark night
while he was being hunted like an animal.

The longer Alex thought about it, the more convinced he became that Sherry had been right. With
his life ebbing away, a man very likely *would* con-
jure a sweet-voiced, radiant-featured female guide to
help him.

In actuality, he had probably followed his nose
through the forest to the inn, guided by nothing except instinct.

That made far better sense. Alex even believed it.
But when he fell into a restless sleep, it was to dream
of glowing eyes and the sweetest voice this side of
heaven.

Spring filled the night air with the scent of flowers, but Alex hardly noticed. This was the second
time in three months he had encountered trouble on
the English side of the Channel, and he made a men-
tal note to plan a different route home for the next
trip.

In the meantime, however, he had to get home *this*
trip.

The smugglers had chosen a moonless night for

their activities, which had been reasonable and intelligent of them. And since Alex was concerned with sins far greater than the smuggling of brandy into England, he was not at all interested in seeing them brought to justice. Besides which, estate owners near the coast had long turned a blind eye to such activities for the secretly offered and accepted price of a few kegs left on the doorstep, and he had enjoyed "run" brandy too many times to be a hypocrite now.

And though he might, under other circumstances, have welcomed an opportunity to even the score, he even bore them no malice for being, he was virtually certain, the same ones who had left him with cracked ribs and a bullet in his shoulder the last time he had encountered them.

But damn their eyes, they were in his way!

As far as he could tell, there was only one path up the cliffs, and the smugglers were making use of it. And if Alex was any judge of such matters, they were going to require the remainder of the night to unload their boats and transport the kegs up to whatever conveyance waited at the top of the cliffs.

He had drifted ashore silently under the cover of fog, and his small boat was beached out of the smugglers' sight behind a rock. But now the fog was gone, and he dared not return to the water to attempt to find another landing point, because they would surely see him. He had little choice except to wait them out, a delay that would make getting to London as soon as he needed to virtually impossible.

Alex hesitated, then gathered himself. If he moved quickly enough, he *might* be able to get up the path before they could shoot him—

"This way."

He jerked in surprise, turning his head toward the

almost inaudible voice just behind his shoulder, and let out an unconscious breath of satisfaction. In the months since, even though he had convinced himself it had been a dream, he had forgotten nothing. It was her.

"This way," she repeated softly. "There is another path. I'll show you."

Alex didn't move. "Tell me who you are," he demanded, keeping his own voice as low as possible.

She moved just a little nearer him, so he could barely make out delicate, glowing features framed by her dark hood. "Please come with me."

"Tell me who you are," he insisted.

She glanced past him, clearly worried about the smugglers, and finally said, "I am—Maggie." And as soon as the reluctant words were out of her mouth, she was backing away, beckoning to him.

He followed her, careful to keep to what cover there was until she led him around a huge boulder and out of sight of the busy smugglers. He kept his gaze fixed on her shadowy form, determined not to let her out of his sight on a dark night when vanishing would be all too easy; this time he meant to find out what a lady of her quality was doing in the middle of the night, miles from anywhere, and aiding a stranger.

She led him to a narrow path that was virtually hidden due to the arrangement of rocks, and he realized they would reach the top of the cliffs a safe distance from where the smugglers would be.

"Maggie." The name felt oddly *right* on his tongue. "Why are you doing this? Why are you helping me?"

She paused on the steep path, perhaps to give him a breather since she herself seemed completely unaffected by the climb, and looked at him. Though she was still more than an arm's length away, her features were more visible to him than they had yet been, and he could only stare at an exquisite face in which those haunting, luminous eyes beckoned to him like lodestars.

She seemed puzzled by his question, surprised. "Because you needed me to help you," she replied.

"Do you know who I am? Do you know . . . what I am?"

"I know . . . you needed to be safe. I needed you to be safe."

"Why?"

That question seemed to puzzle her most of all.

"Why? Because . . . I did. Because I could not allow you to die."

"But who are you?" he demanded insistently. "Why does my life concern you?"

She began to back away, clearly distressed now. "I—you must follow me, please. One of those men . . . will find this path in a few minutes. He must not find you here."

Without making a conscious decision, Alex followed. But he was even more baffled than before. "In a few minutes? How can you possibly know what hasn't yet happened?"

"I know. You must trust me." She continued to glance back at him over her shoulder, remaining just out of his reach.

"How can I?" He tried to close the distance between them, moving faster, but she somehow managed to keep just ahead of him, almost but not quite close enough to touch. "You won't trust me."

"I trust you." Her voice softened even more and took on a quality he could not have defined in words and yet instinctively understood to be the sound of utter certainty. "I have always trusted you."

"Always? How can you possibly—"

"Don't you remember the lake? Don't you remember that summer?" They had reached the top of the cliffs now, and she turned to him with an absent little gesture indicating they had reached their goal. "The coach awaiting you is just over that hill. You must hurry; those men will come this way soon."

"For God's sake, wait!" He held out a hand unconsciously. "I have to thank you for—"

"You don't have to thank me, Alex. But ... I wish ..."

He took a step toward her. "You know my name?"

"I wish ... it wasn't always night. ... Good-bye, Alex."

"Maggie—" Between one heartbeat and the next, she had vanished.

Into thin air.

Alex didn't move for long minutes. He stood perfectly still, looking around him with the careful gaze of a man who needed to be very sure of the facts. There was nothing she could have used to hide herself from him, not rock or bush or tree, for fifty feet in any direction. And in any case, she had not moved. She had simply disappeared.

He was not wounded, not exhausted or cold, and not dazed. He was wide-awake and in full possession of his faculties. And he did not believe in ghosts.

The distant sounds of voices forced him to move away, toward the coach awaiting him, and it was not until some hours later, bowling toward London, that Alex had a sudden jolt of memory.

Don't you remember the lake? Don't you remember that summer?

He did remember, now. Long ago, when he was a boy, he had chanced to be near a lake when he heard cries for help and discovered a young girl fighting to stay afloat in the water. Though not a strong swimmer himself, he had plunged into the water and had managed to pull the girl out. She had thanked him between gasps, and alarmed by her shivering, he had run to get help. But when he had returned minutes later, she was gone.

He'd had no idea who she was, and to his knowledge he had never seen her again. Until ...

Until it had been her turn to save his life? Absurd! And even if an absurdity could be true, it hardly explained how she had managed to vanish before his very eyes.

Still, he remembered now, vividly, that delicate little girl he had rescued so many years ago. And what he remembered most clearly of all was that she had possessed luminous eyes and the sweetest voice this side of heaven. . . .

TWO

"I hesitate to suggest it," Lord Sherringham said somewhat dryly, "but perhaps you saw what you wanted to see, my friend. Isn't that at least possible?"

Alex had faced that possibility too squarely himself to be offended now by Sherry's doubts. "No. She was there, as real as you are. I saw her—I spoke to her. I was wide-awake and not wounded, and I did not imagine her." He stood by the window of his library and looked beyond the gardens to the mist-enshrouded rooftops of London.

"Yet when you returned to the coast and searched, you found no sign of her." Sherringham paused, then added somewhat wryly, "Tell me you didn't go from cottage to inn, knocking on doors."

Alex laughed shortly and came away from the window, returning to his chair across from Sherringham's. "No, I was not so addled as that. I was ... discreet. Perhaps too discreet, for I found virtually nothing of any help to me. She said her name was Maggie, and I found no one by that name—or Margaret or Meg, or any other version I could think of. She spoke like a lady, convincingly so, but there are only farmers' cottages for more than ten miles of where I saw her."

"And if she isn't a lady?"

"I considered that. Unless I am far wrong in my estimation, she can be no more than twenty-one or so; among the families in the area, none has a girl of anywhere near the right age living there—or visiting that night. I found an excellent source of information for the area, a doctor; doctors and vicars can always be trusted to know the people around them. She was not there. She was not anywhere."

Slouched in his chair, Sherringham eyed his friend a bit guardedly. "Alex, suppose you *do* find her—and she isn't a lady? Suppose she's a serving girl or a milkmaid, some wench in a tavern who taught herself to speak like a lady. What then?"

Alex heard himself laugh and wondered if Sherry found the sound as unconvincing as he did himself. "What difference would that make? It isn't as if I mean to marry the girl. She is a puzzle, a mystery—and I owe her my thanks. But nothing more than that, Sherry."

"I wonder if you really believe your own words," Sherringham murmured. He got to his feet before his friend could answer, and added, "Do you attend Lady Northgate's ball on Friday?"

"No. I shall be out of town."

Sherringham frowned. "Another trip so soon?"

"I have work to do. Information," Alex responded lightly, "is no use to anyone if not current."

Lord Sherringham was on the point of reminding his friend that he was not the only man working to acquire that information, but something in those level gray eyes stopped him. Having known Alexan-

der Drake since childhood, he was all too aware that
he was not a man who could be swayed once his
mind was made up—as it obviously was now.

He would return to the dangers of France and the
perils of crossing the Channel, risking his life in haz-
ardous deeds for king and country, and he would do
so so quietly that fashionable society would never
know that there was, in their lethargic midst, a genuine hero.

"Be careful, Alex," Sherringham heard himself say.

"I am always careful," Alex replied in a tone that
deliberately made light of a friend's worry and his
own characteristic recklessness.

Sherringham made a rude noise but said nothing
further, merely taking leave of his host.

Alone in his library, Alex moved restlessly to the
window once again and stood gazing out. It was
only midafternoon, but one of those occasional late-
spring days made dark and dreary by rain and fog,
and so it seemed much later. Or perhaps, Alex
thought, he was merely anxious for this day to be
over so that tomorrow would come and he could
start on his journey back to the Channel.

It had been two weeks now since he had seen
Maggie. Two weeks since she had, for the second
time, come to his aid when he had most needed help.
And not a day of those two weeks had passed without his thoughts turning to her at least a dozen
times.

Maggie. Who was she? Where did she live? How
had she known he needed her help, and known
where to find him? *Maggie.* Was she the girl he had
saved from drowning nearly fifteen years ago? No,
too absurd. But ... if she was *not* that girl, why had
she said she had always trusted him and then reminded him of a lake and "that" summer? *Maggie.*
Why did his life matter to her? Why did she "need"

him to be safe? And where in God's name had she vanished to in the blink of an eye?

"My lord?"

Alex glanced back over his shoulder, vaguely surprised since he had not heard the door open. "Yes, Stames?"

"A message, my lord." The butler came forward bearing a silver tray, on which reposed a letter.

Alex picked it up and glanced at the seal. "Thank you, Stames."

"The messenger awaits a reply, my lord."

Frowning, Alex carried the letter to his desk and sat down before opening it. The message was brief, as was his consideration of the information. He drew a sheet of notepaper forward and wrote a terse reply, and a moment later handed the sealed missive to his butler.

"Send this."

"Yes, my lord."

"And have my curricle brought around. The grays."

"Yes, my lord. Will you be out to dinner, my lord?"

"No, I'll dine in tonight."

"Very well, my lord."

Alone once again, Alex sat at his desk and read the message a second time, more slowly now. A year ago, even a few months ago, it might have given him pause, but now he absorbed the warning of likely trouble on the forthcoming trip and felt himself smiling.

Lord Sherringham did not encounter his friend again until the following Tuesday evening, when they met at a party given by Alex's widowed mother, the Countess of Marsden. As was usual at her popular affairs, the countess's rooms were filled

to bursting with guests; the food was excellent, the
music perfect, and their hostess as charming as always. Polite society was pleased to attend.

"Frederick, you should be dancing," Lady
Marsden said, tapping him lightly on the arm with
her fan.

Sherringham, reflecting somewhat ruefully on the
ability of older ladies to discover the hiding places of
young gentlemen at dancing parties, smiled at her
with his accustomed amiability. "Yes, ma'am. But I
wanted to have a word with Alex first. He *is* here?"

Lady Marsden's still-pretty face showed a mo-
mentary shadow. "Yes, he's here. Frederick ... has
he seemed different to you? Since he was wounded,
I mean."

Sherringham was aware that Lady Marsden knew
of her only son's secret activities; Alex had felt it
only right that his mother know, since he was, in effect, risking the future of an earldom. What the
countess's response had been, Sherringham did not
know, but after the disclosure she had seemed the
same as before. A sensible woman, she never allowed her adoration of her son to cause her to try to
hold him close to her or control his life, and she had
successfully hidden the anxiety his recent activities
must have given her. Until now, at any rate.

Cautiously, holding his voice low in deference to
those around them who certainly did not know of
Alex's activities, Sherringham said, "He seems to
have healed quite well, ma'am—"

She shook her head, a bit impatient. "I know that,
Frederick. I am not speaking of his body, but of
his ... his mind, his heart. He is different. Something has happened to change him."

Sherringham knew very well that Alex had not
confided in his mother about the mysterious Maggie,
and he was certainly not about to reveal that

information—or his own worries. He conjured a smile. "Shall I talk to him, ma'am?"

Lady Marsden eyed him shrewdly, obviously aware that the young viscount had avoided a direct response. But it was equally clear she knew better than to press for one. "Very well, Frederick, speak to him. Try if you can persuade him to remain in town for a few weeks this time rather than barely giving his valet time to repack his bag."

"Yes, ma'am." Sherringham bowed and took his leave of her, beginning to search for his friend in the crush of people. He spared little time for searching the ballroom, knowing Alex too well to expect to find him either dancing or otherwise entertaining one of the many young ladies his mother had invited to her party.

Even before his puzzling encounters with Maggie, Alex had avoided such pursuits; he was a sportsman rather than a dandy, impatient with Society's rules and customs, and he had never shown much interest in the petticoats. And since meeting his mysterious lady, his interest in other women, unless Sherringham was much mistaken, was virtually nil.

It was most worrisome.

Alex was, characteristically, out on the veranda where several men had gathered to smoke cheroots and talk politics. Not terribly fond of parties himself, Sherringham joined them with a feeling of relief.

" 'Evening, Sherry."

Sherringham nodded in response to Alex's greeting and those of the other men.

"I still say the War Office is wrong," Lord Allynby said, obviously continuing an argument the viscount's arrival had interrupted.

"Why?" Jack Billingham demanded with a touch of impatience. "Because you don't believe a good general would move his troops in such a manner? Even good generals make mistakes. I say Bonaparte miscalculated, and we were lucky enough to get wind of it."

Sir Charles Moreton uttered a sound that, in a lesser individual, would have been termed a grunt, and said, "I doubt luck had anything to do with it, Jack. I spoke to Edward Blake at the War Office the other day, and he told me we would all be much surprised if we knew the names of some of the men risking their lives to bring information out of France."

Alex tossed the stub of his cheroot over the balustrade and into the garden. "We should drink a toast to their health," he suggested calmly. "Every evening, in fact. Gentlemen, if you will excuse me, I must return to my mother's party before she sends someone to find me."

Sherringham excused himself as well and followed his friend back into the house. "Alex—"

"My friend, take my advice and never become a gambler." Alex paused before a mirror in the hallway to briefly check his appearance, then glanced aside at his friend with a rueful smile. "Your face would reflect every card in your hand."

"I never claimed to be inscrutable," Sherringham said, not entirely truthfully. "Alex—"

"Not only are you not inscrutable, but if anyone had chanced to note your reaction to Sir Charles's remark just now, they would have been given food for thought. Too much food for thought. Did you *have* to look at me with such guilty knowledge?"

"No one noticed. Alex, did you encounter her again?"

Alex glanced into the mirror once more and touched his cravat as though to make a minute adjustment that appeared wholly unnecessary. His own face was merely reflective, seemingly indifferent to the question asked him. "No." He continued down the hallway.

Sherringham was not about to be put off. Following, he said, "Do you wish me to shout my questions across the crowd, Alex?"

Alex stopped and looked at him, then gestured toward the library. "After you."

They found the library empty of guests, and Sherringham shut the door carefully behind them, watching as his friend stood before the fireplace and gazed up at a portrait hanging above it.

"My father loved this room," he said rather absently.

Sherringham glanced at the portrait of the late earl as he joined Alex. "The older you grow, the more like him you are," he noted.

"All the Drake men tend to resemble the first of our line—and he was, by all accounts, a half-Spanish pirate." Alex leaned a shoulder against the mantel and looked at his friend with a slight smile. "A tale you know. What are these questions you were prepared to shout across the crowd, Sherry?"

"You didn't see the girl—the lady again?"

"No, as I've already told you."

"You expected to see her," Sherringham suggested shrewdly.

Alex hesitated, then shrugged. "I've only seen her in times of trouble; this time my journey went without a hitch."

"As all your journeys should." Sherringham wanted to continue discussing the lady he was very much afraid his friend had imagined under stress, but something in Alex's eyes or pleasant tone warned him to drop the subject for the time being. So, instead, he said, "Alex, your mama has noted a—difference in you since you were wounded. She asked me just now if I knew the cause."

After a moment Alex said, "I trust you told her there was nothing for her to be concerned about."

"I didn't know what to tell her," Sherringham admitted frankly. "You *are* different, whether or not you can see it for yourself."

Alex smiled. "I see the concern of a friend, for which I am grateful, and the anxiety of a mother, which is perfectly natural. And both of you worry needlessly. Sherry, I am no different from the man I was before that unfortunate incident."

Sherringham wanted to argue about that, but before he could frame the words to describe his vague uneasiness, a young couple came into the room, most improperly seeking privacy, and the moment was lost. Alex returned to his mother's guests, and Sherringham found himself dancing with a succession of hopeful young ladies, every one of whom seemed disposed to view him with unnerving approval.

He made good his escape only an hour later, without having again spoken privately to Alex.

And without being in the least reassured.

"Alex."

He felt his heart stop and then begin pounding like a drum in his chest. "Maggie!"

It was she, cloaked and hooded as always, luminous eyes fixed on his face. She was closer than ever before, her sweet voice so low it was nearly a whisper. "This man you are meeting tonight . . . this man means to betray you, Alex."

Standing at the edge of a thicket by the road, his horse tied several yards behind him, Alex looked at her and tried to concentrate on what she was telling him. "I've trusted Jenkins for nearly a year now. He's never given me false information."

"They know about you in France," she said. "Your activities have been noted. They've put a price on your head. Jenkins needs money. And he means to betray you this night."

"They know me? By name?"

She frowned slightly. "They know ... *of* you. Please, Alex, you must believe me."

Alex felt an almost overwhelming compulsion to believe her, but still he hesitated. Jenkins had promised to deliver vital information gathered from other fishermen—who were, Alex had discovered, excellent sources of information when it came to activities on and around coastal areas. The War Office needed that information.

"Come with me now," she urged him softly. "Leave this dangerous place. From a safe vantage point, you can observe what will happen and judge for yourself if I am right."

It was a logical precaution. When she eased back into the woods, he followed her willingly. She waited while he untied his horse, then led the way through the dark forest until the trees thinned more than fifty yards away and there was a bit of high ground where it would be possible to observe his former position unseen.

After tethering his horse again, Alex turned and, for a moment, thought himself alone once more. "Maggie?"

"Here."

The moon was hidden for the moment behind clouds, and since she wore a dark cloak, it was difficult to see her very well in the dimness. But he caught a glimpse of glowing eyes and let himself be drawn by them until he reached her. She was standing at the edge of a small clearing atop the hill, where the road below, and his previous position, could be easily seen.

Alex dared not approach more than an arm's length from her, and even that was closer than ever before. He sensed rather than saw an agitation within her, and had the certain knowledge that she was wary of him in a way he didn't understand.

Seeking to keep her from disappearing once again, he kept his voice low and as unthreatening as possible. "Maggie, how do you know Jenkins means to betray me?"

"I know."

"But how? Do you know him?"

"No."

"Did you see something? Did you overhear a conversation between him and someone else?"

She stirred slightly, clearly uneasy. "Does it matter?"

Alex drew a breath. "Maggie, we are at war. I cannot afford to trust information if I am uncertain of its source."

"Trust me."

He was conscious of another almost overwhelming compulsion, this one to reach out and touch her, and fighting it was the hardest thing he had ever done in his life. With an effort that was almost painful, he managed to remain still. "Trust you? Trust a woman of mystery? Who are you, Maggie? I must know."

Instead of answering him, she pointed, and Alex looked down at where he had waited before to see a horse and rider approach slowly. The rider dismounted and stood for a couple of minutes, then led his horse into the thicket. Only a minute or so later he reappeared, and every jerky motion he made indicated rage.

"Jenkins," Alex murmured.

"Yes."

"But he's alone as we agreed—"

"Wait."

In less than five minutes three other riders approached cautiously, and they joined Jenkins at the thicket. Even at this distance Alex could hear the sounds of voices raised in anger, and he wasn't much surprised when one of the men struck Jenkins, knocking him to the ground.

"They expected to find you there. He failed them," Maggie said softly. "Now they cannot trust him either."

The others rode away, and Jenkins climbed slowly to his feet and remounted his own horse, riding away with the speed of a man hunted—or one fearing he was about to be. Alex watched in silence, utterly convinced that he would have found himself captured or killed had Maggie not come to warn him. When the road below them was empty once again of life, he turned and looked at her.

"Who are you, Maggie?"

She turned her head to look away from him, and the moon reappeared just then to give him a better view of her profile. Beautiful, delicate, her features were oddly familiar to him, especially since this was the first time he had gotten a clear look at her. It was as if he had seen her many times before, in his mind's eye—or in his dreams.

"I ... am myself."

That sweet, sweet voice ... it was a siren song calling out to the deepest part of him, an echo in his soul. And his reaction to it made thinking almost impossible. But he tried. He did try.

"Why do you want to help me? Or—is it England you want to help?"

"You. I need you to be safe, Alex."

"Why?"

She turned her head again, a little toward him, and a frown flitted across her exquisite face. "Why do you keep asking me that?"

"Because you won't give me an answer. Maggie . . . this is the third time you've helped me, coming to me in the middle of the night, miles from anywhere, saving my life. How did you get here? I haven't seen a carriage, a horse. I haven't been able to find anyone who knows you. Where is your family, where do you live? How do you know what will happen before it happens?"

She began to back away as his voice grew harsher with frustration, and Alex held out a quick hand.

"No! Please—please don't leave."

"You ask questions I cannot answer." Her voice was low, distressed. "I—I only know what I know. I only know that I need you to be safe."

"All right." He would have said anything to keep her there. "I'm sorry; I didn't intend to distress you. You have done nothing but help me, and I am grateful. Please believe that."

She nodded a bit hesitantly, but there was still a perceptible tension in her. "I must go—"

"Must you?" Alex made use of all the persuasive charm he could command and kept his voice low. "Could you not remain just a little while? I shall have to return to London in an hour or so—I would welcome the opportunity to talk to you."

"I cannot answer your questions—"

"I understand that." He did not, but lied deliberately. Anything to keep her here. *Anything.* "But surely there is no harm in simply talking to me for an hour or so? You choose the subjects, if you wish. We will discuss—the latest in ladies' fashions if you like, or whether London is bearable in the summer heat."

She was, clearly, amused by the subjects he offered. "Fashions? Am I to believe a man such as yourself takes note of ladies' fashions?"

He offered her a slight bow. "*All* men take note of ladies' fashions, I promise you. We may not understand the finer points of such an intricate subject, but we view the results with pleasure."

Maggie uttered a low laugh, a musical sound that affected him as acutely as a physical caress. For a moment he could only stand there, dizzy, his heart pounding. He gazed at her with a hunger greater than anything he had ever known.

She did not seem to notice.

"A discreet answer, I would say. As for the heat of London in summer, what makes you so certain I have experienced it? Or that I have any knowledge of London at any time?"

"True, I have no way of knowing." His voice sounded normal, he thought. "In fact, I doubt that you have visited London at all, for surely we would have met at one of the parties or balls." It was not *quite* a question.

"I love to dance." Her voice was wistful. "It has always been one of my most favorite things in the world. But it has been so long since I've attended a party."

"Why?" Immediately he regretted asking such a pointed question.

She turned her head away from him. She appeared both confused and uneasy, as though confronted with an alarming puzzle she could not hope to understand. "I—I do not know. Something happened . . . I was going to London, but something happened. . . ."

Her distress hurt him. Though he badly wanted to press for more details, he could not bring himself to upset her further.

Instead, casually, he said, "This time of year, London is quite pleasant. But when the heat comes, it becomes oppressive—hot, dusty, and uncomfortable. Like so many others, I prefer the country during the summer months."

She looked at him and offered a faint smile, a bit uncertain but no longer so distressed. "My home is in the country. It is very peaceful and beautiful. There are meadows and forests, and a lovely lake."

"A lake? You mean the one where ...?"

Maggie's smile widened. "Where you saved my life? No, I was away from home then. We were visiting friends that summer, when you pulled me from that lake."

Alex drew a breath. So it *had* been Maggie he had rescued. Not that he had ever really doubted it ... "I wasn't sure you were unharmed, and you seemed so frightened. I went for help. But when I came back, you were gone."

"Yes. I'm sorry I didn't wait; you deserved far better than that. But I'd been forbidden to go near the lake, you see, and I didn't want my father finding out I'd been so disobedient—and so foolish. I managed to sneak into the house and change before anyone saw me. So no one else knew what you did for me that day."

He shook his head ruefully. "I had nearly convinced myself that it had never happened, and that you didn't exist."

"You—looked for me?"

"That day. And for more than a week afterward," Alex said, remembering only then that he had indeed searched for that little girl with her glowing eyes and haunting voice. "I suppose I didn't ask the right questions of the right people; I assumed you lived in the area, even though I had never seen you before."

In a wondering tone, she said, "You seemed to me

something out of a dream that day. I was drowning, dying, and I knew there was nothing I could do to change that. I hadn't the strength left to save myself. But then, just when I had given up all hope ... you were there. And I knew the moment you touched me that everything would be all right."

Alex couldn't prevent himself from saying honestly, "I did nothing more than anyone else would have done, Maggie. I saw someone in trouble, and I helped her."

"Nothing more than anyone else would have done?" She smiled. "It's hardly a common thing to risk one's life to save another's."

"I didn't think about risking my life," he confessed.

"But you did risk your life. And by doing so, you saved mine." Her luminous eyes seemed to glow even brighter, and her voice was impossibly sweet. "If not for you, I would have missed so much. So many birthdays. So many spring flowers and winter snows and thunderstorms. If not for you, I would never have known my baby sister. I would not have been there to nurse my mother when she was sick, or help my father when he needed me. If not for you, I would never have seen the miracle of a foal being born, or been granted the years to watch it grow. If not for you, I would never have experienced the joys—and confusions—of growing into a woman."

Alex had to clear his throat before he could speak, and even then his voice emerged with a husky rasp. "Then it was the best thing I have ever done in my life, Maggie. Because you've grown into an exceptional woman."

She caught her breath audibly. "You—cannot know that."

"Can't I? I know it as surely as you knew I needed your help tonight."

Maggie was very still for a moment, her eyes fixed on him, and then she sighed raggedly. "I wish . . ."

"What do you wish?" He eased a fraction closer to her.

She shook her head in bewilderment, and her soft voice was filled with poignant longing. "I wish . . . it wasn't always night. I wish I could see you in the sunlight. And, most of all, I wish there was a party where we could dance."

"Then come back to London with me," he urged quietly, moving another infinitesimal bit nearer to her. "London is filled with parties. I'll take you to my mother—"

"I cannot."

"Why? Maggie, it will be all right, I swear to you. I will do everything in my power to make you happy. If there is someone I should ask to be permitted to pay my addresses to you, tell me who it is, and I will go to him tomorrow. Tonight."

She gave a little sob. "Oh—oh, no. You cannot wish to—to—"

"I wish to marry you. Maggie, I love you." He had not known it until the words left his lips, but once he heard them he knew beyond any shadow of a doubt that it was true.

"No," she murmured in a voice beyond surprise.

"My sweet love . . . you know so much—how can you not know that?"

She lifted a slender hand as if she would have reached out to him, then drew back. "It—is so with you too? Alex . . ."

He was finally close enough, and despite an inner voice shouting a warning, he listened instead to the overwhelming longing to hold her in his arms. He reached for her. "Maggie—"

She cried out, a sound of pain and utter desolation—and vanished.

Alex stood there, staring at the spot where she had been, his hand still reaching to touch her. And only the night heard him whisper, "No. No, you have to be real. I can't bear it if you aren't real."

THREE

"*I* can't allow it." Edward Blake, his distinguished face wearing a rare frown, turned from the window and went back to his desk. He sat down, still frowning, and gazed across the desk at the man sitting in one of the two visitors' chairs in the office.

"Why not? Have I ever failed you in the past? Have I ever been anything but successful?"

Blake shook his head. "That is hardly the point, Alex, and you well know it."

"Then what is the point?" Unconsciously, Alex drummed long fingers restlessly against the arm of his chair. "You can get the information as far as the coast of France and require someone to bring it from there back across the Channel—a journey I have made a dozen times. There is no reason why I should not be—"

"The point is that you aren't fit for another assignment," the older man put in baldly.

Alex stiffened. "I beg your pardon."

With a faintly sour smile, Blake said, "I won't give you a fight, Alex, so don't bother to poker up and glare at me. I have been in this game too long not to know when a man is spoiling for a fight in order to dissipate various ... frustrations. As you are now. Forgive me if I don't oblige you."

"Edward—"

"I stand by my assessment of your condition. In the past month you've gone to the Channel—and across it—five times, which is four times more than any other man working for the War Office during the same period of time. Your physical resources are stretched so thin the strain has become visible; your friends and acquaintances are beginning to remark it. Do you realize that, Alex? Do you realize that you look like a man who has just come off a long stint on the battlefield? It is all too obvious that the last thing you need at present is another assignment."

"I," Alex said politely, "am quite well, I assure you. And not a scratch in months. So I don't quite see—"

"I know you don't see." Blake's voice was sober. "That worries me more than anything. Alex ... to every man doing the type of dangerous, nerve-racking work we ask them to do comes a point of ... diminishing returns. A point when instincts have been ... overused, burned away, at least temporarily. And after that, he's simply no good to us any longer, not unless and until he heals himself. On that last trip, you risked the lives of yourself *and* your contact, even after discovering that the information he carried was virtually useless."

"I got the information," Alex pointed out.

"Yes. And it was useless."

"I couldn't be sure of that."

"A year ago your instincts would have led you to abort the meeting—because whatever information *might* have been gained was not worth the risk to you and your contact. You know that, Alex. Or, at least, you did know it once upon a time. It was one of the qualities which made you so effective in your work for us."

Alex attempted a laugh that did not quite come off. "So that's it? One misjudgment on my part and the War Office wants nothing more to do with me?"

Blake leaned forward, his forearms resting on the immaculate blotter. "Alex, I understand how badly you want to aid England. I know very well that you would be in the Peninsula fighting in the field right now, today, if not for your obligations to your family's future. But rest assured, you *have* aided England, more than perhaps you realize."

"Edward—"

"No, hear me out. If not for you, we would not have had any warning of French plans to occupy Portugal two years ago, or their invasion of Spain last year—and those are only two instances where the information you attained for us made a tremendous difference in the war. Your help has been invaluable, Alex, believe me."

"But you want no more of it," Alex responded flatly.

Blake sighed. "London is already miserable in this summer heat, and the fighting in the Peninsula will not be shortened by any information you could get for us. For the time being, we must leave things to our generals in the field. Take advantage of the time, Alex. Go to your country house, where the air you breathe is at least clear of dust and soot. Open Marsden Hall and entertain your neighbors; host parties for the countess. School the horses you're becoming famous for, or strike a wager with Sherringham to find which of you may break the record for a race to Brighton."

"Waste my time?"

"Enjoy your life." Blake smiled faintly. "If we are still chasing our tails come autumn—then perhaps we will need men with your experience to gather information for us. But until then, stay away from this office, Alex. Forget about the war."

Alex rose to his feet, reluctant but all too aware that Edward Blake's refusal was final. He managed to take his leave of the older man courteously, and to hide the riot of emotions inside him as he left the War Office—discreetly, as usual, by a side door.

It was only mid-June, but even so the day was hot and offered a miserable mix of dust, soot, and humidity that seemed to cling to everything in the city. But Alex noticed little of his surroundings. He walked to where his curricle awaited him—again, with the discretion of a man who wanted his actions to pass without remark, two blocks away from the War Office—and climbed into the seat with no more than a nod for his groom.

He drove to his London house with the same abstraction and entered without a word to his butler to closet himself in his library. He sat down at his desk, but did not reach for any of the paperwork with which he might have occupied himself. Instead, he merely folded his hands on the blotter and stared into space.

Despite having a number of close calls during the past few weeks, he had not seen a sign of Maggie. With each trip to the Channel, he had grown more reckless, risking his life without a moment's hesitation, and even though he could have used someone's help on more than one dark night, she had not appeared.

Appeared. An apt word, that. Appeared like a ghost—disappeared like a ghost. Saving his life and yet vanishing into thin air when he would have

touched her. Her sweet voice and luminous eyes
haunting him until he could think of nothing else. A
woman he loved beyond all reason.

A woman who existed only in his mind, at best—
and at worst had long since departed this life.

"No." He heard his voice in the quiet of the room
and was unsurprised by the harsh pain it held. He
had been living with the pain for long weeks now,
ever since the night he had tried to touch her. It was
an ache inside him, inescapable no matter where he
went or what he did.

There was no madness in his family. No tales of
ghostly visitations even at Marsden Hall, the country estate where a long, unbroken line of earls had
spent their time away from London. There was, as
far as he knew, nothing in his heritage to make him
susceptible to a haunting he could explain as nothing
else.

He had saved Maggie's life when she was a child,
and because of what he had done, she had lived to
reach adulthood. But what then? Had she, on the
point of beginning a journey to London, been involved in some kind of accident? She had been "going to London . . . and something happened."

What had happened?

Alex wanted that answer. And yet, at the same
time, he did not want it. Not if the answer would
tell him that Maggie was not flesh and blood as he
was himself, but was, somehow, a creature of spirit,
an angel guarding his life because he had once saved
hers.

Or, at least, that she had guarded his life until he
had attempted to touch her, and in so doing had
shattered some fragile reality—or even, God forbid,
her very existence . . .

No. No, he was not yet prepared to believe such
a thing. Not without making every attempt to find

out for certain what it all meant. His intellect was not ready to accept the unthinkable, and his heart most surely was not ready to love in vain.

Which meant that he had to see Maggie again.

Edward Blake had made his position clear, and since Alex had no intention of doing anything to hinder intelligence efforts for England, he was not about to, on his own, take the assignment Blake had refused him. But that did not mean he could not, on his own, attempt to gather other information vital to England's interests. He possessed the means, and the contacts, to act independently.

It would mean far more danger than he had ever faced before. He would be truly alone this time, without official backing or resources, and he would have to penetrate deep into enemy territory. The odds against him being able to do so and still escape were absurdly high.

Unless he possessed a guardian angel.

Without hesitation, Alex drew forward paper and pen and began to rapidly jot a list of the items he would require for the journey, followed by a list of things he needed to do before he left. Just in case, he told himself, he was wrong. Just in case Maggie *was* a figment of his imagination.

Just in case he did not make it back to England.

When Lord Sherringham entered Lady Marsden's drawing room, it was with a quick step and a worried frown. Even so, with manners drummed into him by a firm mama, he did not forget to bow punctiliously and greet the countess with all the respect due a lady of her rank and years.

"Never mind all that," the countess told him with a dismissive wave of her hand. "What have you discovered, Frederick?"

"Alex isn't working for the War Office, not this

time," Sherringham told her worriedly. "In fact, Edward Blake specifically refused to give him another assignment more than a week ago—told him to go to the country and rest for the summer."

"Then . . . ?"

"He is doing this on his own," Sherringham said. "According to what Edward has been able to discover, Alex left England and crossed the Channel days ago. He is apparently gathering information himself, on French soil."

Lady Marsden caught her breath. "In France? But—if he is discovered, captured—"

"He'll be shot as a spy," Sherringham finished grimly.

He crept through the undergrowth cautiously, trying to make as little noise as possible. It was damned difficult to do, since the summer heat had baked tree and bush until every leaf crackled at the slightest touch, but despite everything, Alex had no wish to die, and so he was very, very careful.

At least some in the company of soldiers had seen him, not clearly perhaps, but well enough to arouse suspicion; he was too whole and healthy in appearance not to have been pressed into service by the army when every able body was badly needed, so they naturally wished to know why. Or, at least, Alex supposed that was how their thinking went. He had already run into suspicion for not being a soldier, and though his excellent French had gotten him out of a couple of awkward situations, he knew his luck could not hold out much longer.

He needed to leave France.

He had accumulated good information about French troop movements and plans that he planned to convey to the War Office—after which he half expected Edward Blake to lock him up for, at least, the duration of the war—but none of it would be of any use to anyone if he didn't get himself back across the Channel.

Alex was exhausted, covered with dust, hungry, and almost overwhelmed by the grinding disappointment of not having seen Maggie. Even though he had always before seen her on English soil, he had been certain she would appear to him even on this side of the Channel if he were to encounter deadly danger. But there had been no sign of her. No sign at all.

And he could not afford to remain here any longer. He had been slinking through the French countryside for more than two weeks now, far too long for safety's sake, and he had no choice but to make for the Channel.

If he could only slip past the soldiers searching for him . . .

It was nearly midnight, and the moon kept vanishing behind racing clouds, which at least aided him rather than the soldiers, but Alex was depending on his sense of direction to keep him heading toward the coast, and he was so weary he knew only too well that none of his senses could be trusted. But he had little choice except to keep going.

"Alex . . ."

"Maggie." It was shock rather than caution that kept his voice no louder than a whisper, overpowering relief that held him immobile, so that he didn't lunge toward her.

"This way." She backed away, gesturing for him to follow.

Alex didn't hesitate. With his gaze fixed on her, he followed her silent progress through the forest, hardly blinking for fear she would vanish. She led him in a seemingly directionless route, but the sounds of the soldiers grew fainter and fainter, until finally he could not hear them at all.

It was only then, more than an hour after she had found him, that Maggie stopped, on the edge of the forest where the moonlight was no longer forced to penetrate dense foliage.

"From here, you can find your own way to the coast." Her voice was strained.

"Maggie, look at me." He didn't try to approach any nearer, having learned that lesson. But she had her back to him, and Alex badly needed to see her lovely face.

She turned to him, finally, and the moonlight changed the tears on her cheeks to silver.

"Maggie . . ."

"You must stop," she told him shakily. "Please, you must stop doing this. Do you think I can bear to watch you risk your life over and over?"

It was a knife in him to see her tears, hear her pain, but Alex forced himself to say, "If this is the only way I can see you, then so be it. Maggie, what choice do I have?"

"Please, Alex, don't do this to me!"

"I must see you, talk to you," he said intensely. "I must, Maggie, do you understand? It has become as necessary to me as breathing. And this is the only way I know to see you. Am I wrong? Is there another way? If so, then tell me, please."

She put one of her hands up to her throat in a curiously moving gesture. "There—there is no other way. I cannot—"

"You only come to me in times of danger. No other time." He laughed roughly. "If there were some other way for me to call you, believe me, I would have found it by now. If the longing of one heart for another could cross distance . . . or time . . . or even death itself, you would have heard me calling your name. I have thought of little but you since the night you found me wounded and saved my life." He drew a breath. "The life you saved belongs to you, Maggie."

"I give it back to you," she said unsteadily.

"No, you cannot. The rest of my life is bound to you. The rest of my days are yours. My nights ... my lonely nights. Dear God, how badly I want to hold you. . . ."

She caught her breath audibly. "Don't, Alex."

"Don't? Don't long for you? Tell me how I may change that, Maggie, because I don't know how to. Tell me how to rip you from my mind, my heart. Tell me how to empty myself of you. And when you tell me that, tell me what I did to deserve this terrible fate."

"No, Alex," she protested.

He hardened himself to the pain in her soft voice. "It is terrible, this fate you've shaped for me. To love a woman I can never touch, a woman I see only when my life is in danger and then only for brief moments. A woman who will never walk by my side ... or dance in my arms. What worse fate could any man suffer?"

Maggie took a jerky step back, almost as though he had struck her. "Oh ... oh, no. I never meant ... anything like this to happen. I never meant to cause you such pain. I only needed you to be safe."

Alex played the only trump card in his hand. "If you truly need me to be safe, Maggie, tell me how to find you, tell me where you spend your days away from me. Because if you do not, I shall continue looking for danger as often as I can. I swear to you I will." He held his breath, very afraid she would not answer, or would answer that she had no existence apart from him. Very afraid she would confess that whatever she was, the Maggie he loved had no flesh-and-blood reality.

She was still and silent for a long moment. Finally she drew a ragged breath. "All right. Then ... then come to Avonleigh."

"Avonleigh." Even as he whispered the word she became something insubstantial, like heat shimmering off pavement, and he found himself alone once more.

"Go away, Sherry," Alex told his guest absently.

Sherringham, who had spent the better part of half an hour giving his reckless friend a piece of his mind, and without mincing words about it, threw up his hands in disgust. "Have you heard a word I've said?" he demanded irately.

"I am stubborn, insanely rash, heedless, foolish, a very bad friend, and doubtless mad as a hatter." Alex looked up from his desk with a faint smile. "I believe that was the gist of it."

With little regard for his fine coat, Sherringham collapsed into a wingback chair near the desk and sighed. "Damn you, Alex." After a scowling moment his natural curiosity got the better of him, and he asked, "What on earth are you searching for? I've never seen so many maps in my life." He sat up with a jerk. "Alex, if you mean to—"

"No, no," Alex soothed, "I don't mean to return to France. Unless ..."

"Unless?"

"Unless *that* is where Avonleigh is," he murmured to himself.

"Avonleigh?"

Alex looked at his friend. "Yes. Do you know it?"

"It's got a familiar ring to it, but ... no, I don't think so. What is it? A town?"

"I have no idea. A place, but beyond that ... It

does not sound like a village, does it? A town of some size, then, surely." He bent his head once more, searching the most detailed map of England he had been able to procure.

Though Sherringham's frown faded, it did not entirely disappear. The spy he had days ago set to watch this house—a sharp-eyed young groom eager to earn a few extra coins—had reported that Lord Marsden had returned very late last night, on horseback and dressed more like a thief than a lord. After hearing that, Sherringham had barely been able to contain his impatience long enough to wait until a decent hour for a morning visit. He had arrived to find his friend up and dressed, and apparently hard at work at his desk. Searching, it seemed, for a place called Avonleigh.

Under orders from Lady Marsden, Sherringham knew he would have to report Alex's return to London to her this afternoon, but he had no idea if he would be able to reassure the countess as to her son's condition.

In one sense, Alex seemed better than he had before this most recent mad journey to France. He was clear-eyed and seemed clearheaded, and was not nearly so tense as he had been the last time Sherringham had seen him, but he did seem ... changed. His face had the curiously stripped-bare look of a man whose entire future depended on the next turn of a card or roll of the dice, as though he had staked everything that he had and everything he was on a whim of fate or fortune.

And *that* Sherringham found very, very disturbing.

"Did Blake threaten to throw you in jail?" he asked.

"For half an hour or so last night when I got him out of bed," Alex replied, his tone absent once more.

"But the information was good, even he couldn't deny that."

"I'll bet he threatened you with worse than jail if you venture out of England again."

"He said something about a ship headed for America, and mentioned indentured servitude."

"Alex, tell me you don't mean to cross the Channel again," Sherringham begged, knowing Edward Blake well enough to believe he was not a man to make idle threats.

"I don't mean to."

The words and the voice uttering them were mild rather than emphatic with the sworn vow Sherringham had hoped for, but he accepted them with a sigh. "Thank God."

"Avon*dale*," Alex muttered. "And Avonmore. But no Avonleigh."

Sherringham's uneasiness returned. "What is this place?"

"I don't know."

"Then why search for it?"

"Because I must find it."

This Avonleigh, the viscount realized, was the hand of cards Alex had before him, the dice he was about to cast; that was evident in the set of his shoulders and the determined tone of his voice. He had, somehow, staked far too much on this Avonleigh.

Sherringham, not a gambling man, grew even more worried. "Is it a property you mean to buy?" he asked lightly.

"No. Perhaps not a town. Perhaps it's an estate." Alex pushed the map aside and drew forth a thick book with *Burke's Peerage* stamped on the spine in gold lettering.

"Alex, what is Avonleigh?" Sherringham demanded. "Why is it so important to you?"

Looking up at his friend at last, Alex said, "Maggie."

"You saw her again?"

"Yes." Alex returned his attention to the book lying open before him.

"And this Avonleigh is ...?"

"Where I'll find her."

Sherringham digested that briefly. "How do you know?"

"She told me. Damn and blast this book—why is there no separate list of estates in England? Will I have to read about every title dating back to the Conqueror?"

"Probably. Did she vanish again—before your very eyes?"

"Not until she told me what I wanted to know," Alex retorted.

"You mean what you wanted to hear. A small distinction, but an important one, I would say."

"Sherry—"

"Alex, will you for one moment *think* about what you're saying?" Sherringham kept his voice level and matter-of-fact. "A girl appears to you in times of danger, apparently saving your life. And then *disappears* literally into thin air. Before your eyes. Like a soap bubble." He drew a breath. "How can you even entertain the *idea* that she might be more than a figment of your imagination?"

With his own voice calm and matter-of-fact, Alex said, "Sherry, perhaps I am mad as a hatter. But *if* she exists, I intend to find her."

"And if she doesn't exist?"

A bleakness tightened Alex's features, but his voice remained composed. "Then you will be able to say *I told you so*, won't you?"

After a long moment Sherringham rose to his feet with a sigh. "I have any number of maps and charts in my library. Perhaps one of them knows your Avonleigh."

Alex smiled faintly. "Thank you."

The viscount waved away thanks, his amiable face wearing a rueful expression. "If I find anything, I'll let you know at once. And if *you* find anything, do me the honor of informing me before bolting London again, will you? I find these abrupt departures and postmidnight arrivals quite disconcerting."

"I will try to remember that."

When the door closed behind his friend, Alex bent his head once more to the book before him. Perhaps the spelling he assumed was wrong? He found a sheet of notepaper and jotted down the alternate spellings he could think of, muttering under his breath a word that had become, for him, a talisman ... or a siren song.

"Avonleigh ... Avonley ... Avonly ... Avonlie ..."

"No need to announce me, Stames," Lady Marsden said, already three quarters of the way into her son's library. She found him, his coat off and cravat loosened, sitting at a desk piled with books and maps. "Alex, what in the world ...?"

He looked up, his face thinner than it had been when she had last seen him several weeks before, a tired frown drawing his brows together. He got to his feet a bit stiffly and absently flexed his shoulders. "Good afternoon, Mother."

"Afternoon? It's gone seven o'clock, Alex. Didn't your staff bother to feed you?"

"I told them to leave me alone," he said dismissively.

"Which, obviously, they have done. This room is terribly hot and stuffy, and you," she told him frankly, "look like something the cat dragged in."

"I beg your pardon, Mother."

"As well you should. I should like to know why you refused my request that you dine with me tonight?"

Alex remembered, vaguely, receiving a note not long after Sherry had left, and recalled jotting a brief response. "I didn't refuse, Mother; I merely said that another night would—"

"I know what you said, and a refusal by any other name is still no! Alex, you have been gone for weeks, and I was hoping you would be ... kind enough ... to spend a bit of time with me before you jaunt off again."

He eyed her thoughtfully. "It is not like you, Mother, to employ tactics designed to make me feel guilty."

A mischievous smile curved her mouth. "Well, I daresay other mothers have success with such tactics. They might even be asked to sit down when visiting their wayward sons."

"We'll be more comfortable in the parlor," Alex told her imperturbably, coming to take her arm and guide her toward the door.

Lady Marsden said nothing else until she was satisfactorily installed on the settee in her son's front parlor, a room that was cooler and far less stuffy than his library had been. Declining a polite offer of refreshments, she studied her son for a moment before finally deciding not to pry, even though she badly wanted to know what both he and his friend Sherringham were keeping from her.

She knew her son very well, and even though his recent activities on behalf of England had tried her fortitude sorely, she was determined to allow him to live his own life. He would tell her what he wanted her to know; she could only trust that it would be what she needed to know.

"Darling," she began briskly, "I realize you must have a great deal of work to do, particularly since you have been out of town, but I really would like to spend some time with my only child."

"Mother—"

"I do not ask for much, after all. Just a brief moment of your time. A small portion of your attention for a little while. And surely that is not too much to ask from the woman who brought you into this world?"

"Mother."

She smiled. "It really is not much, Alex, I promise you, and should require no more than a week or so of your time. It is only that I promised to spend a few weeks with an old friend, and I should feel so much more comfortable on the journey if you were to accompany me."

"An old friend?"

"Yes, Beatrice Findley—Lady Ormsby. We have known one another since we were girls, though we've barely spoken in years. She married Albert Findley, and when he succeeded to the title and became Viscount Ormsby, they moved to a drafty old place up in Lincolnshire—the back of beyond, I assure you."

"And quite a journey," he said rather mechanically, already calculating how much time such a trip would require. He was a dutiful son, and his mother rarely asked such things of him, but still he had to fight the urge to refuse her outright. He had yet to find Avonleigh, and he knew only too well he would resent any time spent away from that search.

"Yes, I know, but I had not the heart to refuse Beatrice's invitation. She had only recently begun entertaining at all. She lost Albert two years ago, and they both had to endure the death of their eldest son two years before that; he was killed at Trafalgar, the

poor boy. She has a younger son who inherited the
title, and two girls to help manage things for her, but
Anne is barely out of the nursery, and I'm sure
Sarah will marry soon—why, she must be past
twenty, though I haven't seen the child since she was
a toddler—and I have no doubt Beatrice is lonely
way out there. She invited me for the summer,
though I promised only a few weeks, and I was so
hoping you would accompany me at least on the
trip. I know Beatrice would love to see you—I don't
believe she ever has, how dreadful! But—"

"Mother," Alex interrupted, accustomed to his
mother's habit of rattling on whenever she was uncertain of his response, "you would not have match-
making in mind, I trust?"

Lady Marsden laughed in honest amusement.
"For you? Darling, don't be absurd! Though
Beatrice didn't mention it in her letter, I would be
much surprised if the oldest girl is not betrothed;
Sarah was a beautiful child. As for Anne, if she is
yet sixteen years old, I will eat my best hat! No, I
assure you that neither I nor Beatrice has any such
plans in mind. She is far too placid to scheme, and
I know you too well to suppose you either want or
require my help in finding a wife."

"I am glad you realize that," Alex said somewhat
dryly, wondering what his doting mama would have
to say if he told her he was head over heels in love
with a lady who might well turn out to be a ghost.

"I am hardly a fool," his mother said with dignity.

Alex smiled, then said, "When do you plan to
start on this journey?"

"I told Beatrice to expect me by the end of the
week. That would mean starting day after tomorrow."

He hesitated, feeling guilty. "Mother, if you were
going later in the summer, even in a week or two, I

would be delighted to escort you, but I have ...
something I must do right now. I am sorry, but—"

She reached over to pat his arm, hiding her disappointment behind a smile. "Say no more, darling, I
understand completely. I shall be safe enough with
outriders, and though I would welcome your company on the journey, my maid will suffice."

"I am sorry," he repeated. And when she rose to
her feet, he did the same, adding, "Mother, why not
dine with me tonight? I am sure Stames has already
advised the cook, and—I would like to spend some
time with you before you go."

"Thank you, I accept," she said promptly, sitting
down once again. "Your cook is better than mine. In
fact, I don't doubt he is better than the one I will
find at Avonleigh. The really good ones seem to prefer to work in the city, don't you think? And they
complain so when they are asked to work at country
houses or remote estates—"

"Avonleigh?"

Lady Marsden eyed her son worriedly. "Darling,
are you all right? You have gone quite pale."

"I am fine, Mother." His tone was normal, he
thought. Shockingly normal. "Avonleigh?" He sat
down carefully.

"Yes, Beatrice's estate. Actually, her son's now, I
suppose, though I gather she means to continue living there. David has not yet married, so I suppose he
welcomes her help in running the house—"

"Mother." Alex was surprised his voice was still
so calm; his heart was thudding wildly, and he was
certain he was not breathing. "If you don't mind
starting your journey tomorrow, I would be delighted to escort you to Lincolnshire. And to
Avonleigh."

FOUR

When Alex saw the lake, he had to force himself not to gallop forward on his horse, leaving his mother's lumbering coach far behind. The lake was beautiful, water shimmering in the sunlight and dotted with a number of ducks peacefully swimming. And around it lay more beauty—tall, stately trees, summer flowers blowing in the slight breeze, and green, green grass.

My home is in the country. It is my favorite place in the world, very peaceful and beautiful. There are meadows and forests, and a lovely lake.

Would he find Maggie here? He had told himself he was braced for disappointment, but knew only too well that if he did not find her here, the failure would be devastating.

As for what his mother thought, he hardly dared to imagine it. After surprising her with his sudden decision to accompany her on her journey, he had insisted they leave London scandalously early the next morning and had to be persuaded much against his will not to try to complete the one hundred and twenty-plus miles in a single day. He had pushed his mother's eight-mile-an-hour coach horses to a straining ten miles an hour, and at every change along the road had demanded the best replacements possible, no expense spared.

As it was, they were now in Lincolnshire in the middle of the afternoon only two days after leaving London—and Alex had to resist the urge to order the horses to be put to a gallop.

"What Beatrice will think, I do not know," Lady Marsden had murmured when they left the inn very early that morning. "I am days early, Alex."

Alex, impatient of such social niceties in his state, merely said, "If she is as placid as you say, Mother, I doubt she will notice anything amiss."

Now, so close to Avonleigh—and, one way or another, to his fate—Alex acknowledged to himself that their arrival would indeed seem abrupt to all but the most oblivious of persons. He had expected his mother to question him, at the very least about his haste, but she had said little. She had, however, eyed him speculatively, and he had no doubt she would be watching him very closely at Avonleigh.

Not that he cared. He was far beyond the point of being concerned if he betrayed himself.

Within five minutes of the lake, the coach turned onto a private road winding among tall trees. Alex, riding his horse with outward patience beside the coach, kept his gaze directed ahead, and when he caught his first glimpse of Avonleigh, fresh tension wound through him.

What Lady Marsden had described as a "drafty old place" was, in fact, very near to being a castle, complete with what looked like a turret. It was fashioned of weathered gray stone that should have looked cold and yet appeared curiously warm and inviting, and both the house and grounds were in excellent repair.

As his mother's coach bowled briskly up the drive, Alex took a quick but intent look around, noting a rolling green pasture containing several horses he judged to be fine ones. Then he turned his full attention to the house, and when the coach pulled up at the bottom of the front steps, he swung down from his horse.

Their arrival might have been earlier than expected, but Avonleigh was a well-run household even in the face of an unexpected arrival: a groom tenderly took charge of Alex's weary horse, another stood at the heads of the coach horses, and a third opened the coach door and stood ready to assist the countess.

Alex helped his mother to alight, conscious of a giddy sort of amusement at himself; it was astonishingly difficult to keep himself from dashing up the steps and shouting Maggie's name at the top of his voice. He wondered almost idly what his mother would think of such a display, but pushed speculation aside as their hostess came down the steps to greet them happily.

"Catherine! I am so happy to have you here. My dear, you look simply wonderful!"

"Beatrice, my dear . . ."

Introduced a moment later, Alex bowed to his hostess. "Lady Ormsby."

She smiled up at him, an obviously sedate woman, still trim and very pretty, with a relaxed air he found very pleasing. "Oh, call me Beatrice, please; we do not stand upon ceremony here, I promise you."

Despite his tension, he could not help smiling at her in return. "Thank you, ma'am. My mother most kindly shortened my name to Alex, so I would be pleased if you called me that."

"Alexander *is* a mouthful," she agreed cheerfully. "And Alex suits you, if I may say so. This way, this way—the staff will see to your baggage and take care of the coachman."

She went on talking as she led them into the house, addressing most of her remarks to Lady Marsden—so that Alex was able to let his own anxious thoughts range free.

Where was Maggie? She had told him to come to Avonleigh, but she had not precisely claimed to live here. Perhaps she lived on the place, in a cottage? Or perhaps she did live here. Perhaps she was—oh, a paid companion, perhaps? A governess? No, for there were apparently no small children here. What, then? A ladies' maid, perhaps to the young daughters of the house?

Alex considered the possibility that the woman he loved was a servant in this house. Society might gasp in horror, and his mother would be shocked—at least at first—but Alex did not care if he found Maggie to be a scullery maid. He meant to marry her.

Just let her be alive. Please, God, let her be alive.

"Alex, I do hope you mean to remain with us for a while," Lady Ormsby said, recalling him to his surroundings. "David would be so disappointed if he returned on Friday to find you gone. He has ridden out to see about some of the outlying property, you see, and it was simpler for him to stay at an inn on the main road. You will stay, won't you?"

"Thank you, Beatrice, I would be most pleased to remain here—for a few days, at least. You have a beautiful home."

It *was* beautiful inside as well as outside, but Alex hardly noticed the high-ceilinged rooms and old, well-cared-for furniture. The drawing room to which their hostess had led them was splendid, he noted—but he couldn't wait to leave it and begin searching for his Maggie.

"Why, thank you, Alex. It *is* a fine place, isn't it? My Albert loved it dearly, and David is just the same. As for the girls— Ah, speaking of whom, here is my youngest. Anne, greet Lady Marsden and her son, Lord Marsden."

The countess would not be forced to eat her best hat, Alex reflected, because the young Lady Anne had at least some months before her sixteenth birthday. She was a slender, fair girl, with wide greenish eyes and a pretty face, and she was not in the least shy of either of her mother's guests.

"Oh, you are early, how nice! And just in time for tea! We have the nicest teas, with bread and butter and the *best* cake you ever tasted—"

"Anne, for heaven's sake," her mother interrupted, but with affection rather than exasperation, "how you do run on! Where is Sarah?"

"She's riding Shadow, of course," Anne replied. "Probably she'll be late to tea again. She's always late to tea," she added in a conspiratorial voice to Alex.

"I quite understand how that could happen," he told her gravely. "I myself love to ride."

"If you've ridden most of the way from London," Lady Ormsby said with a laugh, "I doubt you will feel much like riding again very soon. But we have some very fine horses here, you know. My oldest daughter, Sarah, took over the running of the stables when her father became sick, and David says he does not know what he would do without her now."

"Is she betrothed yet, Beatrice?" Lady Marsden asked.

Lady Ormsby sighed. "No, and I begin to doubt she ever will be. Three and twenty, but does she want a husband? No. That stubborn girl! One would think, with all the splendid young men in the county after her, that she would choose one and settle down. But will she? No, indeed. I don't know what I shall do with her, I do declare."

"*I* think she has lost her heart to some mysterious stranger," Anne declared in a knowing tone.

"Anne, for heaven's sake!"

"Well, I do, Mama. For months now she's looked all dreamy-eyed, and she cries for no reason at all. That isn't like Maggie—"

Alex felt everything inside him go still. Looking at Anne's guilty face, he was not even sure his heart was beating. "Maggie? But I thought her name was—"

"Sarah Margaret," Lady Ormsby explained.

"Maggie is my name for her," Anne added. "Since I was a baby."

"Anne, go and see if you can catch sight of her in the field," their mother instructed. "Otherwise, she *will* miss tea, and—"

"Allow me." Alex rose to his feet. He knew that both his mother and his hostess looked at him in surprise, and Anne in pleased speculation, but he simply did not care. "I will . . . introduce myself to Lady Sarah."

He did not wait to answer whatever questions might have been asked, but left the drawing room quickly. He had to exercise the most severe control to keep himself from running across the entrance hall and out the front door, taking the shortest route outside.

The coach had already been removed to the carriage house, and he could see no one in front of the house. For a moment he was unsure which direction to take. Then, for no reason apparent to him, he found himself turning to the left. He moved along the front of the house and then through a small grouping of trees between the house and a rolling green meadow, heading toward the stables he saw in the distance.

He was about halfway there when he heard the hoofbeats.

She raced across the meadow on a night-black horse, her long black hair streaming out behind her. Bent forward in the sidesaddle, wearing a white blouse and a riding skirt rather than a habit, she was slender and lovely and a little bit wild.

Alex could not move. Standing in the shadows of the trees, he watched her unseen as she rode the powerful stallion toward the stables. She pulled up with a laugh, sliding from the saddle before a groom could do more than grab the horse's reins, and had a brief word with him before turning to hurry down the path toward the house—and toward Alex.

Her riding whip tucked beneath one arm, she was pulling off her gloves and did not see him until she was no more than a couple of yards away from him. Then, looking up, she stopped as though she had run into a wall.

Beautiful green eyes, so alive they seemed to glow with a life all their own, looked at him in shock. She was pale with astonishment, yet the day gave her lovely face delicate colors and textures the night had only hinted at. And her glorious black hair was held off her face with a simple green ribbon, allowing it to flow down her back past her waist.

She took a hesitant step toward him. "Are—are you real?" she asked in the sweet, haunting voice he loved so much.

Alex drew a breath, his first in a long time, he thought, and asked huskily, "Are *you* real?"

Maggie took another step toward him, still uncertain but with dawning joy in her eyes. "But . . . how can this be? How can this be when I am not asleep? When I am not ... dreaming?"

"Is that when you come to me, Maggie? When you're dreaming?" It was no less incredible than any of his imaginings, that in her dreams she might send a part of herself to walk the night, and yet he believed it implicitly.

She tilted her head a bit, as though listening to far-off music, and murmured, "I could never remember your name once I awakened. But now I think ... I think your name is ... Alex."

"Yes. Alexander Drake." His heart was beating now, thundering in his chest, and he wanted to laugh out loud in sheer delight.

A smile curved her lips slowly, and in a wondering tone, she said, "You found me. I didn't think you would come here. I didn't think you were real, Alex. How could I, when you were in my dreams?"

He stepped closer and then held out his hand silently, waiting.

Without hesitation, she put her hand in his, and both of them caught their breath at the unanticipated shock of flesh touching flesh.

"I—I almost—I thought you might vanish," she murmured. "The way you did in my dreams."

"I know." He halved the distance between them with a step and lifted his free hand to touch her cheek very gently. She was warm, her skin silky and so *alive* under his touch. He looked deeply into the luminous green eyes and thought he had never in his life seen anything so beautiful.

"This is ... most improper," he murmured, his head bending.

"Yes," she whispered in return, "most improper." But her face was lifting, her eyes drifting closed.

There was a dimly terrified part of Alex that expected her to vanish when he kissed her, gone like a wisp of smoke in a cruel version of the fairy tale. But she did not. Her lips were soft and warm beneath his, opening for him with an innocent's diffidence and a woman's awakening desire, and that heady mixture went to his head like raw spirits.

All the months of longing coiled in him like something with a life of its own, and it required all his self-control to force himself to lift his head. He felt like a man dying of thirst who had been given a sip—only a sip—of the water everything in him cried out for.

She looked at him a bit dazedly. "That—that *was* most improper," she said uncertainly. "I must be terribly shameless. I know we ... we must go into the house before Mama sends Anne to find us, but ... but would you please be improper ... one more time, Alex?"

Alex knew only too well that his mother was nearly bursting with curiosity all during tea, and he knew that Lady Ormsby observed them with a bewilderment gradually turning into pleased approval, *and* that young Lady Anne had developed a distressing tendency to giggle knowingly, but he only had eyes for Maggie. Indeed, he knew he was wearing his heart on his sleeve for all the world to see, and gave not one damn about it.

Meeting her gaze was very nearly as stirring to his senses as a physical touch, and he could not stop himself from staring at her.

As for Maggie, with the first shock of his sudden arrival worn off, she was both a little shy and obviously delighted, stealing glances at him and wearing a delicate color that made her even more beautiful.

They could not speak privately, of course, not then, but as soon as tea was finished he suggested she show him around Avonleigh, and though Anne

choked on giggles and Lady Ormsby's agreement
was just a bit too knowing, it sufficed to get them
out of the room.

"They must believe us mad," Maggie murmured
as she led the way from the drawing room.

"Undoubtedly," Alex agreed, catching her hand in
his and drawing it through his arm.

Maggie caught her breath. "On the second floor is
the—the portrait gallery, if you would care to see it,
my lord."

Alex was about to protest that form of address
until he saw a stately butler lurking about in the
foyer, and though he himself cared little for the
opinions of any observers, he definitely did not wish
to overwhelm Maggie. "That sounds fascinating,
Lady Sarah," he replied politely.

They walked up the sweeping staircase with dignity, though Alex spoiled the effect by chuckling
once they were out of sight of the butler. "Did that
satisfy your notions of propriety, love?"

She glanced up at him quickly, the soft color in
her cheeks deepening at the endearment. "Oh,
Alex—don't tease me, please. This is all so—so un-
believable!"

"I cannot argue with you about that," he agreed
dryly.

"I was thinking about it, you see." She walked
slowly beside him, her hand tucked in the crook of
his arm and her head a little bent. "And wondering.
So many things. How could I dream about an experience you were living? How is that possible? And
if—if you were not in my dreams—then where were
you?"

They had reached the portrait gallery, a long, narrow corridor lined with paintings that, for the moment at least, afforded them some privacy, and Alex
stopped and turned to gaze down at her.

"I was wide-awake, I can assure you of that."

"Then how could I be with you?" She looked up at him anxiously. "Alex, I never left Avonleigh. I never left my *bed*."

He touched her cheek gently, stroking her silky skin with just the tips of his fingers. "Some part of you did, love. Your . . . spirit, I suppose. I never saw your face as clearly as I wanted to, but I saw your beautiful eyes and heard your sweet voice. I believed you were there, with me."

"The first time, you were—were hurt?"

"I would have died if it had not been for your guidance, your determination to keep me safe."

"I needed you to be safe," she said, and then looked startled by her own words. She repeated them softly and shook her head. "I remember feeling that nothing else mattered except keeping you safe. At the same time I was sad, because even though I didn't know it was a dream—or that I was a dream, I suppose—I knew you were somehow beyond my reach."

"I began to suspect you were beyond mine," he told her rather ruefully. "Especially when you vanished before my very eyes. And then you told me that you had been about to go to London when *something* happened, and I was terrified that the something had been your death, and that I was in love with a ghost."

"Not my death," she told him. "Richard's, at Trafalgar; how could I go to London after that? I had to remain here, and be of what comfort and help I could to Mama and Papa. And then, just two years ago, Papa died. Mama needed me, and there was so much for poor David to deal with. Making my curtsy to Society seemed unimportant compared to other things. So I remained here."

"I wonder what might have been different if you

had gone to London," he mused. "We might have met at some crowded ball or theater party, or perhaps I would have seen you riding that magnificent black stallion of yours in the park one afternoon."

"Or perhaps we would have not met at all." She shook her head a bit. "I have never thought much about fate, but it seems to me that some things are meant to happen just as they do."

He smiled. "So I was meant to pull you from that lake when we were children so that you could in turn save my life and win my heart years later?"

"It sounds so . . ."

"Fantastical? Yes. But it happened, Maggie. It all happened. Doubtless no one else would ever believe us, but you and I know the truth."

"That we were . . . destined to be together?"

"I believe that." He slipped his arms around her and gently drew her against him. "Don't you?"

A little shyly, her arms stole around his lean waist. "How could I not believe it? That first morning, when I woke up, and for days afterward, all I could think about was you. I knew I loved you. I knew it as surely as I knew my heart was beating."

"My love . . ." He kissed her, gently at first but then with increasing hunger as she responded. He wanted to hold her forever, kiss her forever, certain it would take at least that much time to satisfy his need for her. Her slender body in his arms fit him so perfectly it was as though she had been designed for him alone, and a deeply buried, primitive part of him insisted that it was so.

She was his. His mate. And both his soul and hers had known it even all those years ago when a boy had saved a girl's life.

For a time, an all-too-brief time, he forgot where they were. There was nothing in the world except the exquisite torture of her yielding body pressed to his, her mouth returning his kisses with innocent hunger.

But a clock somewhere close by chose that moment to announce the hour in ringing tones, and it brought Alex back to his senses. He managed to tear his lips from hers and raise his head.

"Maggie ..." He framed her face in unsteady hands. "I need you so badly, my love. Marry me. Marry me quickly."

"Yes," she said, as though it had never been in question. But then she blinked and added, "Oh, Alex—my mama. And yours! Annie and—and David. They'll think us mad!"

"I think us mad," he retorted with a faint grin. "As for the rest of them—my mama already has her doubts, and I have at least one friend who is convinced I lost my senses months ago. What does it matter? We will tell our respective mothers now, and if your brother hurries back here by Friday, he may be in time to give me formal permission to marry you before the vicar pronounces us man and wife."

She blinked again. "Are you going to be a masterful sort of a husband?" she asked somewhat warily.

"I will be any sort of husband you desire, milady," he told her with another grin and a brief kiss. He tucked her hand back into the crook of his arm and turned them away from the portrait gallery neither had so much as glanced at anyway. But then he paused and looked down at her very, very seriously.

"What?" she asked involuntarily.

"There is a vow I want to make to you now, Maggie. I promise you that I will love you through all the days of this life. And if there is any kind of life after this one, I will find you and love you again."

She stared up at him for a long moment, her vivid green eyes darkened to emerald. Then she drew a

breath and gave him a smile so tender it nearly
broke his heart. "I love you, Alex. And I always
will."

"Always," he said, "might just be long enough."

"By Friday?" Lady Marsden said dazedly. "Alex,
you cannot mean—*this* Friday?"

He glanced over to see that Lady Ormsby was in
a similar dazed condition, and he felt a slightly
amused pang of sympathy for both of them. It did
not, however, lessen his determination in the slightest. "This Friday," he told them. "Three days from
now. Since we passed a little church some miles from
here, I know there is a vicar close by. Nothing else
is truly necessary, so—"

"The banns," Lady Ormsby ventured, eyeing him
with fascination.

"I have a special license," he told her. "We won't
need to call the banns."

Lady Marsden, who had been sitting in a rather
boneless condition beside her friend on the settee,
stiffened with a jerk. "A special license? Alex, how
on earth could you come by such a thing in the"—
she looked at the clock on the mantel and winced
visibly—"four hours and ten minutes since our arrival at Avonleigh?"

"Naturally, I had it in my possession when we arrived," he said.

Maggie, standing beside him with her hand in his,
looked up at him with a faint gleam of laughter in
her bright eyes and murmured for his ears only,
"Oh, now you've done it!"

He had, indeed.

"Alex," his devoted mama said severely, "I insist
you tell me at once why you bought a special license
before you even met Sarah!"

He debated for a moment silently, but Alex was

not quite brave enough—or reckless enough, perhaps—to tell her the truth. Instead, he told her what he and Maggie had agreed was the only tale possible.

"I had met her, Mother. We met months ago."

Lady Ormsby nodded, satisfied and blessedly unconcerned with details. "Ah, that would explain it, then," she said comfortably.

"*Where* did you meet?" Lady Marsden demanded, being made of sterner stuff than her friend.

Alex gave his mother a faint smile. "Mother, you know how often I've ... traveled these last months. All over England."

She frowned but, after a glance at her friend, nodded reluctantly. She had never asked for details of Alex's "trips" for the War Office, and so had no way of knowing where he had gone. And she was too conscious of his wish to keep those activities secret to betray his trust by exposing the secret to Lady Ormsby.

Satisfied with the reaction, Alex went on. "We met one day while Maggie was out riding. That was how I knew her, by the way, as Maggie. I did not know her surname *or* where she lived, because—"

"I wanted to be mysterious," Maggie contributed in an apologetic voice.

Young Lady Anne, who had been listening in stunned silence, gasped suddenly and said, "Oh, how romantic!"

Judging that the mothers at least had been given all they could absorb for the time being, Alex finished simply, "I fell in love with her. And, Mother, when you asked me to escort you to Lincolnshire and mentioned Avonleigh—which I had finally determined to be Maggie's home—I was more than willing to do so."

Lady Marsden blinked several times, obviously

filled with questions she could not put into words, then said, "But, Alex, *this Friday*? Could you not at least wait a few weeks—"

"No, Mother, we wish to be married on Friday."

Before his mother could object again, Lady Ormsby said to her younger daughter, "Annie, would you go and fetch Mama's notepaper from the library, please? I believe I will write a note to David and have him come home right away."

Anne went from the room with lagging steps, reluctant to miss anything. However, that was just what her mama had intended, for she was no sooner out of the room than Lady Ormsby turned to her friend and spoke with brisk matter-of-factness.

"Catherine, you know your son better than I do, but I don't believe either of us doubts that he means to marry my daughter. They are both of age, and may marry whom they wish."

"Yes," Lady Marsden admitted. "But—so soon!"

"The sooner the better, I should say," her friend stated frankly. "If you haven't noticed they mean to have one another as soon as possible, I certainly have."

"Mama!" Maggie gasped.

"My dear, it is perfectly obvious," her mother told her. "And," she added, looking at Lady Marsden once more, "as it should be."

Lady Marsden looked at her son and his betrothed for a long moment, and then smiled. "Yes. As it should be."

Young Lady Anne returned to the room just in time to see her sister receive a warm hug from her soon-to-be mama-in-law, and she exclaimed in disgust, "There! I knew I would miss something!"

The bright summer sun was beginning to set when Alex and Maggie walked out onto the terrace much later that evening. It was the first time in hours they had been alone together, and for a time they simply stood there, hand in hand, and looked out over the gardens of Avonleigh.

"I have not rushed you, have I, my love?" he asked suddenly.

She turned to look up at him, smiling. "No. Have no fears on that score, Alex. I need no more time to be sure of how I feel about you, and as for the traditional trappings of weddings, I don't need them either. I will wear my mother's wedding gown, and I will marry the man I love in a place I love—and no woman could want anything more."

He lifted his free hand to cup her cheek gently. He was smiling, but he was still just a little worried. "Do you understand why I am moving so fast, Maggie? For so long you were out of my reach. And then, for a time, I feared you were forever lost to me. When I wake up tomorrow morning, it will be with the fear that I dreamed this day, and I will have to see you, touch you, to convince myself that you are indeed real."

"Don't you think I feel the same way? Alex, I *did* wake up each morning to find that you had been no more than a dream. And in those dreams, you were always in danger. Every moment now is precious to me, and I want to spend them all with you. I want to marry you as soon as we can arrange it." She laughed shakily, but then a shadow crossed her face and darkened her eyes. "Alex ... those times you put yourself in danger ... it frightened me."

"I'm sorry, love." He tipped her chin up and brushed her lips with his. "But it brought us together, didn't it?" He kept his hand resting along her neck, his thumb stroking over her cheek, and he felt her quiver a bit. Her eyes were grave as she gazed up at him.

"Yes, it did bring us together. I will always be grateful for that. And I know you were doing something important, Alex. I know you were helping England. And I know that if you feel you should, you will do those dangerous things again."

"If I'm needed," he admitted quietly. "But if I am, the trips will be few and far between, my love, I promise you that. And I also promise you that I will never again risk my neck without desperate cause. I have far too much to lose now."

She remained grave for a moment, but then smiled slowly and slid her arms up around his neck. "Then perhaps I have, after all, discovered the way to keep you safe."

Alex bent his head to kiss her tenderly, knowing she was right. Her spirit had guarded his, and now, because they were inextricably entwined, his would guard hers.

For the rest of their lives.

One of today's top romance writers, Kay Hooper has over 4 million books in print. Her next book will be a work of romantic suspense published by Bantam Books in the fall of 1995.

Guardian

of the

Heart

Sandra
Chastain

PROLOGUE

*S*he was standing in the same place she always had, the place where she talked out her problems and found solutions. Her glorious red hair was blazing like hot coals as the pink glare of the setting sun ricocheted off the canyon walls.

Hungrily, he watched her, as he had day after day, for three long empty years.

And she never knew.

For a long time he didn't understand what had happened. He was there, yet he wasn't. He could see her, feel her thoughts, and experience her joy and despair. At first he'd reached out to her physically, running his fingers tentatively across her skin, whispering to her at night when he'd lain beside her. Sometimes, when he kissed her cheek, she'd smile and quiver beneath his touch. Sometimes she'd cry. But she never spoke or seemed to know that he was there.

Finally he understood the truth.

To Lauren McBride, he was only a longing, a

memory she held on to in her dreams. She couldn't see him. Or feel his touch. Or hear his voice. And he was caught between the life he'd once lived and the hereafter.

Through the years, she'd changed; she'd learned to herd the cattle, to plant and grow, and to market what she produced. But she grew more and more lonely and she longed for a child.

Though it ripped his heart, he knew that he must find a way to help Lauren let go of the past. She deserved a man, not a shadowy presence who was no longer real.

He had to do one final thing for the woman he loved.

Irish McBride would find a man for Lauren.

ONE

Finding a husband was hell.

Particularly if you didn't want one. Lauren McBride had given up on finding a hired hand, for none of the men in the village would take orders from a woman. A husband was what she needed. That's what the village priest had told her. A husband to protect her from what was to come. And, the priest had added, her five hundred acres of good land should buy her some sort of husband.

Lauren hadn't thought she'd ever marry again. The first man she'd married had fallen in love with her and brought her to Texas, where they'd been happier than she'd ever dreamed.

But when she'd lost Irish she'd learned that a woman living alone in a hostile land had to change in order to survive. The priest was right. She'd take a husband. But this time the marriage would be a business arrangement, nothing more.

Chappay, the ancient Comanche who was Lauren's only ranch hand, had warned her that the only men in San Felipe Del Rio were Mexican laborers, cattle thieves, and murderers. It appeared he was right. She'd searched every place in the settlement—except the saloon.

Lauren slid her split-skirt-covered leg over the horse's mane and vaulted to the ground. She was out of time; she had no choice. Unless she wanted to face the Comanche alone, she'd have to settle for the best man available, whoever he was.

It was August, the time the Comanche called the month of the Mexico moon, and August would bring the return of Night Rider's band of renegades.

For three years, since Irish went to the saline lakes for salt and disappeared, the Comanche hadn't bothered her. But two days ago Chappay had a vision of impending danger. He'd been so disturbed that he'd begged Lauren to move into the settlement until the time was past, but she refused to abandon her farm. It was all she had left.

Still, Lauren had long ago accepted the old man's special ability to foretell the future. She couldn't have been married to Irish McBride for five years without accepting that there might be some things beyond her comprehension. Irish had firmly believed in the Little People.

Lauren didn't tell Chappay, but for days she'd felt uneasy. For the first time she'd become afraid. The priest was right. The practical thing to do was marry. That way the man would have a stake in facing the Comanche.

But so far, in spite of the priest's assurances, Lauren hadn't been able to find anybody who was willing to take her offer of marriage. She was about to give up and return to the valley when the tinny sound of a piano drew her to the Faded Rose Cantina. This place was her last hope.

Outside the saloon, Lauren took a deep breath and offered a silent prayer: *Irish, if there really are Little People watching over me, please, ask them to send me a man.*

The music blaring through the swinging doors changed tempo, softening for a moment into a bell-like sound that drew her to the door. Once inside, she paused, allowing her senses to become accustomed to the din. With its dirt floor and boarded windows, the interior of the room was dark and airless. The few candles stuck in bottles only added to the heat, and the mass of unwashed bodies gave off such a stench that it almost took Lauren's breath away.

As she waited a hush fell over the saloon. Every eye was focused on her and it was all she could do not to turn and run away. The only way to do what she had to was to show them she was a woman without fear. She'd have to take the offensive, an action foreign to her while Irish was alive. It wouldn't be easy.

For a long time she'd refused to face the truth—that the gentle laughing man she'd followed from Colorado to the wild new state of Texas was dead. Then she'd learned that he'd been killed helping a farmer's family ward off a Comanche attack. According to the priest, the leader of that same Indian band was again on a brutal rampage through west Texas. She felt it in her bones that he wouldn't bypass her farm this year. If she didn't find help, the Comanche would destroy Irish's dream.

The saloon was her last hope.

But as she looked around the room that hope died.

"Whooeeee!" One of the drinkers let out a Texas cry of appreciation. "If you're looking for a good time, sweet thing, you've come to the right place."

She took a step closer, studying the men slowly, one face at a time, ready to concede that the most she could hope to find here was a vaquero with several friends looking for work. But so far, the only interest she was raising was from a scrubby laborer who offered a proposition she didn't even dignify with an answer.

She continued her slow walk around the room. *Too old. Too young. Too dirty.* She eliminated them one by one.

Until she came to the last man: either asleep or passed out; his head was resting on his arms. The table held one empty whiskey bottle, one half-full, and a worn gun belt, sheathing a well-oiled Colt .45.

He was her only hope. At least he appeared to be an American. "You there, at the table." She rested her hand on Irish's pistol in the gun belt strapped around her waist. Irish was the only one who'd ever been able to fire it, but no one knew that except her. "Stand up!"

He didn't move.

"Stand up, I said. Are you hard of hearing?"

The stranger raised up and took a long swig straight from the bottle. "No, ma'am. But unless the military or the law has started recruiting women, I don't have to follow your orders."

"They haven't, and it wasn't an order."

"Then, if you don't plan to carry through on using that gun, you might try asking."

The ripple of laughter behind her told her that she was losing control. Obviously the man in the shadows met one of her requirements: he didn't back down.

Neither did she. "Are you drunk?"

"I'm working on it."

She took a step closer. "You looking for work?"

"Not till I run out of whiskey."

Lauren took a firm grip on her temper and forced herself to be calm. The crops from her harvest would provide a lot of whiskey. "I may have a job for you—if you fit my needs."

The stranger lifted one booted foot and dropped it on the table. "And I might consider it—if you fit mine."

The crowd went silent.

With a black-gloved hand, he struck a match against his pants and put the flame to the end of the thin brown cigar he held between his teeth. In the quick flash of light before the match died, Lauren caught a glimpse of a face shadowed by a week's growth of beard, a pair of piercing dark eyes, and a wicked smile.

In the shadows, Holton Cade took a long pull from the cigar and let the smoke drift free as he studied the woman standing before him. She was an odd combination of western homesteader and Spanish señorita. Along with the gun belt, she wore a black sombrero with small red balls hanging from its brim, the kind vaqueros wore, to brush insects away from their faces when they herded cattle.

A man's shirt was tucked into the waist of a brown split-skirt edged with dust. But it was her hair that caught his eye. Tendrils of fiery red snaked down from beneath her hat, falling across a face that was used to being exposed to the elements.

She was a woman accustomed to being in the sun. From the sound of the spurs that jingled when she walked, she was equally skilled at riding a horse.

Cade didn't have to be told her name. The priest he'd visited yesterday morning had already told him about the legendary Irish colleen Lauren McBride and her husband, who had homesteaded five hundred acres along the Rio Grande at the end of the War Between the States. The word was out that she was looking for a husband, and Cade wasn't interested. But he was about as close to being drunk as his money was going to get him, and her farm was as good a place as any to sober up until he was ready to leave. Besides, he liked her style.

San Felipe Del Rio was a place where a man survived only by minding his own business and staying on guard. It was a gathering place for bandits who preyed on the traders moving between Mexico and the United States, and outlaws on the run. Cade could take care of himself. He always had, but he'd come a long way and he was tired. Her farm had to be better than spending another night here.

"What did you have in mind, ma'am?" he asked, in an exaggerated southern drawl while he took another drink from his bottle. "Or are your needs more—private?"

"You're crude!" she retorted.

"That, too, but I still know my manners. Care to join me?"

He had a rough whiskey voice that seemed to curl around her face and lie against her cheek like warm smoke. "I don't think so," she said, trying hard to cover her agitation with an air of disdain.

"Too bad. I'm about out of whiskey. I could get you your own glass."

He was laughing at her.

This wasn't going the way she'd expected. For a moment she was sorely tempted to call off her search. There had to be another way. Maybe she'd ride over to the fort and find a soldier ready to muster out and make him the offer. At least he'd be familiar with fighting Indians.

"Never mind," she said. "I don't think you'll do after all." She whirled around and started back through the door, anxious to put as much distance between herself and the man as possible.

"Then take me, *chiquita*." A swarthy short man with a bushy mustache reached out and caught her arm. "I work cheap and I guarantee my services."

"Let me go, you hoodlum!" She tried to jerk out of the man's grasp.

"Garcia is my name and I'd be glad to give you a sample of *my* wares," he said, taking her chin in his hand and tipping it down so that he could study her.

Lauren felt a wave of revulsion sweep over her. "What in God's heaven makes you think I'd be interested in anything *you* have."

A flash of cold anger narrowed the Mexican's eyes. Lauren realized she'd gone too far.

"Nobody talks to Garcia that way. I will have to teach you a lesson." He lifted his arm to strike her.

The black-gloved hand came out of nowhere, caught his wrist, and twisted it forcefully. Everyone in the saloon heard the bones crack.

Garcia looked at his wrist in shock, then at the barrel of Lauren's pistol leveled directly at his heart, the cock of its hammer loud in the silence.

"Let him go, cowboy, I don't need anybody to take up for me. I'll shoot the next man who gets out of line. *Comprende?*" Lauren's eyes swept the room. She was rewarded with a step backward from the patrons who'd crowded closer to see the show.

Except for the cowboy in the black hat. He released Garcia, then stood, holding the nearly empty whiskey bottle in his other hand. His legs were spread wide, his cigar clamped between his teeth, his eyes wry with amusement. Only a slight sway suggested his intoxication.

"Fine with me," he said, dropping his cigar, and crushed it with the toe of his boot. "Have at them." Still carrying the whiskey bottle, he turned and stumbled away.

Lauren's mouth dropped open as he left the saloon, leaving her at the mercy of the men inside.

"Now just a minute, you! Don't turn your back on me." She whirled and chased after, catching up with him at the hitching rail in front of the saloon, where he was untying the reins of his horse.

"I apologize, Mrs. McBride," the cowboy said, taking a deep bow and catching the rail to keep from falling. "I didn't intend to offend."

"You know who I am?"

"Everybody in San Felipe knows the beautiful Widow McBride, the woman who leads a charmed life, though I didn't expect to see you in the Faded Rose. If you'll excuse me now, I'll be moving along."

He mounted the black stallion and nudged him into a slow walk. "Let's go, Rajar."

"But—but what about my job offer?"

Lauren dropped her gun back in the holster, mounted her own horse, Star, and urged her to catch up with the stallion who'd settled down into a slow walk.

"I didn't hear you make one."

"What would it take for you to agree to work for me until winter?"

"What are you offering?"

"Good food and fair wages."

After what he'd been through, he was ready for both. But even the whiskey didn't stop him from knowing that there was more than she was saying.

"Not enough, ma'am. You wouldn't be looking for a farmer in a saloon. What are you really after?"

Star had sidled closer, almost bringing Lauren's leg in contact with the stranger. Lauren studied the cowboy openly. Obviously, he drank too much, but he seemed confident with the gun he was wearing. He had come to her rescue fearlessly and he hadn't turned her down.

"First," she said, "I have a couple of questions."

"Fine, as long as you answer mine."

Lauren bit back a sharp retort. She was hiring him, not the other way around. Still, she'd run out of options and he did seem to be her best choice.

"Can you use that gun?" she asked.

"I can."

"Will you use it?"

"I'm not a hired killer, if that's what you're asking. But if it means the difference between life and death, yes. I can kill."

He'd killed his first man, long ago, not in a war, or an Indian attack, but to save his mother and his little brother from being beaten again. He'd buried his father, and to protect his family from the shame, he'd hit the road. The next killing had been easier.

The cowboy's words chilled Lauren. He'd given her the answer she needed to hear, but the underlying amusement in his voice had turned cold and dispassionate. Maybe she was making a mistake. Maybe he wasn't as drunk as she'd thought.

"Who do you want killed, Miz McBride?"

"Nobody. I don't *want* anybody killed. But I have reason to believe that my farm will be attacked. I need help to protect what is mine."

"And do you know who the enemy is?"

There was a long silence. Was she doing the right thing? Did she have any choice?

"Every August," she explained, "the Comanche come down through the western part of the state of Texas, crossing the Rio Grande south of our ranch into Mexico, to steal cattle, horses, and gold. They live off the land and those unfortunate enough to cross their path."

Cade knew that only too well. All the way from Oklahoma he'd trailed the Comanche, searching for the kidnapped wife of the owner of the ranch on which he'd been working. Yesterday he'd found her, near death. When the Indians built their bonfires and began their war dance, he'd rescued her, but it was too late. He'd brought her body to the priest and they'd buried her. He ended up at the Faded Rose, determined to get falling-down drunk with the last of his pay. He'd been well on his way when the redhead came into the cantina.

Now, for a reason he couldn't fathom, he was riding off in the opposite direction with her instead of heading back to claim his reward. "But you've managed to survive their attacks?"

"Yes. The Honey Eaters have never bothered the canyon where my husband built our cabin."

He gave a hollow laugh. "The Honey Eaters?"

"An innocent name for such a violent, destructive people."

"And do they have a leader?"

His question told her that he wasn't from west Texas, for everybody along the Comanche Trail knew about the Honey Eaters. If he wasn't from Texas, and he wasn't a hired killer, why was he in the Faded Rose? The only ranch in San Felipe belonged to a wealthy Spanish family who employed their own people.

"The leader is a violent savage called Night Rider. Unlike others of his kind, he rides at night. He even paints himself black like his horse."

Lauren's horse had taken the lead, prancing saucily along the edge of the canyon, in which, over the centuries, the river had cut a steep ravine.

"One more question, ma'am. Why, if you've never been harmed, do you fear Night Rider this year?"

"It's Chappay. He has seen a vision that this year the Comanche will come."

Cade couldn't hold back a snort of disbelief. For a woman who seemed to be invincible, she was ready to believe in visions?

"And that's it? You want me to hold off a tribe of Comanche on the warpath?"

"Not alone. There will be—three of us."

This time he didn't pretend to hold back. "No, ma'am," he said, swaying as he laughed. "There'll be two of you. Ain't no food good enough pay for taking on that outlaw." He pulled on his horse's reins and started to turn him back.

"No, wait. There's more. If we're successful, I'll offer you half the ranch."

He released the pressure on his boot heels. "Why should I trust you?"

Lauren drew in a deep breath and gave him her last offer. "Because you'll be my husband—that is, if you're not married."

Cade let out a whistle. The priest had been right. He just hadn't expected Cade to be the one receiving the offer. Or maybe he had. He'd been the one to direct Cade to the cantina. Cade turned up his bottle and took a long swallow while he tried to clear his head.

Marriage? Half of a five-hundred-acre farm *and* a beautiful woman? He was tempted. What did he have to lose?

His life, that's what. Such as it was. No harm, he decided, in asking a few more questions. Then he'd take her up on her offer of a bed and some food. Tomorrow he'd give her an answer. But first—

"Who is Chappay?"

"Chappay is a Comanche. He claims to be a descendant of the Ancient Ones who once lived along the river. He has"—how could she explain?—"special powers."

"And you believe him?"

"When my husband, Irish, brought Chappay home, he was near death. He'd been wounded in a raid and Night Rider had left him behind. After he recovered, he stayed on, protecting the ranch by telling his own people that the Ancient Ones had given him the task of keeping this place safe from harm. They haven't bothered us since, even after Irish died. Until now."

"This Chappay must be some kind of medicine man."

"I don't know. He swore that the Ancient Ones appeared to him when he stood at death's door and turned him back to protect me."

Not only did Cade scoff at the supernatural, but he was also beginning to feel very sleepy. Only her voice was keeping him from falling off his horse. "Well, I don't believe in the Ancient Ones. There has to be another reason why Night Rider leaves you alone."

"It could be the Little People," she said softly.

"The Little People . . . as in leprechauns?"

"Something like that."

"You don't seriously believe in all that, do you?"

"A person believes whatever she needs to in order to survive, Mister . . . ? What is your name?"

"It's Cade, Holton Cade at your service, Miz McBride. But Cade'll do fine." He took a sip from his bottle, then wiped his mouth with his sleeve.

"How far is it to your place? I haven't eaten anything in two days and I'm thinking I'd better get out of this sun and take a little nap before I pass out."

"Don't you dare pass out. We have to get back to the canyon before dark. Besides, we have to reach an agreement on my—offer."

He reined in his horse and glanced around, his eyes blinking furiously as he held on to the saddle horn. "You mean about us getting married? Sorry, ma'am, but I don't think I'm going to be able . . ."

Before her eyes his bones seemed to liquefy and he slumped forward across the saddle, his face against the horse's neck and his arms flailing on either side. The bottle fell to the ground and emptied the last of the whiskey in a pool that dried up almost as soon as it hit.

His horse danced nervously for a few minutes as if uncertain what was expected, then grew still.

Lauren swore again. She'd used more of Irish's colorful language in the last two hours than she'd ever used before. What on earth had made her think this man would be the answer to her problems?

What was she going to do with him? She couldn't leave him out here unconscious in the heat. What she wanted was to strangle him. What she did was dismount and climb up in the saddle behind him, holding his waist so that he wouldn't slide off his horse.

With Star in tow, she rode back toward her ranch. At least, if the cowboy didn't see the path she took to the canyon floor, he wouldn't be able to leave as quickly.

As the big black stallion picked his way to the

bottom, Lauren tried to rationalize her actions, actions she didn't quite understand herself.

"Ah, Irish, what would you say about the man I'm bringing home?"

I'd say he's just what you need now, darlin'. I just wish with all me heart that it was me.

TWO

Lauren stopped at the river, allowing the horses to drink.

She shaded her eyes from the hot pink glare of the setting sun and looked down the canyon. Nothing moved. Normally a breeze swept up the flat wide basin downriver, bringing sand and, sometimes, a hint of salt from the Gulf of Mexico beyond. She looked the other way, where, through the hollowed-out cliffs, the water of the Rio Grande churned and swirled over rocks into deep pools, then grew shallow as it moved sluggishly toward the sea.

There was nothing to disturb the canyon's peacefulness—not yet—except the odd noises coming from the man she was cradling against her. What was she going to say to Chappay? How on earth was she going to justify bringing Cade home.

And what was she going to do with him when he came to?

He was heavy. His body rubbed against her breasts and the inside of her thighs, setting off waves of prickly irritation. He'd lost his hat back there on the trail, and as a small measure of punishment for his drunkenness, she'd left it.

Pressing one hand against the small of her back, Lauren stretched her shoulders.

Dear Irish. He'd been a gentle giant. Like Papa, he'd claimed to know the Little People personally. Irish swore they announced their presence through the bells on their feet. As long she heard them, she would be safe.

Tonight the bells were silent.

Once the horses had satisfied their thirst, Lauren rode toward the cabin and the barn. She tried not to think about Holton Cade for the time being. Instead, she concentrated on her garden. Lauren liked growing things. She even liked the herd of awkward red cows with the long, graceful horns that had started with a few wandering into the canyon, and grown into almost more than her hay could feed. Everything in the Upper Rio Grande Valley reproduced with abandon. Except Lauren.

She regretted that she and Irish had not had a child. She didn't know why they hadn't been blessed. Irish hadn't seemed to mind, saying only that "My life is full. To ask for more would be a sin." Perhaps he'd been right.

Chappay stepped out of the barn and watched her progress. Though his expression didn't change, she knew that whatever he'd expected, it hadn't been a man sprawled over his horse in a stupor.

"Señora? Are you all right?"

"I'm fine. This man isn't. He's drunk."

"I'm not drunk," Cade protested as Chappay helped him get off the horse. "I was just enjoying the beginning of a potentially close relationship."

Lauren shook her head in exasperation as he

leaned on the old man. "Get him in the barn and find him a place to sleep it off."

Chappay nodded. "Tonight I'll keep watch, señora."

"I'll keep watch," Cade said, sounding suddenly sober. "Just point me to a bed and give me a couple of hours of sleep."

Chappay frowned, glanced at Lauren until she nodded. "You use my cot in barn," he said.

Stiffly, as though he'd break if he bent, the cowboy made his way inside. Moments later Lauren heard his collapse on the cot and subsequent snoring.

Lauren's head ached. Nothing had gone as she'd planned. She didn't know what would happen when the cowboy sobered up. But she couldn't worry about that and she couldn't allow herself to dwell on his continued insinuations, calculated, she suspected, to keep her off balance. Even if he were inclined to accept her proposal, she wasn't sure she could go through with a marriage, even if it was only a business arrangement.

He was too irritating and he drank too much.

By morning he wouldn't remember anyway. She'd simply tell him that she'd offered him a job and he'd accepted.

The sun began to sink behind the ridge, the moon already visible in the eastern sky. A breeze kicked up, bringing with it faint bell-like sounds.

"Will he help us?" Chappay asked, coming up behind her as she walked back outside.

"I don't know. I've offered him a . . . job. He was the only man I could find."

"I see." As if listening, he tilted his head in one direction, then the other. "The spirits are talking among themselves tonight, señora," Chappay said. "I sense trouble comes with the darkness."

Lauren shivered.

As if the sun had heard Chappay's words, it disappeared to the other side of the mountain and the bells hushed.

Lauren went inside the cabin, closed the door, and fastened it with the pole that held out any intruder. She removed the gun belt and hung it on its peg. Changing from her travel clothes, she donned a regular work dress, sliding Irish's pistol in her apron pocket.

She couldn't depend on any help from the cowboy tonight. Maybe never. Tonight it was up to her and Chappay ... and maybe the Little People.

At midnight Holton Cade fought back a pounding headache and walked toward the river, where he would get rid of the dust and grime of the trail. The last thing he ought to be doing was taking on Night Rider. He'd seen the Indian in action. Cade's discovery of the rancher's abducted wife was enough to get him killed. Besides, there was no way in hell that two men and a woman could stand off the Honey Eaters.

Somewhere in the back of his mind he vaguely remembered an offer of good food and wages—or was it marriage? Either one smacked of more permanence than he was interested in.

This wasn't his fight. He didn't even know why he'd come. He'd slept off more than one drunk in a bar. Something about the woman had touched him and he'd awakened in her barn, not sure whether he'd agreed to a job or a wedding.

Suddenly he felt the hairs lift on the back of his neck. Someone or something was watching him. At the same time the cattle began to move about, setting off a melody almost like the chime of bells.

It was all that talk about the Ancient Ones that

had him looking over his shoulder. That and bad whiskey.

But it wasn't the cows creating the music. Cade finally decided that the sound came from the wind moving down the canyon, bouncing off the rocks, brushing the surface of the water. There was something calming, reassuring about the bell-like sound.

Cade shook his head. How in hell could he protect a woman like Lauren McBride? He'd been a farmer, a mapmaker, a soldier, and finally a cowboy. He'd been a lot of things, but never a savior. At least not since he was a boy.

Cade glanced up at the bluffs. At that moment, like the reflection of stars in the water, pinpoints of light burst into flame along the ridge. Signal fires had been set by the advance scouts, marking the way for the Honey Eaters, frightening the ranchers and settlers by announcing their arrival to the valley.

The question was, would Night Rider's band cross over or would they stop on the Texas side of the river to dance until, fired to a fever pitch, they attacked anyone they came across—as they'd attacked the ranch where he'd worked.

Since 1867, when a reservation had been established for the Comanche in Oklahoma, the government had tried to contain these Indians. Weary of war, most of the tribes had settled down to a life of farming and misery. But not Night Rider. He and his band of renegades continued to raid and plunder the plains from the reservation to Mexico.

Lauren McBride was in grave danger—for she had food and cattle and the thing the Comanche prized above all else—horses. She'd be captured, just like the woman Cade had been sent to rescue. The Ancient Ones couldn't save her.

Cade wished he had better cover, but the moonlight was unrelenting now. The light reflecting off his silver belt buckle was like a beacon. So bright was the water that he could see himself: gaunt, bewhiskered, wild looking after weeks in the saddle.

Even at his best, Cade was no match for Night Rider, and tonight he was not yet at his best. But he couldn't abandon the woman. He had to stay.

The sound of the bells stilled and a sense of urgency swept over him. He'd better get to her quick.

He had almost made it when he heard the ungodly shriek of rage uttered by the savage who'd painted himself black to match the horse he was riding across the sand, his companions behind him.

"Night Rider," Cade whispered. He didn't bother to draw his pistol. He knew it was too late when a bullet grazed his thigh and a burning pain slammed into his head. He fell, swearing, to the ground.

Night Rider had already killed one woman. The proud red-haired beauty would be next. Some savior he was. He'd been wounded and he hadn't even gotten off a shot.

As he felt the blood puddle under his shoulder, he gave a silent laugh. In the end, he'd never kept anybody safe. His mother and brother had survived his father's brutality only to be killed in a flood. The rancher's wife was dead, and the gun-toting beauty who'd taken him home would be next.

Here he was on the floor of a canyon, miles from any well-traveled route, struck by a renegade's bullet. Night Rider dismounted and towered over him like the angel of death. The avenging angel. His black figure was silhouetted against the moon. He was completely nude, the light revealing an erection that came from pure adrenaline.

Then Cade heard them again, the bells. Except now they were ringing furiously, in unison as if a hundred head of cattle were moving in different directions, each with a different rhythm.

The Indian heard them too. He glanced uneasily around. His companions began to speak furtively, studying him with questions on their faces. Night Rider leaned back on his heels, raised one fist to the heavens, and began to chant.

Cade didn't understand what the Indian was saying, but it appeared to be some kind of prayer. Then, as if he'd been given an answer, Night Rider's arm came down and slapped his thigh.

Moments later Night Rider and the Honey Eaters mounted their horses and rode away, disappearing into the darkness that was stealing the last of Cade's vision.

His scalp had been spared and he owed it to the sound of bells.

He needs you, darlin'.
Lauren came suddenly awake. Her chair was rocking for no reason and her heart pounded furiously in the darkness.

She came to her feet, Irish's pistol bumping against her thigh. What had she heard? Some kind of demon cry? A gunshot? Irish's voice, calling to her.

Had she been dreaming?

Lauren's hand cradled the weapon in her apron pocket as she crept toward the window, leaned against it, and listened.

Nothing but silence.

It must have been the heat that had woken her, that and a lingering case of nerves. With a determined shrug, Lauren opened the wooden shutters to let the cooler night air inside.

Even that didn't stop the sense of dread that settled over her. She was uneasy. She wondered whether the cowboy was still sleeping. And where was Chappay?

But there was no answer in the darkness, only a

heaviness in the air, close, smothering. She couldn't breathe. She lifted the bar across the door and moved out into the night.

The heavens were rippled with black clouds, tracking the moon across the sky, almost a reflection of the waves in the water of the Rio Grande below. Lauren felt dizzy from the mirrored movement. The world seemed to be running away, laughing at her loneliness.

The breeze picked up, humming down the narrow canyon, teasing her with the soft muted sounds of its movement. Lauren focused on the cliffs, which acted like a funnel. As the air reached the narrow cavern through which the river flowed, it brought what Chappay called the moon music, the bell-like sounds that bounced off the canyon walls in the darkness. The music seemed to be speaking to her.

Hurry now, darlin'!

She hesitated for only a second, then turned toward the river. Irish's Little People, she thought, and catching her skirt in her hand, she began to run. Black clouds billowed across the moon and lightning scissored the heavens.

"Señora! Wait. You must not go. There is an intruder in the canyon," Chappay called out, from where he'd been told to wait.

"I have to go. Something is wrong. I'm sure of it. Help me." Though she didn't know why or how, something called her to the bank of the river.

The bells increased, chiming now in a steady musical chant. Another bolt of lightning split the sky. And then she saw him, the cowboy sprawled across the riverbank, his bloody face turned toward her as if he were asleep—or dead.

"He's hurt, Chappay, help me."

Suddenly the wind died and the moon reappeared, casting a silver light across the man's body.

Chappay gasped, crossed himself, and fell to his knees. "It's the Ancient Ones," he said, "warning us."

"Nonsense, it's a late-summer storm." She knelt down and reached out to touch Cade. He was breathing. But there was blood matting his hair and splotching his clothing. "Chappay, bring his horse. I'll find two branches. We'll rig up a travois and drag him back to the cabin."

At that moment Rajar tore out of the barn, frightened by the thunder. Then, almost as if he were being directed by some unseen presence, the horse turned and backed toward his master, waiting patiently while Chappay used the reins to secure two tree limbs to the saddle stirrups.

Lauren stepped out of her petticoat, ripped the ruffle from the hem, and tied it between the poles.

"Careful. We don't know how much blood he's lost. We don't want to start him bleeding again."

Chappay took one arm and Lauren the other, lifting him slowly against their makeshift conveyance and tying him in place with the last of her cotton strip.

Cade groaned but didn't open his eyes. Warily Lauren studied the bluffs overhead for some sign of an intruder. She felt as if she were being watched. But because of the overhang she could see nothing except a smoky moonlit night sky.

Holding the horse's bridle, Chappay led the animal back to the cabin. The clouds had blown away, allowing moonlight to shower across the canyon, turning the mica-covered riverbed into a swirl of sparkles.

Together, she and Chappay moved Cade inside. When Lauren turned to light the lamp, Chappay said, "No, señora. No light. It would not be safe.

Not tonight. We must not draw those who would do you harm."

"Nonsense. I have to see to this man's wounds. I can't do it in the dark." She found a still-smoldering coal in the fireplace and set a dry stick against it. Once it flared up, she touched it to the wick of the lamp and adjusted the flame.

"Take the horse back to the barn and keep watch. Whoever did this could return."

Chappay shuffled his feet, reluctant to obey.

"But first," Lauren continued, oblivious to Chappay's hesitation, "bring his saddlebags and any weapon he might have inside."

She touched Cade's forehead. Still cold, still damp. He shivered beneath her touch. "Hurry, Chappay. I might need your help."

The old Indian finally turned to comply. By the time she'd coaxed the fire into a bright flame, Chappay returned with dusty, worn saddlebags, propped a rifle against the wall, and left to keep watch once more.

Lifting the lamp to shine on her patient, Lauren took a good look at Cade. His face was lined, weathered from the elements. Incongruously long thick lashes feathered his eyes, like velvet against canvas. He was sporting a week's growth of dark beard and she couldn't guess how long it had been since he'd had a haircut.

Then he moaned and licked his lips.

Lauren unbuckled his gun belt, now missing the shiny pistol. She removed his clothes and boots and underwear. Viewing his nude body brought a flush to her cheeks and she hastily covered him with a sheet, willing herself to stop staring at this man who was so different from her husband. Irish had been shy, only coming to her under the cover of darkness, as if he were afraid that his size would frighten her. It hadn't. He was Irish and she'd loved him.

Aye, lass, he's a manly man, all right, maybe too manly. Don't worry, I'll protect you. I pray to the saints that I've chosen wisely.

The familiar voice cut through her and she whirled around. "Irish?" She knew she'd heard him, as she had so many times since he'd left. But as always, there was no one there.

Lauren shook off the odd feeling. She filled a pan with water and washed the river sand from the cowboy's face and neck. In addition to the head wound, she discovered a lump on his forehead, which could account for his unconsciousness. Once she'd cleaned him up, she found a second surface wound on his thigh.

The water in the pot began to boil. She emptied the first basin over her bed of wildflowers near the door and filled her pan with the hot water. Using the last of the hand soap Irish had bought in Boulder City when they started their journey south, Lauren began to wash the man's body.

Weeks of trail dust and blood turned the second pan of water a muddy pink. More hot water and a final wash, then she was ready to take a closer look at his wounds. He was lucky. She sent a silent thank-you to the heavens that neither bullet had done more serious damage. Though he'd bled profusely, both injuries were superficial.

First she packed the wounds with a paste she made from the root of a plant Chappay called the healing tree. Then she bound Cade's head with a strip of muslin. His knee flexed without grinding, though she couldn't be certain there were no broken bones. Finally she treated the leg and bound it.

One of Irish's shirts made a voluminous nightshirt for Cade, covering him sufficiently so that she didn't have to plant her attention on his forehead for fear of what she'd see if her gaze fell lower. Now she'd have to wait.

Mindful of Chappay's warning, she blew out the lamp and sat down beside the bed to keep watch. But her patient didn't rest.

As the night passed he slept fitfully, as if he were disturbed by bad dreams. "Who are you? I know you're there," he called out repeatedly. "Stop ringing those bells!"

At one point he ripped off the oversized shirt she'd dressed him in, screaming out, "Don't hit them, Pa. I'm man enough to stop you now. You're going to treat me like one!" After a few tries she gave up trying to dress him, leaving him naked in the heat.

He is out of his head, darlin'.

It was Irish's voice, but it was Chappay who came to stand beside her. "I fear he will hurt you, señora."

"No, he calms when I speak to him, as if he knows me."

Eventually he grew quiet and slept. Chappay slipped out of the cabin and waited near the trail leading up the cliff. He kept the stranger's rifle ready for firing, should whoever shot him return. Chappay was disturbed by what had happened. As he waited he fell into a light sleep, a sleep in which a shadowy figure moved toward him, a figure who thanked Chappay for his loyalty and told him that the stranger had been chosen to come. Chappay didn't question his vision, for he'd seen it often in recent years.

When Chappay awoke moments later his gaze focused on the heavens, where one bright star seemed to hang just over the edge of the cliff. He hadn't noticed that little star before and knew it was a sign from the Ancient Ones.

• • •

Cade felt cool hands on his body, felt and responded to what he knew, even in his dream, was a woman's soft touch. If only she'd stop caressing him. If only he could sleep. If only he weren't so hot.

He turned, threw off the covers, and tried to move away from the ever-present restraint. He was dreaming that he was in a field of wildflowers with the sun beating down on him. The woman was beneath him.

"This isn't real," he whispered. "It's a dream."

"Don't worry," the soft voice reassured. "I'll look after you."

"But I've been sent to protect you," he said in a voice so low that it was practically a growl. "You need me."

"I'm not going anywhere, I promise," she said softly, taking his hand in hers. "Just rest. I'll be here when you wake."

And he understood the promise she made just as he understood that he'd been searching for her all along. Then he frowned. This was the kind of woman he'd dreamed about, the kind he'd never thought to have. Why, he wondered as he drifted into sleep, was God letting him die when he'd finally found her?

It was midmorning when Holton Cade opened his eyes. He was alone.

The cabin was empty, sunlight streaming through the open doorway, blazing a corridor of light straight through the middle of the room.

For a long minute Cade lay trying to separate reality from the dreams he'd experienced throughout the night. He remembered Night Rider, painted black, challenging the heavens with one raised hand, then nothing else but the dreams of being touched.

Cade tried to sit up and was racked with pain that zigzagged from his head to his thigh. He fell back to the bed and swore. He took deep breaths, willing the pain to subside. Then, more carefully, he began to test his body.

A bandage had been neatly applied to the wound on his thigh, restricting free movement, and his head felt as if a herd of cattle were stampeding across it. He lowered the sheet, taking note of both his nudity and his cleanliness. Someone had washed him.

The hands of Lauren McBride.

That thought cut through him like the lightning that had sliced the night sky before his attack. The woman from the cantina. The woman with the fiery red hair who'd proposed marriage. His head ached, confusion turning his mind into fog. What was real and what was imagined?

"Woman!" he roared, forcing himself up. "Where in the name of glory are you?"

The sunlight was suddenly blocked as a fuzzy silhouette appeared against the glare. "Get back into bed, you idiot! And don't swear! There's nothing glorious about your condition."

Cade swayed. It was her, the voice he'd heard in his dreams. The woman with the soft hands, the woman who smelled like wildflowers.

He started to crumple as she reached out to him, sliding her arm around his waist and pulling his upper body across her shoulders. She staggered under his weight.

"Don't you dare fall! I won't allow you to lie on the floor and you're too big for me to handle."

"I don't think my size will be a problem, ma'am," he said, leaning on her as he forced shaky legs to take him back to the bed. "When the time comes, I'm sure that we'll work it out."

Lauren let him go, watching him spill into the bed, then pulled up the cover, averting her eyes. "Don't move again or I'll tie you up."

"Yes, ma'am," Cade said as his mind began to work. Now he clearly recalled his attacker, and the woman who'd cared for him. It was the time before they arrived in the valley that was still missing, the part he needed to fill in. He started with "I promise, I'm not trying to run away. It's just that my memory seems a bit faulty."

"What do you want to know?" she asked suspiciously.

"I guess what I'm asking is—are we married?"

She felt the air whoosh out of her lungs. What was the fool asking? Did he think that ... did he really not remember passing out? "What's that supposed to mean?"

"Well, the last thing I'm reasonably sure of was that you were offering me a job, which I was about to turn down. Then you sweetened the pot with an offer of a marriage."

"A partnership," she corrected. "That's all. You're just confused."

"Oh, then I guess I'd better get back to the barn. The hired hand doesn't usually share the lady of the house's bed, even if he's been injured."

Lauren realized he wasn't really about to rise. He was simply challenging her with eyes so dark and wicked that she shivered. Smiling sweetly, she moved to the other side of the bed. "You've had an injury to your head and your thigh, Mr. Cade," she said, taking a firm grip on his good leg and arm. "And no good farmer lets the animals in his charge go lame. It isn't good business." Before he knew what she was doing, she jerked him to the middle of the bed.

"Snake eyes and bull—" he swore, feeling a shower of stars descending over his skull with all their points finding their target.

Lauren Alexander McBride, you behave yourself. You need this man. He doesn't know what he is doing.

"He's still addled," she whispered back.

"Not anymore," Cade responded.

Chappay was right, Lauren thought, the stranger was dangerous. Not many men could get up and walk with that kind of leg injury or talk afterward. Yet he had, and what's more, he remembered far more than she'd hoped.

"You pretended to collapse, didn't you?" she said, trying to regain control.

"I did, but I can't apologize for liking the feel of your arm around me, or the effect you have on me, even if I don't seem to have a clear recollection of why I'm here."

There was no mistaking the burgeoning of his manhood beneath Irish's nightshirt. "Why, you—you faker—" Lauren picked up her broom and began to advance. "You can just stop what you're doing. The only thing with permission to rise in this cabin is my biscuit dough."

"I'm sorry. I'm sorry, but believe me I'm in no condition to do anything about it."

Lauren struggled to control the blush that had flamed her cheeks by dropping her broom and turning to the pot of broth she'd made. She stirred it vigorously.

If Cade was to be of any value to her, he had to conserve his strength. That meant food and sleep—in that order.

Using her apron to lift the handle of the iron pot, she poured some of the steaming liquid into the bowl. She took pleasure in adding a few drops of Chappay's sleeping compound to the bowl.

"I've prepared some broth for you, to build your—" She broke off. It had become painfully obvious that he didn't need to build anything. And the less conversation between the two of them, the better. "Open your mouth."

Cade stared at her stubbornly for a moment, then shrugged. He could feed himself, but if it brought her closer, why argue? He opened his mouth.

Lauren's eyes were clear and honest, a color somewhere between amber and hazel. Unlike many redheads, she had dark lashes and her skin was the color of the desert in the sunlight, warm and peachy with a luminous tint. She looked like a shell he'd once found along the coast, all smooth and pearl-colored. Yet there were fine lines at the corners of her eyes that signified her maturity.

"Where is your family, Cade?" she asked.

"Don't have any."

"What happened to them? Was it the war?"

A slash of pain darkened his eyes. "You might say that. The outcome was about the same. Nobody won."

"I'm sorry, Cade, I wanted to know more about you."

"What you see is all there is, ma'am. And from the looks of me, you've seen it all."

She forced another spoon of broth into his mouth.

"I don't know about you," he went on with an impish lilt in his voice, "but I like what I see. What about you?"

"Swallow!"

To her relief the medicine began taking effect at last and he was overcome by sleep. As she stared down at him she heard Chappay come in.

"Señora? The man, is he alive?"

"Yes, he's alive, all right, though I'm not sure he ought to be. Is everything quiet out there?"

"I found the tracks. The Night Rider has finally come to our canyon. I fear that he will return."

She rose and walked to the door, looking out across her land. "Why? Why now?"

"I do not know, unless it was the will of the Ancient Ones," Chappay said, worried but resigned. "I must gather the cabbages before they spoil."

"You must take them into Del Rio, Chappay. We will need the money and medicine for the injured man's wounds."

"I fear for your safety."

Lauren didn't want to think what that meant. The produce had to be sold, and that meant Chappay had to go into town. "Don't worry, old friend. You will take the stranger's rifle. I have Irish's pistol. I'll hide myself and Cade inside the caves if necessary."

"*Sí*, I understand. It has been decided."

"I'll be safe, Chappay. You know I always am."

"Yes, señora. The angel watches over you. Last night he came to me in a vision."

Lauren's eyes widened. "Angel? What do you mean?"

"A presence. I only know that it was there. It is always there. You know it, too, Señora McBride."

Lauren watched him walk away. An odd feeling swept over her. She refused to admit to Chappay that she, too, felt a presence, that she sometimes heard Irish's voice. But an angel?

In her everyday struggle to make a life, to force the land to produce and protect what she and Irish had built, she had learned to rely on herself. If there was an angel up there, it hadn't kept her visitor from harm.

Instead, she'd brought him here and he'd nearly

been killed. It was curiously unsettling. She paced
back and forth, unable to leave him, yet unable to sit
quietly and mend the bullet holes in his clothing.
The tension from yesterday was back and it was
building.

The danger was coming closer.

THREE

For the rest of the day Cade slept, waking only occasionally for more broth and water. Lauren mended his clothes while Chappay gathered the cabbages.

Once Cade asked, "Why didn't you go back home when Irish died, Mrs. McBride?"

"This is my home," she'd answered in surprise.

"And you intend to stay, knowing that you're at the mercy of both the bandits out of Mexico and the Indians?"

"And American cowboys who get themselves shot and become my responsibility instead of my protectors."

"What about the old man?" he asked.

From the pocket of her apron, hanging on the peg beside the door, she took Irish's pistol and pretended to check it to make certain it was ready to fire. "He'll be leaving at first light to take our cabbage to market."

Cade couldn't hold back an oath. Not only was he wounded, but he and the woman would be left to face any trouble alone. "Did Irish tell you to wait for him?"

"No, he only promised he'd be back."

"And you're still waiting. Sooner or later you'll be forced to give up. Believe me, a woman can't survive out here alone."

"I will," she said, adding softly, "You see, I have something others don't. I have the Little People to protect me."

"I can almost believe it—hearing those bells all the time."

She drew in a sharp breath. "So you've heard them too."

"I've heard something. What is it?"

"It's supposed to be the wind. Papa explained it to me back in Colorado. The air currents pick up the small pieces of sand and rock and fling them against the canyon walls. When the conditions are just right, it sounds like music."

"But you don't believe it?"

Lauren sat down in her chair, the rocker creaking in the silence. "Irish said that only the pure in heart hear the bells."

That wasn't the way Cade would have described Night Rider, who'd heard the bells, or something equally disturbing.

She went on. "That says something about you, Mr. Cade."

"There's nothing pure about my heart." He wasn't even certain he had one anymore. He knew why he'd gone after the kidnapped woman—for the reward. If he hadn't gotten drunk, he told himself, he'd have been headed back to Oklahoma by now.

"I don't know about that, Mr. Cade. I only know

that if you hear the bells, your thoughts must be more loving than you know."

They stared at each other for a long moment, Lauren uncertain of what she should say and Cade damned sure that anything he said would be something he'd regret later.

Cade closed his eyes. Loving thoughts? No. Thoughts of *making* love was more honest. After he'd left the priest, his only thoughts had been of a bottle, a woman, and a bed. He'd had the bottle and the bed; the only thing left was the woman, and it looked as if she was going to meet the same fate as the rancher's wife and he couldn't do a damned thing to stop it.

The next day Lauren left food and water for Cade while she worked in her fields, keeping herself away from the cabin. He'd already proved he could move around, but she told herself that he needed time to heal. She didn't like the way Cade made her feel and she was learning that she couldn't trust herself.

She missed Irish, and she felt guilty. Though they'd had a good marriage, the sparks that flashed between her and the cowboy were terrifying.

Tired and dirty, she started toward the storage caves with the last of her fruit and produce. It wouldn't stay as fresh as she liked, but she'd had to find something to occupy her time, something that kept her away from the devil-eyed man who made her skin tingle with a glance.

When everything was stored and she had no excuse to stay away longer, she took a longing look at the river, where she normally bathed, but until Chappay returned she dared not wander too far from the cabin at nightfall.

Finally she washed her face and hands and started

back to the cabin. The walls of the canyon were turning a fiery pink as the sun moved beyond the ridge. It was the time of the day Lauren had always liked best.

Until now, when her safe haven had been invaded by a different kind of presence. She stopped and glanced up at the edge of the cliff. Where was Chappay? He should have been back an hour ago.

Unless there'd been trouble in the settlement.

Unless something was wrong.

She shivered and moved toward the house. There were no bells and she felt a twinge of fear. "Don't desert me now, Little People," she whispered. "Irish promised that someone would always be here to protect me when he was away."

As she reached the cabin Cade appeared in the doorway and gave her a blistering frown.

"I was about to come looking for you," he said, and the sun dipped behind the ridge. "If I'm going to help you, you need to stay close enough so that I can be sure you're all right."

"You're going to stay?"

His answer was a simple "Yes." He was glad she didn't ask him why because he didn't have an answer yet.

She cut a sharp glance at the frowning man. Somehow she wasn't sure that being close was safe at all.

Lauren prepared food for a cold supper: fruit, bread, and cheese. They ate with few words of conversation. Lauren couldn't seem to be still. Over and over she walked toward the door and looked out.

"What's wrong, Lauren?"

"It's Chappay. He should have been back by now."

"He probably stayed in town," Cade said.

"Why would he do that?"

"With Night Rider in the area, he may have decided that it wouldn't be safe to travel at night."

"But he's a Comanche. Night Rider wouldn't hurt him. Besides, Chappay wouldn't leave me alone."

Cade was thinking the same thing but decided there was no point in worrying Lauren even more than she already was. "He knows that you're not alone," he said softly. "Go to bed now. I'll keep watch."

"But you're not strong enough yet," she protested.

"I'm strong enough. Besides, I've spent more time in the last two days resting than I have in five years. I'll be outside."

He looked around for his rifle.

"Where are my guns, Lauren?"

"Chappay only found a rifle and I made him take it with him."

Cade groaned and lifted the old pistol from the peg. "Fine, I'll use this. Don't worry," he said, and went out the door.

But she did worry. He wouldn't be able to fire Irish's pistol. Nobody could. After tossing for half the night, she gave up and went to the window to look out. There was a moon, but it wasn't as bright as it had been the night before. A thin layer of clouds drifted across it, like translucent smoke. She wondered if something was burning, maybe the settlement. Chappay's absence loomed even more ominous.

The canyon was quiet, too quiet. Where was Cade?

She moved toward the door and stepped outside, the night air cool against her skin. The soft fabric of her nightgown rustled as she stood on the porch.

"Cade?" she whispered.

Cade sat holding the pistol loosely in his arms, his back leaned against the barn, his legs crossed at the ankle.

Don't do this, darlin'. Stay inside.

But this time Lauren ignored the unspoken command.

Cade heard the creak of the porch and looked up. He choked back a silent groan as the woman took another step closer.

"Where are you, Cade? You're scaring me."

She was standing there in the yard, her nightgown catching the light like a sail on open water.

He cut his eyes to the cliffs, studying the bonfires he'd been watching. There had to be a lookout. Someone could see Lauren as clearly as he.

"Go back inside, Lauren."

"No, I need to talk with you." She walked toward him.

The first arrow whizzed past just as she reached the barn, lodging in the wall with a thud. She gasped. Cade pulled her into his arms.

A second arrow followed, still wide of the mark.

"Stop that!" Lauren yelled in the darkness.

"Hush, Lauren!"

"But somebody's shooting at us."

"Dammit, woman, what in hell are you doing standing out there like a beacon in the dark?" he asked, pushing her behind him and studying the dark bluff beyond the roof of the house.

"Why didn't you tell me they were up there? I—I thought you'd gone," she said.

"Somebody is up there on that ridge. Somebody who is shooting arrows at us. And I think that was only a kind of warning; otherwise, they'd use guns."

"Maybe it's a lone Indian."

"I don't think we're dealing with a lone Indian. Look, the light of campfires."

She raised her gaze to the ridge, where a series of fires glowed in the darkness. Even from where she was she could see the ghostly shadows moving around the flames. Then came the sound of drums and the low chant of voices.

"The Honey Eaters," she said. "They've come back."

"For me," Cade said with certainty, "not you. I'll make sure you're safely hidden, then I'll try to lead them away."

The tunnel, lass. Show him the tunnel.

She'd always known about the tunnel, but Irish had only allowed her inside it once and that had only been partway. He'd told her to use it only as a last resort. Now he was telling her to go there. Her heart stopped for a moment as she realized what that meant. All they'd worked for was about to be taken. Even Cade couldn't change that.

"There's another way, Cade."

Somehow she'd known from the beginning that this moment would come. But she'd expected the tunnel to protect her and Irish. But that wasn't to be. Irish had been taken away from her and somehow this man had come into her haven, sacrificing his own safety by trying to protect her.

The hungry need that flamed between them had come as a surprise. She'd fought her feelings. Now in some way that she couldn't explain, she knew that everything before had been preparing her for this.

"What way?" Cade demanded. "I don't understand."

"I'll go to the house and get food and supplies. Release your horse and follow me."

"But—"

"Hurry, they're mounting up." She jerked away, and following the darkness along the side of the barn, she made her way to the shadows at the back of the yard, disappearing into the house. Moments later the pale light from inside was doused.

Cade gave a last worried look at the cliff and followed Lauren's directions. He took his horse from the barn and set him free, watching him gallop down the canyon toward safety. Leaving the barn, Cade hugged the shadows along the ridge until he reached the cabin.

At the door he peered in, just as Lauren pulled the cot away from the back wall of the cabin. "What are you doing?" he asked in a loud whisper.

"Come inside and help me," she said.

In the distance he heard a scream, followed by others lifting their voices to the spirit world in a violent threat. Then he could hear their horses as they started down the path to the floor of the canyon. Cade knew he and Lauren didn't have long and he had no better solution than whatever Lauren was planning.

"Close and bar the door and the window," she said, tugging at the wardrobe leaning against the wall. "We have to move this thing."

"A strange time for spring-cleaning, when we're about to be massacred," he said as he got on the other side and shoved the heavy piece of furniture aside, revealing a second door. "What the hell?"

Lauren unlatched the door and pushed it open. "We'll wait until we're inside the mountain before we light the lamps," she said, gathering up her sacks and disappearing into the tunnel beyond.

"Close and lock the door." She struck a match and touched it to the lamp's wick. "It won't hold them back for long, but once we release the boulders, they'll be a while getting through."

He pulled the door closed and latched it on the inside. "Boulders?"

"That's right. Stand back. We never tried this, but Irish was sure it would work."

The sounds of the raiding party came closer as Lauren loosened a heavy hemp rope from the beam where it had been tied, then let it go. A platform overhead tilted forward, releasing an avalanche of rock and debris. Moments later, when the dust had settled, there was no longer any sign of the door.

"Pretty impressive," Cade admitted. "Once they open the cabin door, the rocks will block the opening and crush anybody in their path. Your husband was pretty smart."

"Yes, he was," she agreed.

"And from the size of those rocks, he must have been pretty big. How'd he get them up there?"

"Someone else dug the tunnel, leaving the rocks. He built the cabin in the front of the cave and built the retainer overhead. Then he carried the rocks up, one at a time. And yes, he was a very big man, both his body and his heart."

Cade felt a twinge of pure jealousy. He covered it as he asked crossly, "So, we're inside a mountain, what now? Do we wait for an eruption?"

"We go into the caves. Tomorrow I'll show you the way out." She lit another lamp and handed it to Cade. "Follow me."

Cade knew they'd burned their bridges behind them. He followed Lauren, hoping she knew where she was going, hoping that there was an exit. Irish McBride might have hoisted all those rocks out of the cave opening, but Cade knew he'd never be able to match that feat.

The walls of the cave were damp. The tunnel slanted gently downward, Cade's boots echoing on the stone floor like the sound of the Indian drums.

His leg ached. His head, no longer bound by the strip of muslin, twinged, but he didn't stop or slow down. He'd suffered worse and kept going when there was only his own life at stake.

And this time there was Lauren.

The temperature inside the mountain was growing cooler. But there was a constant sensation in the air currents of being pulled, as if they were being urged along. The silence was eerie. Trailing behind Lauren, Cade held his lamp in one hand and the bag of supplies she'd handed him in the other.

"How far does this go into the mountain?" he asked.

"Far enough."

"It must have taken a long time to dig this out. If your husband didn't do it, who did?"

She held up her lamp, shining the light on the walls. "It was done a very long time ago. Look at the drawings."

Crude stick figures, painted on the wall, came to life, portraying scenes of odd-looking people and animals.

"Irish figured an early civilization must have used the cave as a religious site. Then, later, prospectors came along and thought they'd find some kind of treasure inside. You have to lean over here, then we're inside the first cavern."

Cade followed her lead, bending at the waist as he wedged himself inside the narrow opening. Once there, he could feel the vastness of the cavern before he even lifted his lamp. From the floor cone-shaped rocks layered with colors and odd formations pushed upward. Overhead, the same kind of rock extended from a ceiling so high that it was lost in the darkness.

"I hope you know where we're going," he said,

and listened to his voice echo across the cavernous space.

"I only came in once and it was a long time ago, but Irish always told me that as long as I followed the wall along the left side, I'd be safe. Let's go."

Cade knew they were moving deeper when drops of water fell from overhead, frosting Lauren's hair with jewels that reflected the light of the lamps. Now and then he heard a plop as the drops fell into water. An occasional flap of wings announced the presence of bats, though strong air currents drew the ammonialike odor away from the cave.

The way wasn't easy. Often they had to crawl over fallen pieces of rock and search their way around and through openings in promontories that extended precariously into space. Once, Cade kicked a rock and knew that it was falling. Long seconds later there was a muffled sound as the rock hit bottom.

"Maybe you'd better let me go first," he said, touching Lauren on the shoulder.

"No, we're almost there."

Cade looked past her, searching the inky blackness for some indication of what lay ahead. "Don't suppose you'd like to tell me where *there* is?"

"It's a surprise. I think we start moving up about here." She was right. There was a rather steep incline to the rocky ledge they were traveling. Sometime later a faint glow lit the passageway ahead.

Then, as if a pale sun had come from behind a cloud, they stepped into a chamber suffused with soft light. Cade looked up. High above, there was a crack in the rocks, allowing a jagged pattern of moonlight to shine through, illuminating a shimmering, mirrorlike pool of green water in the center of the cave. Wisps of fog seemed to drift upward.

"Hot springs," Lauren said. "Irish always said he'd bring me here someday to bathe in the water."

Cade let his sack slide to the floor and walked closer. Almost as if the cavern had been built by human hands, the rocks around the pool were smooth and flat. The granite walls were set back several feet, giving the illusion of a cozy, private bath.

"Why didn't he?"

"I guess we never had the time we thought we did," she said wistfully.

"And how do we get out of here? I don't think we can get up there to that opening."

"There's supposed to be a crack in the wall on the other side that looks out over the river. Then there are handholds that will take us up to the top."

"Handholds?" Cade wasn't sure he liked the sound of that. He'd done a bit of mountain climbing during the war and he hadn't been fond of it. This rock seemed to ooze moisture and it was dark.

"We'll wait until daylight," Lauren said. "In the meantime I think we need to get some rest. Unfold the blankets and spread them out. I'll get us something to eat."

"I think we'd better put out the lamps," Cade said, trying to decide on the best spot to make camp before the cave went dark.

"Yes. I suppose we can't know how long we'll have to stay in here. Oh!" She'd obviously thought of something.

"What's the problem, Lauren?"

"Chappay. He won't know where we are. We should have left a note."

"A note telling where we are might be a bit foolish, wouldn't you say?"

"I doubt that Night Rider can read English."

She touched her pocket to make certain that she'd brought along her precious supply of sulfur matches, then blew out the lamp.

Cade began laying out the blankets, arranging them side by side, adjacent to the pool.

"I think I'll put my blanket over here," Lauren said in a tight voice.

"Fine. I'll bring them both over."

"Ah, no. I'd be more comfortable if yours stayed where it is."

"Well, I wouldn't," Cade said, moving around the side of the water. "I can't protect you if there's a bathtub between us."

Lauren gave an uneasy laugh and made her way toward the far wall of the cave, moving her finger-tips along, searching for the end of the wall and the space behind that made the natural escape Irish had described. She didn't want to think about the con-flicting emotions she was experiencing, to admit to the desire that raged within, desire for a wicked black-eyed man.

"Are you afraid of me, Lauren?"

"No, of course not. If you'd been ready to harm me, you would have done it last night. I'm simply looking for the exit."

"Have you found it?"

"Yes, here. I feel it. There's a suction, as if the air is being drawn to the outside. I'll just check it out."

"Not until daylight, Lauren," Cade said in a voice that tolerated no argument. "Without a lamp you could end up in a deep hole and I don't have a lad-der handy. If there is an opening, a light would give our position away."

He was right. She heard the rustle of clothes, but she wouldn't allow herself to speculate about what he was doing to cause the noise. Then she heard the ripple of water and a long, satisfied groan.

"It's going to take Night Rider a while to get to us if he finds the tunnel. Why don't you come into the pool and let this hot water soak that sore back you were rubbing yesterday."

"I couldn't possibly do something like that," she said primly.

"Why not? Nobody will ever know but us, and I'll never tell."

"That isn't it. I—I can't swim," she admitted.

"Your feet will touch the bottom, at least where I'm standing. Take off your clothes and give me your hand. I can't see you."

Actually, he could see her. His eyes were becoming accustomed to the darkness, and the moonlight filtering through the crack was stronger than he'd thought. He wanted to smile. Lauren had both arms wrapped around herself and she was rocking back and forth like a child trying to keep from sticking her hand in a jar of rock candy.

"It would feel good," she whispered. "But I don't dare."

Then she felt it, the sudden turbulence in the air, followed by the distant sounds of musical notes. Not like the bells exactly, but music all the same.

"The bells," she whispered. "Irish said they were here, inside the mountain. I didn't believe him." She turned back toward Cade, wondering whether or not he'd heard them.

"They're here, or something is here," Cade agreed, "and I think it's time that I find them."

She heard a rush of water. Then he moved toward her, feeling his way along the natural bank around the pool. His fingertips touched hers. "Where is the opening?"

"Beyond my left hand. I reach out and there is nothing."

He slid behind her, his body brushing hers in the narrow space in which they had to move. He, too, found the opening. "Wait here, Lauren," he said as he cautiously put his foot behind the wall. Once he turned sideways and slid into the next cave, his feet encountered solid earth.

This cavern was smaller than the one they'd come through, but it was much the same except that there was no moonlight overhead. On the opposite side he could see the outline of a large opening. Sky and stars blinked through the hole. And between where he was standing and the exit were silhouettes of tiny columns, like odd-shaped mushrooms sprouting in the cave floor. He knew when he looked up that if it weren't so dark he'd see the same thing.

For once Lauren had followed his directions and stayed behind. He couldn't see, but in the silence, he could hear. As the crack in the ceiling of the mountain sucked the air from the cave, it swirled across the formations overhead and below, drawing musical notes from them like the melody played by a fine orchestra. He wasn't hearing bells. He was hearing the sound of the wind playing the cones like an instrument, like bells, like bagpipes might have sounded if he were hearing them from far away.

"Okay, Irish," Cade said, "I concede. You've found something special here, but I'm not convinced that it's anything more than an anomaly of nature. There are no Little People down in this hole."

At that moment a rock fell from somewhere to Cade's right. The angle from which it came suggested that it had been thrown instead of falling. Cade had a healthy respect for the unknown, particularly when it was black as pitch, but this seemed a bit too much on target to be a coincidence.

"Is there someone here?"

As the melodious sounds grew louder Cade felt a breath of cold air curl around his neck. He had the distinct impression that he was not alone.

FOUR

Cade studied the shadows. "Is someone there?"

Slowly he began to back through the opening into the cave with the hot springs, straight into Lauren, who was trying to join him. She started to fall and he reached to catch her. Somehow their feet became tangled in the skirt of her nightgown and both Lauren and Cade ended up on the hard floor of the cave.

"Oh," she said.

"Hmmph!" he echoed.

"Are you hurt?" He dragged his arm from beneath her and lifted himself so that he could look down at her face.

"I don't think so...."

As her voice trailed off, he became aware of the sweet wild scent of her. Here they were, in the middle of a mountain, in God only knew how much danger, and all he could think about was loving the woman beneath him. She'd thawed his heart and slipped inside it.

Beneath him, Lauren was filled with need. She was through fooling herself. All those words about how much Irish had meant to her were true. She'd loved him with all her heart. But Irish was gone. She'd refused to accept that until now, until this man had come reluctantly into her life and almost gotten himself killed.

The tunnel into the mountain had been Irish's way of protecting her, and now she was using it for Cade. It felt right for the two of them to be here.

Cade groaned.

"Does your head hurt?"

"No."

"Does your thigh pain you?"

"No," he said, a bit louder.

"Then why is your breathing so hard?"

"Why should it be any different from any other part of me?"

"I don't understand."

He pressed himself against her, his maleness finding that part of her body where it was meant to be. "I think you do, Lauren. If you don't, it's time you understand what I feel."

She gasped. He was handsome, this devil who'd charmed her. In the dark he was even more tempting. Her fingers had found the back of his neck without her permission. Now they ranged across his face, curving around his cheekbones and rimming his lips.

"I think we should move to our blankets," she said, desperate to separate their bodies. "You need rest."

"Stop fooling yourself, Lauren," he said in a hoarse voice. "You may think you can stop this, but your body is having a hard time believing you. And mine isn't even trying."

"Irish always told me that nothing was too hard to deal with if you really put your mind to it."

"I don't want to talk about Irish right now," he said, his hand ranging across her rib cage and untying the ribbons on her nightgown.

Her hands left his face and caught at his fingertips, trying to keep him from going any further. Then, before she could stop him, he'd moved out from under her and pulled her up, letting her gown fall in a swish at her ankles. In the darkness he took her hand and held it against his chest.

The erratic beat of his heart caught her by surprise. His pulse was racing in time with her own, his skin hot beneath her touch. For a moment she couldn't speak.

"Do you know how desirable you are, Lauren?" He lifted her, carried her to the blanket, and laid her down. Then he lay down beside her. Lauren tried to protest, but everywhere they touched, her body felt as if it had been scalded.

"Are you sure about what we're doing, Cade?"

"I'm sure," he whispered. "I was never more sure of anything in my life."

And suddenly Lauren understood. Irish had made a home for her and provided a place of safety. He'd told her that the bells would remind her that he would look after her and he had continued to linger. But that presence was fading now. She wasn't sure at what point she'd realized it, but she knew now that she was alone in the cave with Cade.

Then Cade kissed her and the music of her body found its voice. Touch intensified heat, and her blood raced through her veins to fuel the flame of her desire. His arms came around her, his lips explored, adding fire to every place his mouth touched.

"Please?" she whispered, urgency adding movement to her body. As if she lay in a bed of prickly cactus, she squirmed, inching beneath him, forcing him to move over her.

"Please love me, Cade."

"Yes," he said in a ragged voice. "I do. I could never stay in one place. I was always searching. Until now, I didn't know I was looking for you."

He was lying fully over her now. She parted her legs and he slipped between them. She heard him catch his breath and stop for a long moment. A drop of water fell into the pool, rippling the water slightly.

"I want you beside me forever," he whispered.

"Forever, Cade? You don't have to promise that. I'm not fool enough to believe that Night Rider is gone. The Comanche don't rest until they've made certain that their victims' spirits don't go free."

"I won't give you up now," he said, still holding himself over her.

"Oh, Cade. Tonight may be all we ever have. Let's leave forever up to the Little People."

Liquid heat welcomed him as he moved swiftly inside her. "I'm afraid I don't have any faith in the Little People, Lauren. There is only you, and me, and this."

Then all his restraint, his defenses, his barriers were gone. He was joining his body to hers, taking her power and giving his freedom.

She needed no encouragement, no instruction. Her legs curled around his thighs and she joined his movement, thrust for thrust. "I love you, Cade," she whispered. "I'll take your heart and I'll give you mine."

As his lips claimed hers she knew that she was giving him more than her heart: he filled the empty part of her soul. She molded herself to him. Even her toes quivered as he moved against her, leaving her body writhing in sweet agony. Deep inside, the agony began to build. There was no holding back the tide of pure sensation.

Then she was lost in the spasms of pleasure that welled up inside her, finally erupting like the waters of the Rio Grande plunging over the rocks into the pool below.

Cade gave one final thrust, and she felt his seed filling her. With a groan he collapsed on top of her, resting his face beside her head, his body still joined to hers.

There was a long silence as Lauren allowed herself to examine the wonder of what she'd just experienced. "Thank you, Cade," she said softly.

"You're thanking me? Don't you know that you've just given me life again and I don't have any idea in hell how all this happened, or why?"

"I don't think we have to understand a thing to appreciate it," she said slowly. "My papa always believed that he'd find his river of gold, even when everybody else thought he was crazy."

Cade's hand found Lauren's breast and cradled it lovingly as she talked. Her voice was musical. Her words were like a song and he felt a curious wonder at his need to touch her.

"Did he discover it, his river of gold?"

"Of course. Though the gold turned out to be silver, and he died finding it."

"I'm sorry. No man ought to lose the thing he's searched for."

"Perhaps it's the search that's important, not the finding."

He raised up, looking down at her in the darkness. "God, I hope not. I've been looking for a long time. I just didn't know for what. Now that I've found my pot of gold, I don't want to lose it."

Lauren smiled. Inside her, Cade seemed to be coming back to life, expanding, filling her within.

"Cade?"

"Yes, my love?"

"Are you going to love me again?"

"I think I am," he said, "I surely think I am."

It was sometime later when they washed themselves in the heated pool and even later when they finally wrapped themselves in a blanket and slept.

It must have been near dawn when the sound of falling rocks awakened Cade. It took him a few minutes to figure out that someone was creeping through the cave behind them. Whispered oaths of pain indicated that others had found a way inside.

Whoever it was must have come down from one of the cracks in the ceiling, breaking off the fingers of rock extending downward, which in turn broke those underneath.

Cade dressed and shook Lauren awake, laying a finger across her lips to indicate silence. As she gathered her senses she, too, heard the sounds. Quickly she rose, pulled on her nightdress, and leaving her supplies behind, followed Cade around the pool and through the opening into the cave.

The sky was a soft gray now, aglow with the promise of light from the rising sun. Carefully, Cade stuck Irish's pistol inside his shirt and began to feel his way around the wall. Lauren never questioned him, following silently behind. Finally they reached the opening. Lauren came to stand beside Cade and gasped.

They were high above the Rio Grande, looking out over the valley through which it flowed. The sides of the cliff were smooth, cupping beneath the opening and disappearing from sight beneath the bluff. There would be no climbing down. Moving to the right side, Cade began to feel along the rock beyond the opening. Nothing.

With a smothered curse he felt along the other side. Just as he was about to give up, his hand encountered the trunk of a bush growing out of a crack. He followed the crack downward as it slanted toward the floor on which he was standing.

Behind him the trespassers had ceased trying to conceal their presence. From the sound of their voices, at least one of the men had fallen into a pit and his companions were being forced to rescue him from the hole.

With a desperation born of his new feelings for this woman, Cade caught hold of the trunk of the bush with his right hand and planted his right foot in the earth's crack. The trunk held. His left hand found a handhold in the inside wall of the cave as his left foot searched for purchase inside the fissure. A cautious examination of the crack found another place for his foot higher up and a slight indention in the rock face that allowed him to find the next place for his hand.

Cade started to move back, to whisper instructions to Lauren, when he realized that she was right behind him. As he moved from a space she found it. As they scaled the face of the cliff he was glad that it was not full light. He didn't want to see what was ahead of them or what awaited them if he made a mistake.

Dear God, it wasn't fair. She'd already lost Irish. Now she was about to lose Cade. Lauren closed her eyes. If she were going to die, she'd go to her resting place carrying the memory of the night she'd shared with this man she so desperately loved.

Inch by inch, they moved upward, until a falling rock nicked her forehead and she opened her eyes. At that moment the sun leaped over the edge of the cliff overhead, outlining the body of the savage who was standing there waiting.

Night Rider. They hadn't escaped after all. She glanced down to see other Indians scaling the rock behind them.

"Cade," she said quietly, "I think we've run out of forever."

Cade, too, had seen the renegade Comanche, seen him and weighed their situation. There was no place to go, no escape.

"There's one thing I forgot to tell you, Lauren."

"What's that?"

"About your marriage proposal. If we get out of this alive, I accept."

Suddenly a stiff wind whipped down the canyon, slamming Cade against the rock, almost as if a giant hand were holding him. "You call it, darlin'," he said. "Up or down."

The breeze swept down the canyon again, this time curling up from beneath the overhang, pushing against Lauren, as if she were being lifted. With the second gust of air came the bells, faint at first, then louder.

Night Rider jerked his head around, peering behind him, then over the edge, as if he'd heard someone call his name.

"Up," Lauren said.

As the darkness faded the bells continued. Cade could see the way more clearly, reaching for and finding the next handhold, slowly scaling the wall to the top. Apparently the music came from the fissure in the rock over the chamber of cones. He knew what made the sound, but the Comanche didn't. Though clearly unnerved, Night Rider stood his ground.

Cade was at the top now, at the edge of the cliff beneath the Indian's feet. Night Rider's black body paint was splotched with dust. At some point he'd wiped his face, leaving a smear of skin color that looked as if he'd been slapped. The Indian's face broke into a cruel smile as his eyes met Cade's.

Cade prepared himself to die.

Lifting himself to the surface, he pulled out the ancient pistol and pointed it toward the painted figure.

"Stay down, Lauren," Cade ordered.

Lauren heard the click of the hammer as Cade pulled it back.

"Cade," she cried. "There's something I forgot to tell you too. Only Irish—"

A gun fired. Lauren felt her heart stop as she lunged over the edge, prepared to find Cade fatally wounded.

Instead, Night Rider was crumpled on the ground. A line of Indians on horseback were backing away, their eyes wide with fear, their weapons lowered in submission.

Lauren flung herself into Cade's arms.

"—only Irish was ever able to shoot that pistol," she said.

He held her close. "Not anymore."

The Indians on horseback swiveled and quickly rode away, leaving one rider behind. "Señora!" A stocky figure climbed down from his horse and hurried toward Cade and Lauren. "You are all right?"

"Chappay. Yes! Oh yes."

As they walked back toward the path that led down to the canyon, Cade held Lauren close.

Chappay explained that he had been captured, but once he'd warned the Indians that the Ancient Ones had made him keeper of the bells, Night Rider had been afraid to do more than hold him. It was Cade he wanted to punish. It was Cade who'd set off the spirits' anger and then made Night Rider look bad before his brothers by stealing the woman captive.

Night Rider believed the other man, the big one protected by the bells, who'd prevented him from entering the canyon, had gone. Now Cade was the keeper of the bells.

"You know about the cave?" Cade asked.

"*Sí.* I knew about it long ago." Chappay observed that they would need to rebuild the barrier and restack the rocks inside the tunnel, then left to search for his burros, promising to return the following day.

The sun overhead was bright, and the Rio Grande moved past just as it always had.

"Thank you, Cade," Lauren said quietly. "I owe you my life."

"I can't claim any credit for that. You were the one who got us through the mountain."

She smiled. "That isn't what I meant. I was here, but I wasn't truly alive. I think I was waiting to die. Until you came. You awakened me."

There was a peaceful stillness around them that took away Cade's questions before he asked them. He, too, felt awakened.

The death of his father and the later loss of his mother and brother had killed something inside of him and he'd walled it off, going through the motions of living, feeling nothing but pain. That pain was gone, replaced with a brightness that was more than a reflection of the light. He'd been drifting, alone, and now he'd found a reason to stop and put down roots.

Lauren stood beside him, her head on his shoulder, her hair snaring the glint of the sun and catching fire. She'd taken him in and trusted him, giving her love freely.

"Will you stay?" she asked softly.

"You've convinced me that the Little People are watching after you and this place," he finally said. "Are you sure they'll welcome me?"

How could she explain that it was the Little People who'd led her to Cade—the Little People and Irish. One day she'd tell him, but today she didn't answer. She didn't have to. The joyous sound of bells did it for her.

EPILOGUE

There is an ancient legend [the young woman wrote in her diary] that there is a special place along the Rio Grande guarded by spirits. There are those who argue that the spirit is an angel. Others say the spirits of the Ancient Ones protect the canyon.

My name is China and I know the truth. My grandmother Lauren knew them first, then later my mother, Cheyenne. Grandmother told me about the Little People and of Irish McBride, who loved her and brought her to this place. Irish believed the bells were messengers of love.

He said that if your heart is pure and your love is true, you can hear them.

My grandfather Cade came to the valley when Grandmother was widowed. He heard the bells, fell in love with her, and stayed forever. It is my time now. This afternoon I hurry to a spot by the river where the pink walls of the canyon catch the setting sun, to await the coming of the man I'll love. I don't know him yet, but he will come.

I can hear them, the Little People, calling to me, through the music of the bells.

China closed the book and hid it behind the loose board in the floor of her room, then slipped out the door. There was no spoken voice, though she heard it in her mind as she had a hundred times before.

Go, my pretty one. The Little People will guide you, as they have all those who hear their music.

As she danced away the fiery-haired colleen who was the child of his heart, if not his loins, looked back and laughed in pure joy.

China knew the secret; only special lovers are chosen to come to the valley. Long ago she'd learned that Lauren McBride Cade and all her descendants would be blessed with the luck of the Irish.

In the distance the sound of bells floated through the evening air. Lauren, her hair silvered, her heart full, held Cade's hand. Up the canyon they could see their daughter, Cheyenne, standing on the porch of the old cabin waiting for her husband's return and watching her daughter, China, until she disappeared from sight.

Cade slipped his arm around the woman he loved. "Our granddaughter's time has come," he said. "I only hope that the man she waits for will make her as happy as you've made me."

"He will," Lauren whispered, and turned her lips to Cade to receive his kiss.

Her "thank you, Irish" was only a whisper, but it caught in the air and the bells rang softly with her love.

Sandra Chastain is forging a reputation for funny, romantic, and heartwarming historical romances of the west. Her next romance will be THE RED-HEAD AND THE PREACHER on sale in the fall of 1995.

Angel

on my

Shoulder

Susan
Krinard

New Orleans
January 1850

Ariel had disappeared again.

Standing on the levee in the shade of her somewhat battered parasol, Miranda O'Reilly sighed. Perhaps Ariel had gone in search of Miranda's father, who might have wandered—quite unintentionally—into one of New Orleans's countless taverns. Perhaps even now Miles O'Reilly, Shakespearean actor extraordinaire, was bestowing his inebriated talents upon an unappreciative audience of sailors, cardsharps, and rogues in some dive on Gallatin Street.

Miranda swallowed and lifted her head, brushing a wisp of copper hair from her eyes. It would do no good to be downcast about it. She would wait here, as she'd waited all morning, for Miles to return. And then they would go back to their shabby boarding-house on Magazine Street, another day lost and no engagement secured. Once again she would speak to her father about the drinking and the gambling, knowing how little she could do.

Until then, she had nothing to contemplate but the past.

For a moment she lost herself in the ever-changing chaos of the levee and market, absorbing the performances on every side. Sailors from exotic ports argued in strange tongues while dark-skinned women with overflowing baskets cried out their wares. Servants come to market for their wealthy masters dodged stacked cotton bales and barrels of sugar tossed haphazardly along the levee. A thousand scents mingled in the air.

Miranda turned in a slow circle, refusing to think. All the world was here in New Orleans. She was only a small bit of flotsam carried along the great Mississippi River, soon to be swept on again—

"Pardonnez-moi."

The woman was the epitome of Creole perfection, her pale, finely sculpted face bonneted and veiled against the sun, her walking dress sweeping around her in a rustle of silk skirts. Dark eyes regarded Miranda haughtily as she swept by, trailed by a maid and two male servants laden with packages and baskets.

Miranda gripped the handle of her parasol and stared after the retinue as it disappeared into the crowd.

That arrogant young lady might have been the very one. The woman Damien had married. His *proper* Creole bride.

Turning away, Miranda walked blindly toward the river and the rows of steamboats at dock along the levee. It had been here that she and Damien had first met. Three years ago, though it seemed like yester-

day. Ariel had brought them together, playing unwitting matchmaker between two young people
from very different worlds—aristocratic young gentleman and itinerant Irish actress, never meant to fall
in love.

And Ariel had been with her when Damien had
told her of his duty to marry the wealthy Creole girl
his parents had selected for him. When he had made
his devastating offer ...

Miranda gasped and covered her mouth with her
hand, fighting for control. The past was gone.
Damien Lévesque would be a settled husband now,
with children of his own, running the plantation his
father had given him for doing his duty. She would
never see him again.

I will convince Papa to move on, she thought,
watching the muddy water flow among the hulls of
the gilded steamboats. *We should never have come
back. This is no place for us. We must find another.
Any other* ...

" 'Then westward-ho!' "

Miranda looked up at a flurry of feathers as Ariel
ducked under the parasol and settled on her shoulder. The parrot cocked his head at her, one pale yellow eye fixed on her face.

" 'Westward-ho!' " the parrot repeated, rocking
from foot to foot. He ruffled his gray feathers and
nibbled her ear under the edge of her bonnet.

Miranda shook her head. "Where have you been,
Ariel? And where is—"

"Miranda, my love. Our fortunes have turned at
last!"

Miles O'Reilly stood before her, his ruddy face
flushed. He grabbed her in a sudden hug, ignoring
parasol and parrot. Miranda closed her eyes at the
smell of whiskey on his breath.

"Papa," she said, setting him back. "What has happened?"

Miles did an abbreviated Irish jig. "Why, my dear, I have won us a new life." He held up his hand. His fingers clutched two grimy rectangles of paper. "Tickets—tickets for a steamer bound for Panama, and thence to California!"

"California," Ariel croaked in her ear.

"California," Miranda repeated blankly.

"Yes!" Her father pressed the crumpled tickets into her hand. "It was Ariel who put me in mind of it, my love. There has been endless talk about the gold in California—we have heard it everywhere the past year—and Ariel has picked it up. 'Westward-ho,' he said in my ear. And when these tickets were offered as stakes in the game—"

"You were gambling, Papa," Miranda said sadly.

"Yes." For a moment he looked chastened, dropping his head. But the grin stole back across his face, and he grasped her shoulders.

"Don't you see, Miranda—such tickets have become impossible to find anywhere in New Orleans. But I have two. I have heard that the miners in the west are starved for the benefits of culture. A theater has already been built in Sacramento, and players touring the mines have met with great success. With your talent, Miranda, and a little luck—"

She shivered, hardly hearing the rambling speech that followed.

California. Only a name to her, a word bandied about by eager young men who dreamed of overnight fortunes. A word that put hope back in her father's eyes.

California. A world away from New Orleans— and Damien. A place to start over.

She focused slowly on her father's face. "And

what of your plans to—find our old colleagues and secure an engagement with a company here in New Orleans?"

His expression grew sober. "No, Miranda. It won't do. Returning to New Orleans was only a last resort, when I believed we had no other choice. With nearly all our money gone—" He dropped his gaze and took her hands in his, folding her fingers around the tickets. "These mean a new life, Miranda. For both of us."

That hope was in his voice again, a hope she had no will to destroy. A new life—a new start. Only moments before she had been longing for just such a miracle. Perhaps, in California, her father would give up his drinking and gambling, return to the stage he had once trod so brilliantly.

And she could leave Damien behind forever.

"Please, Miranda," Miles said softly. "I have enough money to get us started once we arrive. I'll even let you keep it for me." He touched her chin gently. "Miranda—"

"A new life," Ariel echoed, bobbing his head.

Closing the parasol with a brisk motion, Miranda looked back at the market and its seething, oblivious crowd. A handsome, dark-haired, dark-eyed dandy mounted on a fine bay stallion caught her eye, tipped his hat to her and grinned. Except for the grin, he might have been Damien.

She closed her eyes. " 'Having nothing, nothing can he lose,' " she quoted softly. "Very well, Papa. California it is."

Miles O'Reilly whooped, and Ariel burst upward with a cry of triumph.

" 'Then westward-ho!' "

Plumas County, California
May 1850

It was not at all a satisfactory situation.

From his perch on a rickety shelf above the table in the corner of the saloon, Ariel watched the poker game progress. Miranda was winning, of course—without cheating, of course. And her opponents were considerably less than pleased.

Ariel hunched his shoulders. *It is not nor it cannot come to good,* he thought on a sigh. This was not why Ariel had urged Miranda and Miles O'Reilly to California—not Miranda's destiny to gamble for enough money to survive because her father's death had left her with nothing but her wits and a single small trunk of clothing and costumes.

Ariel breathed a silent prayer, shifting from one foot to the other. No, this was not the answer at all. Miranda had suffered much on the long journey by steamship to the Chagres in Panama, across the sweltering jungles by primitive boat and mule to Panama City, and northward again by crowded steamer to San Francisco. Her father had suffered as well, weakened by his years of drinking; he had succumbed to ship fever and had grown weaker still in the damp, chilly climate of San Francisco.

The money had been nearly gone, absorbed by the inflated prices of lodging and food and medicine in California, when Miles had been well enough to travel again. Miranda, at her father's urging, had taken to wearing men's clothes as she'd done so often in her roles as Rosalind, Viola, and Puck. In a land where women were rarities, Miranda had ventured into the dangerous city alone to find passage to the Sierra foothills—to the mines where lonely men waited to be entertained, and where the warmer climate might cure her father.

Ariel had done all he could to help. Miranda and her father had reached Sacramento at last. But Miles O'Reilly's time had come. In a dirty, damp, riverside canvas-roofed boardinghouse he had caught the dysentery and departed his earthly suffering.

Now Miles O'Reilly was in a far better place. Ariel had given Miranda all the solace he could in her time of grief, stayed at her side when she took the mule pack train from Sacramento up to the mining camps. But Miranda's chance for happiness still lay before her, if she would but take it. . . .

A long-bearded ruffian at the table below cursed volubly, slamming down his hand of cards while Miranda calmly gathered her pile of gold dust. Ariel shifted his wings and studied the miner's seamed face intently. That one would bear watching. " 'O brave new world, that has such people in't!' " he quoted under his breath.

Ariel glanced about the saloon, at the crowded gaming tables and long bar swarming with slick gamblers and uncouth roughnecks. Something must be done quickly indeed. Ariel had led Miranda to the mining camp at Heaven's Bar, California, for a reason. If that reason didn't walk through the door very soon, Ariel must take a hand—or wing—once again.

But even a guardian angel was far from omnipotent. Ariel had chosen to assume mortal shape to stay with Miranda when her mother had left her years ago, but there was only so much he could do. Miranda must listen to him, must choose to hear him. Her fate was ultimately in her own hands.

She must find the courage to accept what life offered. " 'We must take the current when it serves, or lose our ventures,' " Ariel murmured. And so must a certain stubborn man by the name of Damien Lévesque. . . .

The saloon's fancy wooden door swung open silently. Ariel straightened on his perch, eyeing the tall, lean man who walked into the smoke-filled room. And then, with a soft whistle of approval, Ariel settled back to wait for matters to take their course.

"What'll it be, Your Lordship?"

Damien leaned on the pitted and stained wooden bar, ignoring the familiar ridicule in Cain Sullivan's voice. The Irishman, owner of the Pearly Gates saloon, the finest establishment on the North Fork of the Feather River, raised an eyebrow at Damien's pointed indifference.

"As sociable as ever, I see," Sullivan drawled, his Irish brogue mockingly pronounced. He made a show of cleaning a smudge from the vast, gilded mirror behind the bar and grinned at his own handsome reflection. "You'll not be trying my whiskey today, I'll wager."

Damien straightened and looked around the saloon. The smoke was stifling, and the din was enough to raise the dead. "Claret," he said softly.

"Of course, Your Lordship." Sullivan bowed and poured the wine into a none-too-clean glass. Such minor matters as dirty glasses had long ago ceased to bother Damien. A hundred things that would have horrified a young, untried Creole aristocrat three and a half years ago in New Orleans meant nothing at all to the hardened stranger who stared at his bearded reflection in the mirror.

"And have you finished your business in Heaven's Bar, Your Lordship?"

Damien set down his glass and regarded Sullivan without expression. "Impatient to see me gone, *Irlandais*?"

Sullivan leaned back against the mirror and folded his arms. "Let's just say that I've never taken a liking to your face."

"Nor I yours," Damien said, smiling without a trace of humor. "You'll be pleased to know that Etienne is arranging the final sale of my share in the company. Within a week I'll—"

He broke off at a sudden commotion from a far corner of the saloon, where a small crowd had gathered about one of the gaming tables. The monte and faro tables scattered across the room were suddenly deserted. A babble of voices rose in heated argument.

Damien watched with distant curiosity as the crowd parted long enough for him to glimpse the apparent source of the squabble: a young boy, not yet out of his teens, hunched on a rickety chair against the wall like a lamb among wolves. His thin arms rested on the table, and between them was a considerable pile of buckskin gold-dust pouches.

Sullivan cursed under his breath and strode over to the disturbance.

"The boy does very well," a soft voice commented in French.

Annette's perfume swirled around Damien as she leaned against the bar. The position she took displayed her ample charms just as she intended, but Damien only smiled and kissed her hand absently. He nodded toward the boy as the crowd closed around him again, buzzing like a swarm of angry bees.

"He's a little young to be in this place," Damien remarked.

Annette shrugged. "What is young here in the mines? The boy has already won dust from the best poker players on the North Fork. There are a few who do not appreciate his skill."

"How long has he been in camp?"

"Nearly a week." She plucked at the sleeve of Damien's blue flannel miner's shirt. "You have been too long away, *mon cher*." She sighed. "I have had to seek ... other distractions."

Damien shook his head. "Not the boy, I hope. He's too young for you, Annette."

She pouted prettily. "Perhaps. But *you* are not." She teased the wiry hair of his beard with her fingers. "I remember when we first met, when Heaven's Bar was only a few tents by the river. It seems so long ago...."

How long? Damien closed his eyes, no longer hearing Annette's lilting voice, losing himself in the past.

Two long years since he'd staked his claim on the Feather River, one of the first eager young men to follow the promise of California gold. Three years, nearly to the day, since he'd left his family in New Orleans, abandoning duty and honor and everything he'd been raised to revere, giving up a life of ease and certainty. Three years since his heart had been shattered by a girl he should never have known at all.

Miranda.

He had come to the frontier seeking oblivion, and had found wealth and a new life instead, claimed by the sweat of his own labor from the very earth itself.

Damien lifted his hands and stared at the scarred palms. How his father would have cursed to see his son laboring like one of the *gens du commun*, like one of Miranda's countrymen across the Irish Channel. Just as Benoît Lévesque had once cursed his bookish son for being so little like his dashing, elegant peers. Not a proper Creole gentleman at all, who quoted Shakespeare and would not join his friends in wenching and gambling and dueling over the tiniest slight.

Benoît Lévesque was no longer alive to curse his son—he and his wife had been felled by yellow fever in the summer of '47, a few months after Damien had left New Orleans.

But the past was gone. Damien focused slowly on the thinning crowd across the room. That boy at the table with his pile of winnings was far younger than Damien had been when he'd made the overland passage to California. But the boy had surely lost his innocence just as Damien had done three years ago. In the mines you either became a man quickly or you paid a terrible price.

Damien had become a man, but his family had paid the price. Because of Miranda O'Reilly.

Damien pushed away from the bar, vaguely aware of Annette's cry of annoyance. Miranda O'Reilly had no hold over him now. No woman did. Now he had enough to settle on the land he'd purchased in the Napa Valley and start over.

The saloon door swung again, letting in a welcome draft of cool evening air. Etienne Sevarin, formerly of New Orleans, leaned against the doorframe.

"Ready for supper, *mon ami*?" The lanky quadroon nodded to Annette and met Damien's gaze. "If oysters and champagne are to your taste, of course."

The tension drained out of Damien as he joined his friend and partner. Etienne, son of a Creole aristocrat and a beautiful *placée*, had come by his culinary talents in Paris, and his powerful frame working a claim at Damien's side. After nearly two years their partnership was dissolving, and with it Damien's last tie to New Orleans.

Etienne clapped Damien on the shoulder. "To-night, *mon ami*, we'll bid farewell to the barbarous life."

But as he left the saloon Damien paused to glance at the table where the lone boy hunched over his winnings and scanned the room with wary eyes.

Damien retraced his steps to Annette's side. "Do me a favor, *chérie*," he said. "Keep an eye on the boy."

Annette looked up at him from under blond lashes. "You know my soft heart. But if I do—"

Without a word Damien pulled her into his arms and kissed her, long and hard. He left her staring after him, ignoring the stirrings of lust, knowing he could feel nothing else for a woman as long as he lived.

Miranda picked her way over the broken, pitted ground that passed for the camp's main street, dodging piles of rubbish and open shafts dug into the river bar by hopeful miners. Only the light of the moon, and Ariel's occasional timely warnings, kept her from disaster. Somewhere an amateur violinist was playing a melancholy tune about a home left behind, the melody nearly drowned out by the din from the saloon. A pair of drunken roughnecks staggered out into the lane; Ariel, perched on Miranda's shoulder, nipped her ear.

" 'Beware the Ides of March,' " he squawked in a near whisper.

Miranda sighed and dropped into the shadow of a ramshackle plank cabin, hugging her small package of supplies to her chest. A fourth of the evening's winnings was already gone, spent on a meager supper and another night's lodgings in Mrs. Baker's boardinghouse on the edge of camp. She was tired—

tired of playing this role under dirty clothes and an
ancient hat pulled down over tangled hair, constantly assaulted by fleas and dust.

"Rosalind and Viola never had this much trouble,"
she whispered to Ariel.

Ariel bobbed his head, fixing her with a pale yellow stare. " 'The play's the thing,' " he said solemnly.

Miranda stroked his breast feathers with one
finger. "You disapprove of my gambling, don't you?
But I haven't any other choice, not without revealing my true nature. If I turned actress now, I'd have
no safety at all. You know Papa was afraid for me,
Ariel—a woman virtually alone in a world of men.
He knew I could play this role. And I haven't the
heart to play any other."

Ariel uttered an almost human sigh. Of course he
didn't understand, mere beast that he was, that she
couldn't imagine a life on the stage without Papa.
Miles had groomed her from earliest childhood to be
a consummate actress, the pride of his old age. But
she'd never loved the wandering life that her parents
had led, even though she'd been surrounded by
affection—from Miles, from her mother before she'd
left them, from other members of the company before they, too, had abandoned her well-meaning but
irresponsible father.

Even then she'd never been alone. For years the
three of them—the O'Reilly father and daughter and
an African gray parrot by the name of Ariel—had
wandered from place to place, joining companies
where they could, taking whatever audience they
could find. But Miranda's secret dream had always
been to have a home, a real home. A stable life. A
husband and children.

And when she'd met Damien Lévesque in New

Orleans, she'd thought for a time that such a foolish dream could come true.

"Papa didn't understand, Ariel," she said softly. "He thought the stage was my life as it was his. But the things I dreamed of were not to be. And now that he's gone . . ."

She swallowed, forcing back the tears. Her father hadn't wanted her to grieve. "Go on," he'd said. "Don't waste the glorious life you've been given, as I have. Make a place for yourself somewhere. I know you have the strength—you always did. 'Yield not thy neck to fortune's yoke, but let thy dauntless mind still ride in triumph over all mischance.' "

And so she did as he asked. She went on, no longer comforted by the illusion of security the theater had given her, completely alone for the first time in her life. Except for a small gray parrot.

"Ah, Ariel," she murmured, emerging out of the shadows and into moonlight. "What are we to do now?"

"Well, if it ain't the laddie boy what took all your dust, Bruce."

Miranda blinked up at the three men who towered over her. She recognized one of them as the angry miner she'd beaten at poker earlier in the evening, a foul-tongued Sydney Duck. His mates stood to either side, grinning and prodding their friend contemptuously.

"Such a little tyke, too. Not safe to leave all that gold with a child."

Miranda was already looking for an escape route as the men's cruel laughter rose around her in a cage of sound.

Bruce swaggered closer, blowing foul breath in Miranda's face. "You still got my gold, laddie boy? How 'bout a little loan?"

The three men advanced, forcing Miranda back into the shadows. She worked her hands into fists. "I won the games fairly," she said.

"Fair!" The ringleader spat a wad of tobacco onto the bar at her feet. "Why, we're fair-minded boys ourselves. Just give over what you've got there, and we'll—"

His low-voiced threat ended in a squawk as Ariel flew at his face. Miranda lost not a moment. She sprang forward between two of the men, dodging their grasping hands, and fled. She knew at once that they were right behind her. And she was running away from the boardinghouse and safety.

Slipping into the narrow alley between two frame-and-canvas cabins, Miranda paused to get her bearings. Ariel had still not returned to her. Perhaps he was leading the men away....

The crunch of feet on gravel approaching from the street warned her just in time. Miranda dashed blindly toward the steep hill that rose behind the bar and into the brawny arms of one of the Sydney Ducks.

"Now, now, now," the man said, grinning broadly as he lifted Miranda off her feet. "Me'n the boys just want a friendly little game of poker to square things up. Don't we, mates?"

He clamped his arms around her as his friends closed in with mutters of agreement.

Miranda went very still. If she struggled any harder, the roughneck would know all too quickly that she hid more than gold dust under her baggy clothing.

"Ariel," she whispered. "Where are you now?"

The parrot flew in the open window and landed directly in the middle of a plate of empty oyster shells.

Etienne nearly choked on his champagne. But Damien froze with his glass to his lips, staring at the African gray parrot whose short red tail feathers scattered the remains of their supper onto the rough wooden table.

Ariel.

No. That was impossible.

"Au secours!" The parrot cocked back its head, flapped its wings, and whistled. *"Help!"*

"Diable!" Etienne set down his glass with great care. "Where did it come from?"

"I don't know." Damien pushed back his chair and got up slowly. One African gray parrot looked much like another. In New Orleans there had always been a number for sale in the market, brought over on ships from Africa. But here in the mines . . .

The bird launched up from the table and flew at Damien, landing on his shoulder. A sharp curved beak nipped at his ear. *"Venez! Danger! Help!"* A moment later the parrot was gone again, flying in agitated circles near the cabin door.

Damien exchanged glances with Etienne and walked across the cabin, retrieving his pistol from the shelf beside his bed. He slapped his hat on his head and pulled the brim low. "I'll be right back."

"Where are you going?"

"To follow an old habit, *mon ami.* Later, perhaps, I'll ask you to remind me that I'm not insane."

The parrot darted ahead of Damien as he strode out into the night. By the time Damien had followed the bird to one of the rubbish-filled alleys near the saloon, he hardly noticed its disappearance. His attention was all for the little drama being played out against a backdrop of shadow and moonlight.

The boy was doing a surprisingly efficient job of defending himself against the three ruffians who had set on him. One of the Ducks was on his back in the dust, bent double and moaning. Another was cursing and sucking vigorously on his fingers. The third had hold of the boy, but even as Damien watched, the lad tossed a buckskin bag to the ground and the ruffian released his captive to dive for it.

Pulling his pistol from his belt, Damien walked calmly into the center of the melee.

"Theft, gentlemen?" he inquired. "We have no use for thieves in Heaven's Bar."

The ruffian holding the buckskin bag dropped it and went very still. His companions ceased their howling and moaning and stared at the pistol. The boy, poised on the edge of flight, looked up at Damien with wide eyes in a pale, smudged face. Blood trickled from the corner of his mouth.

"I tell you, I heard something—"

The woman's distant voice broke the tableau. The Sydney Ducks scattered and fled into the night, one of them still bent double with his hands gripping his crotch. The boy knelt to retrieve his pouch and tucked it under his loose shirt. He staggered a little as he came to his feet; Damien moved quickly to grasp the lad's thin arm.

"Are you all right?" he asked, taking the slight weight against his own body. "Are you—"

But he lost the thread of his thoughts when the boy met his gaze. The sensation of recognition, of eerie familiarity, shook Damien to the soles of his boots.

Green eyes, fringed with thick auburn lashes, flicked away from Damien's face. The boy's tongue darted out to touch the bloodied corner of his mouth. Damien's suddenly nerveless fingers loosened their grip.

The boy pulled free and folded his arms across his

chest, staring fixedly at the ground. "I'm fine," he said in the gruff tenor of a child trying hard to act the man. "Thank you."

Damien felt a strange, overwhelming urge to lift the boy's chin in his hand, study the delicate line of cheekbone and jaw once again by the light of the moon. But as he reached out he heard the tramp of footsteps; a small parade of miners crowded into the alley, Annette at its head, twitching her skirts away from piles of refuse. Cain Sullivan strolled in her wake.

"What is this, *mon cher*?" Annette said. Her gaze slid from Damien to the boy, and she gasped. She swept past Damien and enfolded the lad in her perfumed embrace.

"Ah, *pauvre garçon*. Let me see your face. Bruises!"

Watching the boy squirm in Annette's solicitous care, Cain Sullivan smiled wryly. "I knew there'd be more trouble tonight," he remarked, taking a long draw on his cigar.

Damien shoved his pistol back into his belt. "Since when did you concern yourself with the ultimate fate of your customers, Sullivan?"

Sullivan shrugged. "Let's say the boy reminds me of the little brother I left behind in Ireland."

Damien glanced again at Annette and her reluctant charge, frowning. So the boy reminded Sullivan of a younger brother. But that wasn't why he looked so familiar to Damien.

No. Suddenly aware that he'd knotted his hands into fists, Damien unclenched his fingers slowly. The boy resembled someone else entirely.

Annette drew the boy toward Damien, her gaze flicking over his shoulder to Sullivan. "I will take care of him, Cain. He needs washing up. We will let him sleep in the storeroom tonight, *n'est-ce pas?*" She looked at Damien with a secret smile. "Come see me tomorrow, *cher*. Perhaps you can give the boy some good advice on how to stay out of trouble."

Damien stood in the alley long after Annette led the boy away and the miners dispersed, considering the merits of a good stiff drink. Of course it had been foolish to think, even for a moment, that Miranda would be here. The parrot was just a parrot, hardly exotic in a land where fortune seekers of every nation on earth, from China to Chile, were as common as fleas in a miner's blanket.

And the boy looked nothing like Miranda at all.

He turned back for the cabin he shared with Etienne, grimly resolved to put Miranda from his mind once again. Wherever she was now, she was undoubtedly faring well—charming some other unfortunate fool with her finely polished portrayal of a devoted, virtuous, and loving woman. . . .

Etienne met him at the cabin door. "Do you still wish me to remind you that you are not insane?" he asked, arching an eyebrow.

Damien laughed humorlessly and flung himself down on his bunk. "Remind me next week, *mon ami*. I'm going to Sacramento tomorrow to inspect our steamboats. I only ask one thing of you."

"Name it."

"Find the owner of that bird and give him fair warning. I'm not averse to sampling parrot fricassee."

If matters were not progressing quite as quickly—or as smoothly—as Ariel preferred, at least they were progressing.

Ariel watched Miranda prepare in the makeshift dressing room behind the saloon's newly built stage, coiling her rich fall of red hair under the cap she would wear during the night's performance. She paused, staring at herself in the small, very expensive mirror Sullivan had presented to her several days ago.

"Well, Ariel," she said, drawing in a deep breath. "I'm doing what Papa dreamed of all along. Playing for the miners in California." She dropped her hands into her lap. "I suppose you're thinking it's better than gambling."

" 'When fortune means to men most good, she looks upon them with a threatening eye,' " Ariel quoted.

Miranda smiled sadly. "Strange, isn't it, how Papa and I both feared I'd be in peril of my life alone in this land of men. But Cain tells me they see women as sacred here. God alone knows how long that will last." She stood up, smoothing the short black velvet tunic she wore for Hamlet's soliloquy. "After tonight the entire camp will know what I am."

Ariel hopped across the uneven table between the small pots of stage makeup and clucked comfortingly. Annette had been the first to realize the truth, of course—that the boy she tended in the saloon's storeroom was no boy at all. And once Miranda had convinced the Frenchwoman that she had no intention of competing in Annette's profession—for which Annette had the monopoly in Heaven's Bar—the women had agreed to keep Miranda's true nature a secret between them.

Until Cain Sullivan walked in and saw Miranda with her hair down.

That had been that. Ariel clearly remembered the look on Sullivan's face. Miranda had braced herself, but Sullivan had only stared, mouth open, his smooth self-assurance utterly gone. Miranda had shrugged, lifted her chin, and told him the truth.

She was an actress. Her father was dead, and she was alone and penniless. She had gambled because she had some skill at it, and she needed the money to live, make a new start here in California. If Mr. Sullivan would kindly keep the small matter of her gender secret . . .

Cain Sullivan had shut his mouth and begun to grin. And he had made Miranda an immediate proposition—one that Miranda hadn't been able to refuse.

And then the work had begun. Sullivan had closed off the parlor adjoining the saloon's main room and built a stage—crude, to be sure, but a stage nonetheless, curtained on the sides and back. And he'd let the rumors circulate throughout camp, out into the hidden ravines and gulches where the miners worked their diggings.

An actress had come to Heaven's Bar, a brilliant Shakespearean actress come to ease the miners' lonely existence.

Sullivan called her the Fair Incognita, and tonight was to be her first performance.

The Fair Incognita. Ariel looked heavenward. How blind mortals could be. Damien had utterly failed to recognize Miranda that night in the alley—even when he'd nearly held her in his arms. And, amid the shadows and confusion, Miranda had not known the man she'd never stopped loving. . . .

Ariel walked a tight circle around the tabletop, tucking his wings across his back. He had watched Sullivan closely. In his greed for the gold dust Miranda's performances would bring in, the Irishman would provide the means to bring two very

stubborn mortals together again. And if Damien
failed to show up for Miranda's performance—well,
there were ways to encourage him.

I would fain have it a match, Ariel thought, eyeing Miranda.

"How do I look, Ariel?" Miranda said, tugging
again at the hem of her tunic. "I don't know why
I'm permitting a pack of rough miners to discom-
pose me. Surely I've faced more daunting audiences." She laughed, a little hoarsely. "Stage fright, at
my age. If Papa were here—" Her smile faded. She
held out her hand, and Ariel hopped onto her
velvet-clad arm.

" 'Fight till the last gasp,' " Ariel said, rubbing his
beak against her cheek. " 'All the world's a stage.' "

"So it is, my friend," she said. Her voice dropped
and her carriage straightened as she became the
tragic Prince of Denmark. " 'Though this be madness, yet there is method in't.' "

Ariel knew she hadn't even begun to guess.

Damien returned to the saloon a week after he'd
left Heaven's Bar, bone-weary with the long journey
from Sacramento just behind him. Not once during
the days on foot and horseback and steamship had
he been able to put the past out of his mind.

As he walked into the Pearly Gates he thought he
was ready to sample Sullivan's whiskey after all. But
he stopped just inside the door, staring around the
room at empty monte tables and empty bar, hearing
only an eerie silence.

Not quite silence. A murmur filtered from the adjoining room, the parlor Sullivan used for special
customers and guests. For the first time Damien noticed the crudely painted sign propped up on top of
the bar.

"Shakespearean performance in the Pearly Gates Theater at sundown," he read slowly.

Shakespeare—here, in Heaven's Bar. He'd attended performances in the Eagle Theater in Sacramento—but Heaven's Bar? The Pearly Gates Theater?

The roar of male voices rose from the adjoining parlor, accompanied by shrill whistles. Damien walked toward the curtained partition that led to the parlor and paused as silence descended again.

The voice that began to speak—Hamlet's soliloquy, Damien realized with a start—was low and melodious and hypnotic. He found himself listening, eyes closed, as a flood of memories carried him back to New Orleans—when he had first seen Miranda perform on the stage at the tiny leased theater on Camp Street—when he and Miranda had walked in Lafayette Square and played out their favorite roles. Romeo and Juliet. Rosalind and Orlando. Beatrice and Benedick ...

Pushing the curtain aside, Damien strode into the parlor. He hardly noticed Sullivan's henchman, who demanded an outrageous price for the privilege of a ticket; Damien tossed the man a small bag of gold dust and walked past him without a word. His eyes were all for the new stage and the small figure who stood on it.

He froze, as rapt as the miners who watched in fascinated silence from rough benches and the floor and every corner of the room. It was the boy—the boy he'd tried to rescue a week ago. A boy who commanded the stage like the prince he pretended to be.

" 'And enterprises of great pith and moment
With this regard their currents turn awry,
and lose the name of action.' "

As the boy finished, bowing his head, the audience broke into howls of approval. Stamping feet rattled the floorboards. And the boy, looking up with regal pride, reached up to pull off his feathered velvet cap.

Long, lush hair, red as a mountain sunset, tumbled about the boy's shoulders. There was a moment of silence from the miners, and then their shouts redoubled.

A woman. Not a boy at all, but a woman. Damien stepped back, bumping hard into a miner he vaguely recognized as one of the toughest in camp, and leaned heavily against the wall.

Miranda. Miranda, here.

Dazedly he looked about the room for the parrot. It had been Ariel all along. Ariel who had come to him for help when Miranda had been in danger . . .

Danger. Damien ground his teeth together and stared at the rough, unshaven, dirty faces on every side. Where was her father? Why would he let her perform here, in such a place as this? What bizarre twist of fate had brought her to California at all?

"Miranda," he whispered, staring up at the stage, where she stood calmly accepting the accolades and the bags of gold dust thrown at her feet. Without any command from his mind his legs began to move, pulling him toward the stage. He heard Miranda begin to speak again, her voice restored to its lovely, throaty lilt, but he heard nothing, saw nothing but her petite figure so exposed in the tunic and tights, her lips curved in a smile for her adoring audience, her clear green gaze exactly as he remembered it.

A snap of feathers and a rush of air swept by his ear as Ariel landed on his shoulder.

" 'All hail, great master,' " the parrot quoted softly.

And then Miranda looked down, directly into Damien's eyes.

Papa was right, Ariel, Miranda thought.

She gazed down at the sea of bearded faces, breathing a sigh of relief. It had gone exactly as Cain had promised. These men were desperate for entertainment—and not all of them were uneducated louts. They had listened to Shakespeare as if it were celestial music, and the pile of gold dust-filled bags scattered across the stage was proof enough of their satisfaction.

If she felt almost nothing of the pleasure she'd once found on the stage, that mattered not at all. This was only a temporary measure, just as the gambling had been. A few months, perhaps—here and touring other mining camps—and she could begin to make a new life for herself. Somewhere.

But this night's performance was not yet done.

Miranda smiled down at the miners and raised her hand.

"I know there are many among you who have hidden talents. I'm in need of a gallant gentleman to play Benedick to my Beatrice—if there are any volunteers who can read the part?"

There was an immediate murmur of eager voices as one and another miner pushed his way forward to volunteer. Ariel swooped down suddenly from the far end of the room, where he'd observed Miranda's performance with a critical yellow eye, and came to land on the broad shoulder of a black-bearded man at the foot of the stage.

Miranda looked down and froze. She knew the man. He was the same miner who'd come to her belated rescue a week ago—a man whose face she'd never seen clearly, and not once since that night. A man she hadn't been able to thank.

He was handsome, even bearded as he was. Though he looked as tough and hardened as any man in the room, there was a difference about him—something that made her heart race and her breath come short. His broad shoulders and muscular arms were hardly concealed by the plain miner's shirt he wore. Dark eyes regarded her with a flat, unreadable stare.

Eyes she could never forget.

Damien's eyes. Damien—here.

No, she thought. *Impossible.* He had married his Creole girl in New Orleans. She was never to see him again.

Damien. Miranda began to shiver.

He had changed. There was little resemblance between the boy she'd known and this man with his deeply tanned face, the vivid scar seaming his cheek, the wiry beard that obscured his mouth so completely.

And there was no recognition in the gaze that locked on hers. Or was there? Did he know her—finding her, here, in defiance of fate itself? Was this another cruel game?

Damien smiled, idly stroking Ariel's breast feathers with one long finger.

"Well," he said, so softly that only she could hear. " 'You are a rare parrot-teacher.' "

Miranda gave him no reaction at all. Oh, yes, Damien knew her. The quote was taken directly from *Much Ado About Nothing,* part of Beatrice and Benedick's ongoing contest of wit.

But he would not win this battle. He would not see her crumble. It would be as if he were a stranger. Let him wonder if she recognized him, if she'd ever cared enough to remember him at all....

Miranda drew her stage persona about herself,

barring emotion and weakness from her heart. She composed her lips into a professional smile and held out her hand.

"I believe we have our volunteer," she announced. "I and Mister . . ." She stepped back as Damien jumped easily up onto the stage.

"Mr. Lamoureux," he put in.

"Mr. Lamoureux," she repeated, "will perform the opening scene between Beatrice and Benedick from *Much Ado About Nothing.*"

As the audience whistled approval, Miranda ducked behind the stage curtain. Her fingers trembled as she pulled a full skirt up over her tights and fastened it at the waist, making the swift alteration to Beatrice. When she turned around Damien was directly behind her, the curtain at his back.

"You played the boy very well," he said, his voice deep and rich and achingly familiar. How could she not have known him, that night in the alley?

She turned to face him. His expression was cool, disinterested—bereft of warmth or intimacy. *So be it.*

"We play what roles we must," she replied. "I wasn't able to thank you properly, Mr. Lamoureux, for—rescuing me in the alley." Backing away, she hunted for the script she'd left on a makeshift table. "Here. You'll need this—" She thrust the script at him as if it were a weapon, but he only shook his head and smiled.

"I know the role," he murmured. His gaze never left hers.

A miner shouted impatiently on the other side of the curtain. "We must not keep our audience waiting," Damien said, offering his arm. She took it— and felt a rush of overwhelming sensation sweep through her body at that slight contact. His muscles bunched under her hand. Then they were onstage, and Miranda gratefully lost herself in the performance once more.

" 'I wonder that you will still be talking, Signior Benedick—nobody marks you' " she recited, with Beatrice's mocking playfulness.

" 'What, my dear Lady Disdain!' " Damien answered, dark brows arched. " 'Are you yet living?' "

They played through the scene, Damien handling his role flawlessly. Miranda struggled to dismiss the painful undercurrents behind the words, the constant and memory-laden awareness of the man with whom she shared the stage—a man she'd believed she'd known as well as Beatrice knew Benedick. Like Beatrice, she refused to reveal the feelings Shakespeare's heroine hid in her heart for the roguish, self-proclaimed perennial bachelor.

The scene ended to whistles and wild applause. Miranda heard nothing, saw nothing but her Benedick as he drew closer, gazing down at her as if they were alone in the room, and bent his lips to hers. . . .

"Gentlemen!"

Miranda flinched away as Cain Sullivan jumped up onto the stage, taking Miranda's arm and tucking it through the crook of his elbow. He smiled at her with utmost charm and flashed Damien a look of unmistakable warning.

"And now, gentlemen," Sullivan said, "the Fair Incognita requires an intermission. If you'd care to refresh yourselves at the bar—"

The men needed no further urging. They surged en masse through the door that led to the bar, leaving the makeshift theater empty and echoing with the sound of laughter. When Miranda looked around, Damien had disappeared.

"Just as I told you, love," Sullivan said. He looped

his arm around her waist. "The men adore you, as well they should. You'll soon be known as the greatest actress the Mother Lode has ever seen."

Slowly Miranda came out of the spell the performance had cast over her. She looked up at Sullivan, and he caught her hand, lifting it to his lips.

"The men aren't the only ones who adore you," he said. "I—"

" 'Hark, hark, I hear the strain of strutting Chanticleer!' " Ariel said, flying between them to land on Sullivan's forearm. Sullivan grimaced, shaking Ariel off and losing his grip on Miranda's hand. Miranda blessed Ariel silently and retreated behind the stage curtains. For a moment she stood there, trembling, catching her breath, fighting emotions she had never expected to experience again.

Already Cain Sullivan had begun to drop hints of feelings for her—feelings she sensed might run deeper than the lust her father had so often warned her about, the bane of any actress's life. Papa had always tried to protect her from the rougher side of their profession, and she had grown up innocent of the indiscretions her sisters of the stage were so often known to indulge in. Only once had she been tempted to surrender her virtue; even then she'd held firm. And thereby lost the man she loved.

The man she had found again.

Miranda sat down and automatically began to clean the makeup from her face. *No.* Damien's showing up here changed nothing. She had a new life—and it was hard not to feel flattered by Cain's attentions. He had been the perfect gentleman with her. To him she owed this chance to earn a living as she had been trained to do. And he was an Irishman who had struggled up from poor and humble beginnings. He would understand her.

Damien Lévesque was out of her life.

Donning a patched but clean skirt and blouse, Miranda packed the costumes carefully in her small trunk, the only one she'd been able to bring with her to the mines. Tomorrow would be a new performance. She would choose some other play, not one that reminded her so painfully of her brief time with Damien. *The Merchant of Venice*, perhaps—she'd always been good as Portia.

And if Damien showed up again, he would find it quite impossible to extract his pound of flesh.

Miranda closed the trunk's lid with a snap and walked slowly up the uneven stairs to her small room above the saloon.

This time Damien had known her.

Ariel looked over the camp from a bird's-eye view atop a towering pine, near Damien's cabin in a ravine off the bar, watching the comings and goings of the mortals scurrying about in search of worldly wealth.

Damien was going to be stubborn once again. He hadn't attended a single one of Miranda's performances since the night he'd joined her on the stage. In fact, he'd spent most of his time far from camp, wandering the hills when he wasn't settling some business transaction or other.

But he was preparing to leave. The signs were clear. Damien was going to run away, and nothing would be resolved.

But love is blind, and lovers cannot see the pretty follies that themselves commit, Ariel thought. And so he watched, and waited, for the young man who had loved and lost Miranda three and a half years ago.

An angel's memory was flawless, even a corporeal

angel's. Ariel thought back to the day, on the levee in New Orleans, when it had all begun.

Miranda and her father had arrived with their small Shakespearean company to lease a theater in the American sector. Miles O'Reilly had already found the best Irish taverns and a new set of drinking cronies; Miranda, who hid her sorrow from everyone but Ariel, had learned long ago to make her own way at such times.

And so she had gone one morning in October to the levee, with Ariel on her shoulder.

Ariel could vividly recall his first glimpse of the sober young Creole gentleman at the bookseller's stand at the market, a strangely quiet figure amid so much color and chaos. No one else on the levee had given the young man a second glance. But Ariel had seen with more than mortal sight, and he had known at once. Out of all the men in the world, Damien Lévesque was the one for Miranda O'Reilly.

Miranda had never prayed for a selfish thing in all her life. Since childhood her devotion had been focused entirely on her father, whose loving heart could not disguise his many weaknesses. But one day Miles O'Reilly would be gone—and Ariel was, after all, Miranda's guardian angel.

It had been a simple thing to fly to the young man's shoulder, causing him to drop his pile of books. And Miranda, of course, had followed and apologized profusely for her pet's clumsiness, kneeling in the dust to retrieve the gentleman's parcels. With perfect courtesy, the young man had helped her to her feet.

Their eyes had met, and that had been that.

Ariel was a firm believer in the power of love. It was a professional requirement. He hadn't worried overmuch at the vast difference between the lovers' social ranks and backgrounds.

Miranda had always been surrounded by people and treated with casual affection—by her father and the folk of the theatrical world, and by the audiences that watched her perform—but she had never known the security of a hearth and home. The vast love she had to give was wasted, like a light under a bushel. Damien had wealth and position and stability, but all too little love from his judgmental, rigid parents. He had always walked alone.

Miranda had begun to teach Damien what love meant in those months they'd had together. And Miranda had begun to hope that she had found what her most secret heart had longed for.

Until it had all fallen apart.

Ariel ruffled his feathers and smoothed them with an effort. Perhaps he had simply spent too much time in corporeal form. Perhaps he had lost his angel's objectivity. Somewhere he had made a mistake.

But now he had a chance to put it right again. " 'Time's glory is to calm contending kings, to unmask falsehood and bring the truth to light . . .' "

Ariel stretched his neck and loosened his wings as he caught sight of his quarry. Damien walked with a long, brisk stride toward his cabin at the end of the ravine; Ariel had to dive with a certain recklessness in order to make it through the door before Damien closed it.

The expression on Damien's face was anything but welcoming.

"What are you doing here?" he growled, tossing his battered felt hat onto his bunk.

Ariel took a safe perch at the top of a shelf of supplies. Damien needed a stern talking-to, but he had never known Ariel as anything but an ordinary parrot.

" 'O! for a Muse of fire, that would ascend the

brightest heaven of invention!' " Ariel muttered under his breath. He lifted his voice to a parrot's soft squawk. " 'Dwell I but in the suburbs of your good pleasure?' " he asked the man below him.

Damien threw himself down on the bed and looked up at Ariel with narrowed eyes. "Ha," he muttered. "I know *she* didn't send you. She didn't even know me." He ran one hand over his heavy beard, smiling bleakly. "But I'm not surprised. I have changed, bird, by far more than this."

Ariel bobbed his head. Yes, Damien had changed. There was a hardness about him now, the tough hide and grim wariness of a survivor. He had left that bookish boy in New Orleans far behind.

" 'Sits the wind in that quarter?' " Ariel asked.

Damien swung his booted feet to the floor. "You always were a remarkably intelligent creature. Almost—human." Abruptly he got up, pacing across the small room to stand beneath Ariel's perch. "How in heaven's name did you know where to find me when she was in trouble?" He glared at Ariel as if he expected an answer. "How did she come to be here? Where is her father? What was she doing dressed as a boy and gambling in Sullivan's saloon? This is no place for—" He broke off with a bark of laughter. "Listen to me, bird. Etienne would think I've gone mad, talking to you as if you understood."

Turning on his heel, he locked his hands behind his back. His voice dropped to a near whisper. "Some men do go mad, out here. They come expecting to find gold nuggets on the ground, and leave with nothing. I was lucky. I made my fortune early. But I never believed I'd see her again."

" 'O God! that one might read the book of fate,' " Ariel quoted.

"Fate," Damien echoed. "When I saw her on

Sullivan's stage—" He shook his head, but Ariel heard the slight tremor in his voice. "Why did you come for me, bird? Your mistress doesn't require my help."

" 'A poor lone woman . . .' "

"Miranda, poor? I know how well she can take care of herself. She'll have the camp at her feet soon enough." Turning, he scowled at Ariel. "And Sullivan, too, no doubt."

Ariel observed the expression on Damien's face with keen interest. " 'Beware, my lord, of jealousy!' "

"Jealousy!" Damien snapped. Sucking in a deep breath, he leaned against the rough log wall with studied negligence. "I'll never fall at any woman's feet. Miranda cured me of that particular weakness." His brows drew down. "Damn Sullivan, with his smooth-talking ways. Where is her father? If I thought for a moment she couldn't match Sullivan measure for measure . . ."

Ariel strutted along the edge of the shelf. " 'She's beautiful and therefore to be woo'd. She is a woman, therefore to be won.' "

It seemed Damien had not yet revealed his most ominous expression. For a moment Ariel was grateful for wings and a high perch.

And then all at once the grim anger faded from Damien's face. "If I didn't know better, bird," he said wearily, "I'd think you were still playing matchmaker." He flipped back the scrap of red calico cloth that hung over one of the cabin's small windows. Late-afternoon sunlight washed the lines of hard experience from his face. "I haven't forgotten how you brought us together. *Dieu*—" Running his hand through his tangled black hair, he closed his eyes. "I haven't forgotten a single moment."

" 'True it is,' " Ariel admitted sadly, " 'that we have seen better days.' "

"Better days." Damien stared out the window. "I had a fool's innocence then. I thought Miranda was an angel, and when she fell she took me with her."

Rocking from foot to foot, Ariel resisted the urge to nip Damien on the ear. " 'The fool doth think he is wise, but the wise man knows himself to be a fool.' "

Damien let the curtain fall. Ariel watched him pace the length of the cabin and back again. "Ironic, isn't it, bird? I left everything behind because of her, because I thought my heart was broken. I turned my back on my family and my duty and my honor—for the sake of your mistress. Even after she'd betrayed all her vows of love. And now she's here."

He sat down on the bed and tugged off one dusty boot. "I was ready to leave camp anyway, bird. I see no reason to delay my plans. My business in Heaven's Bar is concluded. I owe her nothing." Pulling off his other boot, he threw it across the room. "Those men who attacked her in the alley didn't know she was a woman. Sullivan won't risk his investment now that he knows how much he can earn from her. Women are worshiped here. She'll be perfectly safe—"

Ariel took the risk. He left the safety of the shelf and flew down to the crude bedpost at the end of the bunk. " 'I do perceive here a divided duty,' " he said gently.

The bed rattled as Damien slapped his hand down on the straw-stuffed mattress. "What duty, bird? To protect her, after she rejected everything I offered except the ring I'd given her as proof of my devotion?" He curled his lip. "Oh, no. She's had everything she'll ever have of me." He bent over and pulled a large canvas sack from under the bed and yanked open the tie that held it closed. His movements were jerky and utterly revealing as he began to grab folded shirts and patched trousers from the shelves and stuff them into the sack.

Ariel hopped onto the mattress. " 'Is there any cause in nature that makes these hard hearts?' "

Damien scowled and tossed a rumpled frock coat on the bed. "Ask your mistress, bird. Ask her about the letter and the ring and the answer she gave me. Ask her how easily my father bought her off."

Fluffing his feathers, Ariel bent his head back to regard the man towering over him. " 'Forbear to judge, for we are sinners all.' "

Damien sat down heavily and passed his hand over his face. "*Oui*, bird, I sinned. I sinned in trusting too much, and in that single dishonorable offer I made her. But I would have made it right, in spite of my family's opposition." He bent his head. "Too late now, bird, far too late."

Ariel felt the weight of Damien's sorrow, knowing the man would never reveal it to anyone else. He hopped onto Damien's knee. " 'Some things are med'cinable.' "

"Not this, bird. Not this." He lifted Ariel from his leg and rose.

Launching upward, Ariel gained his shoulder. " 'Alas, how love can trifle with itself!' "

Damien laughed, though the sound was more sad than bitter. "Do you think I still love her, bird? It was a boy's infatuation. I should have taken a *placée* when my father suggested it. The only use I have for a woman now is to warm my bed—and that Miranda would never do, armored in her hypocritical virtue."

Ariel gave an agitated croak. "She's 'as chaste as unsunn'd snow.' "

Their eyes were only inches apart, deep brown and pale yellow. Damien looked genuinely puzzled. "You're a strange creature, Ariel. Are you to be my personal gadfly? Are you her witch's familiar? Will you hound me until I see her again?"

" 'My purpose is, indeed, a horse of that color. I'll not budge an inch,' " Ariel declared, sensing victory.

The vulnerability revealed so briefly in Damien's face vanished. "So I am to go to her again, bird? Swallow what remains of my pride and forget how she tore my family apart?" He knelt down as Ariel balanced on his shoulder, and retrieved another stack of clothing from the lowest shelf, shaking the garments out and tossing them beside the frock coat on the bunk. Dark trousers, fine lawn shirt, silk waistcoat. The attire of a gentleman.

"Very well, bird," Damien said grimly. "Perhaps you're right. I'll have done with this once and for all. But she won't see the rough miner who played Benedick, nor the boy she knew and discarded. I'll shave this beard for her sake, as Benedick did for Beatrice—but unlike Benedick I'll remain a bachelor to the end of my days."

His decision made, Damien moved with admirable purpose. Within the hour, just as the sun began its descent behind the hills, he had clipped his beard and shaved himself down to the skin. The face that glared so fiercely back at him from the small mirror still held the ghost of the boy Ariel remembered.

"Satisfied, bird?" he demanded. "Will she recognize me now?"

"Is it time to remind you you're not insane?"

Damien swung toward the door so abruptly that Ariel had to flap his wings to keep his balance. Etienne stood in the doorway, grinning.

"Still talking to birds?" he quipped. But his grin

faded as he took in Damien's clean-shaven face. He whistled. "*Mon Dieu.* What's this?"

Damien toweled his face one last time and walked to the bed. He held up the black frock coat. "I'm going to see a lady, Etienne."

The tall quadroon rubbed his own clean-shaven chin. "Annette will be pleased—"

"Not Annette." Damien stripped off his shirt.

"And not Mrs. Baker, I'll wager. That leaves—"

"Perhaps one day I'll tell you the entire story, *mon ami*," Damien said. "But for now . . ."

With brisk, practiced gestures he pulled on the shirt and trousers and waistcoat, tied his cravat, and donned the frock coat. When he had finished, Etienne whistled again.

"I was going to wish you luck, *mon ami*," Etienne said softly. "Sullivan's a rival to be reckoned with. But I don't think you'll need it after all."

Damien bowed, a mocking smile on his face. He ran his hands through his hair, nodded to Etienne, and strode toward the door. As he reached it, Ariel hopped from his shoulder to the other man's.

" 'The course of true love,' " Ariel confided, " 'never did run smooth.' "

And he flew after Damien while Etienne stared after him.

Like all the others, the performance had been an overwhelming success.

Miranda knelt to gather up the pouches thrown onto the stage, taking the callused hands extended to her and smiling impartially at every eager male face. It was so easy to control these uncouth men. If she had craved that heady power, she might have thrived here.

And she could easily grow rich. Already she had

enough gold dust to buy decent clothing and food, more money than she'd ever possessed at one time. In a few more weeks, after touring the nearer mining camps, she'd have a stake to start a new life.

Miranda straightened and gave the rowdy men another graceful bow. *A new life.* It was possible. It had to be.

Damien had not returned.

She smiled again at her audience, but her thoughts were sober. Cain had made it clearer with every passing day that he wanted to be part of her new life. He was ready to give up the saloon and the rough miner's existence—he had wealth enough to establish them both in San Francisco. He'd bought a lot there years ago, before land in the city had become impossible to find at any price.

"A grand new theater has just opened in San Francisco," he'd told her. "A place made for your talents, love. You could be the greatest actress in California. And I can help you."

To stay on the stage ... She hadn't considered it until Cain had made it sound so wonderful. It was, after all, the life she had always known. And it had become clear in these past weeks that Cain had the ability to manage her career as Papa had never done.

With a final bow, Miranda swept behind the stage curtains and began to undress. She'd lost Papa, and had given up the hope of romantic love three and a half years ago. But there were other kinds of love— the thrill of basking in the adulation of the audience, the companionship of fellow theater folk—and the passion Cain Sullivan promised with his eyes and his touch.

The stage could become a full life for her. She need never live alone. Sullivan wasn't the type to settle down to a quiet family existence, but he could give her other things in compensation. Perhaps she could learn to love him in time.

If she could only let those last stubborn dreams go at last, and pretend "Mr. Lamoureux" had been just another miner—or a mere shade from her past, no more substantial than morning mist.

Fastening the last buttons on the elegant green Parisian gown Cain had given her the day before—a far grander dress than any she'd ever owned—Miranda gazed at herself in the mirror. Soon she'd have to make the decision. She glanced at the empty place on her shoulder where Ariel usually rode, and shook her head. Even though he was only a bird, Ariel was an excellent listener. Tonight she'd go over it with him, all the pros and cons. Ariel always had a way of turning her in the right direction.

Miranda gathered her skirts and peered out into the theater through the curtains. The room had nearly emptied as the miners resumed their drinking and gambling in the adjoining saloon. She smoothed the curtains behind her and made her way across the stage and down the shallow steps to the wooden floor.

A man was waiting for her there, Ariel perched on his shoulder. He wore a slightly rumpled black frock coat over dark trousers, a white lawn shirt, and a black cravat. He was tall and broad-shouldered, undeniably handsome, with deep brown eyes that met Miranda's with an intensity that made her shiver.

Now he was clean-shaven, and the strong line of jaw, the aristocratic nose, the carved arc of high cheekbones were no longer concealed. Only the eyes were the same.

Damien.

He doffed his top hat and bowed.

"Miranda," he said.

She clenched her fists. " 'What is't? A spirit?' "

she quoted hoarsely, cloaking herself in the role of the Shakespearean heroine for whom she'd been named.

Damien smiled, a slight curl of his lip. " 'No, wench, it eats and sleeps and hath such senses as you have.' "

Miranda stepped back, feeling blindly for one of the crude benches that filled the theater. At once Damien was beside her, easing her down. Ariel hopped to her shoulder.

" 'What's past is prologue,' " the parrot said in a scratchy whisper.

But Miranda hardly heard him. The thud of her own heartbeat filled her ears, and her arm burned where Damien held it. She jerked away.

"Is your little—game finished?"

"My game?" His eyes narrowed with sudden comprehension. "So you did know me before. As usual, you played your role superbly." He bowed again. "Were you surprised to see me, Miranda?"

"Surprised?" She stopped, struggling to strip her voice of emotion.

Damien studied her. "I see that you were. But your astonishment is no greater than mine was when you removed your cap that night, fair Miranda. I knew you'd gone to the frontier, but this seems somewhat extreme."

She folded her arms across her chest to stop her trembling. "What are you doing here?"

He remained standing exactly as a gentleman should. "I could ask the same of you. In fact, I've been in California since October of forty-seven. I see that you're shocked—"

"You—were to marry Sabine Fortier—"

Damien gave a harsh laugh, though his expression remained pleasant. "It should have been a simple matter after you left. But I was still prone to a certain weakness then." He made an eloquent gesture that seemed to encompass the saloon and all the camp beyond its walls. "California has no sympathy for weakness."

Miranda closed her eyes, fighting back a wave of sickness. When she and Papa had been in New Orleans at the levee, taking ship for California, he had been here all along. He had never married his proper Creole wife. After that terrible letter he had sent, and the ring—his *congé* to buy her out of his life—he hadn't obeyed his family's wishes after all. He had caused everyone untold misery. . . .

"I'm a wealthy man here, in my own right, Miranda," he continued relentlessly, in that smooth and hateful voice. "And I see you're doing well enough for yourself. My congratulations."

Miranda raised her head and met his gaze. "Why are you here, Damien? Wasn't what you did in New Orleans enough?"

His pleasant expression faded. "So virtuous, Miranda. So sensitive of your honor. Do you still pretend to be offended at my offer to you the day my betrothal was announced?" He shook his head. "You had what you wanted. I came because your familiar"—he nodded to Ariel—"seemed to insist." He paused, making a show of examining her expensive gown. "But I believe Cain Sullivan is taking good care of you."

Ariel flapped his wings and croaked an inarticulate protest. Miranda shot to her feet. "Why, you—"

"Trouble, my dear?" Cain strolled up to them, his gaze deceptively heavy-lidded as it passed over her and fixed on Damien. "Is this—gentleman—annoying you?"

Grasping at the escape Cain offered, Miranda took his arm. Ariel croaked and abruptly abandoned her

shoulder, taking up a new perch on the rickety back
of a chair.

"Not at all, Cain," Miranda purred. She gave the
Irishman a warm smile and leaned against him, deliberately ignoring Damien. "We were just renewing
an old acquaintance."

"I see." Damien and Cain locked stares like a pair
of bristling dogs. Cain covered Miranda's curled fingers with his hand. "I know you have a lot to do,
Lévesque, seeing as you're leaving town very soon."
His mouth curved under his neatly trimmed mustache. "We wouldn't want to hold him up, would
we, my dear?"

"Not at all, Cain." Miranda glanced at Damien
with feigned indifference. "I'm delighted that you
enjoyed my performance." She let Cain lead her
away, her skin prickling with the awareness of
Damien's stare at her back.

While Cain poured her a glass of claret at the bar
and the raucous bustle of gamblers and miners
flowed around them, Miranda kept her face turned
stiffly away from the place where Damien had been
standing. But even as she sipped her wine, the stem
of the glass trembling between her fingers, she
caught Damien's reflection in the mirror behind the
counter. He sat down at a table with a pair of Chil-
eans and a rawboned Swede, the flash of his teeth
bright in the tan of his face. Annette strolled toward
him, hips swaying, and he pulled her onto his lap
with a laugh.

Miranda set her glass down very carefully. Turning to Cain, she gave him her most dazzling smile.
Cain's gaze flicked once across the room to Damien,
and then he took Miranda's hand and raised it to his
lips.

"Never fear, my dear," he said. "I'll not let him
bother you again."

Miranda picked up her glass, raised it in salute to the Irishman, and prepared to give the performance of her life.

The parrot hadn't said a thing this time. He'd only shown up at Damien's cabin early that morning, fixing Damien with an implacable yellow stare.

Damien had ignored him. Damned if he'd let a bird bully him into chasing after Miranda O'Reilly. She'd displayed her true nature last night, just as she'd done so long ago in New Orleans.

Damn Cain Sullivan. Swinging the ax again, Damien sent the two halves of the pine log flying in opposite directions with the force of the blow. He paused to strip the sweat from his brow with the back of his hand and positioned another log.

Damn Miranda O'Reilly.... He swore under his breath as the ax blade missed the log entirely and buried itself in the old stump. He tugged on it violently; a large brown hand gripped the handle above his and jerked it free.

"Such ferocity, *mon ami,*" Etienne said amiably, handing him the ax, "can only be inspired by a woman."

Damien set down the ax and glared at his friend, sweat stinging his eyes. "This is not the time for advice, Etienne," he growled.

Etienne raised his hands palm out. "*Non.* I wouldn't dream of it. I only wished to tell you that Cain Sullivan is on his way here, and he looks almost as savage as you do."

Glancing over the big man's shoulder toward camp, Damien felt his muscles tense in anticipation. He flexed his hands and wiped them on his trousers.

"When you smile like that, *mon ami,* you make my blood run cold," Etienne said. He produced a scrap of worn calico and plunged it into the water bucket left in the scant afternoon shade beside the cabin door. "Perhaps it's Sullivan I should be warning."

Damien caught the wet cloth Etienne tossed him and rubbed his bare chest and shoulders. "You wound me, Etienne. Mr. Sullivan and I merely have something to discuss."

"That's what I'm afraid of." With a shake of his head, Etienne retreated inside the cabin. Damien settled in the shade of the rough log wall and watched as Cain Sullivan walked along the riverbank and into the ravine.

Sullivan was, as always, dressed impeccably in a frock coat, waistcoat, and fine trousers, but his polished appearance suffered from the perspiration that slicked his hair under his hat and dripped onto his collar. He gave himself away by glancing at the strip of shade and the water Damien sipped from an old tin cup, but he stopped in the glare of sunlight and regarded Damien as he might a particularly unpleasant species of vermin.

"I've come to tell you to keep your hands off Miranda," Sullivan said softly. "She wants nothing to do with you."

Damien pushed away from the wall and dropped the tin cup back into the bucket. "Is that what she told you, *Irlandais*?"

"She didn't have to. Her feelings are clear enough." Sullivan's mustache twitched. "Whatever past you may have with her, it's over. She's with me now."

"With you?" Damien took a step forward, looking Sullivan up and down. "Does she know what you are?"

For a moment it seemed as though Sullivan might take the bait. His fists clenched and raised; with a brittle laugh he dropped them again.

"She obviously knows what *you* are, Your Lordship," Sullivan mocked. "She's made her choice. Yes, I should say she's made it quite clear." His smile was unpleasant with insinuation. "I plan to give Miranda more than my protection. In fact, having her in my bed may not be enough. She may make an honest man of me—"

His words stopped abruptly as Damien clenched Sullivan's cravat in his fist and twisted it into his throat. "Damn you, Sullivan," he snarled. "If you've touched her—"

But Sullivan only laughed, his gaze unflinching. "It's a pleasure to see you so weak over a woman, Lévesque. But I'm no rapist. I don't have to take my pleasure by force. Miranda is a very—passionate woman."

Sickened by the picture that rose in his mind, Damien let Sullivan go. He hardly saw Sullivan stagger back and straighten his cravat with an angry jerk.

Weak over a woman. Sullivan was right. Damien had known in New Orleans, after she played him for a fool, that she couldn't be the virtuous woman she'd pretended to be. She was an actress, after all. But when she'd appeared in Heaven's Bar, like a miracle come to life, he'd become a callow boy again. He'd betrayed his weakness to Sullivan—and to her. How she must have laughed.

Fool. Damien made his face a rigid mask and met Sullivan's hostile gaze. "Get out of here, Sullivan, before I forget I was once a gentleman."

Sullivan had the good sense not to mock Damien again. He turned his back and walked away with insolent ease, whistling an Irish tune under his breath.

It was some time before Damien's breathing returned to normal. He reached down for the bucket and upended it over his head, closing his eyes against the warm stream of water.

"No bodies, I trust?" Etienne said. He poked his head out the door. "No need of my vast medical skills?"

Damien smiled grimly. "Not yet, Etienne. Not yet."

But it wasn't over. Damien followed Etienne back into the cabin and snapped up a clean shirt, jerking it on so roughly that the seams protested. No, it wasn't over between him and Miranda O'Reilly.

Miranda walked along the river's edge in the cooling air of late afternoon, watching the water flow between banks torn apart by miners who had taken what they could and moved on.

Farther up and down the river men built flumes and dams to drain the bed, but here the claims had long since been abandoned, leaving nature in peace to heal itself. Miranda knew there were countless ghost towns throughout these hills, prosperous camps left vacant when the gold played out. Heaven's Bar would likely suffer the same fate.

Nothing is permanent, Miranda thought, turning blindly into a ravine where a smaller stream joined the Feather River beyond the edge of camp. Her old walking boots kicked up dust that swirled in her wake, and she let the hem of her patched skirt—the one she almost never wore now—drag in the dirt.

She found a place to sit down in the shade of an oak, where polished boulders rose like dry bones out of the bank. All her life she'd wanted permanence, security, love that was tied to a place and a person that existed only in her imagination. It had been a cruel twist of fate that she'd met Damien Lévesque. He had put a name and a face to her dreams. And then he'd taken them away.

Closing her eyes, Miranda remembered. Remembered how Damien had come to every performance

Papa's company had given in the theater on Camp
Street, and the first time he had hesitantly shared
with her his love of Shakespeare; how she had seen
him come alive as he began to court her, watched
him grow from a grim, haughty reserve to the
warmhearted, giving man she fell in love with.

Miranda touched her lips, lost in the memory of
their first kiss. That had been the day after she had
learned of Damien's loveless life with a family who
could never accept him. It had been overwhelming
curiosity that had drawn her to the fine house on
Esplanade, to return a book Damien had acciden-
tally left behind when they'd last walked in Lafayette Square; she'd only wanted to glimpse what the
life of a wealthy Creole was like, a life Damien had
never shared with her.

But she'd found an arrogant flock of female rela-
tives taking coffee in the inner courtyard, who
looked her up and down as if she were less than
dirt—an Irish actress, of all creatures, who dared in-
trude in their hallowed domain. Damien's mother
had been icily polite, claiming Damien was not at
home; but afterward, lingering just outside the
porte-cochère, Miranda had heard her berating
Damien for sullying the name of Lévesque, and
shaming them all with his scholar's ways and low-
born acquaintances.

Miranda had fled then, knowing there was no
hope for them—until Damien had come that night
as he always did, and taken her in his arms, and
kissed her. He needed her love, though he would
never admit to it. He had no one else. And so she
had given him the only thing she had—her heart.

Stumbling to her feet, Miranda rubbed impatiently
at her eyes. Papa had needed her, too. She'd loved
him, and he'd still died in the end. She had to look

after herself now. She owed Damien nothing. Nothing at all.

She touched the bodice of her dress where the ring still hung on its silken cord between her breasts. Damien had stunned her the day he announced his betrothal to Sabine Fortier, arranged long ago by his family. He couldn't turn his back on honor and duty, on all the expectations his parents had of him. But he loved Miranda, he'd said, and couldn't give her up.

That was when he'd made the offer, and her heart had shattered. But she might have forgiven that if it hadn't been for the cold, deliberately cruel letter he'd sent after she'd refused him. And the ring she still wore.

With a soft hiss of breath, Miranda dropped her hand. Tonight she'd return the ring to Damien—if she could keep herself from throwing it in his face.

She shook the dust from her skirts and turned back for camp. Once again she'd lose herself in a performance, and Cain would be there at the end of it to offer his friendship. And more, if she would take it.

She'd only walked a few steps when she heard the crunch of boots on gravel behind her. The lowering sun, glinting off the hillside to the west, made the figure no more than a shadow. She raised her hand to shield her eyes, and gasped.

Damien was not dressed as a gentleman now. He wore the same rough miner's clothes he'd had on the day he'd come to her rescue in the alley, before she'd recognized him. And he was still a stranger.

Only minutes before she'd been remembering the boy he'd been, and her naive trust in love. Now it was hard to believe that she'd ever known Damien Lévesque. The man who stared at her was hard, every trace of a privileged life leached away by sun and suffering. The old Damien had abhorred dueling and the more physical pleasures of his aristocratic peers; this Damien was patently dangerous.

"Damien," she whispered.

He said nothing. He took one step toward her, and then another, his expression forbidding. Miranda's heart began to speed. She backed away, her gaze meeting the molten heat of his dark eyes.

" 'Ill-met by moonlight, proud Titania,' " he said softly.

Searching for sure footing among loose rocks, Miranda said the first thing that came into her mind. " 'The moon! the sun: it is not moonlight now.' "

Damien smiled, his expression far from reassuring. "Shall we mix our quotes, Miranda? You know how Katharina fared."

She glared at him, clenching her fists. "I'm not Katharina, and you are not my husband."

His smile vanished. "You're right, Miranda. I was spared that mistake."

Miranda was stunned into silence. He had made it abundantly clear in New Orleans that he would never consider making her his wife. That he dared fling that in her face now ...

"So," she breathed. "Why aren't you in New Orleans with your pure-blooded Creole bride? Wouldn't she have you after all?"

His eyes were unutterably bleak. "Why should it matter to you, Miranda? You made your choice then. My reasons for leaving New Orleans don't concern you." He looked away, lost in thoughts she had no part of. "It isn't the past I've come to discuss."

"There isn't anything else between us, Damien," she said, fighting the tremor in the words.

"You're wrong. It isn't over between us." His gaze met hers again, as emotionless as his voice. "It seems I still feel some—need to see to your safety. I heard that your father died in Sacramento, and for that I'm sorry. But California is no place for a woman alone."

Miranda lifted her chin. "I can take care of myself."

"By relying on the 'protection' of a rogue like Cain Sullivan?"

The way he emphasized *protection* made his meaning abundantly clear. Miranda shook with the force of her anger, but she drew upon all her acting skills to hide it from him.

"Cain Sullivan," she said coldly, "is a friend, and a gentleman."

"A gentleman so long as it suits him—and as long as you're useful to him."

Miranda looked him up and down. "In that, then, he's exactly like you."

Damien advanced another step; Miranda glanced over her shoulder and found herself teetering dangerously near the water's edge. She looked back to find that insufferable smile on Damien's handsome face.

She held herself absolutely still as he reached out and touched the curve of her jaw with callused fingers. Betraying heat washed through her. "Then you won't be surprised to learn that I'm prepared to renew that offer I made to you that last day we were together in Lafayette Square," he said.

Her hand flew out before she could think, striking his cheek with the flat of her palm. He turned his head with the force of her blow and went utterly still.

"To be your mistress?" she hissed. "I wouldn't be your whore then, and I won't be now."

Damien regarded her silently, the red mark of her slap fading against the deep tan of his skin. It took all of Miranda's discipline to keep from running her fingers over the hurt, to trace the strong contours of his face. She felt behind her with her foot, finding empty space.

"Tell me, Miranda—have you told Sullivan you love him as you once told me?"

She sucked in her breath as if he had given her blow for blow. She could lie—oh, yes, she could lie and make him believe it. . . .

"In what way am I inferior to Sullivan?" he said relentlessly, giving her no time to answer. "Or is it just that you finally found yourself without the choice of turning down any reasonable offer?" His hands shot out with the speed of a striking rattlesnake and caught her arms. "I'll make you a better one, Miranda."

Before she could prepare herself to resist, his mouth came down hard on hers. The kiss began with heated ferocity, but as she gathered her will to fight him it gentled, becoming a caress steeped in memories. Memories of how good it had once been between them, but a thousand times more potent.

"Miranda," Damien murmured against her lips, his tongue tracing each curve. "My sweet Miranda—"

She groaned, going limp in his hold. God help her, but it was as if they had never been apart, as if nothing had ever come between them—not even Damien's cold rejection. His ring burned between her breasts. Her heartbeat shook her body so that she had to cling to Damien for balance.

Damien tangled his fingers in her hair, loosening it about her shoulders. "Now, Miranda," he whispered fiercely, exultantly, his dark eyes bright as obsidian, "can Cain Sullivan give you this?"

His words broke the spell. Miranda gasped, and as his mouth descended again she jerked back and free of his arms. Her feet slid on gravel, struggled for purchase, and betrayed her. With a little squeak of shock she tumbled backward into the river.

Damien froze for a single, heart-stopping moment before he plunged in after her.

The river was not overly deep here, but the late-spring runoff from the mountains covered the larger rocks that would later be exposed. Damien's first fear, that she might hit her head on a rock, was eased as she came up out of the water, red hair plastered to her flushed face. She swore—an Irish-tinged curse that a lady would not have recognized—and sat down hard on her rump, sodden skirts floating around her.

She had never looked more beautiful.

Miranda glared up at him, stripping wet hair out of her eyes and daring him to laugh. But he had never felt less like laughing. Ignoring her awkward attempt at retreat, he bent down and gathered her into his arms. Her body went stiff as it had been at the beginning of their kiss; cold water from her clothing and tangled hair soaked through his shirt. When she shivered, he held her tighter and lifted her carefully onto the bank.

"Let me go," she said breathlessly, pushing against him. "Put me down."

"You're soaked through," he murmured, "and the sun has already set."

He saw her expression change as she became aware of the growing darkness. Already a cool wind was pushing its way through the ravine, searching out openings in wet clothes. Miranda shivered again.

"I have a performance tonight," she said, her voice growing stronger.

"Your audience will have to wait." Damien shifted

her to a more secure position in his arms and turned back into the ravine.

She began to struggle, small hands slapping against his sodden shirt. "Put me down at once. I can take myself back to the saloon—"

"It gets cold in the hills at night," he told her gruffly. "I won't let you take a chill, not in this wilderness. My cabin is just back of the ravine." As she stiffened again he shook his head. "If you fear for your—'virtue,' " he added, "you'll have a chaperon. Etienne's undoubtedly preparing our dinner at this moment."

That silenced her, though she remained rigid as a statue in his arms. But when he reached the cabin door and set her down, he knew that Etienne was gone. A fire burned in the stone hearth, but there were no signs of cooking and none of Damien's partner.

Miranda wedged herself in the doorway and looked around the cabin. Damien wondered what she saw: the primitive, rough lodgings of an uncivilized woodsman, perhaps? Yet he and Etienne had taken the trouble to make the place livable, as few miners did; they had real glass in their small windows, a wooden floor, chairs and a table, and mattresses on their beds.

Damien stared at his bunk and away before Miranda caught the glance. But the damage had been done; his body ached with the arousal that had never eased since he'd kissed her.

Dieu, he still wanted her desperately.

He pulled Miranda into the room and positioned her before the fire on the three-legged stool Etienne had made. He rummaged through his clean clothes until he found an old shirt, one that had long ago become too tight for his chest and shoulders, and a pair of patched cotton trousers.

"Put these on until your clothes dry," he said, handing the bundle to her. She stared at him blankly for a long moment, and a slow flush worked its way from her throat to the burnished copper of her hair. He waited for her to protest, shout at him, leap up, and sweep toward the door in her drenched skirts. But she only held the dry clothes in trembling fingers and dropped her gaze to the fire.

"I'll be outside," he said, turning on his heel.

The night was as cool as he had told her it would be, but the heat raging through his body burned like a fire in dry chaparral. He leaned his head back against the log wall, breathing through clenched teeth.

He did not love her. What he wanted from her was no more than Sullivan claimed to have taken. And he could care for her as Sullivan never would. As Miranda had never given him the chance to do ...

Slamming his fist against the wall, Damien turned and plunged through the door. Miranda looked up, her fingers still on the buttons of the shirt, her drying hair haloed by firelight. Her chest rose and fell rapidly, breasts full and nipples erect under the loose, worn fabric.

Damien caught his breath. The trousers he'd given her still lay folded beside the stool. The soft, pale skin of her legs emerged from beneath the shirt's trailing hem, unshielded from his gaze. In New Orleans, he had never seen her in any state but fully dressed. He had done no more than kissed her lips and her fingers. He had thought then that he understood desire.

They stared at each other in a haze of pain and need and memory.

"*Tu es belle*, Miranda," he whispered.

She swallowed, and her pulse beat in the hollow

revealed by the open collar of the shirt. "Damien ..."

When he went to her this time she didn't resist, didn't struggle, didn't look at him with contempt in her green eyes. She flowed against him, melted into him like snow in the sun, and her face lifted to his.

He kissed her gently this time, as he would touch a wild creature that might flee at the slightest provocation. He didn't want her to run. Her heart beat as rapidly as a bird's against his chest.

"Miranda," he murmured. Her breath shuddered as he kissed away the water drops that trembled on her face. He ran his hands down her arms, slid them to the small of her back. He knew she felt his arousal; nothing protected her now but the thin shirt and his own trousers.

But she did not flinch away. She pressed into him, her fingers clutching his shoulders—a passionate woman, just as Cain Sullivan had told him, as he had always known.

For a moment he stopped, holding her quiet in his arms. If Cain Sullivan had taken her ... But the thought only roused him to hotter desire, the need to put his mark irrevocably on the only woman he had ever loved.

He had never intended this; he could still let her go. But she looked into his eyes, and the green of them shone with a reflection of his overwhelming hunger.

Tonight she would be his alone—and no other man would ever have her again.

Miranda knew there was no turning back.

Damien's next kiss was hard and possessive. There was anger in that kiss, a silent repetition of the words he had flung at her by the river. But she had seen the pain in his eyes, a boy's pain beneath the tough exterior the years had given him.

And she could not think. She could only feel: his breath on her neck as he stroked the moisture from her cool skin with his tongue; the finely honed strength of his body; the insistent caress of his hands sliding down to cup her buttocks. He lifted her against him easily, so easily that she felt like a feather in his arms.

His mouth found the flutter of her pulse at the base of her neck and dipped lower. He reached the edge of the shirt and made a low growl in his throat; suddenly he swung her up and set her down on his bed, kneeling between her legs so that their faces were level.

As he kissed her, his tongue tracing her lips, his fingers moved to the buttons of her borrowed shirt. *Now, now is the time to end it*, Miranda thought, but her limbs were helpless to obey her in anything but holding him close, her mouth incapable of resisting his kisses. She closed her eyes. Hot, callused palms found her breasts. She arched back, and Damien accepted what she unwittingly offered, taking her nipple deep into his mouth.

Miranda had never imagined that such a sensation could exist. The shock of Damien's intimate touch reverberated through her body, settling between her thighs. Even as he suckled and kissed her breasts Damien continued to unbutton her shirt until nothing at all lay between her bare skin and his hands and lips.

He murmured some hot, dark phrase in French, but she could no longer hear anything but the pounding of her heart. His hands traced the arch of her ribs and moved inexorably downward. Miranda, who had always prided herself on her exquisite professional control, had lost every shred of it now.

Her eyes flew open as she felt the first touch at the juncture of her thighs. Part of her knew what was happening; she had lived too long in the world of theater not to be well educated in matters between man and woman, matters a protected young woman would never have understood. But no whispered talk or brief glimpses had prepared her for this.

This was what her father had warned her against, this all-consuming fire that had taken her mother and lured so many women in her profession to surrender their virtue. *This*—the sigh of skin on skin, Damien's hard chest against her breasts, his fingers stroking her to madness, his hands between her thighs, lifting and separating them to accept his body.

She wanted him. She wanted him to be joined with her forever, to bind him to her as she had failed to do before. In a moment it would be over. Damien held himself above her on rigid arms, and all she need do was reach up and pull him down.

But something was wrong. She looked blindly over Damien's shoulder at the small window set in the opposite wall. Gray-and-red feathers fluttered against the glass.

Ariel. It was Ariel, perched awkwardly outside. A single stern yellow eye fixed on her.

"No," Miranda whispered.

Damien did not hear. His eyes were black with desire, muscles taut and straining.

"No," she said, finding her voice. The sound of it severed her body's primitive dominion over her mind. She wedged her hands between herself and Damien and pushed; Damien's chest tensed under her palm.

"Please, Damien," she said shakily. Meeting his stranger's stare, she wondered if it was too late. This man who looked down at her with such fierce, implacable possessiveness would never let her go after she had permitted him so much, after all that had passed between them.

"Let me go, Damien," she said, willing him to hear. "This is wrong. I can't give myself to you this way."

His eyes changed. They focused on her, and sanity returned to them slowly.

"What?"

She pushed again, and this time he gave with her pressure, rolling away from her and off the bed in one motion. He snatched up the rumpled shirt and tossed it at her, turning his back. She caught a glimpse of his beautifully muscled body before he pulled on his trousers with sharp, savage jerks. When she looked toward the window, Ariel had disappeared.

Miranda's fingers trembled as she struggled into the shirt and pulled the coarse bedsheets up over her legs. Damien strode to the other end of the cabin and braced himself against the wall, staring at her without any expression at all.

"So," he said. His voice shook, so heavy with bitterness that Miranda felt like weeping. "Is this some petty revenge, Miranda? Or is Cain Sullivan's lovemaking so superior to mine?"

Miranda was grateful to Damien then. His hateful words released anger, waves of it that drowned shame and regret and sorrow.

"I've never given myself to any man," she snapped, pulling the sheets up to her chin. "Cain Sullivan is a friend who has always dealt honorably with me. Which is far more than can be said for you."

He gave her that grim smile again. "You didn't seem to object, until now." His gaze raked her as if the sheets were transparent. "I'm no monster, whatever you may choose to believe. I didn't plan this. But your response was not that of an innocent, Miranda. You wanted me."

Tugging the sheets off the bed as she rose, Miranda strode toward him and nearly tripped in her haste. "Have you had so many innocents, then? I share the blame, Damien. I'll not deny it. But I'll not prolong this farce."

Damien's chest rose and fell rapidly under his folded arms. "Are you claiming I would have taken your virginity, Miranda?" he rasped.

Heat washed over her, but she met his gaze without flinching. "I wouldn't let you have it in New Orleans, and my reasons are the same now as they were then. I'm an actress, but I won't sell my body or give it outside of marriage."

He said nothing, but he was listening—truly listening, as he had refused to do years ago. Miranda felt her anger fade. Was there a chance of making him understand, healing the wounds between them at last?

Miranda backed away until her legs touched the stool and sat down. "My mother," she began slowly, "was a fine actress and a passionate woman. She loved me, Damien. The last words she spoke were of me. But she betrayed my father again and again because she could not control her passions. She died when one of her lovers killed her in a fit of jealous rage." She closed her eyes. "I was only a child then. But when I understood, I swore to Papa I would never do what she had done. That I would be no man's outside of marriage."

She didn't know what she expected Damien to say. He was silent so long that she opened her eyes and forced herself to look at him, afraid of the mockery she would see on his face.

But he slumped against the wall, his own eyes closed. "Do you believe Cain Sullivan intends to marry you?" he asked softly.

"I don't know." Miranda swallowed. "I know he cares for me."

Very slowly Damien turned his back on her. "Get dressed, Miranda. Go back to the saloon before Sullivan comes looking for you."

She obeyed him. There was nothing left to say. *And what did you expect?* she asked herself, fastening her bodice and smoothing her wrinkled skirts. *An offer of marriage? A declaration of love from the man who threw you away three years ago?*

But she knew in her heart of hearts that she had nursed that very hope, in spite of everything. For she had realized a terrible truth when she had surrendered to Damien's kiss.

She was still desperately in love with him.

Annette rose from her crouch beneath the cabin window, wincing at the stiffness in her knees and the dirtied hem of her full skirts.

But such minor inconveniences were as nothing after what she had heard going on within Damien's cabin. It was fortunate indeed that Cain had sent her looking for Miranda when she hadn't shown up for her nightly engagement in the Pearly Gates Theater.

She prefers another stage, Annette thought bitterly. *And Damien has fallen for her performance.*

A soft rustle from the roof caught her attention, and she almost started at the sight of Miranda's parrot.

"What are you doing here, *bel oiseau*? Waiting for your mistress?" She laughed, but the sound was forced. "It seems she is otherwise occupied. Who would have thought it?"

The bird cocked its head at her, looking for all the world as if it understood.

"He was mine until she came here, bird. I had many others, but I never loved any of them. And now she will take him away."

The parrot made a soft sound, almost like a sigh, and Annette smiled sadly. "Do you find it strange that a whore can love? I was not always what I am now. For Damien I would change. But not if he leaves me."

Annette turned back to the window, but there was only silence within the cabin. The thin glass let every sound escape. She passed her hand over her eyes.

"She has convinced Damien of her virtue, hasn't she, bird? Yet, before, he believed Cain to be her lover. I saw them by the river. Damien once offered to make her his mistress, and she refused him—as she has refused him again." She heard her own voice shaking and despised her weakness. "She hasn't given herself to Cain, but Cain wants her. I've seen it in his eyes. And he won't lose her now when he has so much to gain from her skill. He would be very interested to hear what passed this night. *Oui, très intéressé.*"

The parrot hopped from one foot to the other, squawking soft words, but Annette was not listening. She was already wondering how Cain would react when she told him where Miranda had been—and what he would do with the information.

Gathering up her skirts, Annette crept away from the cabin. The door swung open just as she passed beyond the reach of the flickering candlelight that shone from the two small windows.

Miranda emerged from the doorway, her dress still damp and her thick red hair twisted in a loose knot at the nape of her neck. Annette crouched behind a manzanita bush and watched as Damien followed, lantern in hand, and began to guide Miranda toward camp.

Annette needed no lantern to find her way back to the Pearly Gates.

"He won't have her," Cain Sullivan said between clenched teeth.

Ariel hunched down as small as he could in the corner of Sullivan's private parlor, where Annette had just finished telling her employer what she had heard outside Damien's cabin.

It was inevitable, of course, that complications must ensue where humans were concerned. Ariel's guardianship extended only so far; Miranda's usual good sense merely required nudging from time to time. She was no longer in danger of making a choice that she would deeply regret—but the fragile peace she'd made with Damien was threatened once again by human folly.

These are the forgeries of jealousy, Ariel thought, shaking his head. *Truth hath a quiet breast.*

But there was no quiet in Sullivan's expression, or in Annette's troubled eyes.

"I'll not let that Frenchie aristocrat best me now," Sullivan said. He downed his glass of whiskey, spilling several drops on his immaculate frock coat. He cursed and brushed his sleeve. "Not when she's almost mine."

Annette glanced up from her folded hands. "What will you do, Cain?"

For a long moment he only stared over her shoulder, his expression black. Slowly a smile lifted the corners of his mustache. Annette dropped her eyes again.

"Set a trap, of course. A trap His Lordship will walk right into. He seems to value her virtue as highly as she does. If he believed she was stringing him along ..." He set his glass down on the imported sideboard. "What we'll do, my dear, is show Lévesque that Miranda is not worth his efforts—and leave Miranda no choice but to turn back to me."

Annette was silent. Sullivan strolled over to the chair in which she sat and twisted a golden lock of her hair between his fingers.

"Of course you'll help me, Annette, when the time is right. You'll find I'm appreciative of this little favor you've done me. Perhaps I'll even take a year off your contract."

She looked up, her pretty face expressionless. "I will help you, Cain," she whispered.

"And we'll both have what we want." Sullivan released her hair and smoothed his cravat. "Perhaps after tonight's performance ..."

From the shadows, Ariel stretched his wings cautiously. He had heard enough. Now it was only a matter of whispering a few well-chosen words of warning in Miranda's ear.

He waddled close to the half-open window, awaiting his chance to fly.

"It's bloody cold in here," Sullivan muttered. He strode to the window, nearly stepping on Ariel, and slammed it shut. Ariel hopped out of the path of a booted foot and into the candlelight.

Sullivan froze, staring down. "Well, well. If it isn't that bloody bird."

"I saw it at the cabin," Annette said, rising quickly. "It must have followed me. Don't hurt it, Cain."

"Hurt it?" Sullivan shrugged out of his coat and knelt close to Ariel, spreading the coat like a net. Ariel clacked his beak in warning, and Sullivan's expression turned ugly. "I won't hurt it if there's any chance I can use it. And since I don't trust this bird any more than I trust Lévesque—"

Ariel flapped upward too late. The coat descended on him like a cloud of despair.

"—I think I'll hold on to it for a while."

Staring up at the cabin ceiling, Damien knew he had never stopped loving her.

He'd tried to convince himself that he despised her. When his parents had died of yellow fever a few months after he'd taken a steamboat for the Missouri frontier, it had been easy to hate Miranda O'Reilly. If he had never known her, he would have married Sabine Fortier and given his parents satisfaction before they died.

But it had never been Miranda's fault that he'd turned his back on the Lévesques, that he'd abandoned duty and honor to make his own way rather than tamely become what society decreed he must be—the same society that had come between him and Miranda. Guilt at his parents' deaths had mingled with the bitterness of Miranda's rejection, had festered like an old wound that never quite healed.

Damien covered his eyes with the back of his hand, listening to Etienne's snores. He could brood on it until the end of time, and it would make no difference. Miranda had refused to marry him three and a half years ago, preferring his father's money to a life of possible poverty with the man she claimed to love.

But could he blame her?

Rolling from the bed, Damien began to tug on his boots. When his father had come to tell him of the offer he'd made to Miranda, Damien had been chilled to the bone. "I bought her off, Damien," Benoît Lévesque had told him coldly. "I told her I would disinherit you but not prevent your marriage if she chose to stay and accept your offer. She preferred my money to you. They are all alike, the *gens du commun*. Now you understand."

Damien had thought he did understand.

He had never felt more alone in his life. He had raged inwardly, but he had never revealed his emotion—until the day he'd left New Orleans and his promised Creole bride, vowing never to risk loving any woman again.

An entirely useless vow, he thought, splashing his face with water from the cracked bowl on the washstand by the window. *I never stopped loving her.*

Damien walked to the door and flung it open, breathing in the crisp air of early morning. Last night it had all become clear. What he felt for her was more than lust. Holding her in his arms had been like finding his heart again. And when she had claimed to be a virgin, he had believed her.

In all this time she hadn't given herself to any man, not even Cain Sullivan. She was not the whore his father had claimed. Perhaps her shock at his original offer in New Orleans had turned her utterly against him, blinded her to his second, honorable offer. Perhaps she had been unable to turn down Benoît Lévesque's money, when she had lived so long on the edge of poverty and had the care of an irresponsible father. She could not have remained an actress as Damien's wife.

But if she had despised him then, she didn't now. He hadn't imagined her response—a response she'd given to no other man. Did she regret the choice she'd made in New Orleans? Had they both changed enough to begin again?

He smiled, imagining what Ariel would say. The parrot had a remarkable facility for mimicking a true conversation.

" 'And ruin'd love,' " Damien murmured, " 'when

it is built anew, grows fairer than at first, more strong, far greater.' "

Was it possible? To ask her to marry him again . . .

Damien snatched up a shirt and buttoned it absently. Etienne rolled over in his bunk and blinked at Damien.

"Qu'est-ce que—"

"Go back to sleep, Etienne. I'm going out to the hills today."

Etienne yawned. "Ah. Thinking to do, I see."

"I'll be back by evening. There's a certain performance I won't miss tonight."

Etienne flopped back down on his lumpy pillow. *"Bonne chance,"* he said, wishing Damien luck.

"Dieu du ciel, I may need it."

As she completed Rosalind's epilogue from *As You Like It*, Miranda's gaze was all for Damien.

" ' . . . and I charge you, O men, for the love you bear to women—as I perceive by your simpering, none of you hates them—that between you and the women the play may please. If I were a woman, I would kiss as many of you as had beards that pleased me, complexions that liked me, and breaths that I defied not: and, as I am sure, as many as have good beards, or good faces, or sweet breaths, will, for my kind offer, when I make curtsy, bid me farewell.' "

She curtsied, and the miners stamped and whistled their approval. But she heard none of them. Her ears rang with only one voice, as her very skin hummed with the memory of one touch.

Before she had gone onstage, Damien had come to her and asked her to be his wife.

His wife.

Miranda retreated behind the curtains, and the spell of the performance fell away. She sat down heavily on the chair before her dressing table, pressing her hand to her heart.

Is it possible? she thought. *Can this be happening?*

But it was. They had kissed backstage—gently, hesitantly, knowing how much had yet to be resolved. Damien had held her hand and asked her the question without ceremony, without drama. And he had not demanded an answer.

Miranda rose and paced across the length of the room and back again. What would her answer be? Once there would have been no question at all. But now . . .

Oh, Ariel, she thought. *Where are you when I need you most?*

But she hadn't seen Ariel since before she'd gone to Damien's cabin last night. She was on her own.

Biting her lip, Miranda began to remove her makeup. Damien had truly changed, in mind as well as body. He had not said he loved her—not yet. But she had seen it in his eyes. And nothing in her own feelings had altered over the years, though for a time she had made herself believe they had.

Last night . . . Her body quivered with sensual memory. Last night he had let her go when she asked, and accepted her reasons for ending their tryst. What had happened in New Orleans—what had happened by the riverside last evening, when he'd asked her again to be his mistress—no longer mattered. Nor did his accusations. Those had sprung from anger, and a profound hurt.

He loves me, she thought wonderingly. *Is it possible he suffered as much as I did? Did he regret his choice? He left New Orleans, left his family and the only life he knew rather than marry a woman he didn't love. . . .*

Miranda moved in a daze from her dressing table and walked up the short flight of stairs to her room on the second floor. He had not asked her forgiveness for the cruel things he'd written in his farewell letter three and a half years ago. It was almost as if that letter had never existed. And yet, if they were to be happy, they must confront the past. Miranda had long ago thrown away the letter, but she still had the ring.

" 'Fire, that's closest kept, burns most of all,' " she whispered, closing the door to her room behind her. Her bath was waiting—the one Cain always had ready for her after every performance.

Cain. Miranda sighed, unbuttoning the doublet of her costume slowly. Cain would be hurt. He did care for her, she knew that. It was more than merely the money she could bring in with her acting. And Cain would find it doubly painful that he was losing her to a man he clearly disliked.

I'm not a gold claim to be fought over, Miranda thought defiantly. *And Cain is a survivor.* As she was. He would surely understand.

Easing into the steaming water, Miranda closed her eyes. All her thinking led her around in circles to the same conclusion. "As Ariel would say," she murmured, " 'There's beggary in love that can be reckon'd.' "

Her love for Damien could not be reckoned or destroyed or squeezed out of existence. There was a rightness to this, a sense of fate Miranda felt to the depths of her soul.

She had known all along what her answer would be. And she would give it to Damien this very night.

"Thank you, God, for giving us another chance—"

The door to her room swung open and rebounded against the wall with a crash. Miranda gasped, starting violently.

Cain Sullivan leaned against the doorframe, his tall

body bent and his expression mournful. The smell of whiskey filled the room.

"Ah, Miranda," he said, his brogue thickened by drink. "It's breaking my heart you are."

Miranda crossed her arms in front of her breasts and ducked lower in the water. He was clearly drunk—and unpredictable. "Cain, I'm bathing," she said calmly. "Please leave the room—"

He took a step forward, swayed, and spun around. "I won't look, Miranda." Leaning against the wall with both hands, he dropped his head between his shoulders. "I have to—talk to you. Before it's too late."

Miranda rose hastily out of the hip bath. She reached for the filmy peignoir draped over a nearby chair and put it on. "Cain—"

He turned around sharply and staggered toward her. "Miranda, my love. You can't leave me."

Miranda backed away. "We must talk, Cain—but not now. Let me dress, and we'll go down to your parlor—"

"Talk!" Cain flung back his head and closed his eyes. "About Lévesque?" He laughed hoarsely. "Miranda ..."

She forced herself to stand still as he stumbled across the space between them. His arms came around her, and his breath sobbed. "Forgive me, Miranda. When I saw—you and Lévesque—I waited too long, didn't I?"

Holding herself still in the heavy circle of his arms, Miranda heard the very real pain in his voice. "Oh, Cain," she whispered. "I don't want to hurt you. You've been a good friend—"

"Is that all?" Cain pulled back without letting her go, his face contorted into a mask of almost childlike desperation. The polished, sophisticated saloon owner had vanished. "Is he so much—better than I am? Don't you—care for me at all, Miranda?"

"Of course I care. We're—"

"Give me a chance, Miranda," he said, his gaze suddenly lucid. "Let me prove how much I love you—" He shifted his hands awkwardly, tugging her peignoir partly off her shoulders. It was obvious that he wasn't himself, didn't know what he was doing. Miranda had to think clearly for both of them, just as she had once done for her father.

Oh, Lord, what am I to do now? Miranda thought.

He had become a lovestruck boy again, and he didn't care.

Damien waited impatiently in the saloon, finishing his third whiskey of the evening. Soon Miranda would be down, and she would give him her answer.

He knew what it would be, what it *must* be. Grinning, he saluted his reflection in the mirror behind the bar and signaled the bartender.

"Drinks all around," he said, setting a pouch of gold dust down on the counter. A ragged cheer went up from the miners and gamblers within hearing, and one hearty fellow slapped his back. As the bartender began to distribute whiskeys around the saloon, Damien got up and walked to the foot of the stairs leading to the upstairs rooms.

The bartender had told him that Sullivan arranged a hot bath for Miranda every night. Damien set his booted foot against the bottom step and frowned. After tonight, Miranda wouldn't be accepting any more favors from Sullivan. She would be Damien's alone.

He felt his body tighten in anticipation of holding her naked in his arms once again—his lover, his wife. *Miranda . . .*

"I thought you were upstairs."

Damien looked up at the sound of Annette's voice. She descended the stairs slowly, one hand on the railing and the other holding her skirts. Her fingers clenched and unclenched on the ruched satin. She paused a few steps from the bottom, biting her full lower lip.

"I—must have been mistaken," she said. "I thought I heard your voice in Miranda's room."

Damien stared at her. "My voice?"

She wouldn't meet his gaze. "The sounds—I must have been mistaken," she repeated. All at once she smiled brightly and hurried down the last steps to take his arm. "Buy me a drink, Damien. Let's celebrate your—"

But he shook her off, hardly realizing what he did. His mind was utterly blank. He took the stairs two at a time and strode down the hall to the door of Miranda's room. He grasped the tarnished brass knob and opened the door without a word.

His heart stopped beating. Miranda was in Cain Sullivan's arms, her sheer peignoir worked halfway down her bare shoulders. Her arms were around him, and he was kissing her.

Damien dropped back against the doorframe, his fist slamming the wall. Miranda jerked in Sullivan's arms and looked sharply toward the door.

"Damien!" she gasped. Her face was frozen in a mask of shock and horror. She pushed at Cain, and as he let her go he turned to look at Damien with a grim and mocking smile.

"Damien—" Miranda tugged at the edges of her peignoir with shaking fingers. She stumbled away from Sullivan, reaching out in a gesture of supplication. Damien saw only a blur of motion as he turned on his heel and strode back down the hall. If she called him again, the sound was buried beneath the clamor in the saloon. Bearded faces and flashing teeth turned toward Damien as he passed, but he acknowledged none of the affable greetings.

He didn't stop walking until he had gone deep into the hills.

Ariel paced across the length of the crate once again, peering between the uneven boards that served as bars for his cage. The storeroom was dark now; a full day had passed, and no one had come to release him.

" 'Delays have dangerous ends,' " he muttered to himself. " 'It hath been the longest night, that e'er I watched, and the heaviest.' "

He bent his head to pull a loose feather from his mantle. The time had come to stretch his wings again. He had delayed taking precipitous action, but now . . .

The storeroom's crooked wood-and-canvas door swung open on leather hinges. Annette's face was illuminated by the candle she held; Ariel walked to the front of the cage and pushed his beak through the widest opening.

"*Bonsoir, bel oiseau,*" she whispered, moving close to the crate. She set the candle down carefully on a second crate and produced a small canvas sack. "I've brought you food. I think Cain would leave you to starve."

Ariel cocked his head, examining her face. She had been crying, and he knew when a mortal most needed to talk.

" 'Speak to me as to thy thinking,' " he said softly.

She bit her lip. "You are not an ordinary bird, are you? Your mistress—" Her breath caught on a sob. "Oh, I have done a terrible thing. My conscience will not let me rest." She dropped the sack and paced the room in agitation. "It is because I love him that I did it. But now—since Damien fell into Cain's trap, no one has seen him. And Miranda will not eat, or do anything but stare...."

Ariel held his silence. Annette whirled around, pressing her palms to her cheeks. "Oh, bird. What should I do? I cannot bear to lose Damien. And if I defied Cain, he would surely hurt me for it. But when I saw Miranda run through the saloon after Damien—in nothing but her dressing gown, as if she had gone mad—I could not bear it." She bent her head. "I was not always as I am now, bird. *Dieu merci*, I was not. If I could only go back—"

" 'Now 'tis the spring, and weeds are shallow-rooted; suffer them now and they'll o'ergrow the garden,' " Ariel said gently.

She stared at him, her eyes wide and moist in the candlelight. "What are you saying, bird? *Dieu*, what must I do?"

Ariel nodded to himself. She had asked. He was long out of practice, but the situation called for drastic measures. Bobbing his head in concentration, Ariel summoned his long-unused angelic powers.

" 'Unthread the rude eye of rebellion,' " he pronounced, his voice growing rich and deep, " 'and welcome home again discarded faith.' "

Annette's expression changed as he did. She crossed herself and fell to her knees. Her face was that of a child beholding a miracle, innocent and filled with hope.

"*Mon Dieu*," she breathed. "I understand. Yes, I understand."

She rose to her feet and smiled with her heart in her eyes. And then she was gone.

Ariel relaxed, letting the glow fade. Yes, the small demonstration had been all that was needed to show Annette the truth she already knew within her own soul. He had not exceeded the proper boundaries. But he was sadly out of practice. And—

He had entirely forgotten to ask Annette to let him out of the cage.

Ariel shook his head and settled in for another long wait. The rest was entirely up to love.

Etienne came to the door of the cabin, his usually cheerful face set in serious lines.

"Annette!"

"Is Damien here?" she said, peering past him into the cabin.

He moved out of her way. "You're looking for Damien? He's gone. Left before dawn this morning with most of his things."

Annette froze. "Gone?" she echoed.

He sighed. "*Oui.* Almost without a word to me. Only that he was headed up north, into the mountains, along the Cameron trail." He ran his fingers through his short, curly hair. "I don't think he intends to come back."

Annette swallowed, staring blindly at the neatly made bed in the corner. The shelves beside it were empty of all but a few odds and ends.

Damien had not waited. Believing himself betrayed by the woman he loved, he had run. And Annette knew he would not return.

"Then I must go after him," she murmured.

"What?"

"Nothing, Etienne." She summoned up a smile for him. "If he comes back—if he comes back, give him this." She handed him the letter she had written earlier, folded into a tight square.

Etienne pocketed the letter, frowning. "What's wrong? Are you—is it because he's gone—" He broke off awkwardly, staring down at his scuffed boots. "*Je suis désolé*, Annette. I couldn't stop him."

She closed her eyes. Etienne believed she had come searching for personal reasons. Not because she had finally come to her senses ...

"Don't worry, *mon ami*," she said, touching Etienne's arm. "All will be well in the end."

Annette walked swiftly away from the cabin, her mind already whirling with plans. If she was careful, Cain wouldn't realize one of his horses was missing until she was far from Heaven's Bar. Within a few hours she should have everything ready.

God give me courage, she asked silently. *I must make it right again....*

She prayed the angel would be with her on the long ride ahead.

It was done.

Miranda smiled at Cain and let his words wash over her, withdrawing into herself once again. There was nothing more to say. She had consented to be Cain's wife, and she knew what her future would hold.

A glorious career on the stage, managed by Cain Sullivan. The adoration of audiences in a new, growing land. A home one day—perhaps children, if Cain kept his promises.

But not love. Never what she'd believed she'd had, so briefly, with Damien Lévesque.

Love brings only pain, she thought, retreating up to her room when Cain finally let her go. But now she could no longer feel even that. She went through her days calmly, quietly, expecting nothing. In the week since Damien had left, she had learned to play a new part.

She could remember very little of that terrible evening when Damien had seen her in Cain's arms. She knew she had run after Damien, oblivious to staring miners, intent only on making Damien understand.

It was not what you thought. Not what you thought ...

And she remembered waking in her bed, Cain sitting in a chair beside her, holding her hand, apologizing again and again. She had collapsed in the street, he told her; Damien had disappeared.

"I did this to you," Cain had said, his eyes filled with sorrow. He had begged her forgiveness, utterly sober. He had sworn to give up drinking forever. He would do anything, anything to make it right.

He had offered to go after Damien. Even that he would do for Miranda. But she had refused. Damien had made his choice—to scorn her, to believe the worst of her, to condemn her as a liar and whore, unworthy of his love.

So be it. She had no more will to fight.

Miranda drifted around her room, searching aimlessly for something to occupy her hands. Her belongings were already packed; she and Cain would be on tomorrow's stage, bound for Sacramento. A steamer would take them to San Francisco, where Miranda would begin her new career.

Where she would become Cain's wife.

Removing a costume tunic from her trunk, Miranda shook it and refolded it absently. *I am practical now,* she thought. *I shall be what Papa wanted, and I shall have security at last. Cain will see to that. In his own way, he needs me. He was poor himself once. He knows what it is to struggle. And he loves me....*

The arguments were almost comforting in their familiarity. She had spoken them over and over to herself since Cain had begged her to marry him. "I will make you happy, Miranda," he'd said, a boy's touching earnestness in his face and voice. "You'll be the toast of San Francisco. And I will be a better man for loving you. . . ."

She had tried to be honest with Cain, to explain that she loved him only as a friend. Friendship was a fair basis for marriage. And she was so tired of being alone. After Damien had left, she'd had no one—not Annette, who had disappeared a day after Damien, and not even Ariel. That had been another blow, another reason to wrap up her heart and store it away.

Ariel had deserted her. Perhaps he had even gone with Damien. Everyone she had loved was gone. The only one who stayed by her side was a man she did not love.

But that meant he was safe.

" 'For many men that stumble at the threshold are well foretold that danger lurks within,' " she quoted softly. She should have known in New Orleans that Damien could bring her only sorrow. That her most secret dreams would never come true.

Miranda replaced the folded tunic in the trunk and closed the lid. She had grown beyond the role she'd once thought would bring happiness. Onstage she could be anyone, feel everything but a heart broken past mending. The theater would be her life from this moment on, Miranda O'Reilly only another part she must sometimes play—no different, no more real than any other.

Walking to her narrow bed, Miranda lay down and closed her eyes. She would not dream of Damien tonight. She would not wonder where he was, if he looked up at distant stars and thought of her.

She could not grieve bereft of her heart.

● ● ● ●

The stars were cold and brilliant and perfect. Damien began to count them again, welcoming the impossibility of the task he'd set himself.

He had lost track of the time since he'd ridden up into the mountains. A week, he thought; it hardly mattered. No count of days would ever be enough to make him forget.

The fire flirted with a passing breeze, and his gelding stamped restlessly just beyond reach of the light. Nearly everything Damien possessed was in the pack the animal carried, but Damien's own burden was a thousand times heavier.

He had ridden far and fast, but his memories refused to be left behind. They weighed him down with terrible certainty.

I still love her.

He rolled over onto his stomach, resting his cheek on folded arms. His last image of Miranda in Cain's arms was forever burned behind his eyelids. It made no difference at all.

He could never trust her, never believe anything she said with her soft lips and brilliant eyes. But he loved her still.

"Bon Dieu," he whispered. There would be no more comfort of self-deception. He would go on and find a new life, knowing he loved her, and that she had betrayed him—not once, but twice. Twice she had made a fool of him, and though they would never meet again, he would remain her fool until he died.

Damien pushed himself to his feet and walked to his gelding, dropping his forehead against the animal's arched neck. If Miranda remained in California with Cain, Damien knew he could not. This was to have been his new life—a ranch in a gentle valley north of San Francisco, where he'd bought land with the gold dust he and Etienne had pulled out of the jealous earth.

But if Miranda stayed ...

Damien slapped the horse's withers and shook his head. "I've no heart for wandering, *mon ami*," he told the animal. "The land is in my blood. If I can't settle here, I'll find another place."

Another place, but never home. Never home when Miranda was not with him, sharing his life, bearing his children. Loving him as he loved her.

He crouched beside the fire and began to gather up his things. It was still hours until dawn, but he had no hope of sleep and no desire to stay here another moment. He'd backtrack along the trail until it became light, and then strike directly west to avoid Heaven's Bar before turning south for Sacramento. In San Francisco he'd be able to sell his land, sever all ties to this new territory he'd once thought to make his own. ...

The gelding tossed up his head and whinnied. Brush cracked and rustled; Damien grabbed his gun and took careful aim as a dun horse plunged into the small clearing.

The horse had a rider. He clung to his mount's back like a monkey, arms locked around the horse's neck, clothing ragged and torn. Blond curls were matted with burs and twigs. He lifted his head as Damien holstered his gun.

"Damien," the rider gasped in Annette's voice. "*Dieu merci ...*"

And then Annette fell into Damien's arms. He held her close, brushing hair away from her scratched, dirty face.

"Annette!" He eased her down beside the fire, grabbing his tin of water and holding it to her cracked lips. "Annette—"

She grasped the tin in shaking hands and drank

deep. When the water was gone she looked up at him through half-closed eyelids. "I found you," she repeated. "The angel must have guided me. It took so long. . . ."

"Don't speak, Annette—"

"I must." She tried to sit up, and he took her weight gently. "I rode after you—to tell you the truth. You must go back to her—"

Damien's heart stopped. "Back," he whispered.

"Yes." Annette lifted one hand to touch his cheek. "She never betrayed you, Damien. The angel showed me how I—could make it right again."

She told him, haltingly, what had happened in Miranda's room that night in Heaven's Bar. And when she had finished, Damien stared into the dying fire and cursed his damnable pride.

"You must go back," Annette said softly. "There is no time to waste."

"But I—betrayed *her*—"

Annette smiled, her face radiant under the dirt. "There is always forgiveness, Damien. For all of us."

"You can't ride—"

She pushed at him and stood up shakily, jaw set. "I will, Damien. I'll borrow the angel's wings."

Damien prayed fervently that Annette's angel was with them now.

"It sounds like that bird."

Ariel heard Etienne's voice outside the storeroom and redoubled his squawks. The door swung open, and Etienne ducked his head under the low lintel. Morning light filled the room like hope.

"*Que le diable m'emporte!* It *is* that bird. What are you doing here?"

Ariel hopped from foot to foot, bobbing his head.

Etienne walked into the room and glanced around. "Do you know how much you've missed, bird? How did you get to be here? I wonder." He scratched his jaw, frowning. "In Cain's storeroom, no less."

Ariel flapped his wings and fixed Etienne with his most commanding stare.

"However you got here," Etienne muttered, "it's clear you wish to rejoin your mistress, *n'est-ce pas?* I don't much care for cages, myself."

Ariel paced back and forth impatiently as Etienne studied the makeshift cage and began to pry off the slats.

"Damien would laugh, bird," the big man said as he worked. "Here I am talking to you, and he once asked me to remind him that *he* was not insane." He sighed. "A great pity, bird. I had thought that Damien and your mistress—" He shook his head, tossing broken wood to the ground. "Yes, a pity. Sullivan and Miranda are leaving camp at this very moment. But I believe your mistress will be glad to have you back—"

Etienne stepped out of the way just as Ariel launched himself from the crate, leaving a trail of molted feathers behind him.

Ariel flew as he'd never flown before, out the door and heavenward, spiraling up and up until he could see all the camp and the river and the hills for miles in every direction.

A stagecoach was drawn up in front of the saloon. Miranda stood beside it, eyes downcast, as the driver secured her trunks. Cain Sullivan rested his hand possessively on Miranda's shoulder and whispered in her ear.

Ariel flew higher. Just a mile away, on a trail winding east and north among the hills, dust rolled in a cloud headed for Heaven's Bar.

Whistling triumphantly, Ariel dived. Sullivan uttered a startled curse, and Miranda's wan, pale face turned up.

"Ariel! Where—"

But he had no time to answer her. He flew directly to the horses harnessed to the stage. The mare on the right rolled her eye at him. Ariel leaned close to her flickering ear. She tossed her head and whinnied.

"I'll be damned!"

The driver dropped the trunk he was holding and dashed after the stage as it careened away behind bolting horses. Ariel nodded to himself and found a perch well out of Cain Sullivan's reach, calmly grooming his tertial feathers.

The delay was just long enough. By the time the stage driver returned, panting and cursing, with his horses in tow, there was a new commotion on the bar. Etienne ran into the street, grinning from ear to ear.

"Welcome back, *mon ami*," he said.

Damien, wreathed in dust, handed Annette down into Etienne's arms and swung from the saddle of his bay gelding. Without a word he strode to where Cain Sullivan gaped at him, planted the Irishman a solid blow to the jaw, swept Miranda into his arms, and kissed her for all he was worth.

For a moment Miranda melted in his arms, and then she became a spitting fury, beating him back with a rain of blows from clenched fists.

When he released her, she glared at him, eyes brimming and skin flushed. Loose tendrils of red hair crackled about her face like flame.

"How dare you?" she whispered.

Damien reached for her and she slapped his hand away. "How dare you come back?"

Staring into her eyes, Damien silently rejoiced. If

she'd met him with indifference, he'd have known he'd lost her. But as long as she felt so deeply—

"Why did you come back?" she cried.

"Miranda," he said. "I know the truth. I know how Cain used you—and deceived me."

She blinked, and tears spilled over onto her cheeks. "What?"

Damien gestured to Annette, who leaned heavily against Etienne. "Annette rode after me, Miranda. She nearly killed herself to find me and tell me how wrong I was in believing—"

"I know—what you believed," Miranda said bitterly. "What you've always chosen to believe of me—"

"Miranda!" He took her arms, trapping them against her. "Listen to me. It was all Cain's plan from the beginning, to feign drunkenness, get into your room, and put you off guard. He sent Annette to see that I came in at just the right time."

Miranda stood very still, looking from Damien to Annette. Her expressive eyes revealed every thought that passed through her mind, the anguish of her realization. The color leached from her face.

"Cain—"

"Yes," Damien said gently, longing to touch her face, brush the tears from her cheeks. "He wanted you for himself at any price, and so he betrayed your friendship. It was all a ruse—"

"And you fell for it." Miranda shook her head, swallowing back sobs. "You didn't even wait to hear what I had to say. You stood in judgment and found me unworthy, just as you did in New Orleans."

Her words made no sense, but Damien let them pass. He willed her to meet his eyes. "I was wrong. I was the worst kind of blind, arrogant fool." Slowly, deliberately, he dropped to his knees, catching her hand in his. "Forgive me, Miranda. Give me another chance—"

"Another chance?" she said, eyes wide with pain. "A third time, Damien? After I've tried so hard to let you go—" Her voice broke, and she looked around as if for escape.

But he would not let her go. Never again.

"Marry me, Miranda," Damien said fiercely, refusing to release her hand. "Forgive me, and marry me."

"It's too late, Damien," she whispered.

"No." He lifted her trembling fingers to his mouth, his forehead, praying for the right words. "I love you, Miranda. I've always loved you. Nothing else matters."

Miranda closed her eyes, pulled her hand free of his. "You need a ring when you propose marriage, Damien." She reached into the reticule hanging from her elbow and withdrew a small pouch. "Perhaps you can use this."

She took his hand, turned it over, and dropped a ruby-and-diamond ring into his palm.

Damien stared at the ring, closing his fingers around it convulsively. The ring he had sent her years ago, when he'd offered marriage. The ring she had taken with her when she'd accepted his father's money rather than become his wife . . .

"You kept it," he whispered.

"Yes. I kept it, fool that I was. I hadn't the heart to sell it, even though you'd used it to buy me off—"

"Buy you off?" Damien surged to his feet. "Is that what you call an honorable offer of marriage?"

She stared at him, the color ebbing and flowing in her face. "What? You offered to make me your mistress when you told me of your betrothal, and when I refused—" She broke off, breathing heavily.

Damien dropped his eyes, staring at the dusty ground between his boots. Old shame stabbed through him. "Within a day after I'd made you that infernal offer," he said hoarsely, "I realized what a fool I'd been." He opened his hand and held out the ring. "I sent you this ring with the letter, begging you to become my wife. Did you hate me so much, Miranda?"

"Hate you?" she echoed. "The letter—the letter I received said nothing of marriage." She swallowed. "You told me you never wanted to see me again. . . ."

Damien looked up. There was no dissembling in Miranda, no deception. "I never wrote—"

"I left New Orleans, just as you demanded. But I never thought to see you again."

The ground shifted under Damien's feet. "Miranda," he said slowly, "when my father learned of my feelings for you, that I intended to offer marriage in spite of my family's opposition—he said he'd gone to see you himself."

She stared at him. "I never met your father."

"He said," Damien persisted, "that he gave you a choice. He wouldn't oppose our marriage if you would take me without my inheritance, without wealth or position—that he would give us nothing. Or he would pay you richly to leave New Orleans forever. He said he knew what you'd choose, and you did as he expected. You took his money and the ring I'd sent, and left New Orleans."

Miranda's lips parted as she struggled visibly for words. "I never met your father," she repeated. "I never took his money."

"And I never wrote a letter casting you off, Miranda." Damien reached for her hand, and she let him take it. "The letter I did write never reached you. But the ring did, and a different letter." He closed his eyes. "One my father must have written. He would have done anything to protect the family honor."

"He succeeded," Miranda whispered.

Damien shook his head. "No. Because after you left, and I believed you'd refused to become my wife—I deserted my family. I couldn't bear to live as if I'd never known you. You changed me, Miranda."

"You—left them, because of me?"

"Yes. I took a steamer to Missouri and journeyed overland to California, found work with Sutter's men months before gold was discovered in these hills. I wanted a new life, to forget everything else."

Miranda looked up at the bright morning sky. "You found it," she said. "And yet you came here because of a terrible deception. And I—" She covered her eyes with her other hand. "I came because my father wished it, just before he died."

"If only I'd known, Miranda," Damien said. "If I had trusted you, and my own heart—"

Miranda silenced him with a finger to his lips. "How could you, believing your father bought me off after I'd claimed to love you? You knew little enough of love."

Damien's throat tightened. Miranda had taught him what love was, and he had thrown the lesson back in her face.

"My father—" he began. He forced the words out, voicing the guilt and grief he'd never spoken aloud. "My father never believed I was a proper son, a proper Lévesque. But he didn't savor his victory after he drove us apart, Miranda. I left him with no heir at all. And after I'd been a few months in California, I received a letter from my father's factor in New Orleans. My parents—died in a yellow fever epidemic the summer after I left New Orleans."

Miranda gasped, her eyes bright with new tears.

"Oh, Damien," she murmured. She walked into his arms, hugging him with all her strength, her cheek pressed to his chest. "I'm sorry. So sorry."

Damien held her close, feeling the depth of his loneliness only now that he held her again. "I need you, Miranda," he said against her hair. "Can we forget the past? Can we regain the happiness we had in New Orleans?"

Miranda grasped the collar of his dusty shirt, shaking her head.

He set her back gently, tilting up her stubborn chin.

"Will you take this ring from me again, and do me the honor of becoming my wife?"

"Damien—"

"This is a new country, Miranda. There are no aristocrats here, no barriers between two people who love each other. It's a place made for beginnings." He heard the urgency in his own voice and cast aside the ragged remnants of his pride. "I have land north of San Francisco, enough for a ranch, a farm—a home for both of us—everything we would need—"

Miranda covered his mouth with her hand. "Are you asking me to give up the stage, Damien?" she asked.

He froze, meeting her clear gaze. "I want a home—with you, Miranda," he growled. "I thought that was what you wanted—"

A smile curved her lips, touched with a hint of mischief. "I can't give up acting entirely, Damien. It's in my blood. In fact, I'd been hoping to acquire a new company of performers—"

With a soft oath, Damien grabbed her and pulled her close. "Miranda—"

She chuckled. " 'You and I are too wise to woo peaceably,' " she quoted. "I'll need your help to put together the company I had in mind, Damien." She dropped her eyes, suddenly demure. "The sooner we marry, the sooner we can begin."

Damien sucked in his breath and let it out again on a ragged laugh. " 'Time goes on crutches,' " he murmured, " 'till love have all his rites.' "

They gazed at each other, oblivious to the world.

" 'Do you love me?' " Miranda asked at last.

Damien smiled, remembering the lines from *The Tempest.* " 'I, beyond all limit of what else i' th' world, do love, prize, honor you.' "

" 'I am your wife, if you will marry me.' " She held out her hand. " 'My husband then?' "

He took her hand, folding her fingers around the ring. " 'Here's my hand.' "

" 'And mine, with my heart in't.' "

Damien lifted her small fist and kissed the knuckles one by one. " 'Lady, as you are mine, I am yours.' "

A sudden roar of applause and ragged cheers rose up around them. Miranda blushed, and Damien realized for the first time that they had a very appreciative audience of miners who had witnessed most of the performance.

Etienne strolled over to join them, Annette in the crook of his arm and Ariel perched on his shoulder. "Bravo," he said, grinning broadly. "Surely the finest work of your career, mademoiselle—though I don't see the villain of the piece—"

Brought firmly back to earth, Damien pulled Miranda close and looked at the place where he'd left Cain Sullivan lying on his back in the dust.

"He's gone," Miranda said. The joy faded from her face. "I wish—"

Damien kissed her temple. "I would have spared you this pain, *ma chérie.* But if I see him again—"

"No." She touched his arm. "The time for anger is

past, Damien." When he would have protested, she stood on her toes and brushed his lips with her own. " 'Peace, I will stop your mouth,' " she murmured.

She succeeded very admirably.

The interested crowd broke up at last, the miners going back about their business with grins and unsubtle comments aimed at Damien. Etienne and Annette disappeared into the saloon, closing the door firmly behind them. A few minutes later Etienne reemerged, beckoning to Damien and Miranda.

"Our friend Sullivan has fled, apparently—with his gold dust, his horses, and whatever valuables he could snatch up on the run." He looked at Damien. "Sullivan sold the saloon two days ago, but the new owner has not yet taken possession—and Sullivan left the liquor stores intact." He lowered his voice to a conspiratorial whisper. "*Venez,* you two—before the miners realize they can have all the free whiskey they can drink."

Ariel hopped from Etienne's shoulder to Miranda's, nipping gently at her ear as they walked into the saloon.

"And where have you been?" Miranda scolded, stroking his breast feathers with a fingertip. "I missed you, Ariel. I don't know how I managed to go on without you."

" 'All's well that ends well,' " Ariel said, nodding his head.

"It's a very wise bird," Etienne commented. He smiled at Annette. "*N'est-ce pas?*"

Annette, sitting at the bar, lifted her head from her arms. Ragged and dirty, she looked more radiant than Miranda had ever seen her.

"*Mais oui.* A very wise bird."

Miranda gathered her skirts and sat down on the

stool beside Annette. "I owe you a great debt of thanks," she said, touching Annette's scratched hand. "If you hadn't gone after Damien—"

Annette smiled a quiet, secret smile and glanced at Ariel. "I wronged you and Damien both, Miranda. I thought I understood what love was, but I had much to learn."

Miranda squeezed Annette's hand and looked around the deserted bar. "What will you do now, Annette? Will you—work for the new owner when he arrives?"

She tried to keep the disapproval from her voice, but Annette reddened and dropped her gaze.

"*Non.* I can't go back to that life again."

Damien came up beside them, putting his arm around Miranda. "We'll help you, Annette, in any way we can—"

"That won't be necessary, *mon ami.*"

Etienne leaned against the bar and winked at Annette. "I've already spoken to the lady. You remember my plan to open a fine restaurant in San Francisco, Damien? Since I've lost my former partner, I'll need a new one."

"I can cook," Annette murmured, almost shyly. "And I have saved my money. Enough to start over." Once again she looked directly at Ariel. "Thank you for showing me the way."

Miranda glanced from Etienne to Annette and smiled up into Damien's eyes. "I think perhaps this is cause for celebration!"

The walls and door shook suddenly with a hail of rapid blows. Male voices joined the racket, demanding entrance and whiskey.

"But not here, I think," Etienne said. He grasped Annette's hand and led them all behind the bar and down a narrow hallway to a back entrance just as the impatient miners broke into the saloon with exultant yells.

Miranda pulled Damien to a stop just outside, cradling his stubbled chin between her hands.

" 'The wheel has come full circle,' " she quoted, loving him with everything she was and would ever be.

And as Damien bent his head to kiss her, Ariel looked heavenward and flapped his wings for joy.

> " 'Then is there mirth in heaven,
> When earthly things made even
>   Atone together.' "

Susan Krinard has "set the standard for fantasy romance" (Affaire de Coeur) with her recent bestselling novels PRINCE OF WOLVES and PRINCE OF DREAMS. Her next romance will be STAR-CROSSED, coming soon in the summer of 1995.

Saving Celeste

Karyn Monk

ONE

Boston, Massachusetts
October 1786

He stepped out of the stale curtain of smoke that hung thickly over the tavern and into the cold, brine-laden air of the waterfront. He faltered slightly and grabbed hold of the door for support, his head swimming from the effects of too much brandy. He cursed and slammed the door behind him, annoyed that he had been reduced to this condition so soon, and worse, in the company of prospective investors. Normally he was not so lacking in control. He usually waited until he was home before he permitted himself to get drunk.

He scanned the length of the street and saw his carriage rattling toward him across the uneven sea of stones. His stomach lurched.

"Where to, Mr. Barrett?" asked the coachman. "On to the American?"

Nathan slowly inhaled a deep breath of fresh sea air. He shook his head.

"Home, then?" suggested the coachman, sounding faintly hopeful.

Nathan hesitated. "You take the carriage and go on home, John," he replied thickly. "I am going to walk."

John looked at him in astonishment. "Walk, sir?"

Nathan nodded, and his head spun with dizziness. "Yes," he repeated adamantly. "Walk."

"It is three o'clock in the morning, sir," John pointed out. "The streets are full of all kinds of scum. And it is raining."

Nathan looked around with genuine surprise. He held his hand out and felt frigid drops slap heavily against his palm.

"Good," he muttered, adjusting the collar of his cape around his neck. He began to walk briskly down the street. His carriage followed slowly behind him. "Go home, John," he ordered over his shoulder.

John hesitated, then flicked his whip and sent the carriage clattering into the veil of darkness ahead of him.

The air was sharp with the aroma of the waterfront; salt and fish mixed with the bitter smell of pitch from the shipyards. The cold, the air, and the rain quickly extinguished the numbing effect of Nathan's intoxication, and he found he was filled with a heightened sense of alertness as he strode along the slick, uneven streets. The rain began to fall harder, drenching his hair and face and soaking through the heavy wool of his cape, yet he was not uncomfortable. He felt exceptionally vibrant and ready to act, as if he sensed some challenge was about to present itself and he had to be ready to meet it. That was ridiculous, of course. The streets were totally deserted, and the only challenge at the moment was getting home in this god-awful storm. As he approached the bridge that spanned the Charles River, joining Charlestown to Boston, he began to wonder what insanity had made him want to walk on such a frigid, miserable night.

And then he saw her.

She was standing at the center of the bridge, leaning against its heavy wooden balustrade, gazing out into the rain and the darkness of the river. There was nothing odd about that, he assured himself, she was probably just a prostitute waiting for a customer. It was a damn cold, foul night to be out trying to make a living with one's body. But Boston was full of people with wretched lives desperately trying to make it through another night, he reflected bitterly. He could not see her face, for she was shrouded in a dark cloak and hood, but her silhouette was graceful, elegant, and utterly lonely against the black curtain of rain that surrounded her. He knew she could not be as lovely as her profile suggested, for prostitution was a trade that exacted a heavy toll. Her face was probably pitted and scarred from smallpox and prematurely creased with deep lines. She undoubtedly caked herself with heavy makeup in a pathetic attempt to conceal the ravages of her life. Yet somehow he felt drawn to her, as if her loneliness on this miserable evening allied her to him.

He stepped onto the bridge and approached her in silence, feeling a strange mixture of curiosity and anxiety begin to pound through him. She did not notice him, but simply stood there staring at the river. His hands clenched into fists and his heart began to pump faster. It was as though his body were preparing to act, although she had done nothing to precipitate this reaction. He wondered if it was the effect of too much drink.

Suddenly she hoisted herself up onto the balustrade, precariously steadying herself until she was standing. Every shred of alertness and energy within him instantly froze. She looked small and fragile against the enormous sky that stretched dark and endless before her. She gazed up at the ink-stained clouds, as if searching for something. He called out to her, his voice strangely hoarse as it cut through the heavy beating of the rain against the bridge and the river below.

She turned to look at him. Her face was suddenly bathed in the soft, apricot glow of the bridge lamps, and his heart slammed hard against his chest. Never in his life had he seen such a hauntingly beautiful expression of torment. She held the look of someone who was afraid, of someone who has been utterly crushed with despair and cannot bear it a moment longer. In that instant he realized she intended to kill herself, and was simply waiting for God's forgiveness or the final surge of courage she needed to do it.

For one frozen, agonizing moment everything stopped. An incredible wave of protectiveness crashed over him. He was overwhelmed by an unbearable desire to touch her and have her close, to take her in from the darkness and the rain and wrap his arms around her and protect her from whatever was causing her such terrible grief. Forever.

Her eyes regarded him with vacant hopelessness, perhaps even faintly condemning, as if she were saying, *You are too late.* And then she slowly turned to face the river once more.

"No!" he roared, his heart constricting in fear. He began to rush toward her, his arms outstretched, his cloak billowing around him like the wings of a great, dark angel.

She looked at him again, and this time she seemed

afraid, as if by stopping her he was doing her terrible harm. He tried to hold her captive with his eyes, he ordered her not to move, but she did not obey. She turned suddenly and stepped off the balustrade into the blackness, silently, not screaming, simply slipping from his sight into the abyss on the other side of the bridge.

"*Noooo!*" he roared, his protest coming from the depths of his soul.

He leaned against the balustrade and listened to the horrible sound of her body splashing into the icy black water below. He immediately leaped onto the balustrade and threw himself off, his cloak billowing around him as he flew through the rain-drenched air, down into the dark void where she had disappeared. The freezing river closed over his head, hideously dark and suffocating, but he pulled himself to the surface and began to search for her. She had disappeared. He cursed aloud in frustration. He started to swim, his powerful strokes hindered by the iciness of the water and the heavy tangle of cloak about his arms and legs. His heart pounded with fear, but he continued his course, somehow sensing she was close to him. The rain lashed at his face, blurring his vision, so he allowed his instincts to guide him, or whatever force it was that seemed to say that in all the infinite depths of that black, cold river there was only one place she could be. He reached blindly into the darkness, praying to God she was there. And felt his hand close around the fluid fabric of her cloak.

He pulled her toward him and wrapped his arm around her, hoisting her up until her head emerged through the surface of the water. She did not fight him, but lay heavy and motionless in his arms, her eyes closed, her head limp. He began to swim, slowly pulling her with him until he finally reached the bank of the river. He climbed up and hauled her out behind him, laying her sodden form on the wet, muddy ground.

She was deathly pale and utterly still, not shaking with cold, not breathing. She was beautiful in death. Her face was tranquil and resigned, her ashen lips held the barest trace of a smile. It was as if she had found what she had been seeking. Nathan let out a cry of fury and pushed down hard just below her rib cage. Water spurted from her mouth. He pushed down again, and again, and the water started to flow from her lips in a steady stream. He began to talk to her, ordering her to breathe, pressing rhythmically against her until finally the water eased to a trickle. But still she did not breathe. Burning with desperation and rage, he bent low over her, sealed her lips with his, and exhaled deeply into her, forcing air into her lungs, determined to breathe for her if she would not do so for herself. Suddenly she gagged. Relief poured through him as he pulled her to a sitting position. Her eyes remained closed, but she began to cough and greedily suck in great, long drafts of air, her lungs wheezing from the effort.

His own freezing wet clothes reminded him he had to get her somewhere warm and dry immediately, and he cursed his stupidity at sending his carriage home. He wrapped his arms around her and lifted her to his chest, then carried her up to the road that skirted the river. There was no one in sight, and so he began to walk, wondering if he should try to take her to his home or if he should simply bang on the first door he came to and ask for assistance. Thunder cracked loudly across the heavens, and when it subsided he thought he heard the faint, hollow clopping of horses' hooves. He turned and saw a black carriage appear out of the heavy curtain of rain. He strode toward it, gave the driver his address, and climbed inside, cradling her tight against him as the carriage began to race along the rain-slick streets.

Her head rested against his shoulder, and although she was unconscious, he was satisfied that she was breathing steadily. He adjusted his arm so he could better study her. Once again he was overwhelmed by her fragile beauty. Her skin was pale and smooth, like the creamiest of silks, her lips, though ashen, were full and lush. Thick, black lashes swept the top of her cheeks, which were high and delicately chiseled. Although he was certain he had never seen her before, something about her was achingly familiar. He stroked a dark lock of wet hair off her forehead and allowed his fingers to softly caress her cool cheek, marveling at the incredible sensation of protectiveness that still gripped him. He had not held a woman in his arms for over two years, and he wondered if this accounted for his powerful reaction to her. He was filled with the extraordinary sensation that he knew her, although he was certain he had never seen her before in his life.

The carriage came to a stop and he burst from it, racing up the steps and into his home with his precious burden.

"Preston! Mrs. Lindsay!" he shouted as he carried her up the stairs. He moved quickly down the hallway to his bedroom, flung open the door, and laid her gently upon the bed. He undid the heavy silver clasp of her cloak and stripped the soaking-wet garment off her, tossing it into a heap on the floor. Then he turned her over and quickly began to undo the fastenings at the back of her gown.

"Yes, Mr. Barrett?" said his butler from the doorway.

"Build up the fire," ordered Nathan abruptly as he turned the girl over again and yanked her gown

down to her waist. Her wet chemise clung tightly to
her skin.

"May I be of assistance, Mr. Barrett?" asked Mrs.
Lindsay, his housekeeper.

"Make some hot tea laced with brandy," instructed Nathan. "And bring more blankets in
here—as many as you can find." He grabbed hold of
the girl's wet skirts and with one strong pull had her
dress on the floor with her cloak, leaving her only in
her wet chemise and twisted petticoats. He tugged
the ribbon of her chemise and began to ease the
transparent garment up.

Mrs. Lindsay hesitated. "Perhaps, sir, it would be
better if I attended to the young lady," she suggested
delicately.

Nathan stopped, his hands just at the girl's breasts.
A wave of irritation hit him. He could see Mrs.
Lindsay's point, but he was extremely reluctant to
let anyone else attend to the girl. Once again he was
struck by an odd feeling of possessiveness, that
somehow this girl was his, and therefore only he
should look after her. It was ridiculous, of course,
and most unseemly now that there was another
woman present who could finish undressing her.

"Put her in something warm," he muttered as he
turned and left the room.

He quickly changed into dry clothes and returned
some ten minutes later. The fire was blazing in the
hearth and the unconscious girl was lying beneath a
mound of blankets on his bed, dressed in a white
nightgown. She was pale and beautiful against the
linen of the sheets, her damp hair spread around her
like dark, wild waves cascading over the soft pillows.
He sat down beside her and gently caressed her
cheek with the back of his fingers, overwhelmed by
her beauty. She had almost managed to extinguish
her life tonight, he reflected furiously. What could

possibly make an exquisite creature like this want to kill herself? he wondered. And by what strange force did he come to be there at that exact moment?

She stirred slightly and her eyes flickered open. Her expression immediately became wary and fearful, and she tried to shrink from his touch. He quickly withdrew his hand.

"It's all right," he assured her. "You have nothing to fear."

She stared at him a moment, her eyes dark, haunted, afraid. "Why?" she finally whispered. "Why did you save me?" She pulled her gaze away from him. "How could you be so cruel?" Her voice was ragged with pain and accusation.

A feeling of complete bewilderment swept through him. "I could not stand by and let you drown," he told her, almost apologetically. "I had to do something."

She turned to him once more. Her eyes were hard and glittering with tears. "I wanted to die," she informed him, her voice deadly calm. "You had no right to stop me."

He found himself suddenly angry with her. "Rest assured, I did not plan to end my evening by jumping into a freezing river after some silly girl who was acting out a dramatic finale to her life," he announced brusquely. She turned away from him, and he was immediately sorry for speaking to her so sharply. "I believe there were enough deaths in Boston tonight," he continued, his tone gentler. "We did not need to add yours to the list."

She shook her head slowly and closed her eyes, clearly exhausted. For a long time the room was silent, except for the steady sound of her breathing and the occasional snap of the fire. When he was certain she finally slept, he added another log to the hearth and doused the candle by her bed. As he drew the door closed behind him he thought he heard her stir.

"There will be other nights," she assured him softly through the darkness.

Nathan took a long swallow of brandy and stared moodily into the flames. He had taken the room next to hers so he would hear her if she got up during the night and tried to leave, to return to the river and try again. So far all was quiet. He did not mind that he would not sleep, for he never slept much anymore. Since Emmaline's death, night had become a torturous time for him. He dreaded going to bed because no matter how much he drank he still lay there for hours and missed the feeling of her curled up warm and soft against him, her silky arm draped possessively around his chest, her honey-blond hair spilling over him, fragrant with the scent of roses. It has not been that long, he assured himself. Barely two years. The pain of her death was still agonizing to him. People had told him with time it would dull, but those people knew nothing about losing a woman like Emmaline. She was unlike any woman he had ever known. Especially that silly girl lying in his bed tonight, he reflected bitterly. Emmaline had loved life, had embraced its every moment. When she realized she was dying, she had been angry, and vowed she would not let God take her so quickly. And so she had lived on, losing weight, losing strength, turning into a pale shadow of the healthy, glowing, laughing girl he had married. And then, when she finally became too tired to fight any longer, she gave in, leaving him alone with a young son and a hole in his heart so deep he had thought he would go mad from the agony of having to go on living without her.

But he had gone on. He had started what he knew

would ultimately be a successful shipping company. He had thrown himself into his work these past two years as a way of dealing with the pain, of giving himself a reason to get out of bed in the morning, to get dressed, to eat, to go out in the world and talk and conduct business and carry on as if he was all right, as if his life was in his control and unfolding exactly as it should. It was a lie, of course. Inside he was not carrying on. Inside he was dying.

He took another swallow of brandy.

He knew he should spend more time with his son. But Michael looked so much like her, and acted so much like her, every time he saw the boy his heart constricted in pain. Of course it wasn't right, the way he left his son to his tutors and Mrs. Lindsay and Preston. He was his father. He should spend time with him. But spending time with him was an agony, and so he chose simply to close him off, to see him once in the morning or once before he went to bed, somehow managing to get through those awkward meetings without breaking down completely and showing the boy how weak his father really was.

The girl he saved tonight treated life as if it were of little value, something that could simply be tossed away when it was no longer to her liking. A surge of fury heated his blood. Life was precious. Cruel perhaps, unfair, certainly, but precious nonetheless. Emmaline died, when she wanted so much to live, and the girl in his bed lived, when she wanted so much to die. Such was life. But he had been powerless to save his Emma. He had brought her the best doctors money could buy, who had filled her with their foul medicines, weakened her with purgings and bleedings, cutting her and prodding her and forcing her to endure all manner of horrific procedures. She had borne them all stoically, without complaint, praying each time that this one would work, that this one would give her back the life that was so quickly draining out of her. But finally, toward the end, she begged him not to send any more doctors to her. And Nathan had been furious with her for giving up, for not fighting anymore, for deserting him and Michael. She had cried and begged his forgiveness, and he had taken her fragile form in his arms and rocked her, cursing himself for being so selfish, and cursing God for putting her through such terrible agony. And when she finally died he cursed God even more for taking her from him, even though he knew it was better that she finally be released from her pain.

God certainly had a sense of irony, he reflected bitterly. He would not give him the power to save Emmaline, who wanted so much to live, yet he threw this suicidal girl off a bridge in front of him, knowing he had the power to save her. If God thought it evened the score, he was wrong. He poured more brandy into his glass and tossed it back in a single gulp. He did not know what caused the girl in the next room to despair so much she did not want to live. But by God, he would see to it that she did.

If he had to go on, then so did she.

TWO

She awakened slowly, feeling utterly warm and safe and protected, and therefore in no hurry to open her eyes. When she finally did she was greeted with a burst of glorious light. It was streaming through the windows and flooding the room, creating a pool of heat on the soft mound of blankets that covered her. She looked up and saw a flock of angels flying above, draped in magnificent blossoms of crimson and sapphire and violet, their splendid, feathery wings shimmering with gold. An overwhelming sense of relief flowed through her. She gazed languidly around the room. On the wall across from her hung a portrait of an exquisitely beautiful woman. Her hair was spun of the brightest sunlight, and her eyes held the crystalline clarity of a hot summer sky. The woman was smiling at her and so she smiled back, feeling wonderfully peaceful and at ease. Outside she could hear the familiar sounds of carriage wheels rattling over cobblestones, the hollow clopping of horses' hooves, the sweet

laughter of children. It was strange, she mused
dreamily, but heaven was not very different from
earth, except for this marvelous feeling of tranquil-
lity. And safety. Yes, she felt thoroughly, wonderfully safe. She sighed and nestled contentedly into
the blankets.

A clock began to chime on the mantel. She listened to it for a moment, absently counting the
chimes. There were eight. She frowned. Then she sat
bolt upright and stared at the mantel in confusion.
Surely there was no need for clocks in heaven. Icy
panic rippled through her as a dreadful realization
began to take hold.

She was alive.

She threw back the covers and leaped from the
bed, her bare feet sinking into a thick carpet. An
overwhelming sensation of dizziness assailed her,
forcing her to close her eyes. The room began to
spin around her, faster and faster. All at once her legs
could no longer support her and she fell in a clumsy
heap on the floor. Somewhere through the veil of
dizziness she was vaguely aware of a door opening.

"What the hell—"

Strong arms were wrapping around her, lifting her
against a hard chest, then carefully laying her once
again on the soft mattress of the bed. Safety.
Warmth. She waited until the room stopped spinning, then slowly opened her eyes.

A man with frigid gray eyes was glaring down at
her. "What in the name of God were you doing out
of bed?" he demanded harshly.

She returned his glare for a moment, determined
not to be intimidated by the virulent power he ex-
uded as he towered over her. Everything about him
was dark and menacing, his hair, his eyes, the rigid
planes and hollows of his face, and most of all, the
cold shadow he cast over her as his huge form

blocked the sunlight that moments earlier had warmed the bed. She saw angels flying on the ceiling above him. A fresco, she realized with disappointment. There were no angels here.

"Am I ill?" she demanded, her voice a dry rasp.

He turned to the table beside the bed and poured her a glass of water. "No," he replied curtly. He arranged the pillows behind her and handed her the glass. Surprisingly, his touch was gentle, not at all like his appearance. "But it is too soon for you to be up and about."

She gratefully took a sip of water. "Have I had an accident?" She thought of herself falling to the floor and a horrifying possibility occurred to her. "Am I unable to walk?"

The anger in his expression was replaced with confusion. He hesitated. Obviously he was afraid to tell her. "You needn't hide the truth from me," she informed him firmly, struggling to remain calm. "It will be better for me to know."

His confusion was replaced with irritation. "Of course you can walk!"

Relief poured through her veins. "Thank heaven."

"I am pleased to see you are a little more concerned for your welfare this morning than you were last night," he drawled sarcastically as he took the glass from her and set it on the table. "Or were you afraid if you were crippled you would not be able to return to the bridge?"

She drew her eyebrows together in bewilderment. "The bridge?"

"Yes, the bridge," he repeated tautly. "I doubt when they opened the damn thing this summer they had any idea you would consider it an ideal place from which to jump."

She stared at him in disbelief. "What on earth on you talking about?"

Nathan felt another wave of absolute irritation flood over him. "I am in no mood for games," he informed her brusquely. He pulled a chair closer to the bed and sat down. "You will tell me who you are and why you were so desperate to kill yourself last night."

She shook her head impatiently. It was obvious he had mistaken her for someone else. "My name is—" She hesitated, then frowned in confusion. A terrible pounding began in her temples, forcing her to close her eyes. She tried to push the pain aside and search her mind, but everything was suddenly tangled and vague.

"I don't know," she finally admitted, thoroughly mystified by that realization. "I don't remember."

He scowled at her. "What do you mean, you don't remember?"

"I mean I cannot remember!" she repeated fiercely, fighting to control the panic quickly swelling within her. How could she possibly not remember who she was? It was ridiculous. She took a deep breath, closed her eyes, and searched her mind once more, determined to gain access to her memory. Everything was shrouded in darkness and cold. She tried to pierce through the darkness and see what lay beyond it, but she could not. It was as if her existence before awakening in this room had been completely erased. She felt her panic ignite into fear and she struggled to suppress it. There was undoubtedly some logical explanation. She opened her eyes to see the stranger watching her intently, his gray eyes filled with skepticism. "I realize this sounds most improbable," she admitted, fighting to keep her voice calm, "but I am afraid I cannot remember anything."

Nathan scowled. What did she think to gain by playing this absurd trick on him? Perhaps she felt by

hiding her identity from him she could prevent him
from finding out who she was and contacting her
family. Or maybe she dreaded returning to the situation that had driven her to try to kill herself in the
first place. He folded his arms across his chest and
studied her in silence, wondering how far she would
take her bizarre claim.

She could see he did not believe her. She could
hardly believe it herself. Her hands clutched the
sheets in frustration as she fought to remember
something—anything. Surely her name would come
to her if she really concentrated. Or if she simply relaxed and cleared her mind. After a moment she realized it was no use. She had absolutely no idea who
she was or how she had come to be here. The only
thing she could remember was that when she awakened she thought she was in heaven. Which meant
she had believed she was dead. Why would she
think something like that? She pushed the question
aside and lifted her eyes to his. "I don't know who
I am," she told him flatly, her voice slightly taut
with fear.

If she was lying to him, it was a remarkable performance. But he could not allow himself to be misled by an accomplished performance, especially since
she had been so determined to kill herself last night.
He stared hard into her amber eyes, trying to assess
if there was any trace of deception there. Ultimately
he could not be sure. He sighed. Perhaps for the
moment he should give her the benefit of the doubt.

"I am Nathan Barrett," he informed her. "Last
night I saw you jump off the Charles River bridge.
I went in after you and pulled you out. I brought
you here, to my home. When you awakened, you
were furious with me for saving you. You implied
that you were going to try to kill yourself again."

She shook her head and closed her eyes, trying to

make sense of what he was telling her. "I remember being cold," she murmured. "And everything was black. But when I awoke, everything was light." She opened her eyes and looked at him, feeling hopelessly confused. "Why can't I remember anything else?"

"*If* what you are telling me is true, it is probably due to the shock," Nathan surmised, making it clear he was not fully convinced of her claim. "In which case your memory should return very quickly." He stood and adjusted the covers around her. "I will have my doctor examine you so we can be sure you are all right. For now, you are to stay in this bed and get some rest."

"I feel perfectly fine," she declared frostily, disliking immensely the fact that he did not believe her. Also, she was not accustomed to being given orders. At least, she did not think she was accustomed to it.

"Of course you do," he agreed as he rose from his chair. "That would explain why I found you in a disheveled heap on the floor when I came in." He moved toward the door, then turned to look at her again. Despite the formidable glare she was casting at him, somehow she seemed fragile against the mound of pillows he had propped up for her. The sun was streaming across the bed, setting her hair afire with red-and-gold highlights. Beneath her look of dark irritation he thought he saw a flicker of fear in her eyes. Once again he felt an astounding surge of protectiveness. That was only natural, he assured himself. He did not want her to be afraid.

"Everything will be all right," he assured her awkwardly, not really understanding how he could make such a claim. And then, perhaps more to reassure himself, he added, "I will make certain of it."

•　　•　　•

"She is telling the truth," announced Archibald as he accepted a glass of port from Nathan. "She really cannot remember anything."

"How is that possible?" Nathan demanded skeptically as he took a seat across from his old friend.

"Perhaps she struck her head on something when she fell into the river," Archibald suggested. "I could find no evidence of trauma to her skull, but sometimes a blow does not leave a mark." He sipped his port. "Or it could be the result of shock—a combination of her evident despair and the terror of coming so close to death."

"And how do you treat such a condition?"

Archibald sighed. "The phenomenon of memory loss is perplexing. It is as if the mind simply closes the door on its past. The condition can last for hours or years. Sometimes the door opens eventually, but in many cases the mind never retrieves its former life. It is as if a new life begins from this day forward."

Nathan sighed, feeling all at once incredibly weary. "So what the hell am I to do with her?"

"She is not your problem, Nathan," Archibald pointed out. "You have already done more than enough by jumping into the Charles and saving her." He leaned forward in his chair and regarded his friend earnestly. "Let me find a place for her where she can be taken care of. You do not need this extra burden in your life. God knows, you have been through enough already."

He was referring to Emmaline's lengthy illness. Archibald had been his wife's primary doctor. He had done everything he could to save her, including allowing other doctors to come in and treat her. In the end he had supported Emmaline's decision to stop the treatments. At the time Nathan had hated him for that decision.

It was true he had been through more than his share of dealing with illness and grief. He was trying to get on with his life, which meant he needed to focus his time and attention on his new shipping company. Having a strange, suicidal woman staying in his house hardly fit into that equation. She was in all likelihood deranged; normal females did not go running out on stormy nights and jump off bridges. Why, then, did he have this strange attachment to her? And why did the idea of sending her away make him feel like he was betraying her?

"It will take me a few hours to make the necessary arrangements," Archibald was saying as he rose from his chair. "Unfortunately, Boston does not yet have a proper asylum, so we have to rely on the use of private institutions. They are always overcrowded, but I am certain I will be able to find something." He paused at the doorway of the study. "You are doing the right thing, Nathan," he assured him.

The door closed. Nathan cursed softly and drained his glass in an attempt to ward off the familiar sensation of emptiness and failure wrapping around him like a dark, heavy shroud.

She was not going to stay here another minute. She had no idea where she was, or who this Nathan Barrett was, or if anything he was telling her were true. How could she be certain he had rescued her from the Charles River? The whole thing could be some elaborate lie designed to confuse her further. And now he had sent this doctor to her who had talked about finding a nice place for her to stay where she could rest. She might not remember who she was, but that did not make her a complete idiot. She knew he meant to have her locked up with people who were mad. If they put her in one of those places, she was certain she would *go* mad, and then they would never let her out. She had to get away from here, now. She threw back the covers and moved swiftly to the wardrobe. She jerked open the doors and began to rifle carelessly through the men's clothing in it, frantically searching for something to wear.

Suddenly she realized she was not alone. Whoever had come into the room was being exceptionally quiet, but she could sense their presence nonetheless. She slowly turned. A boy of about seven was standing in the doorway watching her. Realizing she had seen him, he immediately retreated into the hall.

"Hello," she called to him. Perhaps he could tell her where her clothes were.

He looked at her, his blue eyes clouded with apprehension. "I—I did not mean to disturb you," he stammered.

"You didn't," she assured him. The boy seemed familiar to her, but she could not remember if she knew him or not. She studied him a moment, taking in his pale, sunlit blond curls and crystal-blue eyes. There was a vulnerability to him, a haunted sadness that touched something within her, something heavy and aching.

"My father did not give me permission to be in here," admitted the boy haltingly. "I should go."

"Your father?"

"Mr. Barrett," he explained. "You are in his room."

This was Nathan's son, she realized with surprise. He looked nothing like Nathan. Nathan had dark hair and gray eyes that seethed with anger and impatience. His features were hard and angular, his lips a grim line. This little boy was pale and delicate and fine, with a quiet sadness to him. His familiarity confused her. She studied him a moment, and then her eyes moved to the portrait of the beautiful, smiling woman.

"Is that your mother?" she asked, indicating the painting.

"Yes," he replied seriously. "She is with the angels."

A confusing sense of loss enveloped her, causing a tightness in her throat. Some memory was stirring within her, but she could not get access to it. "Did she—go to the angels recently?"

"About two years ago," he murmured. "She was very sick." He pulled his gaze away from the portrait. "My name is Michael. What is yours?"

She opened her mouth to answer before remembering she could not. "I don't know," she replied, feeling somewhat foolish. "Apparently I had an accident last night and I cannot remember anything."

His crystal-blue eyes rounded in amazement. "You don't know who you are?"

She shook her head. "Ridiculous, isn't it?"

Michael stared at her in awe. "What kind of accident did you have?" he demanded, clearly fascinated.

"They say I fell off a bridge," she muttered, still not convinced that story was true. "Your father found me and brought me here." She stepped away from the wardrobe. "Do you have any idea where my clothes are?" she asked casually.

He shook his head.

So much for that idea, she thought ruefully. Another thought occurred to her. "Does your father employ a maid?" If he did, she would steal something to wear from her room.

Michael walked over and seated himself in the chair by the bed. "There is Mrs. Lindsay, our housekeeper. If you are hungry, I can ask her to bring you something to eat," he offered politely.

"No, thank you," she replied. As soon as the boy left she would search out Mrs. Lindsay's room and find something to wear. And then she would get away from here. "Perhaps you should go and play with your brother or sister," she suggested, trying to get him to leave.

"I don't have any," he told her with a shrug. He settled back in his chair and folded his hands in his lap.

"I see," she muttered, feeling an unbidden stab of sympathy for him. It was not easy to be an only child and lose one's mother. Once again a memory began to stir within her. She concentrated on it for a few seconds, but nothing more came to her, so she gave up. "Well," she continued conversationally, "you must have lots of friends from school. Perhaps you should go and play with one of them."

"I don't go to school," he informed her. "I have tutors."

"Then whom do you play with?" she demanded, slightly exasperated.

He regarded her with an air of extreme maturity, which was quite at odds with his childlike appearance. "I don't play with anyone," he stated scornfully. "I am too old to play."

She wrinkled her brow in confusion. "Exactly how old are you?"

"I will be eight this spring," he boasted.

"Really?" she said, as if that was extremely impressive. "Well, that is very grown-up indeed. What do you do when you are not studying?"

He thought for a moment and then shrugged his shoulders. "I read."

"What an excellent idea!" she exclaimed. "Why don't you go and read something now?"

"I don't feel like it." He began to idly kick his feet against the legs of the chair.

A new possibility occurred to her. "It looks like a fine day outside," she observed enthusiastically as she gestured at the sun pouring through the windows. "Why don't you ask your father to take you to the park?" That way she could get rid of both of them, and slipping out of the house unnoticed would be easy.

He looked at her as if the idea were ridiculous. "My father is far too busy to go to the park," he scoffed. "He is creating a shipping company." His little voice was filled with pride.

"That is wonderful," she remarked, feeling slightly defeated. In spite of her desire to have the boy leave, she found herself wondering if Nathan took any time to be with his son. It sounded like Michael spent all his time closeted in the house with his tutors and his books.

The sharp sound of barking interrupted her thoughts. "Do you have a dog?" she asked with surprise. Perhaps she could send him off to play with it.

He shook his head. "I wanted one once, but my father doesn't believe animals belong in a house." There was no trace of resentment in his voice, only acceptance.

"Really?" An unexpected spark of irritation flared within her. It was obvious to her this boy was terribly lonely, which explained why he was so intent on staying in the room with her. He had no one to play with, and seemed content to sit and talk with a perfect stranger. What right did his father have to deny him a dog? Surely he was entitled to some childish pleasure in his life. The barking continued, loud and bright and playful. "The dog must be in the street," she remarked thoughtfully. She watched him as he continued to bang the legs of his chair with his feet. And then she sighed. Perhaps they would not try to send her to a madhouse right away. If not, she could afford to spend a few moments with this lonely little boy. She smiled and held her hand out to him. "Let's go and see if we can watch him from the window."

He looked at her outstretched hand in confusion, as if he did not understand what she wanted from him. And then, very hesitantly, he slipped his little fingers into hers.

It was time to tell her he was sending her away.

He had reviewed his decision over a dozen times this past hour, and each time had come to the same conclusion. He had no time to play nursemaid to this girl. He was utterly absorbed by the demands of his growing business; therefore there was no room in his life for a suicidal young woman whose memory was closed off in some dark corner of her mind. It was best she go to an institution where she could be properly looked after. He would see she had everything she needed for as long as she remained there. He was not abandoning her, he told himself fiercely. He was simply relinquishing her to someone else's care.

He knocked once before pushing the door open. Sunlight was flooding the room with such incredible intensity he had to close his eyes to adjust to it. When he opened them, he felt his heart tighten in his chest.

She was standing at the window with his son, her hand resting casually on his shoulder as she laughed and pointed at something on the street below. An easy intimacy reigned between them, which surprised Nathan. He did not share such a relationship with Michael. She was dressed in a white silk nightgown trimmed with lace. It was Emmaline's, one of the many he bought for her after she became ill,

when jewelry and evening gowns had become useless to her. But he had never seen Emmaline wear
this gown. Warm, shimmering sunlight was streaming through the window, creating an aura around
her, setting her hair ablaze with red and gold, flooding the gown with light and rendering it virtually
transparent. He could see every deliciously fluid
curve of her body. A hot surge of desire tore
through him, appalling in its intensity. Shocked, he
quickly suppressed it. He had not felt the least
twinge of desire for a woman since Emmaline's illness began. Shaken and disgusted, he cleared his
throat.

She turned and looked at him in surprise. Michael
also turned, and the smile on his face immediately
vanished. His eyes were slightly fearful, as if he felt
he had been caught doing something wrong.

"What are you looking at?" Nathan asked awkwardly, feeling like an intruder.

"Come and see," she said coolly. The look she
gave him was condemning, and the guilt he felt suddenly doubled in intensity.

He walked to the window and looked down.
There was an ugly little dog on the street, holding a
small stick in its mouth as it sat looking at them.
The animal was mangy and thin, its matted fur
caked with filth. It flipped the stick up into the air
and flew up to catch it. Then it looked at them again
and wagged its tail. She and Michael began to laugh,
a light, musical sound that sparked something within
Nathan, something distant and unfamiliar. He stared
at her in awe. Last night she had been desperate
enough to kill herself. Now she stood beside his son
bathed in sunlight and laughing at the antics of a
filthy street dog.

"He looks hungry," Michael observed sympathetically. He looked up at Nathan, his blue eyes wide and uncertain. "Can we bring him in and feed him?"

His gaze shifted from his son to her, mystified by the effect she was having on the boy. Of course they couldn't take him in and feed him. God only knew what diseases the mangy little cur was carrying. The dog began to chase its tail, and she and Michael laughed again. The sound filled him with unexpected pleasure. But he did not want a dog in the house. He cursed silently and reminded himself why he was here. He must tell her to get dressed because Archibald would be back shortly to take her to an institution. Which was for the best. He scowled. He tried to imagine her receiving the tender care of doctors and attendants, but all that came to mind was her locked in a place with men and women whose minds were broken, who screamed, raved, and tore at their hair. He had heard terrible stories of these places, of patients being strapped down, fed by brute force, even of the women being abused. Christ. What was he thinking? He could no more send her to an institution than he could have stood by and allowed her to drown. He looked down at Michael, whose eyes were filled with longing and disappointment, as if he already knew his father was going to refuse his small request. When had his son started to look at him that way?

"I think you will find a little dog is really no trouble," she informed Nathan testily, as if daring him to contradict her. She glared at him, and her eyes were filled with reproach.

He looked at her in disbelief, feeling himself being manipulated. What on earth did she think she was doing? "One meal," he said finally, totally bewildered by his decision. "He can come in and have one meal."

Michael's face suddenly beamed with childish delight. He raced out of the room, shouting for Preston.

She gave him a faint smile of victory, and then her expression became hard. "What did the doctor say?" she demanded, ready to tell him she would never allow him to have her institutionalized.

He hesitated. He had come here to tell her he was sending her away. Which Archibald had insisted was for the best. Yet somehow he could not do it. He knew he had no right to keep her here, especially if she did not want to stay. But by saving her he had accepted responsibility for her welfare. If not for him, she would be dead. Yet here she was, gloriously alive and wrapped in sunlight, every inch of her pulsing with warmth and challenge. He sighed. He would continue to watch over her, he decided, wondering what madness was making him do this. Just until her memory returned, he assured himself firmly. Then he would happily release her to the care of her family.

"He said your memory will return in a few days," he lied. "Until then, you will remain here, as my guest."

She stared at him in shock. He was not sending her away, yet she knew that was what his doctor had wanted. Instead he was inviting her to remain here. He had stated it more as an order than an invitation, she reflected petulantly, but given her limited choices at the moment, staying here was profoundly more appealing than going to an asylum or running away. "Very well," she agreed stiffly.

He regarded her a moment, with the sunlight streaming through her hair and gown, creating an aura of gold around her. "Celeste," he murmured. "I shall call you Celeste." Another surge of desire

roared through him, heating his blood. He turned
abruptly and headed for the door, suddenly desperate to distance himself from her. "In the meantime
we better get a dressmaker in here and order you
some clothes," he grated out thickly before closing
the door behind him.

THREE

*H*e would not permit her to interfere with his routine, he reminded himself as he pulled on his gloves. He would pay her a brief visit before he went out, just to make certain she was comfortable. And then he would bid her good night, instructing her to ask Preston if she needed anything. If she expected him to stay in with her, it was simply not possible. Since the end of the Revolutionary War, Boston's stagnant economy had started to experience a resurgence, but one had to be shrewd and determined to make a new shipping company successful. Opportunities were abundant, but they waited for no one.

He rapped on her door twice. No response. She was probably sleeping, but the need to be sure she was all right outweighed his ability to simply leave. He turned the latch and quietly pushed the door open, hoping he would not disturb her.

She was not there.

Panic gripped him, irrational perhaps, but there

nonetheless. She had attempted to kill herself last night. He did not know what might trigger her to try again. When she lay in his bed he felt a measure of control over her safety. But at this moment he did not know where she was. He whirled from the room.

"Preston!" he shouted as he raced down the staircase, his massive black evening cloak billowing out behind him. "Preston!"

Preston appeared at the foot of the stairs. "Sir?"

"Where the devil is Miss . . .?" He paused, realizing he had not given her a last name.

"Miss Celeste is in the salon with Master Michael," Preston informed him.

"I see," said Nathan. He felt slightly foolish. "I wish to bid them good night," he explained.

"Of course, sir," said Preston blandly, as if seeing his employer practically fly down the staircase were perfectly normal. "This way."

He led him to the salon and opened the door. Nathan stepped inside and frowned.

All the furniture had been moved to the sides of the room, creating a huge open area before the fireplace. Michael and Celeste were sprawled on the carpet playing with the little dog from the street, who had been washed and brushed and now looked relatively presentable. Celeste was trying to get the dog to speak, using a small biscuit as incentive. The dog accommodated her with three sharp barks. Then he spun around in a circle and leaped over Michael with amazing height and agility. Celeste and Michael burst into laughter. The dog came running up and stood in front of Nathan with its tail wagging.

"He wants to introduce himself to you," explained Celeste. "His name is George."

Nathan frowned as he looked down at the dog.

"How do you do, George?" he muttered, feeling totally ridiculous.

Michael giggled. "Now you must pat him," instructed Celeste.

Nathan lifted one brow and regarded her incredulously. She raised her chin and watched him calmly, waiting for him to comply. He sighed, bent down, and awkwardly tapped the dog twice on the head. George accepted this and then raced across the room to sit beside Michael.

"Isn't he smart, Father?" Michael asked, his little voice beaming with pride as he stroked the mangy creature.

"Utterly brilliant," Nathan agreed.

Satisfied that Nathan had made an effort to show Michael he accepted George's presence, Celeste stood and brushed the wrinkles from her gown. "Now that you are here we can eat," she declared.

Nathan watched in surprise as she moved to a small oval table that had been carefully laid for three. A collection of silver serving dishes was being warmed by low candles, and Celeste began to lift the covers, releasing the delicious aroma of veal roast in pastry, artichokes with butter sauce, and potatoes mashed with pepper and cream. The wonderful scent of the hot food mixed with the informal warmth of the room, awakening an unbidden desire to stay.

"I am afraid I did not expect—"

"I told you he would not eat with us," Michael pointed out to Celeste. "He always goes out at night." His tone was neither accusatory nor upset, simply accepting.

Celeste looked up at Nathan, her eyes glittering with disapproval. During her time spent with Michael today he had told her his father never dined at home, or ever spent more than a few moments with him. She found Nathan's lack of interest in his son

appalling, especially since the child did not have a
mother to make up for his father's neglect. "You are
going out?" she asked, her tone challenging.

Nathan did not know whether to be amused or
annoyed. What exactly was she trying to do? Was
she trying to make him appear uncaring in front of
his son? He saw Michael staring at him, his expression vaguely hopeful. The conflict within Nathan
deepened. He was on the verge of obtaining an important contract with a merchant who was willing to
invest in his company if Nathan's ships could transport his goods to and from the Orient. He felt certain he could close the deal tonight over a game of
cards and a bottle of brandy. But oddly enough, he
suddenly did not want to go. He was not sure if it
was the warmth of the room, the smell of the food,
or the presence of that ridiculous little mongrel, but
for the first time in two years he suddenly found he
wanted to spend an evening in his own home with
his son.

"My plans for this evening have been canceled,"
he announced suddenly as he swept off his cloak and
tossed it carelessly onto a chair. He gave Celeste a
charming smile to confound her. "May I join you?"

Michael looked at him in shock. "You are going to
stay?"

Nathan stripped off his gloves and dropped them
onto his cloak. "Yes."

His son's face glowed with delight, and Nathan
experienced a warm flow of pleasure. He thought he
saw Celeste's mouth curve into a faint smile of triumph, but he could not be sure. He seated her and
then took the chair across from her, with Michael
sitting between them.

"It would appear George is staying for more than
one meal," Nathan observed dryly. Michael had just

gone off to bed with George trotting behind him. Nathan poured Celeste another glass of wine and sat opposite her before the fire.

She twirled the crystal stem of her glass between her fingers. Her plan to have Nathan spend an evening at home with his son had been a great success, but now that they were alone she found herself feeling somewhat ill at ease. "Do you mind, terribly?"

"I do not believe animals belong in a house," Nathan told her firmly. He recalled the delighted face of his son as he played with the scruffy little dog. "However," he mused, "I suppose I am willing to make an exception."

He saw her smiling faintly into her wineglass, and he was strangely content that he had pleased her. He leaned back in his chair and studied her. She wore a gown of emerald silk, which was cut low over her breasts, then tapered to a narrow waist before flaring out in a generous puff of skirts. The color contrasted with her magnificent auburn hair, making it look more red than brown. She had pinned it in a loose arrangement that allowed several curls to spill down and brush against the creamy skin of her shoulders. She regarded him with her enormous amber eyes, and he found himself wishing he could reach out and touch her cheek, which he knew was soft and smooth like the finest—

"Do you like it?"

He cleared his throat, startled by her question. "Do I like what?"

"The gown," she clarified, feeling warm and embarrassed by his intense scrutiny of her. "The dressmaker brought several with her when she came today, and I chose this along with several others."

"It is very nice," he replied thickly. He took a heavy swallow of wine and fastened his gaze on the fire.

Uneasy silence stretched between them. Celeste was not certain what had created this awkward tension. "Michael looks very much like his mother," she remarked conversationally, trying to fill the void.

In that instant Nathan's face was shadowed with a grief so excruciating it hurt her to look at him. And then it was gone. His expression was once again closed, revealing nothing of what he was feeling.

"Yes," he agreed curtly.

She had not expected his pain to be so great. But knowing it was explained a great deal about why he did not like to be at home. "Tell me about your shipping company," she began again, changing the subject.

He sipped his wine and stared thoughtfully into the flames of the fire. "Many have said I am insane to start it at this time," he admitted, his voice edged with contempt. "Since the Revolution, Boston's maritime trade has suffered tremendously. We no longer have the protection of the British navy, and England makes it virtually impossible for American ships to trade in English ports." He took another swallow of wine. "But Europe is not the entire world. There is a vast market waiting to be tapped in the Orient. If we are smart enough to focus our energy there, Boston will regain its status as the greatest shipping port in America."

She could not help but be impressed by his confidence and commitment. "How many ships do you own?"

"Three at the moment. But," he continued, his voice filled with determination, "I have only just begun."

Celeste thoughtfully sipped her wine. It was clear Nathan's shipping company was of supreme importance to him. "Is that why you go out every night? Because of business?"

He nodded. "As ridiculous as it seems, much can be accomplished over a drink and a friendly game of cards."

"I see." Although his business was important to him, somehow she did not believe this was the sole reason he chose to avoid his home and his son night after night. "Is that why you were out last night?" she persisted.

Last night. The memory of her standing alone on that bridge, a fragile shadow against the rain, filled him with a mixture of fear and protectiveness. He did not fully understand how he came to be there at that moment, ready to plunge in after her, to pull her to the surface and force her to breathe, even though she did not want to. He never drank to excess when he was out. And he never walked home, especially in the middle of the night during a goddamn storm. It was incredible, really. Yet if he hadn't been there, she would be lying at the bottom of the Charles River tonight, instead of sitting in that chair across from him, warm and soft and inviting, with her magnificent hair promising to tumble any moment onto her shoulders and the fire dancing across her exquisite face in ribbons of apricot light.

"Yes," he answered hoarsely.

She stared at him, fascinated by the dark intensity of his eyes. His face was sculpted of shadows and light, and he was studying her as if she were some great mystery that had to be solved. She did not turn away, but allowed herself to contemplate the rugged line of his jaw, the fine shape of his nose, the deeply etched lines across his brow, indicating countless hours of anxiety, anger, and pain. His skin was dark and smooth, and she felt herself grow warm as she realized she longed to reach out and touch him with her fingertips, to lightly stroke his brow and ease away some of the tension that caused him to frown almost constantly. He was frowning now, but she knew it was not out of anger or pain. No, this was different, the look he gave her was brooding, searching, and somehow vaguely predatory, causing her stomach to quicken and her blood to flow like hot lava through her veins.

He slowly put down his wine and leaned forward in his chair, moving closer to her, his eyes holding her captive with a mysterious power she did not understand. And then suddenly his lips were on hers, warm, firm, demanding, causing her heart to flutter like the wings of a frightened bird. He wrapped his strong arms around her and pulled her toward him until she was perched on the edge of her chair, forcing her to lay her hands against his massive chest for support. His lips moved hungrily over her as she clung to him, breathless, uncertain, too overwhelmed by the incredible sensations sparking to life within her to question if it was right. His tongue traced a slow, wet line along the seal of her lips, and then gently slipped inside, causing hot, liquid pleasure to burst into flames within her. She wrapped her arms around his neck and moved off the chair until she was kneeling at his feet, intoxicated by the closeness of him, by his clean masculine scent, by the rough feel of his skin against her cheek, by the solid layer of muscle that lay taut beneath his evening jacket. She kissed him back as thoroughly as her rapidly awakening passion demanded, not caring whether it was wise or not, not caring about anything beyond this moment and how wonderfully, marvelously, incredibly alive and safe she felt, wrapped in Nathan's strong arms before the fire.

Nathan felt himself falling, down and down and down, into an oasis of color and warmth and light he had not believed he would ever experience again. The desire pounding through him was uncontrollable, causing him to forget everything as he plunged his hand into the softness of Celeste's hair and plucked out the pins like petals from a flower, freeing the silken mass to tumble wildly onto her shoulders. He kissed her deeply as his fingers threaded through the auburn cape, marveling at its weight, its silky texture, its glorious, summer-sweet fragrance. And then his fingers grazed her bare shoulder and he was lost, lost to the velvety warmth of her creamy skin, smooth and supple and pulsing with life, begging to be touched. He followed her shoulder to her delicate collarbone, as fine and fragile as a porcelain figurine, and then he moved down, sweeping over the lush roundness of her breast, letting it fill the cup of his hand, driving him mad with the barrier of silk that kept him from knowing the coolness of her skin against the heat of his palm. She moaned softly and pressed herself even closer to him, offering herself, and he wanted to take her there before the fire, as he had with Emmaline, that cool autumn evening when they were first married, and she, too, had been glowing with youth and beauty and life—

He stopped. A sickening wave of guilt and despair washed over him, nearly choking him with its intensity.

"Forgive me," he stammered hoarsely as he pulled away from her. She stared up at him, her amber eyes liquid with desire, her brow raised in confusion. She was utterly magnificent with her hair falling wildly about her shoulders and her lips rosy and moist from his kisses. He stood and moved away from her, trying to put distance between them, unable to understand how she had been able to arouse this incredible need within him that had been dormant for so long.

"I should not have touched you," he managed

harshly, moving toward the door. He had to get away from her. He had vowed to take care of her, not seduce her for his own pleasure. For God's sake, he did not even know who she was. "It will not happen again," he swore. He allowed himself one last look at the sight of her kneeling before the fire, all softness and heat and awakening sensuality, and felt himself harden with a speed and intensity that was appalling. "Good night, Celeste."

He closed the door and retreated down the hall, wondering grimly how much brandy it would take to make him forget how very much he wanted her.

FOUR

Darkness surrounded her, black, cold, and end-less. She was running down a narrow, twisting street that was slick with rain. Her heart pounded wildly in her chest and her breath came in shallow gasps, but still she ran, knowing if she stopped he would find her. The street began to grow shorter and the rain fell harder, weaving a heavy, gray curtain around her until finally she could not see. Her foot touched something. She looked down and saw a man lying on the ground, his head surrounded by a crim-son pool of blood. She opened her mouth to scream, but no sound came out; instead she heard someone laughing in the distance, harsh, mocking, threaten-ing. She tried to run again, but her legs had become leaden and would not move. The laughter grew louder, closer. She closed her eyes and began to fall, down and down into an icy black void. Her breath-ing slowed and her heart grew still. Everything was cold and dark and hopelessly silent. Suddenly strong arms were wrapping around her, pulling her up from

*the darkness and the cold, away from the danger and
into a place that was warm and safe and filled with
glorious light.*

"Look what I found!"

Celeste stirred slightly and opened her eyes. Michael's small hand was directly in front of her face,
exhibiting an enormous, wriggling black bug.

"Michael!" she gasped, startled out of her wits.

"Can I keep him?" he asked with excitement. The
ugly creature began to take a leisurely stroll along
his sleeve.

She shook her head. "He won't live if you keep
him," she explained. "He needs to be outside with
the trees and grass and all the other bugs." She
watched his little face fall with disappointment.
"However," she quickly amended, "if you like you
may keep him long enough to show him to your father."

Michael hesitated a moment and then released the
bug onto the ground. "That's all right," he said quietly. "It might be too long for him to wait." He
turned and began to walk toward the back of the
garden with George following at his heels.

Celeste sighed. Neither she nor Michael had seen
Nathan for the past two weeks. Celeste knew he was
purposely avoiding her, but that did not explain why
he did not take time to see his son. At the end of
each day when she asked Michael if he had seen his
father, Michael immediately rose to his father's defense, informing her that building a shipping company was hard work. While that was undoubtedly
true, Celeste did not believe this was why Nathan
never found time for him. As she watched Michael
search the ground for more bugs, she was once again
struck by the boy's startling resemblance to his
mother's portrait. She strongly suspected Nathan's
reasons for not seeing his son had less to do with

business and more to do with the fact that Michael reminded him so much of Emmaline.

According to Preston, Nathan did come home during the night, but he was always up and gone again before the household began to stir. Preston admitted this was unusual; while Mr. Barrett had taken to staying out late soon after Mrs. Barrett's death, he normally breakfasted at home and found a moment to see Michael briefly before going out. So, while Nathan had been far from an attentive father before her arrival, since the incident in the salon he had begun to avoid both her and his son completely.

Thinking about Nathan kissing her made her stomach quicken. She tried to push the unwelcome memory aside, but her mind was treacherous, bringing back the sensation of Nathan holding her, touching her, his lips moving warmly over hers. Her wanton behavior on that evening had simply been the result of too much wine, she assured herself firmly. It would never happen again. If she could only find a moment alone with Nathan, she would explain that to him, and then he could stop avoiding her. She had no interest in pursuing a man when she had no idea who she was. And during these past two weeks her memory had not shown any sign of returning. She kept having that awful dream of being chased and finding a man lying facedown on the ground, but she had no idea what the dream meant, or if it meant anything at all.

It made her uneasy, not knowing who she was or why she had wanted to kill herself, if Nathan's rescue story was true. It gave her a profound sense of powerlessness, and she found that feeling almost intolerable. But since there wasn't anything she could do to instigate the return of her memory, she decided to focus her attention on Michael. They spent every day together, and Celeste took great pleasure

in introducing him to the simple joys of searching
for bugs, lying on the grass studying cloud shapes,
and sitting before the fire spinning magical stories.
She had grown extremely fond of him, finding him
to be a shy, serious, but very bright little boy, who
worshiped his father and secretly longed for his attention and approval. It infuriated her that Nathan
thought he could simply see his son when it suited
him, which was practically never. As she watched
Michael silently prowling the back of the garden for
more bugs with George, she felt her anger harden
into cool resolve. Nathan was welcome to avoid her
if he chose, but he could not continue to ignore his
son. His wife had died and that was tragic. But it
was incredibly selfish to deal with that death by
avoiding any reminder of her. Perhaps he did not
even know he was doing it. It was time someone
made him realize how lonely Michael was, and how
much he needed his father's love and attention.

Nathan clumsily grabbed the banister and used it
to drag himself up the staircase. He had taken to
getting drunk while he was out, hoping the alcohol
would numb him to the fact that Celeste was sleeping in the room next to his. It was not working. Every night as he staggered down the corridor it took
every shred of self-control not to throw her door
open and pull her into his arms. He wanted to hold
her and touch her and kiss her until she was breathless and burning with the same desire that raged in
him. He had thought by avoiding her his need
would subside, but instead it had grown to such feverish intensity he felt he was being consumed by it.
He lay awake every night and sensed her near him,
sometimes even believing he could hear her breathing on the other side of the wall. His obsession with
her was affecting his ability to work, to think, even

to come home, for God's sake. He thought perhaps he was going mad. But he hadn't the slightest idea what to do about it.

He shut his door and leaned heavily against it, wearily closing his eyes. His nostrils inhaled the delicate, summery scent of her, a mixture of citrus and honeysuckle, so clean and fresh he could almost swear she was in the room with him. His mind swirling with confusion, he slowly lifted his lids. She lay curled in a chair before the dying embers of the fire, her red-gold hair wrapped around her like an exotic veil of silk. He knew he was probably dreaming, but prayed to God that he wasn't. And in that moment he knew without a doubt his sanity had abandoned him.

He moved toward her, slowly, not wishing to wake her, but simply wanting to drink in the wonder of her presence. She wore a nightdress of ivory satin, with a ruched white ribbon tied at the neckline, glorious in its elegant simplicity. Her legs were tucked beneath her and her head rested against her arm; apparently she had been waiting for him and had unintentionally fallen asleep. His heart began to pound against his chest as he took in every magnificent aspect of her lovely form, from the dark fringes of lashes that caressed her pale cheeks to the sensual curves of her body, soft and warm beneath the shimmering fabric of her nightgown. She stirred slightly, as if sensing his presence. Her eyes flickered open and he suddenly found himself flooded with a need so overwhelming he no longer trusted his ability to control himself.

"What are you doing here?" he snapped. He turned his back on her and busied himself with adding more wood to the fire.

"I need to speak with you," began Celeste, feeling sleepy and disoriented.

"I believe the day is a more appropriate time for us to engage in conversation," he informed her brusquely. "You may speak with me tomorrow."

The sweet smell of brandy surrounded her, and she realized he was drunk. Anger instantly flared within her, dissipating the cloud of sleepiness. "You are never home during the day," she pointed out heatedly. "And you are never home during the night, except when you finally stagger in to sleep for a few hours and change your clothes."

He turned to her, his expression hard. "And since when have my hours become your concern?" he grated out, his voice faintly menacing.

She drew back slightly, startled by his anger. He seemed different tonight, powerful and intense as ever, but also vaguely threatening, as if something within him were about to snap at any moment. She lifted her chin and glared at him, determined not to be intimidated. "You have a son, Nathan," she announced flatly. "And your son needs you."

He gave her a dismissive look as he removed his evening cloak and threw it onto a chair. "My son wants for nothing," he assured her.

"Your son wants a father," she countered swiftly. "Not just a man who provides a roof over his head and tutors and clothes and books. Michael is a lonely little boy who misses his mother and can't understand why his father is never home. He needs you, Nathan. And yet you purposely avoid him."

He narrowed his gaze on her, infuriated by her accusation. "I do no such thing," he ground out harshly.

"You do," she persisted. "You cannot bear to be with him, cannot even bear to look at him, because he reminds you so much of Emmaline."

Her accusation sliced him to the core, causing dark, agonizing guilt to flow freely from the wound.

"I don't know what you are talking about," he managed, shoving the truth to one side. "Anyway, I fail to see how my son can possibly feel neglected when he now has you to spend his days with. What the hell does he need me for?" he demanded coldly.

She stared at him in surprise. She knew he did not mean to be cruel. In that instant she realized how deeply the loss of his wife had cut into his heart, leaving it scarred and aching with bitterness and pain. She had thought he avoided Michael because he reminded him of Emmaline. But perhaps the slow, torturous death of his wife had drained him, leaving him with no more love to give. It did not matter. He could not simply abandon a little boy who deeply needed his father. And he could not depend on her to make up for his neglect.

"I will not always be here, Nathan," she informed him curtly.

Her declaration shocked him, causing him to reach out and pull her up from the chair. If she still planned to kill herself, he would lock her in a room and never let her out. His hands held her with bruising strength as he stared down at her pale face. "What do you mean?" he demanded in a savage voice.

She trembled in his grasp, startled by his fury. "When my memory comes back, I will have to leave—to return to my home and family," she managed, wincing under his punishing grip.

He relaxed slightly. She was not going to kill herself. But she would still leave him. "And is your memory coming back?" he asked, not relinquishing his hold on her.

His eyes were glittering with fury, dark and accusing. She frowned in confusion and shook her head, not understanding why he was so angry with her.

He did not release her, afraid that if he did he

would never know the softness of her in his arms
again. Of course she would leave him when her
memory came back. She would go, and everything
would return to the way it was. Michael would once
again be lonely and quiet and never laugh. The need
burning within Nathan would cool into anger and
bitter, empty longing. And he would lie awake every
night of his life, not knowing where she was or if
she was safe. The thought was unbearable.

"Tell me, Celeste," he began, his voice oddly
strained, "are you so anxious to get your memory
back?"

She looked at him in surprise, not certain she understood his meaning. "Do you not want me to
leave?" she asked in disbelief.

He stared down into her luminous honey-gold
eyes and felt desire for her flood through every fiber
of his being. Firelight was rippling across her, casting smoky shadows on the cool satin of her nightdress, making her ivory skin glow with the warmth
of a sun-ripened peach. She was small and soft beneath his hands, her slim body trembling against him
like a fluttering autumn leaf. Everything about her
was exquisitely beautiful and warm and filled with
life. He released his hold on her and reverently caressed the delicate contour of her cheek. She had
wanted to die. But he had found her and brought
her back to life. With sudden piercing, crystalline
clarity he realized he could never let her go. She was
his, and he would keep her safe forever.

"No," he murmured, his mouth descending on
hers. "I want you to stay."

Celeste's mind whirled with emotions as Nathan's
arms wrapped tightly around her and his mouth laid
claim to hers. He wanted her to stay. He had pulled
her out of the darkness of the river and given her
back her life. And now he was offering her a new

life, with him. A burst of pure joy flooded through
her, filling her with warmth and light and hope. She
threw her arms around his neck and pressed herself
against him, sighing into the possessive heat of his
mouth. His tongue twined with hers as his hands
began to roam over the cool satin of her nightgown,
gently caressing her back, her shoulders, her hips.
He pulled her down with him until they were kneeling before the fire, and his lips moved across her
cheek and down the column of her throat while his
fingers tugged on the thin satin ribbon holding her
gown closed. The shimmering fabric slid across her
skin like cool water rushing over smooth stone, until
it lay in a shallow, crumpled pool at her hips, leaving
her naked to the heat of the fire and the warmth of
Nathan's gentle touch.

His mouth rained a path of kisses down the pale
swell of her breast, where his tongue flicked lightly
over the petal-soft nipple. Then he closed his mouth
around her and began to suckle, sending ripples of
shivers cascading through her. She threaded her fingers into his dark hair as she held him to her breast,
feeling a strange, wondrous flame spark to life
within her. He moved to taste her other breast before raising his lips once again to hers, and she
found herself reaching up to his cravat and pulling it
loose, desperate to feel the warmth of his skin
against hers. He quickly shrugged out of his evening
jacket, waistcoat, shirt, and breeches, carelessly tossing them aside as she stared in wonder at the mag-
nificence of his lean, muscular body. He wrapped his
arms around her and slowly eased her down to the
floor, until they lay together on the carpet before the
fire. Celeste moved her hands over his back and
shoulders and chest, loving the hard feel of his
heated flesh, steely smooth and warm, like hot marble. He slid her nightgown down her legs and threw

it aside, leaving her no cover except the apricot glow of firelight.

"Celeste," he murmured softly as he stared down at her, "you are exquisite."

He captured her lips with his as his hands began to move restlessly over her, across the velvet mounds of her breasts, down the firm flat of her stomach, along the slender length of her legs. He traced a slow path up her silky thighs, caressing her lightly until she sighed into his mouth, and then he gently slipped his finger inside. She was already slick with hot dew, and a groan sprang to the back of his throat as his need for her became almost painful. He began to stroke her, slowly and lightly at first, causing her to moan softly and raise herself against his hand, and then his rhythm grew faster, harder. She kissed him passionately as he pressed one finger deep inside her, and then her hand began to travel along his side, grazing lightly over his hip and down his stomach before tentatively closing around him. Unbearable pleasure swelled within him as he pulled his lips from hers and began to kiss her cheek, her eyes, her throat, quickly moving down to pay homage to her breasts and stomach before pausing to inhale the sensual, feminine fragrance of her. And then he lowered his mouth and flicked his tongue inside her hot, sweet wetness, making her cry out with startled pleasure. He lapped at her delicately at first, teasing, persuading, and when he felt her soft thighs close around him, he grew bolder, tasting her and loving her until her body was writhing and she was calling out his name. Then he raised himself over her, cradling her face in his hands as he positioned himself just inside her wet heat, staring into her amber eyes, which were sparkling with life and passion.

"Tell me you are mine, Celeste," he demanded

roughly, feeling like he was losing himself to her and somehow needing to be reassured.

It was impossible, what he was asking her. Surely he could see that? Even if she said the words, how could she be certain they were true? But his request was so incredibly touching, she found she could not deny him outright. She reached up and tenderly stroked his jaw, her eyes silently telling him, *I am yours, Nathan. I am yours because you pulled me from the darkness and brought me into the light.* And then she pulled him down to her and slid her tongue deep into his mouth, dark and warm and brandy sweet. He groaned and arched his body into hers, joining her to him, filling her until she felt certain she could bear no more. And then his hand moved down to where they were joined and he stroked her, making her feel restless and hot and strange. Her breath began to come in soft little pants, her body was flushed with liquid pleasure, and suddenly she was raising herself against him, needing him to move within her. And so he did, slowly sliding in and out as his hand caressed her, tormenting her with pleasure, shameless and wonderful. He stroked her and filled her and kissed her until she was burning with a thousand exquisite sensations, lovely, torturous, frightening. And then they were all melding into one incredible flame, which grew hotter and wilder and brighter, and suddenly burst into a million stars, causing her to cling to him and cry out in wonder.

Nathan drove into her again and again, feeling her close around him like a velvet cape, and suddenly he could bear it no longer. He groaned and thrust into her as deeply as he could, pouring himself into her. She clung to him and whispered his name, and in that moment he felt as if all the darkness and bitterness within him were flowing out and being replaced

with Celeste's sweetness and light. He wrapped his
arms possessively around her and rolled onto his
side, holding her soft form against him as he stared
at her in wonder.

"I cannot let you go, Celeste," he whispered
hoarsely.

She felt her heart fill with tentative joy. Nathan
wanted her to stay. And she wanted to stay. She had
no idea who she was or what she had been running
from, but at this moment she did not care. She belonged here, with Nathan and Michael. They needed
her. It was entirely possible her memory would
never return. That thought did not frighten her. She
felt as if her life was beginning anew. Nathan would
take care of her. And she would help him heal from
the agony of Emmaline's death. She ignored the
gnawing uneasiness that lay coiled heavily within
her and pressed her lips to his, silently pledging her
devotion to him.

He lifted her against his chest, where she curled
sleepily against him. He carried her back to her bed,
carefully tucked her in, then hesitated a moment before climbing in and wrapping his arms protectively
around her.

"I will always take care of you, Celeste," he whispered solemnly.

And then, for the first time in over two years, Nathan Barrett fell deeply, peacefully asleep.

FIVE

"Michael, don't run!" Nathan shouted as his son went racing across the park with George yapping at his heels.

"Little boys need to run, Nathan," Celeste pointed out. "He will be fine."

Nathan looked at her in disbelief. "He could fall and break his neck."

Celeste laughed. "You worry too much," she teased.

Nathan frowned at her and she laughed again. He sighed. Perhaps she was right. "My apologies," he said, offering her his arm. "For the remainder of our walk, I shall try not to worry."

She linked her arm with his and they began to stroll down the mall that was part of the extensive green park known as the Common. The mall was lined on either side by two rows of majestic elm trees, which were ablaze with crimson and gold. It was a glorious day. The sun was strong and the air was sweet with the tang of drying autumn leaves.

But the most magnificent sight for Nathan was Celeste, who wore an elegant walking outfit of deep russet that made her auburn hair shimmer like polished copper. He sighed with pleasure, feeling light-hearted and carefree for the first time in years. Everything had changed since Celeste had come into his life. And after last night he knew he could never let her go. Memory or no memory, she was his, and he would make sure no one would ever take her from him.

"Celeste," he began, his tone serious, "we need to talk."

She lifted her eyes to his.

Nathan nervously cleared his throat. "I realize this is sudden, and of course you may require time to think about it, but would you do me the honor of—"

"Celeste! Father!" Michael shrieked as he raced toward them. "George ran away!"

"What happened?" asked Nathan, mildly exasperated at being interrupted.

"We were running and George saw a squirrel, and he started to chase it," Michael rushed out breathlessly. "I called and called, but he wouldn't stop, and then I couldn't see him anymore." His blue eyes began to well with tears. "I lost him," he announced brokenly.

"Don't worry," soothed Celeste. "We'll find him."

"He can't have gone too far," Nathan suggested, in truth having absolutely no idea how far a little dog could go.

"Of course not," agreed Celeste. "He probably chased the squirrel into a tree and is now looking for us. I suggest we split up and look for him. Nathan, you go with Michael back to where he disappeared, and I will continue this way in case he changes direction."

"I think we should stay together," Nathan protested, not liking the idea of leaving Celeste alone.

"Nathan, that is silly. We have a much better chance of finding him if we separate."

"But—"

"You worry too much," Celeste called teasingly as she started down the path.

Nathan sighed. He supposed she was right. "Come on, Michael." He awkwardly placed his hand on his son's small shoulder. "Let's go find your dog."

Celeste moved off the mall and onto the green, calling George's name. After a few minutes she decided he had not taken this direction after all. She was close to the edge of the Common, where it was bordered by a street, and she did not believe George would venture into traffic when he had all this green park in which to play. She turned to make her way back to Nathan and Michael, not noticing the enormous black carriage that was slowing to a halt on the street near her.

"Genevieve!" called out a man's voice. "Genevieve!"

She looked about in confusion to see whom the man was calling. There was no one nearby. Her heart beating rapidly, she slowly turned. A tall, thin man climbed out of the carriage and began to stride across the grass toward her, his brown eyes filled with anger. A streak of apprehension raced up her spine.

"Where the hell have you been these past three weeks?" the stranger demanded furiously.

Panic began to course through her, causing her instinctively to back away from him. She did not know him. She *could not* know him. But he seemed to recognize her, and that filled her with alarm. "I am sorry, sir," she began, fighting to remain calm. "I believe you have made a mistake." She started to turn away.

"Enough of your foolish games, Genevieve," the man snapped impatiently. He lunged forward and grabbed her arm, wrenching it painfully. "You are coming with me." He started to pull her toward the waiting carriage.

Celeste struggled to break free, but she was no match for the man's strength. Her mind began to swim with shadows, dark and spinning and terrifying. She did not know him, she told herself desperately. But something about him was horribly familiar, causing her stomach to clench with fear. Nathan. Where was Nathan? She closed her eyes and began to scream, feeling herself falling into blackness as the man dragged her across the sun-warmed grass.

"What the hell do you think you're doing, you bastard?" Nathan snarled. He grabbed the man and violently spun him around, forcing him to lose his grip on Celeste. Then he smashed his fist into his jaw.

The man staggered back a few steps and glared at Nathan in surprised outrage. "This is not your affair, sir," he spat furiously. He fixed his gaze on Celeste. "It is between the lady and myself."

A sickening dread rose within him, but Nathan fought to remain calm. "The lady does not know you," he stated coldly, not bothering to look at Celeste.

The man snorted with amusement. "Of course she knows me. Genevieve, tell this man who I am," he ordered, his tone vaguely threatening.

Celeste looked at him in confusion. She desperately searched her mind as she stared at him, trying to remember his straight brown hair, his furious brown eyes, the slightly crooked nose that looked as if it had once been broken. If not for his predaceous manner, some women might have considered him handsome. She turned her gaze to Nathan and Michael, who were watching her closely. Little George was standing beside Michael, his fur raised as he glowered at the stranger. Home. They were her home. She needed them. Just as they needed her.

"I do not know you, sir," she announced flatly, her mind swimming with fear and uncertainty.

The stranger stared at her in disbelief. "What insane trick is this?" he demanded, taking a menacing step toward her.

"No trick," Nathan intervened, moving in front of Celeste. "She had an accident and has lost her memory."

The man looked at Nathan, dumbfounded. Then he narrowed his gaze on Celeste, as if trying to ascertain whether or not Nathan spoke the truth.

"Perhaps you could tell us who you are, and what your relationship is to the lady," suggested Nathan, his chest tightening with apprehension.

The man regarded Celeste intently for a moment. Finally he spoke. "My name is Victor Garrick," he informed them. "And this lady," he continued, his gaze locked on Celeste, "is Genevieve Langport Garrick."

A roaring began in Nathan's ears. "Your sister?" he managed.

The man gave him a cold smile. "No," he returned harshly. "My wife."

"Drink this," ordered Nathan, handing her a glass half filled with brandy.

Celeste accepted the glass with trembling hands and numbly took a sip. She felt she was on the verge of hysteria, and only Nathan's air of authoritative calm was keeping her from screaming.

"Now listen to me," Nathan began firmly as he pulled over a chair and seated himself in front of her. "I am not about to release you into the custody of a man you do not recognize, regardless of who he claims to be."

"He is my husband," Celeste murmured in disbelief.

"So he claims," returned Nathan. "But I believe he is lying."

She looked at him in surprise. "Why do you say that?"

He reached out and gently brushed a silky lock of hair off her forehead. "I may not be an authority on the subject," he began tentatively, "but I don't believe you had ever been with a man before last night."

She colored slightly, then frowned in confusion. "How do you know?"

He hesitated. In truth he was not positive she had been a virgin last night. He had been overwhelmed by his passion and wanting to pleasure her. There was also the fact that he had been fairly drunk. But he was almost certain she had been untouched.

"It's just a feeling I have," he told her evasively. "So when Garrick comes here tonight, we shall take a look at whatever he wants to show us. But unless something there triggers a strong memory in you, there is no way in hell I am letting you walk out that door with him. Is that understood?" he demanded.

She felt tears spring to her eyes. She did not want to leave, regardless of what this man showed them. She did not want to find her old life. She wanted her new life, here, with Nathan. She carefully placed her drink on the table beside her. "I am afraid, Nathan," she admitted in a raw whisper.

He leaned forward and pulled her into his arms.

"Don't be afraid, Celeste," he soothed as he lowered his lips to hers. He kissed her possessively, surrounding her with his protective warmth and strength, heating her with his desire. She threw her arms around him and kissed him back with tormented passion. Don't be afraid, he repeated grimly to himself. Let me be afraid for both of us.

"Good evening, Mr. Barrett," said Victor Garrick as Preston escorted him into the study.

"Garrick," Nathan replied curtly. He gestured to a chair.

Victor sat and looked around in confusion. "Where is Genevieve?"

"*Celeste* will not join us until I have had a chance to evaluate the so-called proof you have brought," Nathan informed him. "If I am not satisfied by what you show me, I see no reason to further distress her. She has already made it abundantly clear she does not recognize you."

"Well, perhaps this will make it clear that *I* recognize *her*," Victor ground out impatiently as he reached into his pocket. He produced an oval-shaped miniature framed in gold and handed it to Nathan.

Nathan held the small painting in his hand and felt his chest tighten. The woman in the miniature looked exactly like Celeste. He turned it over. *Genevieve Langport, 1785*, was engraved in fine script on the back.

"This may make her Genevieve Langport, but it doesn't make her your wife," he pointed out, struggling to quell the apprehension stirring within him.

"Quite right," agreed Victor. He reached into his pocket and produced a folded sheet of paper. "This does."

Nathan took the paper and opened it. It was a marriage registration, showing that Genevieve Claire Langport and Victor Francis Garrick were united in holy matrimony on October 4, 1786, at Trinity Church on Summer Street. The document was signed by the Reverend Samuel Parker.

"It can't be," he uttered in disbelief.

"And why is that?" Victor inquired pleasantly.

Nathan swiftly lifted his head. "Because your *wife* was a virgin," he informed him casually, anxious to see his reaction.

Dark fury erased Victor's previously smug expression. He sprang from his chair and stood trembling with rage. "You bastard!" he swore fiercely, his hands clenched at his sides. "I should kill you right now, you worthless, rutting *son of a bitch*!"

Nathan calmly folded his arms over his chest. "Your performance is admirable, Garrick, but you have failed to explain how you could be her husband for two weeks before I found her, and not have managed to see to the business of consummating your vows."

"I didn't touch her because she was mourning the loss of her father!" he snarled, his voice taut with fury. "Oh yes," he continued, seeing the surprise register on Nathan's face. "Her father was Frederick Langport, who shot himself less than two months ago, just two weeks before our wedding was scheduled. Since Genevieve had no other family, we decided to go ahead with our marriage, but obviously I could not demand my husbandly rights with a bride who was so grief-stricken. We took separate rooms. Naturally I was prepared to allow for a suitable mourning period. But Genevieve wept inconsolably for days. She refused to eat. She could not sleep. Finally I sent for a doctor, who told me her hysteria was temporary and not to worry about it.

He gave her some sedatives to help calm her. But she continued to weep day and night. And then she disappeared."

Nathan felt his apprehension suddenly rush through him with sickening intensity. It was an entirely plausible explanation. But he could not accept it. To accept it meant he would have to give Celeste up, and he could not do that. "If she wanted to marry you so much, why did she run away and try to kill herself?" he demanded.

Victor regained his control and took his seat. "Genevieve adored her father," he began with measured calm. "Her mother died when she was little, and she had no brothers or sisters. Her father was her entire world. When he killed himself, she felt as if she had lost everything. The depth of her grief was almost inconceivable. By going ahead with our marriage, I felt she would be close to me and I could look after her. But I never suspected she was despondent enough to try to take her own life. For that, I have only myself to blame," he admitted, his voice heavy with guilt.

Nathan stared at Garrick coldly, giving no hint of the turmoil raging within him. Everything Garrick was saying made perfect sense. Despite his wish that it were not so, Nathan had no doubt Celeste was the woman in the miniature. And according to this marriage registration, she was married to Victor Garrick. He suddenly felt trapped, as if the walls around him were closing in. She was not his. She was Genevieve Langport Garrick, and this man had every right to take her from him. He wondered bitterly why he had allowed himself to think, even for a moment, that God would have permitted him to have something as wonderful as she.

"I have told her she does not have to go with you," he began, his voice taut, "unless you can show her something that makes her remember. And I intend to stand by that promise."

Victor stared at him in disbelief. "She is my wife!"

"Be that as it may," Nathan continued, struggling to accept the idea, "for the moment she is under my care. If none of what you show her or tell her sparks a memory within her, then she remains here. You will be allowed to visit her every day if you wish, until her memory begins to return. But she will only go with you when she is ready. Is that clear?"

Victor narrowed his gaze on him. "Bring *my wife* in here," he grated out evenly, "and we shall see what she remembers."

Nathan went to the door and instructed Preston to bring Celeste into the study. She appeared a moment later, pale but extremely calm. She gave Victor a frigid nod before taking a seat.

"Celeste, Mr. Garrick has some things he would like to show you," Nathan began calmly.

Celeste turned to Victor and regarded him with icy disdain. She did not like him. She did not like the fact that he had come here to take her away from Nathan and Michael. And she *would not* recognize anything he showed her. "Very well, Mr. Garrick," she remarked stiffly.

Victor smiled and handed her the miniature. She studied it for a moment. She turned it over and read the engraving on the back. Then she shrugged her shoulders and handed it back to him. "This might be me," she allowed, carefully hiding the spark of fear it had ignited within her. "Or it might be someone who happens to resemble me," she finished indifferently.

"I can assure you, it is you, Genevieve," Victor replied with a patient smile. He handed her the marriage registration.

She fought to control her trembling hands as she

stared blankly at the paper. Something about it disturbed her, but she could not understand why. "I don't remember you," she announced finally as she handed it back to him. "And I certainly don't remember marrying you. May I go now?" she asked Nathan, who was watching her intently. He had promised her if she did not remember anything, then she would not have to leave. And she knew Nathan would keep his promise.

"Not quite yet," Victor interjected as he reached into his pocket. He pulled out a magnificent wood-and-silver pipe, which he carefully placed in her hands. "Think, Genevieve," he pleaded in a low voice as he looked into her eyes. "Don't you remember whose pipe this was?"

Her heart began to pound faster as she ran her fingertips over the smooth wooden stem. She hesitantly turned the pipe over to examine the exquisite silver workmanship decorating the bowl. Angels. The bowl was decorated with a wreath of silver angels. Suddenly something within her began to shatter, as if she were a delicate piece of crystal that had been smashed with a heavy object. She felt herself splintering into fragments, stabbing her with painful shards as she fought to remain Celeste. Darkness, thick, black, and suffocating, wrapped around her like a heavy cloak. She closed her eyes and sobbed, mourning the loss of something she did not understand, a grief so deep and raw and painful she did not think she could bear it.

"Celeste," she heard Nathan calling through the darkness, his voice rough with concern. "Celeste!"

Slowly she opened her eyes. He was kneeling before her, his expression worried. He reached up and tenderly caressed her cheek. Hot tears began to stream down her face, wetting his fingers.

"This pipe was my father's," she whispered. "And

my father is dead." A terrible sob of grief escaped her as she held the pipe to her breast.

He continued to stroke her cheek as she wept, her tears glistening like drops of gold on his hand, her cries tearing through his heart and into his soul. He searched her magnificent amber eyes, which were filled with hopeless torment, as they had been that first moment he saw her on the Charles River bridge. And in that moment he knew Celeste was gone. He had lost her, and he had no choice but to let Genevieve Langport Garrick go.

SIX

*N*athan waited a moment for Michael to continue his story before he realized his son had fallen asleep. He looked over to see him stretched out on the carpet before the hearth with scruffy little George curled up beside him. Nathan rose from his chair and went over to them, taking a moment to watch his son's sleeping face before kneeling and gently lifting him into his arms. In a way he was sorry Michael had fallen asleep. He was actually curious to know whether the evil wizard in Michael's story ever did get his powers back.

"Excuse me, Mr. Barrett," said Mrs. Lindsay from the salon door. "I have come to put Michael to bed."

"That's all right, Mrs. Lindsay," returned Nathan softly as he held his sleeping son against his chest. "I'll do it."

He carried him up the stairs and into his room. Michael protested sleepily as Nathan undressed him, but the practice he had received over the past few nights enabled Nathan to quickly get him into his nightshirt and under the covers. Then he sat down beside him and gently brushed a pale blond curl off his forehead. He wondered absently how he could have ever found it difficult to be with his son. Since Celeste had left, he could not seem to spend enough time with him.

At first the pain of losing Celeste had seemed almost more than he could bear. For two years he had steeled himself against any emotion but the empty, bitter fury he felt over Emmaline's death. It had not been pleasant, but at least he knew he could endure it. And then Celeste burst into his life. She had shown him there were still feelings within him, feelings of love, of joy, and of desire, and she had flamed them all to life with glorious intensity. For one brief, wondrous moment he had been glad to be alive. His shroud of grief had lifted, and he had suddenly looked forward to the rest of his life because he knew it would be with Celeste.

What a fool he had been, he reflected bitterly. He should have known better than to believe fate would have allowed him to keep something as wonderful as she was. Now he was empty once more, empty and furious with God or fate or whatever it was that seemed to take such cruel pleasure in offering him love and then snatching it away again. There was also this oppressive feeling of helplessness he had come to know so well when Emmaline lay dying. The infuriating frustration of knowing no matter what he did, he could not save her.

He had never been one to accept feeling helpless, he reminded himself coldly as he adjusted the covers around Michael more to his liking. Even though Celeste had turned out to be another man's wife, somehow that did not change Nathan's desire to protect her. From the moment he realized he had no choice

but to let her go with Garrick, he had been plagued
with unease. It was as if he were still bound to her,
as if in some way she was his and therefore he was
responsible for her. Over the past few days he had
constantly questioned his decision to release her into
the care of Victor Garrick. Nathan had not liked the
man from the moment he met him, but what disturbed him more was Celeste's apparent dislike of
him. He found himself wondering if she was running away from more than just the pain of her father's death on the night he pulled her from the
river.

At first he assumed these questions sprang from
his inability to accept that she would never be his.
But the more he thought about it, the greater his apprehension became. If Celeste, or Genevieve as he
now had to think of her, had been *his* wife when her
father killed himself, Nathan would have done everything in his power to make her feel wanted and
needed, to make her realize that in time her anguish
would fade and that a life with him was worth living. And knowing how intense her grief was, he
would have insisted on sleeping with her. Not making love to her, but holding her in his arms and comforting her in the lonely silence of the night when
the loss of a loved one becomes almost unbearable.

Why did Genevieve try to kill herself that night
on the bridge? he wondered. It was a full month after the death of her father. Surely the initial shock of
his suicide had worn off by then. If she loved Garrick, that should have been enough to get her
through it. *If* she loved him. And if she truly had
wanted to marry him in the first place. This was
what bothered him. And until he knew the truth,
until he fully understood why she was so desperate
to kill herself the night he saved her, he could not

give up feeling she was still his. And therefore he had to protect her.

"Excuse me, Mr. Barrett, but Mr. Caldwell is awaiting your presence in the study," Preston announced quietly from the door.

"Thank you, Preston," Nathan returned. Henry Caldwell was the investigator Nathan had hired to look into the background of Genevieve Langport Garrick. He had instructed him to find out everything he could about her father and the circumstances surrounding his suicide. He had also told him to find out more about Victor Garrick. Nathan rose from the bed and paused to adjust the covers one final time around Michael. Perhaps tonight he would finally have some answers.

"Forgive me for disturbing you at this hour," Henry Caldwell apologized as Nathan entered the study. "But I have some information I believe you will find interesting."

"Sit down," said Nathan, indicating a chair. He seated himself behind his desk. "What have you been able to learn?"

The investigator withdrew some folded sheets of paper from his coat pocket and adjusted his spectacles. "Frederick Langport was a prosperous Boston businessman whose investments began to fail miserably some three years ago," he began as he unfolded his notes. "He was forced to borrow heavily from creditors, taking the money and sinking it into new ventures which at the outset seemed promising, but which ultimately dragged him further into debt."

"What kind of investments are we talking about?" asked Nathan curiously.

Caldwell referred to his notes. "He purchased a newly discovered coal mine which showed excellent production potential. But a few months after he bought it an explosion occurred in which several workers were killed. The remaining men believed the mine was unsafe and refused to go back to work, rendering his investment in the mine virtually worthless. It is now abandoned."

Nathan reflected on this a moment. "And this drove him to suicide?"

"Not on its own," explained Caldwell. "But every investment Langport made after that was plagued with catastrophe." He consulted his notes again. "Langport believed in the recovery of Boston's maritime industry. He financed the building of a merchant ship which would carry goods from America to various European ports, and return with luxury items to be sold here."

"That was a sound investment," Nathan remarked. "What happened?"

"The ship sank on its maiden voyage," Caldwell announced. "And took all its expensive cargo with it, as well as the lives of its entire crew."

"Christ," Nathan muttered in disbelief. How the hell could one man have such incredibly bad luck?

"There is more," continued Caldwell. "Langport's final investment was in a factory that was to produce cotton fabric. He believed as the population of America grew there would be less inclination to weave fabrics in the home or purchase them from abroad. He sank everything he had left into outfitting this factory with the very latest equipment. And then it burned to the ground."

Nathan frowned. "How did the fire start?"

Caldwell shrugged his shoulders. "No one seems to know. It began in the middle of the night. There was an old man who was hired to stay in the building at night to make sure it was not vandalized, but he burned to death in the fire."

"And was that when Langport killed himself?"

Caldwell nodded. "At that point he had nothing left. He had sold his country property, and all the artwork and furnishings of any value from his home in Boston. His debts at the time of his death were staggering. About a year ago he tried to arrange a marriage for his daughter, hoping it would ease his financial troubles, but apparently she refused to go along with it. Then, as his debts grew, no one was interested in marrying her."

"No one except Victor Garrick," Nathan pointed out.

"Victor Garrick was the man Genevieve refused to marry," Caldwell stated. "He was a business associate of Frederick Langport's. He came to Boston a few years ago. He claimed to have come from New York, where he owned several successful businesses, but I could find nothing to support this story. At any rate, he met Langport just after he purchased his coal mine. Garrick wanted to buy the mine, but Langport refused to sell. A short time later the explosion occurred and the mine was closed. Garrick then began to lend Langport money to help him finance his new ventures. As each one failed he advanced him more money, until finally Langport was hopelessly indebted to him."

A pounding began in Nathan's temples. Why would Garrick continue to lend money to a man whose businesses were failing? Victor Garrick was not a fool. He *wanted* Frederick Langport to be indebted to him. But why? What did Langport have that Victor Garrick wanted? The only thing he owned of any possible value was the title to an abandoned coal mine. But perhaps Garrick knew more about the mine's potential than even Langport. A disturbing thought occurred to him. It was possible

Garrick was involved in the catastrophes that struck
Langport's investments. Maybe he was orchestrating
Langport's downfall so he could eventually get title
to that mine.

"Who owns the mine now?" Nathan demanded.

"For years it remained in Langport's name. But
shortly before he shot himself he transferred it to his
daughter's name, presumably so it could not be
taken over by his creditors."

Unease swept through Nathan in a sickening wave
as he absorbed this piece of information. Something
was wrong. Genevieve. He must go and see Genevieve immediately. He rose from his desk.

"I made another discovery which is extremely
troubling," Caldwell continued. "You said Garrick
and Miss Langport were married three weeks ago.
This evening I went to Trinity Church to see if the
minister who married them noticed anything strange
about the union." He regarded Nathan seriously.
"He told me he never performed the marriage. It
was scheduled to take place on the twentieth of October, but neither the bride nor groom showed up.
He sent a boy to find out if something was wrong,
and Garrick penned a note to him explaining Miss
Langport had taken ill and the marriage would have
to be postponed."

Nathan stared at him in shock. He had found
Genevieve on October 19. The day she had been
scheduled to marry Victor Garrick she had been lying upstairs in his bedroom, unable to remember
who she was. The pounding in his temples became a
deafening roar as the pieces suddenly fell into place.

Victor Garrick was not her husband. He was the
man who had destroyed her father, ultimately driving him to suicide. He wanted Langport's mine,
which now belonged to Genevieve. A sickening

mixture of dread and cold, hard fury churned within him as Nathan realized what he had done.

He had sworn to protect Genevieve. Instead he had unwittingly turned her over to the bastard she had tried to kill herself to avoid marrying.

SEVEN

Genevieve laid the heavy silver hairbrush down and lightly traced her fingers over the elegantly scripted *GCL* engraved on the back. Genevieve Claire Langport. She supposed she should arrange to have the monogram changed to reflect her married status. She wearily lifted her gaze to the mirror and regarded her pale reflection intently. The dark circles under her eyes were becoming more pronounced each day. She had hardly slept since she arrived here five days ago. You are Genevieve Garrick, she told herself stiffly. You are married to Victor Garrick and this is your home. Maybe if she said it enough she might start to accept it. But instead the depression she had been wrestling with these past few days suddenly boiled violently to the surface, tearing apart the carefully constructed facade of calm she had been struggling so hard to maintain. Feeling hopelessly trapped and dejected, she grabbed the hairbrush and hurled it with all her might at the mirror, causing the silvery wall to shatter. She stared vacantly at the myriad of Genevieve Garricks trapped in each tiny fragment. Maybe Nathan's doctor was right after all, she reflected dismally. Perhaps she did indeed belong in an institution.

She could not understand why everything here was so foreign to her. Part of her memory was coming back, but its return was slow and confusing, and she could not be sure how much she was actually remembering and how much was the result of what Victor told her. He had explained that they were married only two weeks before she disappeared. During that time she had been despondent over her father's recent death and was often sedated. That accounted for why she found the house so unfamiliar, he assured her. But the clothes and accessories in this room were obviously hers. And although it pained her to do so, she found she was starting to recall memories of her father and how utterly devastated she had been by his suicide. She was even beginning to remember Victor, who had been her father's friend and business associate. Why, then, could she not recall marrying him? And worse, why did she dislike him so much?

Victor had been most understanding of her condition. He had considerately taken the room next to hers, telling her he did not wish to rush her into her marital duties until she was ready. She was profoundly grateful for that. Because the thought of sharing her body with him the way she had that glorious night with Nathan absolutely sickened her, and she had no idea why. Victor was the man she had chosen to marry. He had told her they married for love. Yet try as she might, she could not unearth any tender feelings for him. Although he was polite and solicitous with her, his presence made her extremely ill at ease. Something about him was vaguely threatening, causing her to shrink from his touch when he reached out to her. She suspected he had sensed her revulsion, but if he had, he chose to ignore it. She sighed and laid her forehead against the coolness of her palms, oblivious to the broken glass at her elbows.

She missed Nathan and Michael terribly. It was strange, but during the weeks she spent with them she had a far better sense of who she was than she did now. She had loved introducing Michael to the childish pleasures he had missed since the death of his mother. And Nathan had awakened the most wondrous, incredible feelings of joy and passion within her, making her feel thrilled to be alive. She knew she would never experience those emotions again. When she was Celeste, she had been filled with energy and purpose, and a love of life she wanted to share with Nathan and Michael. She had not known who she was, but somehow she had felt vibrant and whole. Now she was Genevieve Garrick, and she felt utterly cold and empty.

A heavy knocking on the door pulled her from her thoughts.

"Genevieve," called Victor, "may I come in?"

She hastily sat up and pulled her dressing gown closed. "It is late, Victor," she replied haltingly. "Can it wait until tomorrow?"

"I need to talk to you now," he persisted. "Just for a moment."

She hesitated. She did not want to let him in, but if she didn't it might create a confrontation and she did not want that either. She went to the door and opened it.

"Good evening, wife," he murmured thickly as he pushed past her and sauntered into the room.

The stench of whiskey emanated from him, filling her with a mixture of disgust and wariness. "What do you want, Victor?" she demanded abruptly.

He looked at her in feigned surprise. "I don't

want anything, Genevieve." His gaze moved slowly over her, openly enjoying her state of undress. "I have everything I want," he drawled with satisfaction.

She fought to suppress the revulsion rising in her throat. "I am tired, Victor," she announced frigidly. "I think you should leave now."

He ignored her and began to prowl around the room. When he came to the dressing table, he stopped and stared in surprise at the shattered mirror. He picked up one of the jagged fragments and slowly turned it over in his fingers. And then he smiled. "Genevieve," he murmured, his voice low and filled with amusement, "it would appear your temper is coming back."

"It was an accident," Genevieve lied.

"Really?" he said mockingly. "Somehow I can't quite believe that."

He circled behind her and laid his hands on her shoulders. She flinched and he responded by firmly increasing his hold on her. "Genevieve," he breathed hoarsely, moving closer until she could feel his chest pressing against her back, "your beauty could drive a man insane."

His touch absolutely sickened her, and she had no idea why. He was her husband, after all. But something within her was rejecting the idea that he should be touching her. It was intuition rather than logic, but she decided to listen to it. "Forgive me, Victor," she began, "but it is very late—"

"I have been more than patient, Genevieve," he snapped. He released one shoulder and allowed his hand to wander possessively over her. "I have not pushed you these past few days. I have given you time to accept your situation." He roughly turned her around. "But I find I cannot wait any longer," he informed her harshly.

Her heart began to pound against her chest as

panic streaked through her. "Victor, you must understand, I need more time."

His expression grew dark. "You did not need much time with Barrett," he spat furiously.

She stared at him in shock. "What do you mean?"

His lips curled into an ugly sneer. "For two years I lusted after you like a fool, thinking you were so pure, so goddesslike. I never rushed you, Genevieve. I waited patiently for you to need me, until finally you had no choice but to agree to marry me. And then I find you spreading your legs for some cretin you have known but a few weeks." He buried his hand in her hair, holding her steady as he glowered at her. "Your 'little accident,' my dear, revealed you to be the filthy whore you really are."

He released her suddenly and gave her a violent shove, causing her to stumble backward and fall onto the floor. She struggled to get up, but he was already lowering himself onto her, imprisoning her with his weight as he viciously wrenched her arms up and pinned them above her head. "Come, my lovely little Genevieve," he said, sneering. His other hand reached down and began to wrench up her nightgown. "Don't be shy. Show me what you so readily showed your gallant protector."

She struggled wildly against him, frantically kicking her legs in an effort to throw him off her, but she was no match for his weight and superior strength. She felt the roughness of the carpet grate her bare skin as her nightdress was jerked up to her hips.

"Imagine," Victor drawled as he freed himself from his breeches, "that Barrett was fool enough to jump into the river after you." He regarded her with contempt. "Whereas I, while perhaps cheated of what should have been mine, would have been just as content to let you drown."

Genevieve's mind began to swirl with horror as

she felt him probing between her legs. Everything
was moving too quickly, overwhelming her with
panic as she tried to grasp what he was saying.
Memories began to flood through her, terrifying,
painful, angry, loving, all racing through her with incredible speed and intensity, creating a vortex of
blackness and cold and utter despair. She hated Victor. And suddenly she realized she had *always* hated
him. In that instant her mind cleared and she was
standing on the bridge staring at the river, afraid to
die, yet knowing she could not bear her life one second longer. She opened her mouth and began to
scream, a scream born of agonizing desperation and
unmitigated fury, and somewhere through the
scream she could hear Victor laughing.

A terrible roar of rage suddenly filled the room,
and in one violent motion Victor's heavy weight was
torn off her. Genevieve opened her eyes to see Nathan smash his fist viciously into Victor's startled
face. Victor let out a sharp yelp of pain as a scarlet
fountain of blood spurted from his broken nose.

"You cowardly *son of a bitch*!" Nathan snarled
with murderous fury. Never in his life had he been
so consumed with hatred and rage. He held Victor
by his shirtfront, pulled his fist back, and smashed it
into his face a second time, relishing the crunch of
bone against his bloodied knuckles.

"No more!" shrieked Victor meekly.

Nathan regarded the sniveling little bastard with
contempt. He wanted to beat him to a crimson pulp,
but for the moment he was more concerned about
Genevieve. "You sicken me," he ground out with
disgust. He abruptly released his hold on Victor and
turned to Genevieve.

She had pulled herself up off the floor and was
standing by the bed, watching him dazedly. He held
one hand out to her, but she did not go to him. Her

eyes were huge with confusion and fear. "It's all right, Genevieve," he soothed. "I—"

Suddenly a chair smashed against his back, cracking into his ribs with savage force. Nathan let out a soft curse and turned, but Victor was ready for him. He brought the chair crashing over Nathan's head, momentarily stunning him.

"This is not your affair, Barrett," Victor spat fiercely as he dropped the chair. He dabbed at the blood leaking down his face with his shirtsleeve. "How I treat my wife is entirely my own business. Now get the hell out of my house."

With a roar of fury Nathan straightened up and threw his entire weight against him. The two men fell to the floor and began to roll, groping and clawing, knocking over furniture as each struggled to gain the advantage. Nathan grasped at Victor's neck, wrapped his hands firmly around his throat, and then rolled onto him, pinning him helplessly against the floor.

"*She is not your wife, you spineless bastard,*" he grated out savagely. Burning with rage, he began to squeeze, tightening his grip as Victor tried in vain to throw him off. He watched with cold indifference as Victor's eyes widened, first in surprise, then with fear. He held him down as brutally as Victor had held Genevieve down, feeling a kind of hopeless, bitter revenge as he watched Victor realize he could not save himself now that Nathan had the advantage. His hands continued to squeeze until Victor's eyes closed. He knew he should stop, but something within him was blazing with uncontrollable fury. He could not forgive Garrick for what he had done to Genevieve and her father. Suddenly he felt a hand lightly grip his shoulder and a voice softly pleading, "Please don't kill him, Nathan."

Startled, he released his hands from Garrick's neck

and moved off him. Victor rolled onto his side, coughing and gasping for air.

"Victor Garrick, you are under arrest," announced a voice from the doorway.

Nathan turned to see two constables enter the room with Henry Caldwell behind them.

"On what charge?" Victor sputtered in disbelief.

"Kidnapping," replied one constable as he pointed his pistol at him. "You took Miss Genevieve Langport from Mr. Nathan Barrett's care under the pretense of being her husband. We also have evidence you were involved in the fire which destroyed Frederick Langport's textile factory some months ago, killing one of his employees. And we are investigating your involvement in the explosion which closed down his mine, and the unfortunate sinking of his merchant ship."

"This is outrageous!" Victor shrieked as the other constable grabbed him and roughly hauled him to his feet. "You can't do this to me, do you hear?"

He continued to protest as the officers escorted him down the stairs and into the street.

"Thank you, Henry," said Nathan. He had instructed Henry to fetch the authorities while Nathan raced to Garrick's house.

Henry nodded. "I have one or two contacts who should be able to provide me with the information we need to see Garrick hanged," he announced. "I think I'll head down to the waterfront and see if I can buy them a drink." He left the room, softly closing the door behind him.

Nathan picked up his cloak which lay in a black heap on the floor and walked over to Genevieve. He gently placed it over her shoulders and wrapped his arms around her, pulling her soft, trembling form against him. He rested his chin on top of her head and began to stroke her hair, drinking in the sweet, summery fragrance of her. "It is over, Genevieve," he told her quietly.

Genevieve stood silently in the warmth and strength of Nathan's embrace, waiting for her trembling to subside. It was almost as if she had known he would come, as if in that terrible moment when her mind took her back to the bridge, she had sensed Nathan would be there. She pulled away slightly so she could look up at him, wondering how he could possibly have known she needed him at that exact moment. Perhaps the love she felt for him somehow united them. Of course that did not explain how he had come to save her the night she jumped into the Charles River. No, she reflected, some other force had been at work that night. His eyes were dark with concern, and in that instant she was filled with a wonderful sense of belonging. Nathan was here, and she was suddenly secure and whole once more.

"I remember everything, Nathan," she began quietly, wanting to share the burden of her past with him. "I was supposed to marry Victor, but he was forcing me into it. I did not want to. But with all my father's debts, I had nothing. I felt I had no choice." Her voice was heavy with shame.

"You own a mine, Genevieve," Nathan told her as he gently brushed a lock of hair off her cheek. "The mine your father was forced to close. That is what Victor really wanted. When your father refused to sell it to him, he set out to secretly destroy him, believing that ultimately your father would be forced to sign it over to him. What he did not count on was your father transferring the deed to your name before he shot himself. The only way for Victor to get his hands on it was to marry you."

A terrible, aching loss flooded through Genevieve as she absorbed this information. "He destroyed my father because of a mine?" she whispered. She shook her head in disbelief. "I should have married him a year ago when he first asked me," she stated bitterly. "If I had married Victor then, he would have cleared my father's debts. He could have had his damned mine. And I would still have my father," she finished brokenly, her voice laden with guilt and sorrow.

Nathan stared down at her, his heart aching. He felt lost, uncertain what to do. He had come to love this magnificent woman as Celeste, and he still loved her, whoever she was. But now that she had her memory back, he had no idea what her feelings were for him. When he first found her that night on the bridge, she had needed him, whether she realized it or not. And then over the weeks she had filled his home with laughter and light, slowly weaving her spell over him and Michael until they both needed her. He did not know if she needed him any longer. But he knew if she walked out of his life, he would not be able to bear it.

"Do you want me to take you to your home?" he demanded, his voice rough with dread.

She slowly nodded, and Nathan felt his heart shatter. He forced himself to release his hold on her, setting her a step away from him. He knew he had to let her go. His heart began to weep, and the pain was so great he wanted to die. But he knew he would not die, and somehow that made it even worse. He had hoped she might have come to love him the way he loved her. Perhaps, for a brief, shining moment, when she had been Celeste, she had. In the years to come he would tell himself this was so.

"Do you know where your home is?" he asked hoarsely, his mind black with loss.

She drew her brows together, as if she was surprised by his question. Then she took a step toward him, looped her arms around his neck, and pressed herself against the length of him. "With you," she answered simply. She gave him a tender smile.

Nathan looked down at her in disbelief. Then he lowered his head and took her lips in his, knowing in that moment that the glorious light flooding into his heart was there to stay.

Karyn Monk is a gifted author whose first romance SURRENDER TO A STRANGER has just been published. She is called "a remarkable new voice in historical romance" by the nationally best-selling Jane Feather.

The Trouble

with

Angels

Elizabeth
Thornton

Lady Hannah Marchmont stood at the long window of the dimly lit study and looked down on the scene below. It was three o'clock in the morning, though no one would have known it from the crush of carriages and sedans that choked the street, as well as the throng of masked ladies and elegant gentlemen who were coming and going through the front doors of the house. Gaming houses, Hannah had discovered, especially magnificent places like this one, were as quiet as churches until the wee hours of the morning. That's when respectable balls and parties came to an end, and society matrons and their dutiful daughters trooped home to their beds. That's when their menfolk and the more dashing ladies of their acquaintance began a round of less innocent pleasures, pleasures that the granddaughter of a duchess should know nothing about. And she wouldn't have known anything about them if her grandmother hadn't sent her to Aunt Patty's in

London, as a last resort, to find herself a husband. Instead of finding a suitable husband to bring home to her grandmother—perish the thought!— she'd found Flynn and adventure with the fast set. That's why she was here now.

When she thought of the coming interview, a quiver of alarm danced along her spine. By sheer force of will, she shook off her fear. She must appear calm and in command of the situation. To show weakness with Flynn was to invite failure, and that was something she refused to accept. The stakes were too high. Besides, what could he do to her? If he wanted to see a penny of the money she owed him, he must do as she asked.

He was keeping her waiting on purpose, that aggravating man, anticipating, no doubt, that she would be reduced to a quivering mass of jelly by the time he got around to seeing her. It was a tactic to which she had become inured through long association with her grandmother. Intimidation never worked on Hannah Marchmont, but only provoked her to give as good as she got.

To divert her thoughts, she began to take stock of her surroundings. Gaming, evidently, was a lucrative business. The candelabra on the desk and mantelpiece were sterling silver; the paintings on the walls were by masters whose names were well-known to her; the carpet beneath her flimsy satin slippers was Persian; and the furniture was good, solid English oak. The duchess would have approved of this restrained masculine sanctuary. What puzzled Hannah was the row upon row of leather-bound books that lined the walls. She would never have taken Flynn for a literary man.

Richard Flynn, or simply Flynn, as everyone called him, always made her think of pirates and sailing ships. She could quite easily picture him climbing the rigging with a flat-edged sword between his teeth, or forcing some poor wretch (such as herself) to walk the gangplank into a shark-infested sea. He was the sort of man whom, in her own little village of Warwick Campden, mothers would warn their daughters to avoid like the plague. He made no secret of his background. From very humble beginnings, through hard work and a stroke of good fortune, he'd risen to his present position as proprietor of London's most glamorous gaming house. On the way, he'd had a varied career—pugilist, government agent, spy, or so rumor had it. What was indisputable was that at one time Flynn had been a footman, and he never let anyone forget it. In spite of this, or perhaps because of it, he was universally liked, and society hostesses vied with each other to secure his presence at their balls and parties. He rarely accepted the invitations that came his way, and Hannah thought she knew why. Flynn had a healthy respect for the unspoken rules that governed their world, and he preferred to mix with his own kind.

As she wandered around the room she caught sight of her reflection in the pier glass between the two long windows. There was nothing to be seen of the real Hannah in the elegant lady who stared back at her. Her own grandmother would not have recognized her, not with the elaborate powdered, silver wig that covered her dark tresses, and the white feathered mask that concealed most of her face. It was the disguise she had adopted to hide her true identity these last few months, ever since she'd taken to slipping away late at night to be with her friends. A month ago, when Flynn had discovered who she was, those exciting adventures had come to an abrupt end. Not one of her escorts, blue bloods all of them, would dare go against Flynn's express orders. Hannah surmised it was because either they owed him money or they feared he would banish them from his club, as he had done with her. Not to be outdone, she had found other friends to share her adventures, only to be thwarted by Flynn at every turn.

Tonight, however, she was the one who had out-witted Flynn. Without benefit of an escort, she'd talked her way past vigilant footmen and operators and in the space of only thirty minutes had managed to create quite a stir at the hazard table. A five-thousand-pound stir, to be precise. Surely that should bring Flynn running?

The enormity of what she had done gave her a few unquiet moments, but her nerve steadied when she considered her options. She really had no choice. The first step in the elaborate scheme she had con-cocted was to lose a large sum of money at Flynn's hazard table. She'd accomplished her objective. It was too late to regret it. Deep in thought now, she painstakingly began to rehearse in her mind each step of the course she had set for herself.

Without warning, the door opened, and the man himself crossed the threshold. Pirate, thought Han-nah, and felt the familiar ripple of feminine aware-ness. She was tall, but she always felt diminutive in Flynn's presence. Tonight his broad shoulders and trim waist were superbly molded by a green silk coat that was heavily embroidered with white thread on the great turn-back cuffs and the flared hem. The lace at his throat and wrists was Mechlin, as it al-ways was with Flynn. His abundance of fair hair, unpowdered, was brushed back from his broad brow and tied with a black ribbon. On his left ear, an emerald winked rakishly. His face might have been called handsome if it were not for his nose. It was slightly out of joint, having been broken several times in pugilistic contests to which, she had been told, Flynn was incurably addicted.

"If you 'ave quite finished appraising the merchandise, Lady 'annah," said Flynn curtly, "I suggest that we get down to business. I 'aven't got all night to waste on this."

He was dropping his aspirates. Quite deliberately, of course. That meant he was going to be difficult. If she had not been in such desperate straits, she would have been tempted to turn tail and flee. Flynn in a temper was no laughing matter. But she *was* in desperate straits, and she was bound and determined to see this thing through to its end.

"As it 'appens," she responded, mimicking his accent with what she hoped was droll exactitude, "I 'aven't got all night either." She went further, baiting him. "Flynn, where are your manners? Haven't you heard of amenities? It's one of the boring rules of etiquette I was taught as a child." She went on with relish, "A rich, pampered child, living in the lap of luxury with doting grandparents and an army of servants, especially footmen, to indulge my every whim." Those were the very words he had flung at her the last time they had been together.

It seemed to her that a gleam of amusement flashed in those incredibly green eyes before he remembered she was out of favor. "I take back none of it," he retorted. "You are still a spoiled, pampered child, and a willful one to boot, else you would not be here with me now."

At least he was speaking normally. That was a good sign, she hoped. "What?" She flung her arms wide in a gesture she had picked up from Flynn. "In this notorious gaming house, alone, with no one to protect me from London's most celebrated skirt chaser? Flynn, this is Hannah, remember me? When did you get to be so straitlaced?"

He smiled, a slight, insolent curving of the lips. "Since I discovered that you were not who you pretended to be, but a member of that voracious race all right-thinking bachelors heartily despise." To her raised brows, he responded, "A lady on the hunt for a husband."

Without opening her mouth, she laughed. "You and I, Flynn?" She pretended to give the matter serious consideration, then said, "I hardly think so. At any rate, I'm *not* on the hunt for a husband. Why should I be? I value my independence too much. I enjoy the single state as much as you. No, Flynn, a husband would add nothing to my comfort and only become a burden."

Flynn was not amused. "A husband, my girl, would keep you in line. You've been sailing too close to the wind, Hannah. Do you realize that if it gets out you were one of Viscount Redmond's set, you will be ruined? You'll never make a match then."

Again she laughed in that provoking way. "If you believe that, then you know nothing of the aristocracy. Flynn, I'm an heiress. For what it's worth, blue blood runs in my veins. If I were in my dotage, with a string of lovers to my credit, I'd still be considered a matrimonial prize. That's how it is in my world."

He was holding a chair for her. Mustering a determined smile, she seated herself, taking particular care to arrange her hooped skirts. She debated about removing her mask and decided to leave it on. Flynn was obsessively determined that no one should know she had ever set foot in his gaming house. Flynn took the chair on the other side of the desk. As his eyes raked over her the flat line of his mouth became tighter, and Hannah straightened her shoulders.

"Five thousand pounds, Hannah," he drawled

softly. "That's an expensive evening's entertainment, even for you. If you're thinking you can worm your way out of this little scrape, I would advise you to think again. I never allow anyone to welsh on his or her gaming debts, least of all spoiled, pampered, indulged society darlings who never think there are consequences to their actions."

" 'Spoiled'? 'Pampered'? 'Indulged'? Really, Flynn, all this flattery is going to my head."

He ignored the gibe. "When may I expect payment?"

It was time to move on to step two. She licked her lips. "Very soon, on my twenty-fifth birthday, I come into my fortune. It will be mine outright. I can do whatever I want with it. I swear to you, Flynn, I'll settle my debts then."

"How soon?"

"Three months. In September to be exact."

There was a long silence as Flynn digested her words. "Three months?"

She nodded vigorously.

Something cold and unpleasant glinted in his eyes. "You do realize that I have ways of dealing with those who welsh on their bets?"

Visions of pirates swarming over innocent captured merchant vessels floated through her head. Not for the first time she began to question the wisdom of what she was doing.

"Well?" asked Flynn.

She swallowed the lump in her throat. "Flynn, I'll be perfectly frank with you. . . ."

"That'll be a change."

"There is one small obstacle standing between me and my fortune."

"I thought there might be," he murmured.

"My grandmother, Flynn. She's determined to see me married before I come into my fortune because she knows that once I do, I'll be my own mistress and may choose never to marry. I'll be free to do whatever I want, and I won't follow the path she has chosen for me."

"And what do you propose to do when you come into your fortune, Hannah?"

She gave him a slow smile. "Why, I shall have adventures, Flynn. Perhaps I shall go on a grand tour, or become a patroness of poets and actors, or open my own salon. I might even open my own gaming house and give you a little competition. But that can only happen if I escape my grandmother's machinations for the next three months. If I do, I shall pay off my debt to you with interest. Otherwise, I don't know how I'm going to pay it off."

She paused, looking for some sign that her words were having an effect. There was a change in him, but she wasn't sure whether it was to her advantage or not. He made a steeple of his fingers, slouched in his chair, and brought both feet up on the flat of the desk, crossing them at the ankles. White silk stockings and black satin breeches were molded closely to the hard muscles of leg and thigh. The muscles flexed, and something fluttered in the pit of Hannah's stomach. She felt quite giddy.

"Now this," said Flynn, "is more like the Lady Hannah I know so well. Let's dispense with the preliminaries, shall we, Hannah? I know what you're going to offer in lieu of hard cash, and the answer is no. Delectable as your beautiful body undoubtedly is, I'm not interested. I make it a rule never to bed society ladies unless they are widows or have complaisant husbands."

For several long moments she was sure she must have misheard him, but a glance at his insufferably gloating expression convinced her there was nothing wrong with her hearing. A woman with less to lose might have been tempted to swing at that crooked blade of a nose and whack it back into shape. A woman with less control of her emotions might have been tempted to dissolve in a fit of hysterics. A woman who hadn't spent several sleepless nights concocting an elaborate scheme to achieve her ends might have been tempted to thump him on the head with her reticule. But not Hannah Marchmont. *Calm and in command of the situation*—those were her watchwords.

With a cry of rage, she lurched to her feet and swung at him with her balled fist. His hand lashed out, capturing her wrist, and she was hauled unceremoniously across the desk, hooped skirts billowing up around her. As that misshapen beak lowered, coming perilously close to her own patrician little nose, she froze.

Flynn's green eyes glittered down at her. "Don't pretend you're insulted. I know the crowd you run with. There isn't a virtuous woman among the lot of them."

"How was I to know until you pointed it out to me? They all looked like ladies, didn't they? And I don't understand why you're complaining. You were one of us, weren't you? I liked you better then, Flynn. You never used to find fault with me."

His voice increased in volume. "That's because I didn't know who you were."

"Is that why you tried to seduce me?"

He made a sound that made Hannah think of a lion with a thorn in the soft pad of one paw. "Your memory," he growled, "is playing you false. I was the one who was damn near seduced."

She tugged on her wrist, but he held her fast. "Stuff and nonsense!" she exclaimed. "You know perfectly well that I would never offer myself under any circumstances. You're just saying these things to punish me. It was all innocent fun. I enjoyed myself until you appointed yourself my cursed guardian angel, as Jack puts it."

Between his teeth, he said, "Oh, Redmond would. That's because he had hopes of bedding you, but I prevented it."

She stopped struggling. "No," she breathed. "Did he? How famous!"

When the hand on her wrist tightened cruelly, she cried out, "Have done, Flynn! I don't run with that crowd anymore. You saw to that. In fact, they refuse to have anything to do with me. I haven't a single friend I can count on. If I had, do you suppose I would have come here, to you, for help?"

There was a short, taut silence, then Flynn let her go. She lost no time in scooting back to her own side of the desk, where she glared at him in simmering fury.

"You lost that five thousand pounds on purpose," said Flynn.

She could tell from his expression that there was no point in maintaining her little deception. "Yes."

"Why?"

"I thought you would help me, if only to get your money back."

Once again, he adopted his indolent pose, steepled fingers resting on his broad chest, ankles crossed on the flat of the desk. Hannah was too angry to be moved by the creature's undeniable beauty. She focused on his broken nose and wished she could shake the hand of the man responsible for it.

"I'm listening. Out with it. What scrape have you tumbled into now?"

"I haven't tumbled into a scrape, not this time. I told you, it's my grandmother. You must know she sent me to London to find myself a husband. My time has run out. I've failed her. That's how she sees it. So now she has issued an ultimatum. Either I choose one of the local swains and announce my engagement on midsummer eve, or she will send me to live with my stuffy, dreadful spinster aunts Theodora and Priscilla in Inverness. It's all a ploy, you see, to force me to marry. But, Flynn, I'm only twenty-four years old. I haven't even begun to live yet."

She edged forward in her chair and went on persuasively, "If I can convince my grandmother that her fears are groundless, and that I've finally found myself a suitable husband, she'll leave me in peace. It's only for three months. Then, as I said, when I come into my fortune, you will receive the money I owe you, and I shall be free to do as I please."

"Hannah—" He passed a hand over his eyes. "I'm confused. Where do I . . . ?" His hand dropped away. "Oh no! Tell me you're not asking me to pose as your husband!"

"My *future* husband," she corrected earnestly. "I've thought this out carefully, Flynn. All you need do is accompany me to Warwick Campden, say how d'you do to my grandmother, and be my escort for the week of the Midsummer Festival. Then, at the ball on midsummer eve, we can announce our engagement. After that, you may return to London, and after a suitable interval I shall follow you. Oh, not that we need see each other ever again. I'll think of something to explain your absence. Flynn, I don't know why you're looking so stern. It's only for a week. Is that too much to ask?"

"Hannah," said Flynn, staring at his clasped hands as if inspiration were to be found there, "this has all the hallmarks of one of your reckless adventures."

"Is it reckless to wish to be mistress of my own fortune? You know what happens when a woman marries. Her property becomes her husband's to do with as he pleases. In that event, you'll never see a penny of the money I owe you."

"That's not the point. Even if I were crazy enough to fall in with your wishes, your grandmother would never accept a gamester for your husband."

She let out a whoop of laughter. "Oh no, Flynn. We could pass you off as ... well, the Baron Flynn, for example. You'll have to tidy yourself up a bit, dress more conservatively, and so forth. For a start, I suggest you leave off that absurd earring. And of course, no one will know you in Warwick Campden. No one ever goes there, leastways, not the sort of people you know. It's just too respectable and dull."

She couldn't fathom the odd look in his eyes, but she was aware that she had made an unwitting blunder, and she moved restlessly, waiting for she knew not what. Then he smiled, not one of his charming "Flynn" smiles that set a lady's heart to throbbing, but his predatory smile, the one he reserved for his gaming tables, just before he showed his hand and collected his winnings.

Finally he said, "Do you know why my club is so successful, Hannah?" It was a rhetorical question, and she wisely made no attempt to answer him. "I'll tell you why. Because my patrons know they can rely on me to protect their reckless, spoiled, pampered sons and daughters from the consequences of their folly. No young gentleman or lady of gentle birth ever came to ruin in my establishment. I stop them long before they get to that point. If I didn't, my patrons would soon use their influence to close my doors—permanently. They trust me, Hannah, and it's in my best interest not to betray that trust."

She said impatiently, "I don't know where all this is leading. Just tell me whether you will help me or not."

"I'm coming to that. I made a mistake with you, though I will say in my own defense that you were the one who deliberately misled me. However, either way, if it becomes known that we spent some interesting nights together—"

"Innocent nights!" she exclaimed.

"—my patrons are bound to take a dim view of it. A professional gambler and a young lady of quality? I think you understand my dilemma. I've tried to protect you from yourself, Hannah, but by coming here tonight, you have convinced me that something more drastic is required."

Now she knew what she was waiting for. She was waiting for the ax to fall. "So, you won't help me, Flynn?"

"Oh yes, I'll help you. I'll even come to Warwick Campden with you, but not as your betrothed. And once there, I shall look over your suitors and choose a suitable mate for you myself, a man who will know how to manage a spoiled, willful, pampered chit of a girl who is used to going her own way. Then *he* can play the role of your cursed guardian angel, for I tell you frankly, I've had my fill of it."

"But ... but what about your five thousand pounds?"

"You miscalculated there, Hannah. I would gladly *pay* five thousand pounds—no, double that sum— just to be rid of you. Now *this* is what we are going to do. We are going to pass you off as a *real* lady. You'll have to tidy yourself up a bit, dress more conservatively, and so forth. For a start, I suggest you leave off the powder and paint, and that absurd wig. I know this is going to be the hardest role you have ever played in your checkered career, but don't worry, I shall be right there by your side to guide you every step of the way."

"But . . ." She felt as though she had taken a wrong turn. "How can you be there to guide me?"

"I shall be your guardian angel, your *cursed* guardian angel, suitably disguised, of course."

"And what might you mean by that? What disguise?"

He laughed, obviously enjoying himself. "I'm going to be your footman, Hannah, your *personal* footman. I'll be closer to you than your own shadow. Now do you understand?"

She got to her feet and regarded him in pent-up silence. Finally she said, "A most generous offer, Flynn, but I fear I must decline it. I'm quite capable of choosing my own suitor."

"Or finding another way to thwart your grandmother?"

"Meaning?"

He noted the frown on her brow and the pinched nostrils, and he smiled in satisfaction. "I don't trust you, Hannah. Make up your mind to it. I shall accompany you to your grandmother even if I have to drag you there by force."

"By what right—?"

"Five thousand pounds, Hannah. I warned you that I never allow anyone to welsh on a bet. You've brought it on yourself."

Her eyelashes lowered, and after a moment's consideration, she gave a gurgle of laughter.

"What?" asked Flynn.

"You as my footman? My mind fairly boggles with possibilities. Are you sure you can manage it, Flynn?"

He gave her one of his shark smiles. "Why don't we wait and see?"

After he had seen her off the premises with one of his trustworthy footmen to escort her home, Flynn returned to his study, poured himself a fortifying measure of brandy, and then some, and settled himself in the chair behind his desk. There was something about that interview with Hannah that made him uneasy, but he couldn't quite put his finger on it. He thought about it some more, and then it came to him. She'd given in too easily. That wasn't like Hannah. Then what was she up to? It didn't matter what she was up to. He was more than a match for her.

Lady Hannah Marchmont, he reflected savagely, had become the bane of his existence. He'd known from the moment he'd set eyes on her at Lady Heathe's ball that he didn't want to know her. Proud, spoiled, pampered, and used to being fawned over—that's how he had summed her up, and as a consequence, he had given her a wide berth. And he would have continued to give her a wide berth if he'd had the least suspicion that the ravishing creature who had turned up at his gaming club with Jack Redmond and a party of his disreputable friends was not who she pretended to be—Anna, a French mademoiselle, dressmaker to the rich and famous, and an experienced woman of the world.

He'd been captivated by *that* Hannah. Anna was a warm, vibrant woman who knew how to enjoy life. Within minutes of meeting her, he'd made up his mind to have her. She'd proven elusive, but that had only added stimulus to the chase, as had the good-natured rivalry with Redmond for the lady's favors. He'd baited his line carefully. Anna had a taste for adventure, and who better to indulge that taste than a gentleman who was at home in every conceivable sphere of society, from the very proper homes of the aristocracy to the more questionable salons of London's infamous courtesans? She had taken the bait, but had insisted that Jack and her friends accompany them. And so had begun a series of jaunts—to cockfights, pugilistic contests, pleasure gardens, and dens of iniquity—that had damn near ended in catastrophe. Just thinking about it made him gnash his teeth.

On one such jaunt, he'd engineered things so that he had her alone in a closed carriage. The only good thing to be said of that hair-raising misadventure was that Hannah Marchmont had finally come by her just deserts. He'd been wild to have her, and damn her, she had been just as wild to let him. But some sixth sense had warned him that for all her eagerness, the lady was lacking in experience. And when she'd inadvertently dropped her French accent, he had, thankfully, come to his senses before it was too late. He'd forcibly removed her mask, but it had taken him several moments to place her. When he did, his passion had converted to a white-hot fury. As a result, Hannah's dignity as well as the rest of her had been severely shaken, quite literally. She deserved a lot worse than that for leading him astray.

That's what rankled, of course. She'd been toying with him for her own amusement, and that rackety ne'er-do-well, Viscount Redmond, had aided and abetted her just for the sport of the thing. An unmarried girl of Hannah's prospects did not make friends of men like Richard Flynn, much less embark on affairs with them. And they had been friends, or so it had seemed to him. He'd told her things about himself he had never confided to another soul. What he had received in return was a pack of bare-faced lies that had wrung his heart. Poor Anna, he'd thought, orphaned before her second birthday and raised by a stern grandmother until she was old enough to strike out on her own. Just remembering that she had damn near brought tears to his eyes made him want to wring her neck. He'd always had a soft heart, and Hannah had deliberately played on it.

After he'd found her out, he'd wanted nothing more to do with her, and had warned his employees to turn her away at his doors. Redmond and his cronies would have found themselves in the same position if they had not fallen into line. He should have known that Hannah would look upon his meddling as a challenge. She'd found herself another set of rackety friends to share her adventures. But the worst of it was, she'd used *his* name to gain entrance to the same notorious salons and dens of vice to which he had originally introduced her. After that, it was open warfare between them. He thought he'd carried off the victory until the events of this evening.

He didn't know why he was smiling. Hannah was well on the way to ruining her life. She couldn't go on like this. That girl was in sore need of a strong hand to guide her, but that hand could never be his. A gamester and a lady? They shouldn't even know each other, except from a respectful distance. Marriage. It was the only solution for a girl like Hannah, a spoiled, pampered chit of a girl who followed no rules but her own.

Abruptly rising, he strode from the room and made for the private gallery that overlooked the vast entrance hall of his gaming house. At the rail, he halted and looked down on the throng of fashionables who were moving through various rooms. It was, he acknowledged, as fine a setting as any to be found in London. In the last ten years, since he had acquired the house, he had made few changes. White marble, decorative Greek columns, crystal chandeliers, scenes from Greek mythology painted on every wall—it was a far cry from the hovel in the stews of Whitechapel where he had been born.

Though his origins were humble, good fortune had smiled on him.

He was thirty-three years old, and until Hannah Marchmont had poked her little aristocratic nose into his affairs, he'd been happy with his lot. He *was* happy with his lot, he assured himself. He was proud of what he had accomplished, of who and what he was. He should be. Gaming had brought him more wealth than he knew what to do with. He'd invested in trading companies and properties in far-flung corners of the world. There was a house in Richmond and a plantation in the Carolinas. There was one thing, however, that his wealth could not do for him. It could not make him acceptable as a husband for the granddaughter of a duchess.

Not that he cared. Marriage was quite decisively not in his cards. He enjoyed the carefree life of a bachelor. He never lacked for female companionship. In fact, there were more women eager to bed him than he could possibly accommodate. They didn't find fault with his mode of dress, or try to change him. They were more than happy to accept Richard Flynn as he was. As for the fact that he'd been celibate since he had met Hannah, that was of no consequence. He'd been too busy to indulge himself. His gaming house and business ventures took up an exorbitant amount of time, as had that bothersome chit who was well and truly on the road to ruin. And he would have left her to it, so he told himself, if he had not felt responsible for whetting her appetite by introducing her to a side of London she should know nothing about.

Midsummer eve. That was less than two weeks away. On midsummer eve, Hannah would announce her betrothal to some suitable gentleman. Perhaps then this vague restlessness that possessed him would come to an end and he could move on with his life.

A moment later his lips were twitching. He was thinking of how much he was going to relish his role as Hannah's cursed guardian angel.

Three days later, as previously arranged, Flynn arrived with a hired chaise to conduct Hannah home to Warwick Campden. The plan was that he and Dennis, one of the young footmen from his gaming house, would pass themselves off as crack shots whom Hannah had hired for protection on the long journey. Once they reached Wrole, her grandmother's house, they would stay on as footmen. Hannah had assured him that her grandmother would make no objection to this, since footmen were always coming and going in Warwick Campden. The place was so out of the way that few remained for long.

As the coach pulled up, Hannah and two elderly ladies came out the front doors. Flynn made no move to descend from the box to assist with the baggage, but with a snap of his fingers sent Dennis and the two coachmen to the pavement where Hannah's boxes were stacked. His eyes glinted merrily at the demure picture she presented. For comfort's sake on the long journey, she had left off her hoops, and the low bodice of her plain blue round gown was modestly filled in with a lace kerchief. He had not altered his own mode of dress, quite the reverse, and he knew very well that this was bound to annoy Hannah.

He watched with some amusement as Hannah stood meekly while the lady he assumed was Aunt Patty droned on about highwaymen and the perils of traveling on the king's highways. The other lady, who put Flynn in mind of a plump pigeon, was talking to Hannah at the same time. Hannah had warned

him about Mrs. Fry. She was afflicted with a run-
away tongue that drove her companions to distraction. She was also her aunt's cousin through
marriage, a poor relation who earned her bread by
taking on thankless tasks for her wealthy relations
that no one else would attempt. Chaperoning Hannah to Warwick Campden was evidently one of
those thankless tasks. As the twittering went on and
on Flynn shook his head, marveling that the duchess
could have been so hen-witted as to put a girl of
Hannah's mettle in the care of these two ninnyham-
mers. In his opinion, it was asking for trouble, and
trouble is what they had got.

When Aunt Patty's harangue came to an end and
the farewells were spoken, Hannah turned to go into
the coach. Her face was hidden from Flynn by the
broad brim of her straw bonnet, but he willed her to
look up. She didn't disappoint him. The hat brim
tilted and her dark eyes lifted to meet his. Her
glance roved over him, taking in his unabashed sar-
torial splendor, and those soft brown eyes began to
sizzle. She turned aside to assist her companion into
the coach, and after following Mrs. Fry in, Hannah
shut the door with a decided snap.

Flynn stretched his arms above his head and gazed
up at the cloudless sky with a big smile on his face.
He felt strangely exhilarated, and decided, in some
surprise, that he was looking forward to the next
week with an anticipation he had not experienced in
a long, long time.

They stopped for the night at the Saracen in High
Wycombe. Hannah would have preferred to push on
to Speen, but at the posting houses along the way,
Flynn had heard that on the morrow there was to be
a prizefight at Speen, and the place would be swarming with company that was not fit for ladies. He had

called a halt. Mrs. Fry, who was very vague about Flynn's position in their entourage, but who recognized him as the leader, complimented him warmly on his foresight. Hannah threw him a dark look, which he returned with an unrepentant grin. They both knew why he had called a halt. One way or another, Flynn was going to attend that pugilistic contest, but not in the company of Hannah Marchmont, not this time.

When she came down for breakfast the following morning, it came as no surprise to find the underfootman waiting for her with a note from Flynn. Dennis, a young lad of about twenty, by Hannah's reckoning, blushed to the roots of his red hair as he handed her the note. One of the wheels of their chaise, Flynn wrote, had buckled and it would be some time before it could be fixed on account of the blacksmith having shut down his forge in order to attend the prizefight. He had taken it upon himself to travel to the next village to have the wheel repaired and hoped to return shortly after midday. In his absence, he had left Dennis and the two coachmen to see to the ladies' comfort and protection. On no account were they to go anywhere unaccompanied. This last sentence was underlined.

There was no point in berating poor Dennis for Flynn's outrageous conduct. Hannah was under no illusions. She was quite sure that Flynn had buckled the wheel deliberately. "I'm sorry," she said, "that you're to miss the fight. No doubt Flynn will give you a blow-by-blow description of it when he returns."

The young footman beamed at her, obviously relieved at her calm acceptance of the situation. "If he don't," he said ingenuously, "there'll be another fight waiting for 'im when 'e gets back, and so we told 'im."

Hannah found Mrs. Fry in the dining room, where she had already ordered a substantial breakfast for the two of them. Without comment, Hannah passed the note to her. Though one part of her was vexed at Flynn, another part admired his ingenuity. He'd really clipped her wings this time. Without a carriage, she couldn't go anywhere. So far, the journey had not turned out as she had imagined it would. She'd had visions of having a grand time ordering Flynn about, and had thought him insane, even if they were only playacting, for putting so much power into her hands. Flynn, however, had spiked her guns yet again. He'd given himself airs and graces, pretending it was beneath the dignity of a servant of his exalted position to fetch and carry for her. Whenever she issued orders, he merely yawned behind his hand, snapped his fingers, and sent poor Dennis to do her bidding. There was no sport in that. At this rate, she really would find herself married to one of Warwick Campden's finest, and Flynn would walk away laughing. She wasn't going to let that happen.

As her companion began to twitter Hannah listened with half an ear. Inwardly, she was groping for a way of paying Flynn back for the awful punishment he had inflicted on her. He hadn't spent eight hours the day before shut up in a carriage with only her aunt's cousin for company. She now knew more about the dysfunctions of the human body than it was wise for a young woman to know. She had practically begged Flynn to travel in the coach with her, if only to head the woman off before she got started. He had turned a deaf ear to her pleas. And now, by delaying their journey to take in the fight, he'd sentenced her to another stretch of Mrs. Fry's incessant, boring chatter. She did not know how she could bear it. Richard Flynn must be made to see that he could not ride roughshod over her and get away with it.

"What's that you said?" Hannah asked as something her companion said registered in her brain.

"Our landlord's daughter," repeated Mrs. Fry. "She was riding pillion. I saw them from my window, and when I asked Dennis to explain it, he told me that the poor girl's grandmother, who is very sickly, lives in Speen, and Mr. Flynn had very kindly offered to convey the girl there so she could visit the old lady."

"The landlord's daughter?" said Hannah sweetly.

"A very comely young thing." Mrs. Fry's voice sank to a whisper. "Though a common piece, if you take my meaning."

Hannah could well imagine. "And she was riding pillion with Flynn, you say?"

In the same hushed tones, Mrs. Fry went on, "With her skirts hiked halfway up her bare thighs. Poor Mr. Flynn! It was a vulgar display. I felt quite sorry for him. All the postboys and ostlers were ogling the girl."

"Oh, I'm sure Flynn would have shut his eyes before sinking to that level," said Hannah, smiling, and in a voice that brought an anxious look to Mrs. Fry's face.

The waiter arrived with their breakfast, and when he moved away, Hannah took up where they had left off. In the same lethally pleasant tones, she said, "Now let me see if I have this right. Flynn was mounted, and there was a girl riding pillion behind him?"

Mrs. Fry nodded.

"And where was the wheel?"

"What wheel?"

"The buckled wheel that he was taking to the next

village to have repaired, the same wheel he mentions in the note you just read."

Mrs. Fry thought for a moment. "Perhaps one of the coachmen had it," she finally suggested.

Hannah threw down her napkin and lurched to her feet. "That," she said, and her eyes flashed with temper, "is what I mean to find out."

As she anticipated, she found the chaise with all four wheels intact. Within an hour, the horses were in harness, and they were on the road to Oxford. No one dared suggest that they wait for Flynn.

Flynn was in a mellow mood. He was sitting in the courtyard of the Red Bull in Speen's High Street soaking up the midday sun, with a sonsy lass on his knee (not the girl he had started out with) and a tankard of ale in his hand. His blunt was paying the shot, for he'd bet heavily on Gentleman Jack, one of the pugilists in that morning's contest, and he'd walked off with a packet. Every now and again, he or one of the other gentlemen who were sitting around the table would jump up, dislodging the girls who were hanging on their necks, and pantomime one of the sequences of punches from the fight just past. There was a great deal of good natured argument and much laughter, as there always was after these sporting events.

Flynn drained his tankard of ale and was looking around for a waiter so that he could order a bite to eat, when his eye was caught by a chaise and four that had a familiar look about them. As the chaise bowled past the Red Bull at a fair clip, his eyes became riveted on the red-haired footman who sat on the back perch. Dennis caught sight of Flynn at the same moment, shrugged helplessly, then waved. Flynn's brain finally unfroze, and with a muffled roar, he started to his feet and inadvertently intercepted a punch one of the gentlemen was demonstrating. It caught him square on the nose. Flynn saw stars, then his knees buckled, and he sank to the ground.

He was fit to be tied by the time he caught up with her on the outskirts of Oxford. Nor was his temper improved when the landlord of the Lion took one look at his swollen nose and blood-soaked shirt and barred his entrance. If Dennis hadn't had the good sense to wait up for him and smooth things over, he would have torn the landlord limb from limb.

"Where is she?" he demanded between clenched teeth when Dennis's explanations had finally gained him admittance. He was striding for the stairs, with Dennis hard at his heels.

"Now, Mr. Flynn, don't take on so. She left our direction at every posting 'ouse, didn't she? If she 'adn't, you never would 'ave found us. That says something in 'er favor, don't it?"

When they came to the head of the stairs, Dennis darted in front of Flynn and flung himself across a door halfway down the corridor. With his back to the door, he held out both hands to ward Flynn off.

"Now, Mr. Flynn, get a 'old of yourself. Remember who she is."

The door behind him opened, and a cool, cultured voice, Hannah's voice, said, "What's going on here? Oh, Mr. Flynn. I see you finally caught up with us."

Dennis said, "She knows about the wheel, Mr. Flynn."

"Dear, dear, Flynn," Hannah went on, "if only you had asked my permission, this little misunderstanding might have been avoided." There was a pause, then she gave him one of her close-mouthed, provoking Hannah laughs. "Oh dear, I do believe, Mr. Flynn, your nose is out of joint."

Dennis gasped. This was no way to address Mr. Flynn when he was in a temper. "Milady," said Dennis reproachfully, and got no further. Flynn grabbed him by the collar, flung him clear, and entered Hannah's chamber, locking the door behind him.

Hannah scooted to the far side of the bed. There was a moment when Flynn forgot to be angry. She was dressed in a filmy undergarment that left nothing to a man's imagination. Lush curves, supple valleys, and skin glowing like ivory satin. Her dark hair was loose and fell about her shoulders in an abundance of waves. As his eyes roamed over her, he saw the dark nipples beneath the soft material of her shift swell and harden. His mouth went dry.

Then he saw the smile on her face. She was doing it on purpose, toying with him again, goading him into making a fool of himself. Hannah saw his expression alter, and she reached for the pistol she had prudently borrowed from the landlord for this very encounter.

"If you dare lay a hand on me, Flynn, I'll pull the trigger. I mean it."

She hadn't cocked the gun, but even if she had, Flynn was in such a temper that he didn't care if she blew his head off. He flung his arms wide. "Go ahead. Pull the trigger, for I warn you now, I'm going to do a lot more than lay a hand on you."

She climbed up on the bed. "What did I do that was so bad? You're angry because for once I got the better of you. Where's your sporting instinct, Flynn?"

"I'll tell you what you did. My nose is throbbing from a stray punch that landed when I was distracted by seeing my own chaise take off without me. My arse aches from having been bounced thirty-odd miles on a nag that has yet to be broken to bridle. I'm famished, my best coat is ruined, and my head hurts like the devil. And it's all your doing, you spiteful wretch."

He had hardly finished speaking when her shoulders began to shake. She emitted a giggle, then another. That's when he dived for her. The pistol went flying, Hannah squealed, and they both went rolling on the bed. When they came up for air, Flynn was on top, and Hannah's legs were splayed wide beneath him. She was struggling to throw him off, and the friction against his groin had the inevitable result.

"Oh Jesus!" he said. "Oh Jesus! I've been celibate too long."

Hannah stopped struggling and glared up at him with loathing. "You expect me to believe that when you left with that ... that Jezebel? Get off me this instant, Richard Flynn, or there'll be another part of your anatomy that's out of joint, and that's a promise."

"What Jezebel?" He was gritting his teeth, but not in anger. She was soft and warm in his arms, and the scent of her, a subtle blend of lavender and violets, made his head swim.

"The landlord's daughter. Mrs. Fry saw you leave together."

He wasn't going to give in to his baser instincts. He just wanted to hold her. "I took her to her grandmother."

"I saw her on your knee outside the Bull when I passed in the chaise."

And kiss her. What harm could there be in one kiss? He lowered his lips to hers, not ravishing them, merely testing them. She should stop him. Why wasn't she stopping him? He kissed her again and again, and each kiss became deeper, hotter, more demanding. Her arms wound around his neck; his hands took their fill of her lush curves. They were both rasping for breath.

"Flynn, tell me!"

Tell her. Tell her what? Oh yes. "That wasn't Rosie, that was Mabel."

He was poised to give suck at one tantalizing nipple. Her fingers threaded through his long hair, dislodging his ribbon and suddenly his head was jerked back as her fingers tightened. He let out a yell of pain. She dug him in the ribs with one of her elbows, and when he relaxed his hold, she quickly slipped from the bed.

Flynn blinked up at her as though he had awakened from a deep sleep. Suddenly coming to himself, he leaped from the bed. "You did this deliberately! You were trying to seduce me!"

She stuck her nose in the air. "I like a challenge, Flynn, and you are any woman's for the taking. Go make love to Rosie and Mabel."

Flynn let out a long, relieved breath. That one careless remark had saved them both. He had the wisdom to refrain from provoking her till he had the door open. Looking over his shoulder, he grinned. "If I didn't know better," he said, "I would say that you were jealous," and he quickly shut the door against the hairbrush that came flying at him.

The rest of the journey to Warwick Campden was uneventful and they arrived at Wrole just after noon on the following day. Back in London, Hannah had told Flynn that the house had once been an abbey, and had come into the family's possession in Henry VIII's time, when he'd sold off all the church's properties to enrich his coffers. Since Hannah was the last of her line and there were no males to inherit, the title had returned to the crown. If she had been born a boy, she would have been the Duke of Wrole.

Her Grace, the dowager duchess, was waiting for them in the great flagstoned hall. She was leaning heavily on a cane, and Flynn remembered she suffered from arthritis. Her hair was pure silver, but as abundant as a young girl's; her face was crossed with tiny wrinkles, but flaunted powder and paint. One glance told Flynn that the lady was a force to be reckoned with. He sensed an ally, and that made him like her on principle.

As the ladies greeted each other Flynn turned aside to direct Dennis and Her Grace's footmen to dispose of the baggage. No one questioned his authority. He'd learned from experience that manners not only made the man but also established precedence in the servants' domain. No prince of the blood could have matched his haughty, well-bred demeanor as he commanded the servants with a word and a snap of his fingers.

Mrs. Twitter, as Flynn was coming to think of Mrs. Fry, went off with a decrepit relic of a butler. Flynn made to follow them up the stairs, but the duchess intercepted him. With a snap of *her* fingers, she indicated that he was to follow her.

She led the way to a shabby, sunny morning room done in primrose and white. At a nod from her grandmother, Hannah seated herself. Flynn remained standing while those hawklike eyes in that lined face made a thorough inspection. It wasn't the first time, by any means, that women had looked at him in that assessing way, disrobing him inside their heads till he was down to his underthings. The duchess went further. Damned if the old dame didn't fancy him!

He swallowed a laugh. The duchess chuckled

knowingly, then seated herself. At her signal, Flynn took a chair.

"So," said the duchess, addressing Hannah, "you've found yourself a real man at last. Well, don't dawdle, girl. Introduce the gentleman."

"Grandmama," said Hannah, "this is my footman, Flynn."

"Footman, my arse!" the duchess stated in her plain style. "I know a rogue when I see one. I should. I've warmed my bed with many a one since your grandfather, the lecherous sot, went to his final reward. Yes, and before that, too."

Hannah sent the duchess a murderous glare. "Grandmama!"

"Oh, don't get your bowels in an uproar, gel. Flynn is beyond shocking, or I don't know men. Who are you, Flynn? Out with it, man, and don't try to hoax me."

Flynn said, "I'm a man who lives by his wits, ma'am, that is to say, my services are for hire. Today I'm a footman, tomorrow I could quite easily be a peer of the realm. Lady Hannah engaged me to protect her until she is safely married to the gentleman of her choice."

"Protect her from whom or what?" asked the duchess.

"A most unsavory character, Your Grace. A married man who became enamored of your granddaughter and will stop at nothing to get her in his power. The man's insane, of course."

"Flynn!" protested Hannah, torn between outrage at the story he was spinning and by the notion that any man who was enamored of her must be insane.

Flynn waved Hannah to silence. "I am a shrewd judge of character, Lady Hannah, and I see that nothing but the truth will suffice for Her Grace."

The duchess digested what he had told her. "You're a sort of mercenary. Is that it?"

"More or less."

"Mmm. You're quite sure the gentleman was unsuitable?"

"Not a drop of blue blood in his veins," commiserated Flynn.

"And married, you say?"

"With several children to his credit, and not all of them to his wife." He paused, then went on gently, "In my opinion, it was a mistake to send Hannah to her aunt. Lady Patricia is hardly a vigilant chaperone."

The duchess let out a cackle of laughter. "As though I didn't know it! What you don't seem to understand, Flynn, is that I hoped if I gave the girl enough rope, she would hang herself. Not to mince words, I hoped she would return home with a husband in tow. Oh, not one of the bloodless fribbles who would find favor with her aunt, but someone she would meet on one of her adventures. An adventurous gel is my Hannah, as I think you know. What I had in mind was a real man, one who would set her blood on fire, a man of her own choice, mind you, but someone who was a match for her."

Hannah smiled sweetly. "Instead, all I brought home was Flynn," she said.

"Mmm," mused the duchess, taking a moment to look from one to the other from behind lowered lashes. "As you say, all you brought home was Flynn." There was a moment of silence, then she said, "If what you say is true, Flynn—and mind, I'm not saying I'm satisfied that you've told me everything—I think we should elevate you from the position of footman to some distant relation."

Flynn shook his head. "That wouldn't suit at all. Footmen are allowed liberties that other gentlemen are denied. No one raises an eyebrow when we enter chambers that are barred to everyone else. In short, Your Grace, we go where angels fear to tread."

A long look was exchanged, then the duchess smiled in complete comprehension. "Then a footman it is." When she turned to Hannah, her brows came down, and she rattled her cane. "Well, missie, I gave you your chance and you threw it away. I warned you what would happen if you didn't come home with a husband."

"There's still time, Grandmama. I'm hardly in my dotage. I'm only twenty-four years old."

"Time is something I don't have. I aim to see you settled before I die."

Hannah laughed. "You're a fine one to talk of being settled. You've traveled the world, had all sorts of adventures."

"Nevertheless, I did my duty. I married your grandfather and bore him children. Tell me the truth, Hannah. Are you truly resigned to announcing your betrothal to one of your suitors on midsummer eve?"

Hannah let out a long, telling sigh. "I've almost made up my mind to have Lord Horsham. I suppose he'll do as well as the next man, unless someone else catches my fancy before my time is up, and in Warwick Campden, that doesn't seem likely, does it, Grandmama?"

Flynn's eyes narrowed on the conspicuously innocent expression on Hannah's face. Once again, he felt that flash of unease. This wasn't the Hannah he knew. This was too easy. It put him on his mettle.

Hannah looked out the coach window and reflected that the village of Warwick Campden had changed very little from the Middle Ages. Rich wool merchants had built homes of Cotswold stone, and those homes were still lining the High Street in the middle of the eighteenth century. Even the customs of that bygone era still lingered on. During the week of the Midsummer Festival, every day would be marked by some tradition, beginning with the ball tonight in the assembly rooms, and ending with the bonfire on midsummer eve.

The coach turned the corner of the High Street and almost immediately rolled to a stop. Flynn opened the door and helped her alight from the carriage. Dennis ran ahead to hold the door of the assembly rooms. The duchess's arthritis was acting up and she had chosen to remain at home with Mrs. Fry, having first instructed Flynn not to let Hannah out of his sight. The advice was superfluous. Flynn had every intention of keeping Hannah on a tight rein. He'd made inquiries about Lord Horsham, and what he had discovered had relieved his mind. The viscount was young, personable, and came of good stock. His reputation was spotless. In short, Hannah was lucky to get him, and Flynn was determined she would not ruin her chances for a respectable match.

They had just entered the vestibule of the assembly rooms when Hannah caught sight of the stranger. He was in the card room, dealing cards as if he had been born to it. She had an impression of grace and virile good looks, dark hair, and garments that put even Flynn's in the shade. A pirate, she thought, and her lips turned up. As her eyes lingered the stranger turned, caught her staring, and his bold gaze slowly wandered over her before returning her look. Then recognition dawned and she turned away with a laugh.

"I didn't know he was in Warwick Campden," she said, "and I'll wager my grandmother doesn't know it either."

Tight-lipped, Flynn demanded, "Who the devil is he?"

"That," said Hannah, "is Sir Waldo Manning. I almost eloped with him once, but he was looking for a rich wife to pay off his debts, and I couldn't persuade him to wait until I came into my fortune."

"You *what*?" Flynn moderated his tone. "You almost *eloped* with him? And he *told* you he couldn't wait till you had come into your fortune?"

"To be fair, he was letting me down gently. I was only twelve at the time." A trace of a smile touched her mouth. "He was my first love, and I never quite got over him."

Flynn said dryly, "Even at twelve, you were a precocious chit. Hannah, the man's forty if he's a day."

"He was only in his twenties when I knew him. And he's a well-preserved forty. I don't think he recognizes me. Well, he wouldn't, would he? It happened such a long time ago."

Flynn didn't like the soft look in her eyes and couldn't keep his annoyance from showing. "I presume he married his rich wife?"

"He eloped with an heiress and they settled in the West Indies. My heart was broken, of course." With a soft sigh, she turned to face him. "A week later I met a Gypsy boy, and my heart mended."

Flynn would have laughed if he hadn't seen the way Sir Waldo was studying Hannah. "Where is Lady Manning?" he asked.

"I believe she died last year."

"So, Sir Waldo is looking for another rich wife?"

"It wouldn't surprise me. His aunt lives in the village, and from what she says, he lost his wife's fortune in bad investments. He'll have to marry money, I suppose."

"Well, it won't be your money, my girl."

"Oh? And why not?" She dimpled up at him.

"Look at him! Anyone can tell at a glance that he's an adventurer."

Hannah peeked over her shoulder. "Perhaps," she said, "my luck is about to turn," then she gasped as Flynn caught her by the wrist and yanked her toward the ladies' cloakroom.

At the edge of the ballroom where footmen were stationed, Flynn stood sipping a glass of champagne (which nobody dared question), watching the couples glide down the length of the dance floor in a stately cotillion. Hannah and Lord Horsham were the cynosure of all eyes. Both were dressed in silver and white; both were dark-haired, though Hannah was darker than her partner. Hannah, Flynn decided, was a very fortunate girl. Not only was Perry Horsham tall, dark, and handsome, but he also had a title, and was the biggest matrimonial prize in the county. And the fact that he, Richard Flynn, who didn't have a jealous bone in his body, was seized with an almost irresistible urge to tear Hannah away and thrash the viscount to within an inch of his life truly appalled him.

He didn't abide by many rules, but one he invariably held to was to steer clear of gently bred young women who were destined for marriage. Hannah had circumvented this inviolable rule by posing as someone she was not, and he was paying the toll. He'd tasted her, touched her, unleashed the passion in her, and he burned to do it again. And the knowledge that he was aiding and abetting some other man to take what he was denying himself made him seriously question his own sanity.

"They make a charming couple, don't they?"

The husky comment came from Mrs. Fanshaw, a lady of indeterminate years, whom Hannah had pointed out to him earlier in the evening. The widow Fanshaw, as Flynn remembered. She was almost as tall as Hannah, and far more generously endowed. Her eyes were as busy as his, and told him that she liked what she saw. A distraction, thought Flynn, a heaven-sent distraction, and he rewarded the lady with one of his lazy, Flynn grins. "Very handsome, indeed," he said, his eyes boldly roving over the beauty.

One innuendo led to another, and before long Mrs. Fanshaw asked Flynn if he would be good enough to accompany her outside for a breath of fresh air, her own footman having mysteriously disappeared. What could a poor footman do? Before leaving, however, he quickly assessed the lay of the land. The cotillion would last for a good half hour. Sir Waldo was deep in play in the card room. As a precaution, he spoke to Dennis, who was in conversation with some other footmen at the glass entrance doors. "Watch her," he said, "and fetch me at the first sign of trouble."

Though the night was as hot as Hades, Mrs. Fanshaw intimated that her skin was quite chilled and would Flynn be so kind as to fetch her stole, which she had left in her carriage. The stole, not surprisingly, could not be found, though both Flynn and the lady entered the carriage to search for it. In the Stygian darkness, hands brushed against bare skin. Mrs. Fanshaw fell heavily against Flynn, and in the next instant they were locked in a passionate embrace. He felt the stirring of his senses and could have wept in relief. Since Hannah's entrance into his life, he'd begun to suspect he was spoiled for other women.

"Psst, Mr. Flynn? Where are you? Psst, Mr. Flynn?"

Dennis's voice came to them through the open window. Flynn ignored it.

"Psst, Mr. Flynn. Where are you?"

Flynn came to himself gradually and pried the beauty's hands from his neck. "My underfootman is calling me," he said.

"Let him," she purred, and drew his head down for another stirring kiss.

"Psst, Mr. Flynn?"

Again Flynn pried the widow's hands from his neck. "This will only take a moment," he promised.

She let him go reluctantly. "Only a moment, then, Flynn." Her pique was very evident. "Just remember, I don't wait on any man's convenience."

"I lost 'er," said Dennis when Flynn appeared out of the dark.

"What do you mean, you lost her?"

"She turned 'er ankle and left the dance floor. I waited outside the ladies' cloakroom, but she must 'ave come out by another door."

"Hell and damnation!" Flynn spared one regretful look for Mrs. Fanshaw's carriage, sighed, then reluctantly went in search of Hannah. His first port of call was the card room. When he discovered that Sir Waldo had disappeared also, he was practically foaming at the mouth.

Outside, couples were strolling about on the grounds of the assembly rooms. There were benches and lanterns set out at intervals along the riverbank so people could enjoy the view. Flynn sent Dennis in one direction and he took another. After twenty minutes' fruitless searching, he was coming to think the task was hopeless. She could be anywhere. Then he heard it—laughter that was not quite laughter but more a muffled, provocative siren's call. Hannah's laughter! His head twisted and he saw the line of stationary carriages along the tree lined avenue that led to the assembly rooms. A short while before he had been enjoying himself in one of those very carriages.

The thought that Hannah and Sir Waldo might be enjoying themselves in like manner sent his temper to the boiling point. It came again, Hannah's muffled laughter, and he broke into a run. He slowed when he approached the carriages. Hannah wasn't laughing now, and his imagination was running riot. A soft rustle of skirts and a woman's moan brought his head whipping around. He had them now! With a roar of rage, he flung himself at the nearest carriage door and yanked it open. As he entered the carriage there was a gasp of dismay and a gentleman quickly decamped by the other door. Flynn did not trouble to go after him. That would come later. He reached for Hannah.

"You shameless hussy!" he cried out. He quickly tumbled her across his lap and threw her skirts over her head.

"Flynn!" she squealed, then shrieked as his open palm caught her a stinging blow on her bare backside.

Her cries made no impression on Flynn. He was maddened by jealousy and he did not spare his blows, not until he heard Hannah's voice outside the carriage door. *Then* he froze.

"Flynn!" she said. "What the devil do you think you are doing to Mrs. Fanshaw?"

On the ride home to Wrole, Flynn elected to ride in the carriage with Hannah. As soon as they had left the village behind, he said, "You deliberately engineered that scene with the widow Fanshaw."

"I did nothing of the sort!" Actually, she had played a small part in things, but even she had not hoped for such a spectacular finale. "As I told you,

Perry was showing me his new team of grays." She couldn't preserve a straight face and dissolved in giggles. "If only you had seen your expression when you discovered you were spanking the wrong lady! Flynn, did you really think it was Waldo and I in that carriage?"

"It's what you wanted me to think." He stared stonily out the window.

True, but it was more than her skin was worth to admit it in Flynn's present frame of mind. "You have a lurid imagination. I didn't even know you were there." A lie, but she told it convincingly. She'd seen him slip away with the widow Fanshaw, and knew that they would soon be snug in the lady's carriage. At these assemblies, Mrs. Fanshaw invariably indulged in a spot of dalliance in her carriage with any footman who was willing to oblige. She'd been doing it for years. Hannah had also known that when she gave Dennis the slip, Flynn would come looking for her. That Sir Waldo had left early was a mere stroke of good luck.

"I shouldn't worry about it, Flynn," she said consolingly. "Of course, you've lost your new flirt, but Mrs. Fanshaw won't breathe a word of what transpired. People would ask too many awkward questions, and she wouldn't want that."

He ignored the snickers. "Lord Horsham was showing you his new team of grays, you say?"

"Shocking, isn't it, what the young blades of Warwick Campden get up to? But that's Perry for you. He was showing me his grays, and that's all he was doing."

"He sounds like a most proper young gentleman," declared Flynn.

"A regular slowtop," Hannah agreed dismally. "I tried to hint him into kissing me, but a lady has no chance with Perry when there are horses around.

Now, if I were sixteen hands high, and could carry him over fences and ditches, he would lavish me with caresses."

Flynn raised a brow. "There'll be time enough for caresses after he gets his ring on your finger."

"Now, that's where you're wrong."

"What?" He sat up straighter. "Hannah," he said warningly. The light from the coach lamp gave him enough illumination to see the glitter in her eyes and the provocative smile on her lips. "Just what might you mean by that?"

"I have decided that my grandmother is right. I can't marry a man who doesn't—well, how did she put it?—heat my blood. That being the case, I've made up my mind to put each of my prospective suitors to the test."

"And how do you propose to do that?" he asked, as though he didn't know.

She gave her siren's laugh. "You'll find out," she said, and promptly shut her mind to all his heated remonstrations. Things, she decided, were progressing rather well. Her original plan, of course, had gone by the wayside when Flynn had refused to play the part of her betrothed. It was fortunate that her plan was flexible, fortunate that *she* was flexible. It was time to move on to the next step.

The Midsummer Festival was the most notable event in Warwick Campden's calendar. It lasted for two days and was one of the few times in the year when all classes of people mixed freely together. Apprentices and their masters, maids and their mistresses—everyone left off their chores and flocked to the common, on the banks of the river, where the fair was set up. There was something for everyone—sideshows, maypole dancing, pugilistic contests, boating, as well as the serious business of trading one's stock and produce. And for a self-appointed guardian angel, it was sheer hell.

This was Flynn's thought as he watched Hannah cavort around the maypole with the young blacksmith. If he once took his eyes off her, he could be sure that next time he looked, she would have slipped away. In the last several days he'd managed to foil her every attempt to elude him, but that was before the Midsummer Festival. Today, it was going to be difficult. That was why he had recruited others to help him. Mrs. Twitter for one. Dennis for another. And he could always count on the duchess to keep him informed of where Hannah was supposed to be, just as he could always count on Hannah not being there. Much good it had done her. His spies were everywhere. Today, though Hannah didn't know it, they were assigned to her suitors, and when Hannah slipped away to be with one of them, which she did frequently, those spies reported to Flynn. And Flynn would make posthaste for their trysting place and carry Hannah off before any real harm could be done. Heat her blood indeed! What he itched to do was heat her bare backside.

This thought, naturally, put him in mind of the widow Fanshaw. Strange to say, far from being outraged at the spanking he had administered, the lady regarded it as the act of a jealous lover, and had hinted, coyly, that she was more than willing to take up where they had left off. So was Flynn, and so he would, the first chance he got. The trouble was, Hannah had kept him so busy that he'd had no time left over for the fair widow. All in good time, Flynn promised himself.

"Hannah seems to be enjoying herself."

The comment came from the duchess. Her arthritis had improved sufficiently to allow her to put in an appearance at the fair. Not to do so, she had confided to Flynn, would disappoint all the villagers. It was the one time in the year when they were allowed to hobnob with the nobility. It had not taken Flynn long to discover that there was a lot more to it than that. The duchess and Hannah were genuinely liked by the good people of Warwick Campden. They knew everyone by name and knew all their business too. Hannah, in particular, was regarded with a great deal of affection. Her manners were natural and unassuming, and not what he had expected from the spoiled vixen he had known in London. In fact, he felt quite proud of her.

The duchess, who had been watching Flynn watching Hannah for the last half hour, had a merry twinkle in her eyes. Flynn didn't notice. The blacksmith had ceded his place to Sir Waldo, and Flynn's expression was as black as thunder.

"Handsome devil, ain't he?" said the duchess.

Flynn made a rude sound. "From all I hear, the man is an out-and-out scoundrel." He turned his head and looked down at the duchess. "You don't consider Sir Waldo an eligible suitor for Hannah, I hope?"

The duchess chuckled. "Of course I don't. If Hannah marries him, I make no doubt that he'll fritter her fortune away on riotous living and loose women. It's what he did with his first wife. Even before his marriage, Sir Waldo was a wild one." A shade of admiration had crept into her voice, and Flynn's expression became darker. "How the Mannings came to produce such a demon is beyond understanding. They were so straitlaced, while Waldo was a degenerate from the beginning. Before he reached his majority, he'd deflowered half the virgins in the county. No woman was safe from him, not even me." And laughing at Flynn's shocked expression, she summoned a footman to help her to her carriage.

Flynn looked around for Lord Horsham. What the devil was the matter with the man? Couldn't he see what was going on under his very nose? If he were Horsham, he'd soon get rid of Sir Waldo. Hannah, Flynn was coming to see, had taken Horsham's measure. Horses were all the viscount thought about. He'd wager his last groat that the blockhead was looking over the horseflesh in the stock pens when his interests would be far better served if he were here, looking over the opposition.

The only other swain who was in the running for Hannah's hand was Mr. Simon Featherstone, and he was a dead loss. True, he had some of the right credentials. He was the right age, had the right bloodlines, and the right fortune. But he was all wrong for Hannah. All wrong for any woman was what it came down to. He preferred men to women, or so Dennis had it from Featherstone's very own valet. He couldn't allow Hannah to go to someone like Featherstone. It was Horsham or nobody, and that was the depressing truth.

He mustn't allow himself to feel sorry for her. As the duchess said, Hannah had had her chance, and she'd thrown it away. He could vouch for that. In London, she'd had her pick of suitable young gentlemen, and had turned her nose up at every one. He'd seen it with his own eyes at Lady Heathe's ball. He'd summed her up as a spoiled, pampered chit who was highly conscious of her own worth, and he'd avoided her like the plague. If she'd only played her cards right in London, she might have captured any one of a number of wealthy, titled gentlemen. Now, it had come down to Horsham, and she had no one to blame but herself.

The alternatives were enough to make his hair

stand on end. If she didn't marry, she would come into her fortune and open her own salon for poets and actors, or even open a gaming house. She'd told him so, and he believed her. Then, no decent man would want her. She'd take lovers, of course, and ruin whatever chance she had for children and a normal life. She didn't want a normal life.

God, so much thinking was making his head ache. He'd made up his mind that he would see this thing through to its end, and there was no good reason to change his mind at this late date.

He suddenly realized that Hannah and Sir Waldo were no longer skipping around the maypole. Bloody hell, where were they? He quickly scanned the crowd and a smile lit up his face. Above the heads, like a beacon, bobbed Hannah's yellow parasol, and Flynn blessed her taste for gaudy colors. More than once, her parasol had helped him locate her. Smiling to himself, he hurried to catch up with her.

"Hannah?"

His smile faded when the young lady with the yellow parasol turned and looked up at him. He had never seen her before in his life.

"Where did you get this parasol?" he demanded.

The vicar's daughter quailed before that fierce look. "Lady Hannah loaned it to me," she quavered.

"Oh, she did, did she? And when was this?"

"A few moments ago, when she and Sir Waldo decided to go boating. Is something wrong?"

Flynn didn't answer. His keen eye had picked out Sir Waldo's garish pink coat.

At that moment, Dennis came running up. "They're going boating," he said.

Flynn flashed the young woman one of his rare grins, plucked the parasol from her nerveless fingers, and after sketching an elegant bow, he strode off. Dennis went after him.

Miss Reede, the vicar's daughter, took several moments to gather her scattered wits. There was a dreamy smile on her face when she entered the marquee where the ladies of the church were selling their produce to raise funds for the new pulpit.

"Flynn, this is insupportable!"

Flynn lifted Hannah into the rowboat, jumped in after her, and picked up the oars. "No, Hannah. What this is, is a rearguard action. This is one skirmish you have lost. Besides, you wanted to go boating, and you have your wish, so stop whining."

"But I wanted to go boating with Sir Waldo. You deliberately pushed him into the water so that he would have to change his clothes."

"It was an accident, for which I apologized."

"It was no accident."

Flynn shrugged, picked up the oars and began to row the boat into the center of the stream.

Hannah opened the parasol Flynn had shoved into her hand and stared at him from beneath its concealing brim. Since she'd told him that she was going to put each of her suitors to the test, Flynn had foiled her at every turn. When Sir Waldo arrived in one of those newfangled curricles to take her for a drive, Mrs. Twitter—no, Mrs. Fry—would suddenly appear from nowhere and squeeze in beside them. When Perry accompanied her to the stables to advise her on her stock, the place would erupt with grooms and stable boys, buzzing about like bees in a hive. When Mr. Featherstone invited her to take a walk in the gardens, every gardener at Wrole would turn out in force and start digging ditches. Maids, footmen, stable boys, gardeners, not to mention her own grandmother and chaperone—Flynn had them all in his pocket. She couldn't turn around but she was falling over one of them. And there in the background would be Flynn, flashing her a triumphant grin.

She turned her head so he wouldn't see that her lips were twitching. When the urge to laugh had passed, she turned back to upbraid him and promptly forgot what she was going to say. She was watching the ripple of powerful muscles across his arms and chest as he dipped the oars in the water. He'd told her once that if he hadn't acquired his gaming house, he would have become a prizefighter, and he still kept his hand in at Figg's Academy in Soho Square. Well, this time Flynn was outmatched.

"Flynn," she began reasonably, "this is absurd. How can I make up my mind which suitor to accept if I don't have some time alone with them?"

"I know what you want, Hannah, and you're not going to get it."

"What's wrong with a few stolen kisses and a little fondling?"

"Fondling?" He looked truly shocked, and she pressed her lips together to stifle a laugh. "Fondling!" he repeated.

"Yes, you know, passion. I don't want to marry a man who doesn't stir my passions. What's wrong with that?"

"Passion, let me tell you, my girl, is highly overrated." Even to his own ears he sounded as virtuous as a vicar, but he couldn't seem to help himself. "Character is what counts, not passion."

"And you should know?" she asked sweetly.

He nodded. "I'm eight years older than you, Hannah, and I'm giving you the benefit of my experience. Of all your suitors, only one will do. Lord Horsham, Hannah. You know it too."

"But, Flynn, he's as cold as a fish."

"I'm thinking of his character, and so should you."

She didn't reply because her teeth were clenched. She was thinking of Mrs. Fanshaw and the long, limpid looks she had caught Flynn exchanging with the ripe beauty. If he hadn't been so busy foiling her attempts to meet with her suitors, she had no doubt that he would have been in hot pursuit of Mrs. Fanshaw by now, and by the looks of it, he wouldn't have to run very fast to catch up with her. Oh yes, Hannah thought viciously, passion was highly overrated. Character was what counted. The hypocrite! The bare-faced, low, conniving hypocrite!

When they returned to shore, she saw Dennis and beckoned him over, then turning to Flynn said, "Thank you for the outing, Flynn. You may leave me with Dennis. He will escort me to the assembly rooms."

At the assembly rooms, a cold supper was to be served, and afterward a fireworks display would take place on the banks of the river.

When he made no move to leave her, she went on, "I give you my word that I won't slip off with any of my suitors, unless Dennis is there to chaperon me."

At last he had talked some sense into her. Still, he hesitated.

"Oh, go on, Flynn," she said impatiently. "I know you are dying to take in the pugilistic contest. While you're there put some money for me on Will Bouchard. He's our blacksmith, and he'll give that overmuscled challenger a run for his money."

He grinned. "Hannah," he said, "you're a woman after my own heart."

"Yes, I know," she replied.

He was well out of earshot before she turned to the young footman. "Dennis," she said pleasantly, "what do you think Flynn would do if he knew that *you* were the gentleman he caught in the carriage with Mrs. Fanshaw?"

"What?"

"You heard me, Dennis."

He looked at her in horror. His jaw worked. "No," he finally choked out.

Hannah smiled up at him. "Yes, Dennis. With my own eyes, I saw you jump from the carriage just after Flynn entered it. Your red hair gave you away."

"M-milady," he stammered, thinking of Flynn's temper and his punishing right, "you w-wouldn't tell Mr. Flynn, would you?"

"Of course not, Dennis. How could you think such a thing?" She paused. "That is, not if you agree to my terms."

Sometime later, when supper was over and dusk had settled over Warwick Campden, people began to idle their way out of the assembly rooms in anticipation of the fireworks display. Flynn stood off to one side, his eyes trailing Hannah and her beau, Mr. Featherstone. He dismissed Featherstone with a flick of his lashes, knowing that he had nothing to fear there. Just to be on the safe side, however, he gave Dennis the nod and watched as the three of them left the hall together. Sir Waldo was escorting the duchess, and they were flirting outrageously. Horsham was still sitting at a table with his cronies, arguing the finer points of the latest addition to his stables. No doubt he'd be there till all the candles were snuffed out. The slowtop!

Flynn dipped his hand in his pocket, and his fingers closed around the note that someone had slipped him when he was replenishing wineglasses. It was a note from the widow Fanshaw, inviting him to watch the fireworks display from the comfort of her carriage. This was one appointment Flynn was determined to keep.

For six whole days he had been in close proximity to Hannah, and it was driving him crazy. *She* was driving him crazy. She wanted a taste of passion, and he ached to give it to her. Only, it wouldn't stop at a few stolen kisses and a little fondling. He wanted to fall on her, and tear off her clothes, and pleasure her till she begged him for mercy. Then he would show her how to pleasure him, and make *him* beg for mercy.

Just one more day, that's all he had to endure, and he would accomplish what he'd set out to do. Only one more day to keep his treacherous hands off her, and she would announce her engagement, and it would be all over.

The widow Fanshaw came into his line of vision, and Flynn quickly erased his frown. A long silent look passed between them, and he wiggled his brows suggestively, to show that her message was received and understood. He gave her a few minutes, then he went after her.

The carriages were lined up on the avenue, well away from the spectators who were assembling for the fireworks display. Well away from Hannah. That was very important. He didn't want Hannah to know anything about this. She was a female and wouldn't understand.

Even in that dim light, he had no trouble finding the right carriage. She waved to him with a white lace handkerchief through the open window.

He only hoped he was up to it. It wasn't easy to put himself in a carnal frame of mind when he'd never felt more virtuous. This was, by far, the most noble thing he had ever done in his life. No guardian angel had ever suffered the trials he had been made to suffer. He was doing it for Hannah, protecting her from himself. Only one more day, then he could turn in his wings.

Think carnal, he told himself bracingly, then he opened the carriage door and hopped inside. Before he could say how d'you do, he was seized and dragged halfway across the banquette. God, he liked a lusty wench, but not this lusty. It made a man wonder if he would be adequate to the occasion. He wasn't given a chance to protest. Her lips came down hard on his and kissed him into silence. This wasn't going to work. The thought had hardly crossed his mind when she grasped his hands and cupped them around her breasts. His fingers flexed automatically. Her nipples hardened. Everything was going to be all right.

A soft moan passed from her mouth into his. With a muffled groan, Flynn drove her back against the cushions of the banquette. His hands were everywhere at once. He couldn't believe how lithe and supple she was. He'd always considered the widow Fanshaw a trifle overblown. His hands told him he'd misjudged her. In the dark, it was quite possible to imagine he was making love to Hannah. Even her scent, a subtle blend of lavender and violets ... Lavender and violets? Hannah's scent?

Flynn leaped up as though he'd been bitten by a poisonous asp. "Hannah!" he roared. "What the hell are you doing here?"

That's when she let fly with her fan and caught him a glancing blow on his nose.

When Flynn howled, Hannah quickly flung out of the carriage. Disregarding the pain to his nose, Flynn jumped down after her. "Hannah," he called out, "wait!"

She rounded on him. "You knave!" she railed. "Who was it that said passion was highly overrated? I suppose you slunk off to be alone with Mrs.

Fanshaw so you could admire her character? You low, conniving, lecherous scoundrel! You hypocrite! You filthy . . ."

The rest of her words were drowned out as fireworks exploded overhead, but no one could have mistaken the meaning of those silent words. It was then that the widow Fanshaw came upon the scene, escorted by a blushing, goggle-eyed Dennis. She looked at Hannah's disheveled clothing, then she glared at Flynn, and a spate of obscenities poured out of her mouth. Flynn was glad he couldn't hear them for the din of the fireworks. Then she hit him with her reticule.

And this was his reward for trying to be virtuous? Now he knew there was no God. Summoning the remnants of his dignity, he made an elegant bow to both ladies, and as they continued to revile him, he sauntered off as though he hadn't a care in the world.

Silence, a long unbroken silence, as the sun edged its way down below the horizon. Flynn could feel his heart thundering against his ribs, and feel the throb of his pulse at his throat. They were gathered on the common like worshipers keeping vigil—the girls clothed all in white with garlands in their hair, the young men brandishing their blazing torches, waiting for the signal to light the midsummer bonfire. No wonder people of old believed in magic. Shadows lengthened and deepened, and the odd sounds of insects set him to wondering about ghosties and the little people. And guardian angels.

In just a few hours, he would be relieved of his obligation to Hannah, and some other gentleman would take on that responsibility. It was why he had come to Warwick Campden in the first place. He'd felt guilty for leading her astray in London and had thought it was his bounden duty to see her suitably settled. And he had succeeded. Hannah had finally chosen one of her suitors.

Not that she had said anything to him. After last night's debacle, she'd looked through him as if he were invisible. The duchess had told him, however, that Hannah had sent a note to each of her suitors advising them of her decision. To his demand to know who the lucky man was, the duchess would say only that she approved of her granddaughter's choice.

It had to be Lord Horsham. *It had to be Horsham.* The duchess surely would not see Hannah go to someone like Featherstone or Sir Waldo? Hell, he'd marry Hannah himself before he would let that happen.

His reflections were scattered by the awful, sudden blast of bagpipes that signified the sun had set. Men cheered and thrust their blazing brands into the center of the bonfire. The bonfire crackled into life, and men turned, grabbed their partners, and swung them into a circle of dancers.

As the fiddlers began to play Flynn watched from the shadows. There was nothing stately about this dance, nothing that remotely resembled what went on in the assembly rooms. There were no steps to learn. Everything was spontaneous. Young men, brandishing a torch in one hand, swung their partners off their feet, then kicked their heels high in the air and did it again. Girls taunted their young men with being too slow for them, and their nimble feet flew faster and faster in time to the music.

Blue bloods, gentry, tradesmen, footmen—all classes were represented here; no one stood on ceremony. This was one of the things Flynn liked about Warwick Campden. Men judged each other on their merits, and though there were class distinctions, there was also a sense of community. A man might spend his whole life here and never give the outside world a second thought. Hannah belonged here. People looked up to her, liked her, respected her. If she married Horsham, she could make her life here. He'd done the right thing.

Hannah was partnered by Dennis. The widow Fanshaw had the young blacksmith in tow, and she fended off any presumptuous girl who tried to displace her. Horsham and Featherstone were partnered by girls from the village. There was no sign of Sir Waldo, and Flynn frowned. Somehow, this didn't feel right, and that worried him.

"Come, Flynn. Join the dance."

Hannah was standing before him, holding out her hand to him. There was a sparkle in her eyes and a glow on her cheeks. She had forgiven him for last night. *Hannah*, he thought, *Hannah*, and his throat tightened.

"Why not?" he said.

She gave him a flaming brand and led him to the circle of dancers. "Put your arm around my waist, Flynn."

Flynn did, then he swung her in a circle. It was glorious. It was bittersweet. If this was all he could ever have of her, he would take this memory to his dying day—*Hannah*, with garlands of violets in her hair, looking up at him with love in her eyes. She was so vibrant, so warm and giving; so much more than any man had a right to hope for. And for this brief moment in time she was his and he was hers. He wished the dance would never end. But time has a way of running out. The bonfire burned lower and lower, until it was reduced to a rubble of glowing embers. He couldn't leave things like this between them.

Flynn flung his torch into the embers of the fire and, with a calculated flick of his wrist, sent Hannah spinning out of the circle, then he went after her. With an arm around her shoulders, he swept her behind a screen of rhododendrons.

His arms dropped to his sides. "Hannah," he said, "last night . . . This will sound ridiculous, but I was doing it for you. You see—"

She stopped him by placing her fingers on his lips. "I know, Flynn. Don't think about it. I understand."

He swallowed the tightness in his throat. "Everything I've done, I've done for you. I want what's best for you, Hannah."

"Yes, I know that too." She smiled up at him. "My cursed guardian angel."

There was a long, long silence as they stared into each other's eyes. Finally Flynn said hoarsely, "Which one did you choose? I have to know."

She took a moment to compose herself. "I followed your advice, Flynn. I chose the man with the most upstanding character."

So it was Horsham. He should feel elated. He felt like blowing his brains out. "I'm glad."

Her eyes were swimming. "Are you, Flynn?"

He couldn't repeat the lie, and he said instead, "Then this is good-bye for us. I shall be leaving very early in the morning, long before you are awake."

"Aren't you coming to the assembly rooms for the ball?"

And hear the announcement of her engagement to Horsham? He didn't know if he could trust himself to accept it. "No," he said simply.

"I understand, Flynn."

Hannah. Hannah. He cupped her face with both

hands. His mouth brushed over hers with just a hint of pressure. Then he let her go.

He wandered along the banks of the river and tried to congratulate himself on a job well done. He'd accomplished what he'd set out to do. Hannah was suitably settled.

She wasn't suitably settled. She was a vibrant, passionate woman with a lust for life. If she married Horsham, she would die by slow degrees. Yes, and he held himself responsible. She was only following his advice. Then what else could he have told her? *Marry me, Hannah, and come live with me in my gaming house. We'll have glorious adventures together. Oh yes, and you can preside at my hazard table.*

A gaming-house wench? He wouldn't permit it. Nor could he take up residence in Warwick Campden. Her grandfather had been the Duke of Wrole, and if her father had not predeceased him, he, too, would have been the duke. Richard Flynn marrying into the nobility? The idea was preposterous.

Fine. But there had to be some other way of resolving the problem. He wanted Hannah to be happy, and he knew she could never be happy with Horsham. Deep down, he had always known it. It was only because Horsham was the least unworthy suitor that he had promoted his cause. When there was no Sir Waldo or Featherstone to compare him with, the man was completely ineligible. No, not ineligible. Just wrong for Hannah.

And so it went on. He didn't know how long he had been wandering along the riverbank when he finally came to his decision, nor did he care. If the engagement was already announced, it would just have to be unannounced. Hannah didn't have to wait till she came into her fortune to be free of her grand-mother's machinations. He would lend her the money on the condition that she did not set up her own gaming house. It wasn't the best solution, but it was better than Horsham. The pity was he hadn't thought of it sooner.

He quickened his steps as he approached the por-ticoed entrance to the assembly rooms. Though lights blazed from every window, the place was as quiet as a church. There was no music, no sounds of laughter or conversation, no couples strolling about taking the air. A feeling of foreboding gripped Flynn, and he broke into a run.

On the threshold of the main hall where the danc-ing took place, he halted. People were clustered in small groups, conversing in hushed tones. He did not see Hannah, but the duchess was there, flanked by Lord Horsham and Featherstone. At sight of Flynn, she beckoned, and he quickly crossed to her.

"We thought it was you," she said. "Now it ap-pears it must be Sir Waldo."

Flynn's heart began to beat erratically. "What's happened to Hannah?" he demanded.

"She's eloped," said the duchess. "She left a note, but the fool girl didn't say whom she had eloped with. Now we know."

"I don't believe it."

"Your own footman confirmed it."

It was then that Flynn saw Dennis. "What did you see?" asked Flynn.

Dennis said, "I saw 'er after the torch dance. A chaise and four was waiting for 'er. There was a gen-tleman, but I didn't get a good look at 'im. I knew it was either you or Sir Waldo. Your coats are almost the same."

"And she left in that chaise?"

Dennis nodded.

"What about the note?" asked Flynn.

The duchess handed it to him. "She left it with her maid with instructions to give it to me tomorrow morning. The poor girl didn't know what to do. By the time she gave it to me, it was already too late."

Flynn scanned the note. It said only that Hannah had decided to elope and she hoped her grandmother would forgive her. "We must go after her," he said.

The duchess made a small sound of derision. "What good would that do? She can marry whom she chooses. The girl is over twenty-one. Sir Waldo wasn't my first choice, by any means, but I'll bear it, if I must."

Flynn was conscience-stricken. It was all his fault. This never would have happened if he had only listened to Hannah. She didn't love Sir Waldo. She loved *him*.

He turned on his heel and quickly strode from the hall. After a moment's stunned surprise, Dennis went after him.

The doors to Flynn's gaming house were flanked by two footmen resplendent in maroon-and-gray livery. Flynn descended from his hired chaise, and as he paid off the driver Dennis quickly jumped down, ascended the front steps at a run, and disappeared inside the house. Young Sean O'Brian held the door for Flynn. He was on the point of making some innocuous comment, but one look at his employer's face curbed the impulse. Mr. Flynn was in a raging temper.

Flynn entered the house and paused for a moment in the spacious vestibule. She was here somewhere. She and Sir Waldo had left a trail that a blind man could have followed. They wouldn't have been expecting anyone to follow them, of course. As the duchess said, Hannah was of an age to marry without requiring anyone's consent. Well, Hannah Marchmont could think again. He had not sacrificed his own happiness for this. If she had married Sir Waldo, he, Richard Flynn, would make her a widow, and he didn't care if he hanged for it.

Oblivious to the many patrons who greeted him warmly, Flynn strode toward the room where a game of hazard was in progress. He knew her game. Neither she nor Sir Waldo had two pennies to rub together. They'd come to his gaming house hoping to make a killing at his hazard table. There would be a killing, all right, but not the one Sir Waldo expected.

Just inside the door, he halted. Dennis, the traitor, had got there before him to forewarn them. There was no sign of Sir Waldo, but Hannah was there, wearing one of her flash gowns that left nothing to a man's imagination. Her dark hair was flowing loose about her shoulders, and rouge warmed her cheeks and lips. She wore no mask. Flynn's jaw clenched. She was gorgeous.

Hannah had been making her own inspection. He looked haggard and out of sorts, she decided. Also, in a temper. Everything was going as planned, more or less. She'd had to make a few adjustments to the steps in her scheme along the way, but nothing to overset a seasoned soldier like herself. This was war, and the closing offensive was about to begin.

She opened with the first salvo. "Flynn," she called out gaily. "I took your advice. I just lost ten thousand pounds at your hazard table. You will have to apply to my husband for payment."

At these taunting words, such a look crossed his face that her heart wrenched and she cried out, "No, Flynn. I didn't marry him. I swear it. I didn't marry him! You knew I wouldn't. You must have known I couldn't."

He closed his eyes, and when he had come to himself snarled through clenched teeth, "I would rather see you married to *me* than to that dissolute wretch."

"No," she breathed. "Flynn, is this an offer?"

A hush descended on the throng of players. Only the ticking of the clock on the mantel could be heard. When Flynn continued to stand there, staring, one of his patrons called out, "What's the matter with you, man? Answer the lady!"

The spectators, who had never been half as well entertained in their lives, nodded vigorously, then protested just as vigorously when Flynn grasped Hannah by the elbow and, with one furious glare at his gawking patrons, hustled her out of the room.

Colonel Mowbray, who had been a member of the club long before Flynn's time, and who liked Flynn immensely, was the first to get to his feet. "One hundred guineas says the lady carries the day," he challenged the room at large.

"Done," cried another, who was quite confident that Flynn was not the marrying kind of man.

More bets were laid, and there was an exodus that almost turned into a stampede.

Flynn led Hannah to a short flight of stairs that gave onto the private gallery overlooking the vast entrance hall. At the rail, he turned her to face him.

He said harshly, "I'm not in the mood for jokes, Hannah. My bones ache from the rattling they've taken in that broken-down chaise I hired in my mad dash to catch up with you; I'm tired and hungry; I've been set upon by highwaymen; I haven't slept a wink for three nights and—"

"You were set upon by highwaymen?"

"I was," he said curtly, "or I would have caught up to you sooner. In addition, I had to delay at Oxford for Dennis's sake. He knocked his head on the carriage door and required a physician."

She cut in, "Dennis is a real treasure. Do you know what I think? I think you should promote him to operator. The boy has his heart set on it. In fact, I promised I would put in a good word for him. I owe it to him, Flynn. He has been of immeasurable service to me, and to you too."

"I don't want to talk about Dennis," he roared.

"Yes, Flynn," she answered meekly. "Go on. You were saying? If you caught up to us, what would you have done?"

"What would I have done?" he asked incredulously. "*What would I have done?* I would have run through that unscrupulous fortune hunter with my sword, that's what I would have done."

"Then all I can say is, thank God for Dennis's foresight. You really ought to reward him."

He gnashed his teeth. "Stop trying to change the subject."

"What is the subject?"

"You, of course. Hannah, listen to me. You don't have to marry anyone. I've thought this through carefully. I'll give you the money to make you independent. You don't have to wait till your birthday. You can do what you want, within reason. Take your time in finding the right man for you."

She looked at him sadly. "Flynn, you coward! You heard me. You know I haven't married Sir Waldo. I think you knew all along that I never would. You've lost the war. You know you have. I saw it in your face not a moment ago. It's time to admit it."

He closed his eyes, then opened them wide, blinking rapidly. He was under attack from every side, but he wasn't beaten yet. "Think, girl!" he said harshly. "Look at me. Really look at me. What do you see?"

Her eyes moved over him slowly, lovingly, absorbing the abundance of blond hair tied back with a ribbon, the blade of a nose in that handsome face, the manly physique, and not least, the emerald winking rakishly in his left earlobe. But it was his eyes that held her, green eyes with a touch of mist in them, and fathoms deep with love for her. She never doubted it for a moment.

She dimpled up at him. "I see an angel, Flynn," then more softly, "my cursed guardian angel."

"I'm a gamester, dammit! Before that, I was a footman. I was born in a hovel. I'm not fit to be your husband."

When she touched a hand to his cheek, he drew back violently. "Oh, my love," she said, "you are what you are because of these things. I wouldn't change a single one, else I might change the man I love."

It had come to a last stand. He croaked out, "Think of your grandmother. She would die of shame if you married me."

"Wrong again, Flynn. My grandmother is counting on me to bring you home as my husband."

"I don't believe it!"

She inhaled a long breath. "The truth, Flynn?"

No. No. No. He didn't want the truth. He wanted to save her from herself, and that made him vicious. He forced a laugh. "You're surely not going to say that I loved you at first sight? That is a womanish notion, Hannah."

She laughed in that provoking way that mocked him. "You know it's the truth. I saw it in your eyes when Lady Heathe introduced us at her ball. You, however, fought against our love every inch of the way. You tried to keep me at arm's length by calling me names. Spoiled, pampered, indulged. What could I do when you were so determined not to love me? So I became Anna, the seamstress. And when I was sure you loved me, too, I wrote to my grandmother and told her I had finally found the man I wanted to marry, and if I couldn't have you, I would never marry. She knew I meant it. She wanted to meet you, but she wasn't well enough to come up to London. I had to find a way to get you to Warwick Campden. I knew that once she met you, she would give us her blessing, and she did. In fact, she said if she were thirty years younger, she would give me a run for my money."

Flynn's mind was reeling. "But ... what about your suitors?"

"They were never my suitors. How could they be? I've known them all since I was a child. I misled you there, Flynn, with my grandmother's connivance. I knew you would never let me go to another man. How was I to know it would take you this long to come to your senses? You're such a snail."

"You eloped with Sir Waldo!" he roared.

"No. I sent him on a wild-goose chase to Manchester. Suffice it to say, the gentleman who traveled in the chaise with me was one of my grandmother's footmen. Mrs. Fry came with us, so you see, it was all very respectable. My poor, poor dear. Have you been suffering agonies on the long drive to London? It's no more than you deserve."

He couldn't take it all in. "But ... Viscount Redmond, and all the adventures you got up to with his wild friends?"

"I did it all for you. Surely you don't think I care for cockfights and pugilistic contests?" She suppressed a shudder. "I hope, when we are married, you won't expect me to accompany you to such barbarous sports?"

She edged closer and began to toy idly with the buttons of his coat. "You're the man for me, Flynn. You're the man to help me put my estates in order, make Wrole and our village a place of prosperity, not only for our children and their children, but also for all our people." She saw the stark terror in his eyes, and this made her very tender, very gentle with him. "You can do it, Flynn. You can do anything you want. Look what you've accomplished with your own life. Believe in yourself, Flynn, as I believe in you."

Though her words affected him deeply, he was still thinking of her and only of her. He fired his last shot. "Hannah, you should marry money and a title."

She smiled at this. "Oh, I intend to, especially money. We'll need the profits from your gaming house to set our estates in order. My grandfather wasted his fortune in profligate living. My own fortune ... well, I misled you there, too. I'm afraid I've been a very naughty girl. As for marrying a title, that's already taken care of. When my grandfather died and his title returned to the crown, His Majesty most generously bestowed a barony on whoever would be my future husband."

"A barony?" he said faintly.

"You'll be the Baron Flynn. It has a nice ring to it, don't you think? Now Flynn, don't look as though you had swallowed a hot coal. A title won't change you. Just remember, I'm marrying you for your money. That ought to make you feel better."

"Hannah," he moaned, "what am I going to do with you?"

"Marry her, you fool!" shouted a voice from the floor below.

Flynn and Hannah looked over the balustrade. A sea of smiling faces looked up at them. The hall was thronged with people—elegant ladies and gentlemen of fashion, footmen, operators, croupiers—and as they watched, others, curious about the commotion, joined them from various side rooms.

"Marry 'er!" roared Dennis, and the cry was taken up by all and sundry, until the crescendo filled every corner of that great hall.

Hannah smiled up at him. "Well, Flynn?"

He swallowed painfully. He wanted to do the noble thing, but it wasn't easy, not when he was drowning in the love that was shining in her eyes. Hannah. Children. A home. He wasn't man enough to fight the temptation she was dangling in front of him. "Hannah, be very sure you mean this," he said.

"Flynn, get on with it."

He drew in a deep, shuddering breath. "All right, you win. I've loved you from the first. I admit it. Hannah, will you have me?"

It wasn't perhaps the most eager proposal a lady might expect from her beloved, but to Hannah's ears it sounded heavenly. With a great whoop of laughter, she flung her arms around his neck. "Yes, yes, yes, my love," she cried out, and kissed him fiercely.

Colonel Mowbray, who had somehow managed to hoist himself on top of a table, bellowed above the din, "Three cheers for the Baron Flynn and his lady. Hip, hip . . ."

The crowd went wild. "Huzzah! Huzzah! Huzzah!" they chanted, and the chandeliers began to sway.

Flynn and Hannah broke apart, laughing. "I thought I heard choirs of angels singing," he said, and meant it, but his words were drowned out by the riotous applause.

Elizabeth Thornton is the award-winning author of the best-selling DANGEROUS TO LOVE. About to go on sale in March of 1995 is her next spectacular romance, DANGEROUS TO KISS.

THE VERY BEST IN CONTEMPORARY
WOMEN'S FICTION

SANDRA BROWN

___28951-9 Texas! Lucky $5.99/$6.99 in Canada   ___56768-3 Adam's Fall $4.99/$5.99
___28990-X Texas! Chase $5.99/$6.99   56045-X Temperatures Rising $5.99/$6.99
___29500-4 Texas! Sage $5.99/$6.99   ___56274-6 Fanta C $4.99/$5.99
___29085-1 22 Indigo Place $5.99/$6.99   ___56278-9 Long Time Coming $4.99/$5.99
___29783-X A Whole New Light $5.99/$6.99

TAMI HOAG

___29534-9 Lucky's Lady $5.99/$7.50   ___29272-2 Still Waters $5.99/$7.50
___29053-3 Magic $5.99/$7.50   ___56160-X Cry Wolf $5.50/$6.50
___56050-6 Sarah's Sin $4.99/$5.99   ___56161-8 Dark Paradise $5.99/$7.50

NORA ROBERTS

___29078-9 Genuine Lies $5.99/$6.99   ___27859-2 Sweet Revenge $5.99/$6.99
___28578-5 Public Secrets $5.99/$6.99   ___27283-7 Brazen Virtue $5.99/$6.99
___26461-3 Hot Ice $5.99/$6.99   ___29597-7 Carnal Innocence $5.99/$6.99
___26574-1 Sacred Sins $5.99/$6.99   ___29490-3 Divine Evil $5.99/$6.99

DEBORAH SMITH

___29107-6 Miracle $5.50/$6.50   ___29690-6 Blue Willow $5.50/$6.50
___29092-4 Follow the Sun $4.99/$5.99   ___29689-2 Silk and Stone $5.99/$6.99
___28759-1 The Beloved Woman $4.50/$5.50

THERESA WEIR

___56463-3 Amazon Lily $4.99/$5.99   ___56378-5 One Fine Day $4.99/$5.99
___56092-1 Last Summer $4.99/$5.99

- -

Ask for these books at your local bookstore or use this page to order.

Please send me the books I have checked above. I am enclosing $____(add $2.50 to cover postage and handling). Send check or money order, no cash or C.O.D.'s, please.

Name _____

Address _____

City/State/Zip _____

Send order to: Bantam Books, Dept. FN 24, 2451 S. Wolf Rd., Des Plaines, IL 60018
Allow four to six weeks for delivery.
Prices and availability subject to change without notice.